Kylie Tennant bequeathed an awesome array of literary work to posterity. Her determination to write about life as it was has been likened by some critics to that of John Steinbeck, especially *The Grapes of Wrath*. She was blessed with an incisive eye for character and a wonderful sense of humour which saved her stories of misery and hopelessness from seeming pessimistic.

Kylie Tennant's concern was with the individual's life amidst the wider community and it was the ebb and flow of life which she wished to convey rather than the individual struggles... Whether writing about the tramps moving from town to town or the inhabitants of the Sydney slum, she left us a canon of work that is as relevant today as when the stories were first written."

Richard Mackay,
*The Book Magazine*

# FOVEAUX

## KYLIE TENNANT

SIRIUS

Other novels by Kylie Tennant

RIDE ON STRANGER
THE BATTLERS
TIBURON
THE MAN ON THE HEADLAND
TELL MORNING THIS
THE HONEY FLOW
THE JOYFUL CONDEMNED
LOST HAVEN
TIME ENOUGH LATER

ANGUS & ROBERTSON PUBLISHERS

*Unit 4, Eden Park, 31 Waterloo Road,
North Ryde, NSW, Australia 2113;
94 Newton Road, Auckland 1,
New Zealand; and
16 Golden Square, London W1R 4BN,
United Kingdom*

*First published in 1939
by Angus & Robertson Publishers
Published by Angus & Robertson in 1981
This new Sirius edition 1989*

*Copyright © Kylie Tennant, 1939*

*National Library of Australia
Cataloguing-in-publication data.*

*Tennant, Kylie, 1912-1988.
  Foveaux.*

  *ISBN 0 207 16149 6.*

  *1. Title.*

*A823'.2*

*Printed in Australia by The Book Printer*

# CONTENTS

PROLOGUE                          9

BOOK I:    EBB TIDE              15

BOOK II:   FULL TIDE           101

BOOK III:  THE SURF            215

BOOK IV:   THE ROCKS          317

This is the littoral, the long pale shore,
  The gleaming sand, the cliffs where shallow foam
  Mutes in its murmurings the rousing roar
  Of curved green crests that crashed the proud ship home,
The silver sandhills, where, uneasily,
  The land receives the rejects of the sea.

# PROLOGUE

There is now no Municipality of Foveaux. Its boundaries are obliterated, its identity merged with that of the city of Sydney. But in 1912 Foveaux still had its own council, its own mayor, and even, some maintained, its separate smell. That last, however, might have been due to Ogham Street, basking like a wicked snake at the foot of the fair hill on which Foveaux was set. Upon the network of alleys around Ogham Street and the black chimneys of the factories Upper Foveaux looked down secure in the sunlight. The factory smoke simmered hazily on the skyline, and the factory whistles sounded faintly up Lennox Street, like timid bugles blowing an advance; but the factories, clustered round the foot of the hill, hung back as though daunted by that steep scarp.

Towards Dennison Square — a star-shaped tangle of traffic on the Hilltop, much like any other business centre except for a queer predominance of piano shops and pawn shops — Murchison Street made its way from the city at the foot of Foveaux. Lennox Street, a more direct route from the city, remained a quiet residential road and a suffering in the flesh for those who had to climb it. To stand at the foot of Lennox Street and see it going up and up, as though it would burst against the skyline in a shower of roadmetal, gave you the feeling of watching a fountain or a waterfall — a feeling that it might spout even higher or alternatively pour over you. Particularly was this so after a storm when the brown water came creaming down the gutter and spread roaring, fan-shaped waves across the footpath.

Foveaux had grown used to Lennox Street, the way it spouted up as though to touch the stars, and then dwindled to a miserable little lane that crept to Errol Street between the wall of St Matthew's Church grounds and the garden of

Foveaux House. It was this bottle-neck choking off the traffic
that kept the upper part of Lennox Street such a quiet residential area. Here the Reverend Dr Wilbram, Mr Foxteth, K.C.,
the Agnews and the Hugheses could dwell secure from any
other incursions than that of the rabbit which resided among
the élite. The rabbit was as sure of itself as the pigeons wheel-
ing above the steep slope of the convent roof just around
the corner in Mark Street. There, over the towering stone walls
and the great shut gates, the magnolias dropped their pale
petals; and if you were a small boy standing on tiptoe, you
might just see the white statue in its niche high up where the
pigeons flew, or through a chink glimpse a strip of green lawn
where walked mysterious black-clad women, their beads jink-
ing, their coifs and hoods like strange wings folded.

Young Tommy Cornish always confused the bunny rabbit
in the churchyard with the mythical beast the rector had been
tracking through the Book of Revelations for many studious
years. The rector lived in a legend of the Apocalypse from
which he would emerge each Sunday to lead his flock through
a maze of allegorical explanations and Greek roots. Foveaux
was proud of the rector, his horned beast and his notable
Greek.

In the long summer evenings the rector and Mr Sutton of
Foveaux House would often watch for the rabbit to bob its
white tail amid the grass.

"Did you see him?" Mr Sutton would say placidly over the
fence and his cigar.

"I almost believe I did," the rector would respond, adjusting
his pince-nez on the high bridge of his nose. "He ran from that
honeysuckle."

A deep, golden silence would descend, and then the rector
never failed to remark:

"I must have that bush removed. The place is a perfect
wilderness."

Indeed, except for the path his flock kept clear from the gate
to the church porch, there was little sign of human comings
and goings. The whole church might have been just a great
stone, covered with ivy and crumbling into the grass. The
wooden pickets of the fence, once white painted, were rotted

a dead grey. One in every three was missing while the remainder hung insecurely by a nail each. It was a habit with the Foot of Foveaux to wrench a picket from the church fence any time there was a shortage of firewood.

"Little beast doesn't do any harm." Mr Sutton would break silence. "Eats the roses sometimes."

Mr Sutton's grounds were a great contrast to those of St Matthew's. His house was the finest in Foveaux and the oldest. Hildebrand Edward Sutton had lived in Foveaux House ever since it descended to him from that line of Suttons who had once held all Foveaux as their estate. Not only did he own the big house and its grounds, but there was a large share of the firm of Sutton, Targis and Underwood, Box Manufacturers, at the Foot of Foveaux, to his credit. It was difficult to connect Hildebrand Edward Sutton, very spruce and elegant in his grey top hat and his grey morning coat, with anything so prosaic as a factory. Factories belonged down near Ogham Street and Mr Sutton belonged to his ornamental fountain and his flower-beds. Around him Upper Foveaux breathed a rarefied air, while below it Middle Foveaux, with rows and rows of terraces, separated the higher altitudes from the Foot. In those happy days, when you spoke of people "going downhill" it might literally mean that they were moving into a house below Mary Street or, perhaps, even lower down past Slazenger Street where the horse buses ran. They might even end up in Plug Alley with Hamp and Mrs Sampson and Joe and Chink.

The Rose of Denmark, on the lower left-hand corner of Slazenger Street, was the meeting-place of Middle Foveaux and the Foot. Here presided Jordan True, under whose equal hospitality the dwellers of Plug Alley and Ogham Street might mingle with parched respectability: and Mr Jerrill or Bob Budin, returning homeward with his bag of tools, would find himself gazing over the beer mug into the unlovely visage of Curly Thompson or Blue Jack. A yellow wasps' nest on the corner was the Rose of Denmark; a wasps' nest where gathered not only thirsty souls in search of nectar but dark, weaponed men in search of plunder. The place was a landmark for nervous policemen.

Beside the Rose of Denmark a narrow stone stair ran down

into Plug Alley and from this stair entrance might be gained by knocking in a special manner. It was from this stair that Curly Thompson threw the Rose of Denmark's barman, as shall presently be told.

"I wouldn't mind them murderin' each other so much," Mrs Blore complained, "if they wouldn't throw stones on the roof."

From the stair the iron roofs below made a delightful target.

A little above the Rose of Denmark, but spiritually breathing the air of Upper Foveaux, was the Misses Dimiter's school. The Misses Dimiter had kept their select girls' school in Lennox Street when only the "nicest people" lived there; and refined families who had moved out of Foveaux still sent their little, pigtailed offspring to the Misses Dimiter as their mothers had been sent before them. Year by year the Misses Dimiter won the most famous scholarships. Year by year their girls topped the examinations in Hebrew and German and Greek. The Misses Dimiter believed in Solid Attainments, and they continued to turn out German scholars who would spend the rest of their lives doing fancy work and prodigies of Greek who would forget it all with the arrival of the first baby.

At the head of a sedate crocodile the Misses Dimiter every Sunday led the school boarders up to St Matthew's Church, while half Lennox Street leant admiringly over the balcony rail and the other half stood in an odour, not of sanctity, but Sunday dinner, in the front doorway.

"Never forget," the Misses Dimiter's pupils were instructed, "that a lady is proved a lady by the way she wears her gloves." The Misses Dimiter gave tone.

So did Mrs Isador in a different way. Her establishment, one block above the Misses Dimiter's, was also very select. Her young ladies, if they did not come from the best families, were at least intimately associated with some of them. They were very beautiful young ladies, even better behaved than the Misses Dimiter's. They did not walk out in crocodiles. They seldom went out at all. They spent their time entertaining visitors, very select visitors, who drove up in cabs and had to present their introductions. It is difficult to say which Foveaux admired more, the young ladies of the Misses Dimiter or those of Mrs Isador.

If the Foot of Foveaux had the Rose of Denmark as a land-mark, Middle Foveaux had Mr Keyne's palm-tree. Every time a hurricane thrashed up Lennox Street, and the little terrace gardens went sailing off in a swirl of mud and water, their owners would crouch to the fire muttering: "I wonder if Mr Keyne's palm-tree is all right?" and half expecting to help pick the bodies of Mr Keyne's family from under a deluge of brick and tile when the palm finally fell across the roof.

Someone had once warned Mr Keyne that the telephone department might cut his tree down if it obstructed their wires. Mr Keyne got in first and wrote to the department, telling them to take their telephone away as the wires were interfering with his tree. The telephone department solemnly sent out an expert to see what could be done, and the joke lasted Mr Keyne for years, while the tree soared up and up.

"You go down past Mark Street," the stranger would be directed, "until you come to the place with the palm-tree. Three houses further along is a lane, with the wood-and-coal shop on the corner, and the barber's is just opposite."

There were shops on every corner. Clusters of shops. But of the three hundred houses along Lennox Street most were in the form of clay-coloured terraces. There was a certain quaintness in the ornate wrought iron, gilded and tortured into balcony rails, edgings, cornices, and any possible projection, until the houses looked as though they had been trimmed with mouldy lace. In these terraces the builders had resolutely striven to preserve all the narrow discomforts of Victorian architecture. The doors and windows successfully defended the houses against the entrance of light and air. The halls were measured to allow one human body to pass through at a time, the stairs were steeper than Lennox Street. The great success was the roofs, pitched to allow for the fall of snow; though as Nosey Owen pointed out, "The only 'snow' in Foveaux is what they sniff down in Ogham Street."

Uniformity had been observed even where Lennox Street disconcertingly skirted a sheer drop into Plug Alley. Here the enterprising pioneer builder had apparently taken a lesson from the swallows and, while insisting on his usual three-storey plan, with an area in the basement for the servants, he had utilized a little jutting ledge halfway down the cliff, and on this had triumphantly erected Clarestone Terrace. The attic windows of Clarestone Terrace just managed to peep level with the ankles of people passing in Lennox Street, and the back gardens resembled those little pockets of earth illustrated in story books about the Swiss Alps. Since it would have been not much good attaching a balcony to the front of the house (the front was only a few feet from the cliff face), the builder had constructed an extra balcony at the back hanging carelessly over what at night looked like the bottomless pit.

"You ought to be ashamed of yourself," Mrs Owen scolded when Nosey Owen complained that climbing down to the yard, where he stabled his two cab horses, "wore him to a shadder". "Such a view as we got."

"What's the use of a view when you've got to climb about three miles to get to it?" fat old Nosey grumbled. "I like my views on the ground."

It was not really until poor Linda Montague lived there, however, that the view of "the stairs", as Clarestone Terrace was called, came into its own.

Below the stairs lay Plug Alley, which met Ogham Street at the foot of Lennox Street. The backyards of Plug Alley were well worth watching, even disregarding all the rest of the city, that city which, like a surrounding sea, encompassed and surged upwards towards Foveaux.

Yet, no matter how the tide of the city might flow, Upper Foveaux, impregnable on its peak, stood aloof from the roar of urban progress. On the skyline there sprang up in every direction the dark challenge of factory chimneys, some delicate and fragile as needles of clear ice that might melt to vapour at a breath, others black and abrupt. They sprouted above the road level, as did that ledge of swart thorn beyond the palace of the dreamy princess, as though they had thrust their dark shoots up through the crack where the pavement met the warm blue wall of the sky, as though they would sprout till their shadows were higher over the sunny street than Mr Keyne's palm-tree, and so ever higher and higher into the sweet air, with a quivering of smoke above, and the roaring and humming of their machines below.

# BOOK I

---

# EBB TIDE

# CHAPTER 1

## I

The change in Foveaux, that momentous slow change that was
to creep over it, had just begun in 1912. Perhaps the last time
Foveaux came out in all its old glory was the day of the Eight-
Hour Day Procession. The people of Foveaux loved processions. Men would leave the hotels, boys their games, women
take their children, and all wait for hours, just to see a procession go by. Shopkeepers shut their shops and hung out flags.
Crowds had a habit of gathering in Foveaux on a rumour of
anything noteworthy, from a murder to a marriage, but never
did such a crowd roll up and line Murchison and Errol streets
as for the Eight-Hour Day Procession.

Eight-Hour Day was almost invariably blessed by rain or
wind and some of the unions from bitter experience had taken
to carrying their banners furled. More than once a groan had
gone up from the crowd as over a hundred pounds' worth of
crimson silk split like old sailcloth. But for a miracle the first
Monday of October 1912 dawned a clear quivering blue. No
breath of wind stirred the flags along the route. The pigeons
circled on pale wings above the bustle of the streets where small
boys ran excitedly to and fro, shouting to each other, or breathing smudgily on the shop windows, peering at the draped and
shrouded corpses of the pianos in the piano shops, fighting for
positions in the gutter hours before there was any sign of a
procession. Later, as the crowd began to choke the footpath
behind them, they found themselves under the irate notice of
the hot young policemen trying to be cool and official.

"Keep back there, keep back," one adjured young Tommy
Cornish who, having taken his stand at the foot of the lamp
post he planned to climb when the procession came in sight,
was being slowly but surely squeezed into the road. As the
hour of the procession drew near there were people up lamp

posts, people on veranda roofs, people hanging out of second-storey windows and out of attic windows with flags, people on the very roofs, waving to friends in the street and shouting raucous comments to neighbours at other windows, on other roofs. The crowd murmured and swayed: "Lord, isn't it hot!"

"I wonder how much longer they'll be."

"Look out, Florrie, your hat-pin!"

On the corner of Murchison Square near the water tank a group of old ladies from the Foot were talking together. They formed a compact little squad with their daughters or daughters-in-law, all nursing fat, dirty small children, with parcels in their arms and other children clinging to their skirts and whining to be lifted up.

"I been up all night with me diarrhoea," Mrs Sampson, a massive, white-haired old lady, shouted to her neighbour, Mrs Blore. She laboured under the delusion that everyone was deaf and didn't speak up. "In an' out. In an' out all night long. I felt that weak this morning I could hardly crawl out to see the procession."

"I thought I heard you," Mrs Blore sympathized. "And it makes the night seem so long, don't it? I wasn't so good me-self. I been terrible sick lately, dear. I thought I was going to die."

"What did you say?" Mrs Sampson roared, craning round in front of a young man who had been pushed between them.

"Real sick I been. I was on the whisky, love, and it turned me up something terrible."

"What did you say?"

"The whisky," Mrs Blore shrieked. "What it did to my inside was a crime."

"Here they come! Here they come! No, it isn't," someone cried; and the crowd surged off the footpaths to see and had to be forcibly replaced. It settled down good-humouredly to wait again and concentrated its attention on a photographer on the roof of the hotel, waving hands and handkerchiefs and holding up the baby to make sure it would be in the photograph.

"Me stays'll just about bust in a minute," Mrs Fulcher panted. "I'm that squeezed I'll have red stripes where they're pressing. Has your daughter found a house yet, Mrs Blore?"

"Houses is terrible scarce. Seventeen people come to my door yesterday looking for lodgings. Poor things, I couldn't give 'em any, there being only the three rooms in the house. One man said 'e landed off a boat a week ago and 'e'd been looking ever since. Tramped 'is boots off all round Bondi and Paddington and all."

"Ah, we're lucky, we are," Mrs Sampson put in. "They say they're paying ten pounds for a door-key."

"Keep back there. Keep back there."

"And even if you've got a place, look what you've got to put up with. We been living in Plug Alley seventeen years and that Bross don't take no more notice than a fly on the wall when you want anythin' done. Here have I been with the water pouring through the roof all last week and what's he done about it? Nothing."

"That's not the worst. Why, every time we go out to the lavatory we have to take an umbrella and sit under it, the cistern leaks that bad. It wasn't so long ago Joe caught cold from water dripping down his back. I'm always sayin' I'll leave the place, and I will too."

"Not you. Only way you'll leave is in your coffin. You'll never walk out."

"It's not because I hain't felt like it."

"Processions ain't what they was years ago," Old Mrs Deeps wheezed behind Tommy. "I remember when Hemma was a little girl bringin' 'er and Gertie to a procession and them gettin' nearly trodden to death by the 'orses. Now there ain't nothin' but a lot of policemen."

"The procession isn't come yet, ma," Mrs Deeps's eldest daughter volunteered. "She's that deaf," she confided to Mrs Blore, "she couldn't hear the procession, not three yards off."

"Oh yes I could," Mrs Deeps responded unexpectedly. "And I'll trouble you, Florrie, to keep your remarks to y'self and look after Eddie. 'E'll be trampled. I often wish," she informed Mrs Blore, "that I never 'ad daughters. A lot of trouble to rear."

"Here they come. It's them."

The seventh false alarm brought a fresh surge forward which carried Mrs Deeps several yards away where she continued her conversation with Florrie and Mrs Blore, holding her old umbrella with the crooked handle well up above the crowd. Her black bonnet and its wisp of ostrich feather was submerged every now and then in the hustle of shoulders but she held her own, boots planted well apart on the gutter edge, aged but indomitable.

"Don't you speak to me like that. I may be an old woman but I ain't goin' to have any impudent lads tellin' me—"

"They're coming. Here they are."

Far away the faint echoes of the band could be heard above the noise of the crowd.

"Remember the time, Joe, when the brewery banner split right under the Temperance League's window and them praisin' it as an Act of God and throwin' down pamphlets?"

"Do I bloody well wot!"

There was a glitter of sunlight on brass as the procession began to make its way slowly up Murchison Street. First, the policemen on foot, and then, gods of the small boys, the mounted police, their uniforms glinting blue and silver, their tall horses walking delicately, though somewhat bored and restive from the long hot morning. Then came the marshal on his white horse and — amid cheers — the coach for the Pioneers of Labour. The cheers of Foveaux were all the readier because they felt they were represented. Was not their own John Hutchison, Honest John, riding almost beside the pioneers' coach, very busy and important as some kind of subsidiary marshal.

"There's a lot of people I know in the procession," Tommy Cornish remarked to Billy Noblett.

"Not as many as I do."

"Bet I know more'n you."

"You don't."

"I do."

The deafening thunder of the band nearly took Tommy's breath away. The big drum was almost on top of him before he could shrink back; the sticks seemed to be inside him thudding with his heartbeats, thudding as though they would break his chest. He tried to retreat but the crowd was too dense. Suddenly an arm shot through and gripped him, a path was miraculously cleared. Tommy disappeared among the forest of legs in the clutch of his big brother Bramley.

"Here," Bramley said, very red in the face, "what do you think you're doing? Mum'll have a fit."

"I want to see," Tommy mourned.

"All right. Quick."

The bigger boy bent and hoisted Tommy laboriously on to his shoulders. With Mrs Blore's angular frame pressed into him on one side and Mrs Deeps's umbrella handle on the other, Bramley's chief worry was for his new straw boater.

The floats were approaching, the first drawn by ten great horses, their shiny rumps swaying proudly and deliberately under a web of coloured ribbons. The Eight-Hour Day Procession would have been nothing without the grand big horses, clopping sedately along with their manes in light little pigtails like schoolgirls, their tails looped and tied with ribbons and their silver-studded harness hidden under favours and silk pompons and silver bells. Their great heavy shoes shone, their big silky feet rang deliberately on the pavement. They looked at the crowd with confident kind brown eyes. The fat brewery horses, the dray horses, the cart horses, knew it was their day.

"There's nothing like a good 'orse," remarked Nosey Owen huskily to a friend. He should have been collecting a fare with his cab, but he was waiting to see his son go by in the ranks of the tramway men.

Bramley Cornish, bent under the weight of Tommy, occasionally caught a flash as the firemen's helmets went by or the float of the glassmakers with their mirrors dazzling and dancing on the crowd.

"Look at him! Gov'ment stroke!" roared the blacksmith's friends as the time-honoured float with a docile horse being shod was drawn past.

"Go on, Jim, show 'em what you can do." They encouraged the marble masons chipping industriously at a rock, the basket makers, the stonemasons and the model bakeshop. A terrific jerk that threatened to disintegrate the new boater indicated to Bramley that Tommy had caught one of the buns the cooks were throwing to the crowd.

"Here you are, doughey."

"This way, over here," the small boys begged.

Their fathers had an eye on sample cigars.

"Look out yez don't poison yerselves," someone roared as the tobacco workers went by puffing at their wares.

"Now if the brewers were to give free beer it'd be something like," someone suggested.

"You're out of step, Bob," one of his mates called as Bob Budin with his youngest son on his shoulder came tramping doggedly behind the float of the plasterers with its white pillars and pretty girls all Grecian gold and white. Bob looked down anxiously at his feet and his mates' feet and then caught sight of his adviser.

"Here, I want to see you, Fred," he shouted. "It's about that job of Jerrill's."

His friend ran alongside the procession and continued the conversation in shouts until he managed to shoulder his way into the ranks and join Bob.

"Here comes Mr Jamieson," Tommy yelled in Bramley's ear. "He's over the other side."

The stovemakers and ironworkers, a grim impressive squad in their blue working clothes and leather aprons, marched behind a figure in armour.

"And here's Mr McErchin."

Mr McErchin was shepherding a motor lorry loaded with the Women Workers' Union. His face wore a lofty expression as he contemplated the fat, jingling horses.

"Hey, look at the girls! Done out in style, aren't they?"

The artificial flower-makers' float, a blaze of pink and purple, came rolling behind.

"There's Miss Melston," Tommy called. He had hardly so much enthusiasm, even for the passing of the Theatrical Workers' float with the Indians in warpaint and a live Noah's Ark and Beefeaters in full dress. Miss Melston was Tommy's Sunday School teacher.

Ten grey and white horses in blue ribbons came clopping along with the banner of the Seamen's Union, a band in front blaring "Sons of the Sea". The crowd good-humouredly took up the tune: "For they are the boys of the bulldog breed . . . Look out! Hang on to that rope or she'll pull you over."

"You ought to know more about ropes than that."

"Barney!" Tommy yelled. "There's dear old Barney in the procession." Barney was a big grey draught-horse belonging to the Merrick livery stable. "I wonder how he got there?"

"They probably hired him," grunted Tommy's steed.

"He's got his hair plaited."

Bramley was straining his neck for a glimpse of two carriages, the first full of fat, richly dressed "ladies and gentlemen" placarded "We Deprive and Thrive", and the second of ragged women working at machines with the inscription, "Our Bread is Sorrow and our Cup is Tears". Behind them came a little perambulator with a notice reading "Australia's Dreadnought", which had an uproarious reception.

The procession was beginning to tail down to the Cleaners' Union on horseback with their buckets worn helmetwise and their new garbage collector proudly rolling in front. The crowd surged out into the road to fall behind and follow to the Showground for the day's sport. There was a great deal of confusion because the middle part of the procession, by this time at the top of Errol Street on the boundaries of Foveaux, had fallen into disorder passing the Royal Arms Hotel, a number of loyal unionists feeling that having stood the heat and burden of the day thus far it wouldn't matter if they hopped in for a quick one and rejoined the procession later. Mothers with children and baskets urged on their stragglers with visions of free lollies and fruit and ginger beer.

"If you don't come along, you won't get there till it's all over." Mrs Noblett adjured her young. "Here, Billy, take Freddy's hand and *pull* him."

"I'm comin'," whined the aggrieved Freddy. "I don't like old processions."

Mrs Noblett's good-natured face took on a shocked expression.

"You wouldn't let your father hear you say that," she said severely.

Freddy, who had seen nothing but the legs of those in front, was recalcitrant. "I don't care. Silly ole procession."

"You ungrateful little . . ." Mrs Noblett was speechless. "Here you've got holiday and procession and all and you—"

"Mum, why is there a procession?" Billy asked.

"It's a celebration," Mrs Noblett explained. "The trade unions hold it."

"Why?"

"Well, why shouldn't they? An' don't drag that bag along the ground. They went and won eight hours or days or something, and then they formed unions to celebrate. That's how Eight-Hour Day's a holiday. An' if you dawdle along like that," even Mrs Noblett's good nature gave way, "I'll give you something to go on with, Eight-Hour Day or no Eight-Hour Day."

## II

Hildebrand Edward Sutton had almost missed the procession.

He had been going the rounds of his rosebuds when he heard the bands. Dropping his spray he sallied out and pushed through the iron posts that cut off the top of Lennox Street from Errol Street. Close on his heels trod Sam Merrick from the livery stables.

"Mornin', Mr Sutton," Sam called. "Goin' to the procession?"

"I almost missed it," Mr Sutton confessed. "Oh, here they come. Not marching, Sam?"

"One of the horses is. Old Barney. Was that mulch I told you of any good?"

"It's done wonders. You were right. The soil needed building up."

"Look at that, will you," Sam grunted. "Look who's riding alongside the pioneer coach. If Honest John Hutchison's a labour pioneer, I'm a poached egg."

"What do you think of his chances for the council elections, Sam?"

"He'll get in," Sam prophesied. "Gets into everything. You can't even build a mud-pie in the backyard without he's got a finger in it." He dropped his voice to an undertone. "Do you know why they say he's so keen to get Lennox Street pushed through to Errol?" He whispered the reason huskily in Mr Sutton's ear.

"Is that a fact?" Mr Sutton adjusted his glasses and peered after the pioneer coach. "Wish you could prove it, Merrick."

"He's too cute."

"I've no time for progress and civic advancement," Mr Sutton grunted. "I've seen too much of it. The progress is always of money into someone's pocket. And this time the advance may be through my rose garden."

"It'll mean my livery stable'll come down if they widen Errol Street. That means more to me than roses, Mr Sutton. Though maybe," he grinned, "it don't smell as good."

"Progress, progress," Mr Sutton murmured. "Rolling on? Yes, like Juggernaut. Pretty girls on that float, Sam. Wish I was twenty years younger."

"I wonder how the road'll look if they start this widening and running through. Be a different sort of street for the procession. Anyway, it'll be some time yet before they start on their improvements."

Sam Merrick was right. By the time Lennox Street was gaping into Errol Street in a devastated area of broken houses and torn paving there was a procession streaming the opposite way to that grand motley march of Eight-Hour Day. The procession was going down the hill to the water side. It was dull, prosaic, khaki-coloured, and the people watching stood on the ruins of the broken houses, on the rubble of the improvements, some of them crying, others in the cold grey morning calling, "Good-bye, Good-bye" in thin monotonous voices, farewelling their own sons and other women's sons alike. And the horses marched too, but not in ribbons and bells.

"Well, well," Mr Sutton said brisky. "Mustn't waste a beautiful bright day when the roses need attention. Can you let me have any more manure, Sam? I'm needing a load or so."

The two walked back together through the footway into Lennox Street.

# CHAPTER 2

## I

Between the brown surge of the terraces in Lennox Street and the tranquil upper reaches around Foveaux House was "Mrs Webb's Place", two old stone cottages, isolated by a lane on either side, where dwelt a little colony of folk, with one foot in gentility and a desperate other boot sliding downhill towards the workers of the terraces and the flotsam of the alleys.

The cottages, originally intended for the warders of Darling-hurst Gaol, must have been designed by some ticket-of-leave architect with only his memory and a sense of humour to guide him. They looked sane enough from the outside, substantial works in weatherboard and stone, with deep, paved verandas and green wooden shutters to their long french windows; but inside they went wild. A stairway sprang up like a parliamentary question from an irrelevant nook and continued to tie itself into strange knots amid a jigsaw puzzle of attics and alcoves and deep hidden cupboards, out of which might as fittingly emerge the skeleton of a long dead convict in manacles as Mrs Webb's spare bedding. The dormer windows protruded from the steep roof like a snail's eye; and everything the architect had forgotten to put in the house, such as kitchen, bathroom, laundry, lavatory and second best bedroom, had been added on in the back yard, to the discomfort of a little peach-tree, a feeble and anaemic peach-tree, tenderly surrounded by iron supports like a paralysed leg.

One of the cottages, the one farthest up Lennox Street, was given over to boarders, and the lower one to lodgers. Of course, the boarders who paid a pound a week looked down on the lodgers who paid as little as five shillings. The lodgers, on the other hand, as hard to suppress as the plumbago hedge by the front fence, insisted that boarders might come and go, but they lodged on for ever, an affectionate attitude that became a little cloying when they were behindhand with their rent.

Mrs Webb's favourites among her lodgers were certainly the Cornishes in the left front room. The Cornishes never fell behindhand with their rent, even if they starved for it; though Mrs Webb, when she judged that state to be approaching an actuality, was sure to send her daughter Betty with a message "not to worry about Sunday dinner because Mother's sending some over".

"It's wonderful how they manage at all," Mrs Webb would sigh. "What with his wife, such a nice little woman, and them two boys, there's times it breaks me heart to see the Captain always standin' in that window lookin' out." And she would shake her head and call in young Tommy to give him a cake.

When Captain Cornish stood in the long french window, he saw more by sound than by sight, for Captain Cornish was nearly blind. He was waiting to go blind as other men wait for deliverance, the hospital doctors having promised that with the removal of the cataracts on his eyes he would see again, sail a ship again, in short, live again. Meanwhile he could but wait, and on the afternoon of that clear Eight-Hour Day he was waiting for the return of Tommy who had gone down to the Rose of Denmark to see the results of the last race.

Above the level of Lennox Street the inevitable smokestacks rose like the masts of some strange black ship and the Captain's gaze was bent on them, but unseeingly. As he stood there, a castaway mariner on a cliff top, with his brown beard and kind weatherbeaten face, he was placid and steady. There was, the Captain knew, no rescue ship. All his daring life, since he had run from his father's farm at the age of twelve he had faced storms with a carelessness that was no less with him now when, blind and penniless, he found himself a stranded bit of wreckage tangled in other leftover lives.

"Is that you, Tommy?" he called. "Did Sayforth win?"

"No, dad — Greystone, five to one — not even a place."

"Oh well, better luck next time."

"Shall I take your chair on the veranda, dad?"

"Right you are. And bring the paper. I've an idea that if we back Twofold for a place on Saturday, we're on a sure thing. She's a good horse."

All horses were she to the Captain. He had given up his occasional bottle of beer, and even his tobacco sometimes when things were at the ebb, but he remained deaf to all persuasions to give up betting on horses. There was always the chance that he might make a bit of money and in the meantime the excitement of risking sixpence did something to satisfy the craving for change and chance that ran like tidewater in his blood. On Saturdays Tommy wore a path between Mrs Webb's place and the Rose of Denmark, where the results were posted. Tommy was no mean student of form and would hold solemn consultations with his father over track performances. Very occasionally the Captain won and then there was no holding him till the money was gone on other horses.

" 'The two-year-old colt, Twofold'," Tommy read carefully, when they were settled on the verandah, " 'gives every in-diction'. . ."

"Indication," corrected his father placidly.

" 'Indication of a cre-cretible performance'. . ."

"Creditable."

"Bob Noblett says Twofold's a washout."

"Why?"

"Says he knows a chap that knows a chap who works in the stables, and he says Twofold's being kept for bigger money."

"Well, I don't know." The Captain puffed peaceful clouds of blue smoke. "What does he like?"

"He likes Galatean."

"He's right," the Captain nodded. "Cross out Twofold, Tommy, and put down Galatean."

Tommy laboriously tackled the long word.

"Well, go on reading."

Tommy's attention had been taken by four of their fellow lodgers who were tacking across the street in a jovial though unsteady manner, encouraging each other with loud though somewhat incoherent cheers.

" 'Ullo, 'ullo, 'ullo, 'ullo," their leader, Mr Doust, hailed, as he sent the gate crashing open with a mighty kick. His arms lovingly embraced a brown paper parcel suspiciously resembling bottles. This he dumped on the veranda step.

"Ship ahoy!" he roared. "How's the main brace, Cap'n?"

Fred Doust always greeted the Captain in what he believed to be a nautical manner.

"Do the poor old coot good to think he's at sea again," he would explain in loud whispers to his friends. Doust was the handy man of Mrs Webb's place. A waiter by profession, he was willing to mend anyone's boots by a patent process of his own (so that the sole would flap off in three days' time), play the accordion, cut the hair of the lodgers or nail up a rattling window. He had a reputation for drowning kittens in a scientific, kindly, but very elaborate way. He even repaired the plumbing and investigated the terrible smell of a drain which he found was occupied by a dead parrot. There was nothing Fred Doust would not "have a shot at", as he said, even if the shot went wide. The moist, sparse strands of black hair he had trained over his bald pink scalp seemed to shine with perspiration and good nature. He had a touching though unfounded faith in a patent hair restorer which he purchased by the quart and solemnly recommended to anyone who would listen. His boots creaked as he walked and they seemed to creak all the louder when Mr Doust was expressing sympathy. From top to toe he exuded good nature. He was positively hot and clammy with it.

The rest of the party negotiating the gate came eddying round the Captain's chair, Mr Bishop wandering along in the rear with another parcel of bottles. Old Bishie, apart from his habit of champing his false teeth in a way reminiscent of an aged cockatoo grating its beak, had other resemblances to some wise old bird in his deep-set little black eyes, his long hooked nose, and his stiff crest of white hair. Bishie earned an unenviable reputation and a scanty living by casting horoscopes, communicating with the departed, predicting the future, astrology generally, and the mending of watches when all else failed. He dwelt rather draughtily above the kitchen in an attic which the architect had over-generously provided with two windows, a skylight and a little private stair coming up through the floor. Mr Doust was more often in Mr Bishop's attic than in his own, for they were bosom friends.

"Do you know what he did, the old devil," Mr Doust explained, slapping Mr Bishop so lovingly on the shoulder that the bottles were endangered. "He put me onto a Good Thing.

He did, blast him. The only good turn he's ever done me an' I'll stake my oath on that."

"Now, now Fred," Bishie cackled. "You'll get nothing by ingratitude, will 'e, Duncan? Honour those that do you good."

"Good, eh!" Fred Doust protested. "Look at the time you told me Satin was kissing Mercury an' I couldn't lose an' all I got was a summons for not paying income tax. Call that good? Me, that trusted you!"

"You don't happen to know if my wife's home?" Mr Montague said longingly. He was a big man with a puffy red face, insurance agent by compulsion. "You could bring the stuff into our place."

His rather boiled blue eyes stuck out and his prick-up moustache almost quivered with drouth. He fixed his gaze on the bottles as though daring them to lose as much as their froth without him. Mr Doust did not accept the invitation, however. He gathered up the bottles firmly and made for the Cornish room.

"Come on, Duncan," he called as Mr Duncan made to pass. "Here, take the Captain's arm and we'll have it in here. Now you can't refuse me, Cornish, when I haven't had a win for weeks. Look, I brought some sandwiches. Might get drunk on an empty stomach."

Mr Doust's stomach must have been very empty earlier in the day from his appearance. Tommy seized the propitious moment.

"Can I go out in the billy cart, dad?"

"Yes, you may go, sonny," Mr Duncan patted him graciously on the head as the Captain hesitated. "We'll see that your father comes to no harm. The labourer is worthy of his leisure. Eight hours' work, eight hours' rest, eight hours' recreation. Did I ever tell you Cornish, how I settled the chap at Bendigo in 'ninety-five who was interrupting my speech? Eight hours' sleep, I said, but for curs like you, I said, we're willing to give twenty-four hours' sleep. Let sleeping dogs lie, I said."

He was leading the protesting Captain into the front room where Mr Doust was already busy with the bottles. Mr Bishop began to explain how he came by his special system for predicting winners.

"Cost me fifty pounds, sent specially out from London by a man that's so high up I don't dare say who. You've heard me speak of Ritchie, the bookmaker, haven't you Fred? Well, he's the chap that brought it out here. Course I didn't have the money to pay straight out for it, but it'll be worth its weight in gold. I'm the only man in Australia that can work it, and do you know why? I'll tell you why, because the stars change their position, they never stay still, and if you were counting on the race starting at, say five past two, and one of the horses frisks round at the barrier, and it doesn't start till eight past, then that's likely to throw all your reckonings out, if you don't watch it."

"Here's happy days," beamed Mr Doust who had been too busy arranging the little store of cups to hear a word. "Here's to old Bishie's stars putting in some more good work. All together, boys." With this inspiring speech Mr Doust drank. "Ah," he breathed, "that's the stuff. Fill 'em up again."

"One influence in the wrong place, Captain," continued Mr Bishop, "can throw all your reckonings to the winds."

"Is that so?" said the Captain affably.

"Come on, Captain, you can do with another," Mr Doust urged. "Look at him." He pointed admiringly to Montague. "He was weaned on a salt herring."

"My family," began Mr Montague bitterly. "I don't let on to it often. Always throwing off about my family, my wife is. The Montagues——" He paused, overcome. "Among the bravest and best — the Montagues. Come of gran' ole family."

"There, there, Hec," Doust boomed. "We believe y'."

"And what of it?" demanded Mr Duncan. "Say y' come from a grand old family. Well, what about it?" He eyed Mr Montague fiercely. "Have you ever been president of the Council of the Leagues of Freedom? Ten years I was president of the council and never let down the cause of the workers in all that time. Thirty years I've been fighting the workers' battles and that's more to be proud of than inheriting a lack of guts and a set of blond whiskers from any blooming family."

"Now, now, Duncan," Doust put in, pained. "This's a frien'ly gathering, all frien's."

"Language is unparl'ment'ry, Duncan." Montague's little

moustache quivered. "I'll ask you to withdraw the remark."

"Well, right-o," said Mr Duncan.

As though fascinated he eyed a ship's lantern hanging on the wall. He took it down and swung it by the bit of chain attached. Chuckling in an amused way, he paced up and down the room swinging it.

"What the hell do you think you're doing?" Doust inquired.

"I used to have a little white cotta," Duncan mused. "And curls." He took off his old battered hat and flung it on the table. He chuckled again. "I was an altar boy. Can't believe it, can you? Right-o. Watch this." He paced gravely and absurdly up and down. "Three swings to the altar, three to the priest, three to the servers, three to the congregation." He shook the ship's lantern solemnly. "Think I don't know what to do? Well, right-o." The congregation behind its beer encouraged him. "There was a home for fallen women attached to the church," he said, putting down the lantern. He buried his white moustache in his teacup. It emerged again with a slow washing sound like a polar bear from the foam. "I used to stand at the top of the steps and give out the hymn books. Haw, haw. And the magdalenes going past would always chuck me under the chin and say: 'Ain't 'e a little love?' "

Mr Bishop at this moment chanced to glance out of the window. "Well, well," he said with spurious enthusiasm, "here is your good lady, Captain. And Bramley too. I suppose we'd better be going."

From his expression it might be inferred that the Influence was malefic to hearty drinking. Not that Mrs Cornish, timid little Mrs Cornish, ever said anything. It was just that she vibrated. She would sit quietly radiating disapproval, affection, indignation, grief and any of a gamut of emotions without moving a muscle or uttering a word. The heartiest party would fall to funereal gloom if Mrs Cornish, polite in her corner, began silently to vibrate her feelings about the drink evil. You could feel it quivering out of her. As they filtered out the celebrants could hear her murmuring behind them that of course they must stay, she didn't mind at all, they were welcome: "Thank you so much for the sandwiches, Mr Doust."

## II

It was from his mother that Bramley Cornish must have inherited his shy determination. The Cornish family would have gone under long before had it not been for Mrs Cornish. As a young bride, she had formed an unobtrusive habit of collecting from the dressing-table those threepences and six-pences which the Captain scattered about. When disaster over-took them, she was able to produce a bank balance of two hundred pounds, all saved in silver. Hers was the courage of endurance and tenacity. She always gave the impression that she was seeking cover from some unseen enemy; and it was hard to believe that she had twice rounded the Horn in winter and stood calmly with the baby in her arms while the Captain ordered the mutineers back to the pumps with a levelled revolver. She was not pretty; she was not even young; and she was very worn and worried. But under it all there peeped out of subdued little Mrs Cornish a certain quaint mischief, an old-fashioned gaiety, delicate, light and demure, like lace frills on a petticoat. All her life she had been good; but that did not prevent her from the more admiring the Captain for being quite delightfully wicked before she married him, went to sea with him, and quietly took over domestic command.

"I always had to go every voyage," she would explain. "The men would think there was something wrong with the ship if the Captain left his wife behind. They would have refused to go aboard."

To one who had been used to sailors in port the gentle removal of Duncan and Doust and Co. was a slight matter.

"And what sort of a day did you have?" the Captain asked, kissing her.

"Aunt Eileen insisted that Bramley must have another pair of boots. She says she will pay for them."

"That's a shock," the Captain said caustically. "I thought she bit every thrippence so she'd know it again."

"It's really very good of her, John. It isn't that she's mean. . . ."

"Huh."

Bramley's forehead twisted in a frown. He hated going to see relatives on what was practically a begging mission.

"Why can't I get a job?" he demanded. "I'm thirteen."

"Don't be silly, dear," his mother said firmly. "You must finish your schooling. And don't sigh like that. They say it takes years off your life every time you do it."

"We've got five shillings till pension day," the boy said desperately. "Five shillings to last nearly a week."

"We've been worse off." The Captain's tone was calm. Galatean, he was thinking. Never venture, never win. Perhaps if he put a shilling on instead of sixpence straight out . . . at six to one. "We'll manage," he said confidently.

"But why can't I get a . . ." Bramley was reopening the old debate when Tommy's head popped in at the window.

"Mr Webb's lost again," he shouted.

"Can I go and look for him?" Bramley clamoured.

Mrs Webb always rewarded the finder of her spouse.

"You can't go walking the streets in the dark," his mother replied. "You might catch cold, and it isn't right for you to be wandering about by yourself. Don't frown like that, dear."

Bramley subsided. "But I must get money somehow," he thought, "anyhow."

# III

Mrs Webb's husband was always getting lost and would be gone for days at a time. Half Foveaux would turn out to look for him. The charitable explanation was that he lost his memory since he never knew where he had been or what he had done in his wanderings. Scouting parties would turn out and comb the district systematically and women stand at their front gates keeping watch for sign of him.

"Have they found Mrs Webb's husband yet?" people would call to picknickers returning home.

"Good Lord! Is he lost again? That poor woman must be nearly out of her mind. Here Joe, you go up and see what you can do while I take the children home."

And one more husband would have joined the search party, his wife later sallying forth to condole with the bereaved Mrs Webb.

All the lodgers not taking part in the search waited on their communal veranda for a cab. It was the custom for anyone who found Mr Webb to come home with him in a cab at Mrs Webb's expense, and many a small boy had dreamt of sharing such glory. All the small boys and girls of the neighbourhood assembled outside the Webb gate ready to bear tidings home, and they were employing their time meanwhile with a game of rounders and a game of chasings, the two going on simultaneously and confusedly, the little girls' white dresses showing like moth wings in the dusk as they raced up and down with shrill cries. Young Tommy and his friend Billy Noblett had started a free fight with the opposing gang, the Wallies. It was waging bitterly round the right to own a small plane-tree which the municipal council had planted outside the gate of Mrs Webb's with several hundred other small trees up and down the street. These were intended to provide shade in ten years' time if nothing happened to them before. Over the tree and the little wood-paling fence surrounding it Tommy exercised proprietorial rights. No one could touch it or water it except himself. And here was Bert Wallies swinging on the fence round his tree!

"G'wan," he shouted. "You go home. 'Tisn't your tree. See!"

" 'Tisn't yours."

" 'Tis. And you haven't got anyone lost from your place. See!"

This was felt to be a telling blow and he followed it up with a good swing of the fist that sent Bert howling down the footpath. Mrs Cornish on the front veranda was busy comforting Mrs Webb and did not notice the incident.

"I'm afraid he'll be run over," Mrs Webb mourned. "What with all these cars that are about now. If only we lived further out from the city, Waverley or Coogee, it wouldn't be so hard to find him."

"Now take last time," Mrs Cornish put in, "I thought from the way the man brought him home, he must have some hold over Mr Webb."

"Do you think so, Mrs Cornish?" Mrs Webb quavered like a small child frightening itself with a bogey.

"Well, of course, you never can tell. But did he have his flannels on, Mrs Webb? The nights are still cold and if he's sleeping out. . . ."

"No, he didn't. And Herb takes cold so easily."

"Dear, dear." Mrs Cornish was really more concerned about Mr Webb not wearing his warm underwear than about his being lost.

"It was such a lovely day," Mrs Webb apologized.

"It's not so much him wandering about as what he might catch."

"You can't catch anything," Mrs Montague's little cheerful voice put in behind them. "That's only an error of mortal mind."

Mrs Cornish froze into shocked disapproval. To doubt pneumonia and the validity of flannel underpants was a kind of atheism almost as bad as saying there was no Garden of Eden. Mrs Cornish, if she ever made a mental picture of the Garden of Eden, would have seen that Adam and Eve were "properly wrapped up". Winter and summer Mrs Cornish's menfolk wore their flannels.

"Divine Mind governs," Mrs Montague said, firmly sitting down on the remaining cane chair. "You must remember, dear, that Divine Mind governs all things."

"Not down near Ogham Lane," Mrs Webb responded dolefully. "He might get hit on the head."

"Now you're letting in error," Mrs Montague said with that saintly sweetness that always affected her husband like toothache. "You must know he is quite safe. He reflects Divine Mind."

Everyone at Mrs Webb's place had long since worn themselves out arguing Christian Science with Mrs Montague. They accepted it now as her particular failing, just as they accepted Doust having one too many drinks occasionally or old Bishie's star-gazing. Besides it was felt that if Christian Science comforted her for the calamity of Mr Montague, then it would be kinder and better to let her keep it. Not that Christian Science always sufficed. Mrs Cornish remembered one occasion when she walked into the laundry to find Mrs Montague tearfully washing curry and rice from her hair. Mr Montague did not like curry. "There are some times," Mrs Montague had said bitterly, "I can't overcome the error of disliking my own husband."

Everyone liked poor Mrs Montague: a pretty fair woman, a little wistful, a little faded, very conscious that her youth was going from her and that her unhappiness was hastening its going. "I don't mind being poor," she confided to Mrs Cornish, "if only my husband would take me out sometimes or even be nice to me. But he wants all the money, all the good times for himself." She cheered up. "Oh well, when Linnie and Oscar grow up we'll have good times, the three of us. You see. Only," her face fell again, "I don't suppose they'll want me. I'll be too old."

"Nonsense," Mrs Cornish responded, patting her on the shoulder. "It's their duty to look after their mother." Mrs Cornish disapproved of Mr Montague, who might have been a rich man instead of an insurance agent if he had not squandered all his money and Mrs Montague's as well.

"I don't want duty," Mrs Montague said wistfully, "I want them to want me."

Teaching dancing was no hardship to Mrs Montague. Her idea of paradise was a dance tune and a good partner. Hector had been light on his feet when she first met him. Now that he was going to flesh, he refused to dance. He still went out to visit friends in the evening; but he left Mrs Montague at home to mind the children. "We can't both go out," he argued. So Mrs Montague studied her Christian Science and managed to convince herself that her life was full of gladness, even when her husband sold her piano. "There's no lack of Divine Mind," she said firmly, and took Linnie with her to the little room above the Sunday School hall where she kept up her music on the battered wreck of a piano used for dancing classes.

"It's all in the way you think," Mrs Montague was explaining to Mrs Webb when there was a roar from the hall that betokened the presence of Mr Montague.

"Where are you? Where's Linnie? Dammit, where are you all?"

"Excuse me, dear," Mrs Montague said sweetly. "I think Hector wants something." She went to the front gate and called: "Linnie! Linnie, dear! Your father wants you."

"Let him want," was the ungracious retort, as the hot, panting Linnie flung inside the gate. Little Mrs Cornish quivered reproach at this filial disregard. "S'pose I'd better find out what he's bellowing about," Linnie grumbled as she made her way inside.

"I don't believe in children being rude," Mrs Cornish observed to Mrs Webb, folding her hands in her lap as a kitten folds its paws. "I've always brought my boys up to be well-behaved. One of those men who read your head said that a son of mine would become Prime Minister of Australia."

"I do wish I knew which way he's gone," Mrs Webb fretted. "I'll move, I will truly."

"Oh no, you won't," the Captain put in cheerfully. "I've heard you say that before. He'll come home and you'll forget all about it."

The Captain was sitting just outside the window of the Cornish room with Mr Duncan, having a last peaceful pipe as was their custom. It was too early, too cool for the locusts who later in the year would shrill through the dusk from the convent garden. There was not even the thrilling of a cricket or the mazy dance of the tiny flies around the street lamp to indicate the coming of summer, but the little group on the veranda had sat through so many peaceful evenings that they knew the turn of the year as well as any woodman.

Mr Bishop came out, under his arm the portfolio in which he kept his horoscopes.

"Ha, ha," he croaked. "Enjoying the night?"

He beckoned mysteriously to Mr Duncan who joined him in the hall where whispering and the chink of pennies indicated that Mr Bishop was borrowing his fare. They heard the murmur, "Tomorrow", and "That's all right, quite understand." Duncan resumed his seat and all pretended not to have noticed the incident. They called good-nights after Mr Bishop's retreating back.

There was a muffled crash of crockery and a minute later Mr Montague shot out of the door like a rocket. "Just when I'm trying to digest my tea," he shouted over his shoulder. "You know your damn Science upsets my stomach."

"Evening," he muttered savagely. "Look very peaceful. Wish I could get a bit of peace. Only place I can get it is Out, always Out. No home life."

Mr Montague made a habit of these soliloquies. He liked to represent himself as a much-tried man. He bounced out of the gate and turned downwards towards the Rose of Denmark. The flurry of his passing had hardly died away when around the corner from Mark Street a cab appeared and made purposefully for the gate of Mrs Webb's place. That could only mean one thing, especially with Nosey Owen on the box.

"He's found!" roared Mr Duncan. "Mrs Webb!"

"Thank heaven!" Mrs Webb panted, hurrying to the gate. "Oh, I was that scared."

"Now perhaps you'll realize what Science can do," Mrs Montague rejoiced, quite forgetting that an overdose of it had just sent her spouse rocketing down to the Rose of Denmark. "I've been thinking the right thought all the afternoon."

"And I hope you're quite satisfied with yourself, Herbert Webb." Mrs Webb received the salvage. "I hope you're satisfied with nearly driving me to my grave with worry and anxiety.

Fretting about you all the afternoon and the policeman coming round and all the people running their legs off. You ought to be ashamed the trouble you give. And dinner half burnt, I was that upset in my mind. You don't deserve to have a good home and family."

"Looks as if I hold finder's record," Nosey Bob beamed. "This is the second time, ain't it, that I've beat the field?"

"Comes of having a cab," Mr Duncan retorted. "Gives you an advantage over the rest of us."

Nosey pocketed his reward, waved his whip, and turned the horse's head in the direction Mr Montague had just taken.

"Bet he boozes the lot," the Captain prophesied.

There was a coolness in the dusk that might have been merely Mrs Cornish expressing temperance views.

"It's getting a bit chilly." Mr Duncan knocked the tobacco out of his pipe. "Think I'll go in."

He rose reluctantly out of the creaky cane chair. From the street the children were being called in one by one. Their cries were quieter and they sat in little groups under the lamplight. On the boarders' veranda a desultory murmuring of conversation fell into silence. The Captain knocked his pipe out in a shower of red sparks. "I must call Tommy in," Mrs Cornish thought. But she felt it would be a pity to break the calm. It was all so peaceful.

# CHAPTER 3

## I

The uproar in the Rose of Denmark reached a climax towards the close of Eight-Hour Day. The air in the bar was heavy with the smell of beer and loud with the roar of voices. The canary in its cage above the cash register took its head peevishly from under its wing, scattered some birdseed on the bar floor, ruffled its feathers and burst into full song. The canary was the spoilt darling of the bar and he allowed no one to forget it.

"Ah, dry up, you!" Daisy shouted at him half in earnest as she rushed past with a couple of foaming mugs in each hand.

Eight-Hour Day had made her bad-tempered for, as she pointed out to George the barman, she "only got the blasted procession coming home".

Usually Daisy chirruped blithely up and down the bar, as light on her little stilt heels as the canary hopping on its perch. Her tight black dress set off her pert figure and frizzy blonde hair. Her cheeky face wore an engaging grin as she chaffed the men on the other side of the bar. She knew she could hold her own; but tonight, what with the heat and the worry and the rush, and her feet hurting her, and Curly Thompson sitting with Elsie Snow in the ladies' parlour, she was completely miserable. The shrilling of the canary was the last straw. Wasn't there enough noise without him starting?

"I'd poison your blessed birdseed if the boss wasn't looking," she muttered.

"Marvellous that bird is," Bob Noblett remarked to the proprietor, Jordan True. "You wouldn't think 'e could 'old all that voice in jus' a bunch of fevvers." Bob was standing with a group consisting of Hamp, Jim Kleist and Nosey Owen, all of them slightly the worse for beer.

"The little animal has certainly a gift for mellifluousness," Mr True responded, his pale eyes following Daisy and the money to the till.

Jordan True's eyes seemed to have taken cover in his face as a neutral ground between the heavily greased wave of hair trained down over his forehead and the stiff white collar which had shot up and buried his chin. Jordan's clothes were as ornate as his speech. There was gold in his smile and a heavy gold seal ring on his pudgy red hand. His gold watch chain crossed a fancy vest with white edging; and in his tie, in a gold setting, was a large green stone which its owner fondly referred to as "a gem of purest ray supreme". Behind all this opulence Jordan showed merely as a background. The man himself was visible only in those pale blue eyes that looked out over his red face like strangers.

"My wife," he said, wiping down the counter with a cloth, "has an undiluted affection for that canary."

Hamp's friend, Jim Kleist, was suddenly overcome by a mixture of beer and pathos. "Not that I'm the man to flatter," he murmured huskily, "but that little songster's voice — it brings tears to my eyes." He wiped them with the back of a hairy fist. "Sure as I stand here, Jordy, he . . . he's got me completely knocked up. I'm a lonely man." He sniffed again. "I cry meself to sleep sometimes. Havin' a kidney extracted is what does it." He tearfully insisted on dragging out a handful of shirt to expose the scar in an epidermis resembling Jewish cheese. "Did you know I come from the bush, Jordy?" he asked plaintively. Coming from the bush was almost a profession with Jim Kleist. "I used to pick up the little lambs and carry them on my saddle bow. If it hadn't been for me, Jordy," he paused to wipe the tears away, "they would uv perished."

"Brace up there, Jim." Hamp patted him on the shoulder. "You know," he remarked admiringly to Jordan, "he's a card. Can turn on the waterworks like that any time he wants to. He's up to no end of things."

"Now, don't go saying that, Hamp," Kleist protested, wounded. "People'll get ideas if you go saying a thing like that."

"Hamp wasn't making any interventions," Mr True put in peacefully, at the same time fixing his eye on Nosey Owen near the door. He was thinking of having Nosey put out.

"Jim," said Hamp emotionally, "you know I'm the last man in the world to let any man think anything he wouldn't like me to think."

Having with difficulty mastered this sentence Hamp stretched his huge hand out dramatically. "Old man . . . Jim . . . sure as there's a heaven above I've never wronged you in thought, word or deed. Jim — forgive me."

Jim with the simple emotion of a strong man took his hand.

"My dear old chap," he said tearfully, "I forgive you. But there ain't nothing to forgive."

On this beautiful scene Daisy intruded with a regrettable lack of tact. "George says will he let Nosey Owen have another drink or not, Mr True, and the sandwiches are running out."

"I'll come," Mr True said. Then apologetically, "You'll excuse me, boys." He overtook Daisy. "Where's Mrs True?" he asked in a low voice.

"She's in the ladies' parlour." Daisy hesitated. "She isn't quite herself."

True walked past her down the bar towards the ladies' parlour, his face wearing its customary expression of affability. There were very few people in the parlour. It was comparatively quiet after the uproar of the bar. At a table in the corner Jessie Kerr, under a straw hat overburdened with roses, was warmly extending hospitality to a newly acquired and rather befuddled gentleman friend.

"You'll like it up at my place," she mentioned enthusiastically. "Real home-like. I always do things comfy and home-like. Oh you'll like it. There's a piece of pork I roasted and we got real plum pudding out of a tin. 'Tisn't like a lot of places, just any old how."

At the nearest table Curly Thompson and Jock Jamieson were sitting with Daisy's friend, Elsie Snow. Mrs True, leaning over the table, was shouting jovially to Elsie:

"That's the way to give it to him. Gee, I wouldn't let him tell me what to do, Elsie. You stand up for yourself. Eh, Curly?"

Curly Thompson lolled back in his chair, his waistcoat spread open showing a silk shirt that bulged with the effort of containing Curly, muscles and all. He was handsome in a thick heavy way, but he was not too heavy to move with cat-footed speed if he had urgent reason for it. His hat canted back from a low fleshy forehead on to a greasy swell of coal-black waves. He eyed the scowling Jamieson with a lazy dangerous look.

"If," Elsie was saying in a high, genteel voice, "you think you can come the Holy Willie over me, Jock, just because I came in to have a drink with a friend of my girl friend's, while he waits for her to get off, you can. . . ." She turned appealingly to Curly Thompson. "Isn't that a fact, Curly? Didn't you say you wanted to see Daise, and asked me to have a drink while we waited?"

"Well," Curly said liberally, with a provocative grin at Jamieson, "I don't see why if she's workin' late, you an' I jus' shouldn't have another drink and then go without her. Keep each other company, see? I've always liked you, Else. You know that."

The girl was uncertain whether to be flattered or scared. Curly was Daisy's bloke; he was also a power in the Foot. He was a desirable and flattering catch. On the other hand there was a nasty look in the eye of this pestiferous Scotsman who had attached himself to her.

"Elsie," Jamieson said in a commanding tone, "Ah'm askin' ye to come out of here."

"You weren't invited to come," Elsie said jeeringly, "but since you're here, have one on me?"

He stood like a granite statue. "No worrrkin'-class man or woman," he said, drawing out his r's like a cable from a locker, "can afford to drink." She took no notice. "Else!"

"You take my tip. . . ." Mrs True was beginning noisily, when she felt Jordan's presence behind her and the words died on her lips.

Jordan nodded to the company. He experienced considerable satisfaction at seeing Curly with the handsome Elsie Snow. He hoped Daisy had duly noted that Curly was preoccupied with the other girl. It didn't seem to be any use telling Daisy how fond he was of her. She just didn't seem to know where her best interests lay while Curly was about. If Curly were only removed, Jordan True had often thought . . . but there was always his wife.

He nodded to Curly Thompson affably though. If you had windows in your house, it was wise to be friendly with Curly.

"We need some more sandwiches, Millie," he said to his wife. "Will you accompany me?"

The woman, her hair hanging down, her face flushed, followed him obediently from the parlour down the hall to the kitchen. He shut the door of the kitchen before he spoke.

"You're a nice one," he said quietly. "There's times when I could belt you."

"Ah, don't be a nark, Jordy." She lurched over and put her arms around his neck. "I ain't done nothing, love. What's a few drinks?"

He patiently disentangled himself from her embrace and set about cutting the sandwiches.

"Don't smooge to me. It isn't the drinks, it's the way you carry them. Eight-Hour Day and a rush on, and that's the time you get boozed."

True's love of words was never evident when he spoke to his wife. "Millie has what you might call a vacuity of diction," he once observed. Sober, Millie was a pleasant woman, but nowadays she was seldom sober.

"Come on, give us a kiss an' make up," she shouted, clumsily endeavouring to wrest the bread-knife from his grasp.

"Look out! Let me alone!" True protested. "I haven't any time to be messing about. You go upstairs and have a rest."

As he spoke, she wrenched the knife out of his hand with such force that it sliced downward against her thigh.

"Gee, I'm cut!" she said stupidly, and flopped down in a chair beside the table. True recovered the knife and continued with the sandwich cutting.

"Now Millie," he repeated, "you go on upstairs and have a good rest. I'll fix this and George'll look after the parlour."

His wife rose obediently, if unsteadily, and lurched out of the kitchen.

"Woman," True observed to Hamp, as he set the sandwiches on the bar, "you know the moolidious line of the poet, Hamp. 'Ever since the world began, she's been ruling the Fate of Man.'"

"Them's beautiful words, Jordy." Jim Kleist showed signs

of breaking into tears again. "Beautiful, beautiful words. . . ." He began to sing.

Jordan's light eyes slid sideways and the merest flicker indicated to Hamp that his friend was wearing out his welcome.

"Come on," Hamp said, "we'd better be gettin' home, Jim, old man."

"Always the same," Jim snivelled. "Only the little lambs to love me."

There was a sudden roar from the ladies' parlour where Jock Jamieson had suddenly taken to Curly Thompson with his fists. The table went over with a crash just as the drinkers at the bar crowded to the door to see what was happening.

"What's the game?" Jordan inquired, coolly strolling up. The times when Jordan True had lost his composure could be counted on one hand.

Big George, the barman, having thrust himself into the fray, was endeavouring with argument and muscle to persuade the fighters out the side door on to the stone stairs leading to Plug Alley. A couple of Curly Thompson's friends closed in behind George and they all disappeared with the milling mob from the bar after them. Some rushed out of the front door to get a better view of the stairs. True remained by the cash register.

"An old trick," he observed sardonically. "Start a fight and get everybody away while you extract the auriferous from the till."

Curly and Jamieson might be fighting over the girl, but True wasn't going to take any chances.

"Hey, Jordy!" Jim Kleist stuck his head in the door. "George's goin' crook at Curly."

Through the voices raised in argument outside True could hear George's hoarse bellow: "That'll be enough from you . . . you get out of here. Don't let me see your ugly mug round here again or I'll. . . ." The customers had begun to drift back to the bar when there was a cry from George, a crash, and a rush outside again.

"*Now*, what's up?" Jordan inquired.

"He froo 'im over the railin'."

"Who did?"

"Curly."

Jordan swore and rushed to the rescue. The pale-faced George, shaken, bruised, but hardly hurt, had landed on the roof six feet below and was being advised and vociferously assisted back on to the landing.

"They might uv killed me," he muttered, feeling himself all over. "Might uv broken me neck." His assailants had taken to their heels down the steps. "Come at a man from behind," he grumbled. "Rushin' him when he's not lookin'."

"You're supposed to be the useful, George," Jordan said coolly. "Want me to get you a wet nurse?" But he thoughtfully poured George a whisky.

George, the centre of a small mob of sympathizers, held forth loudly about his injuries and his determination to fix Curly. In the bar the noise continued cheerfully, with the shrilling of the canary rising above the chink of glasses and money, the arguments about the races, the cries of "Two of half and half", "Schooner of new", "Pint of old", and the ping of the cash register.

"Something'll have to be done about Curly," Jordan murmured to Hamp. "He is becoming too obstropulous." His pale eyes flickered sideways to Daisy. It was a pity Daisy was so keen on Curly. If she knew which side her bread was buttered, she would have decided to cut him out long ago. Jordan could tell that Daisy knew he was watching her. She was probably scared he would decide to do something about Curly. She gave him a nervous smile.

"Gee, boss," she shrilled, "that was a near go for George."

If I weren't married, Jordan thought, it might be different. She wouldn't hang on to Curly a minute, if she thought I could marry her.

"Your young man, Daise. . . ." he was beginning, when the terrified face of Elsie signing to him from the ladies' parlour attracted his attention.

"Oh, Mr True," she gasped, "your wife. She's lying on the bathroom floor and there's blood everywhere."

"Send for a doctor," Jordan flung over his shoulder to George. "Here, come and give me a hand. . . . Get Anne from the kitchen."

"If it isn't one thing," George grumbled with lumbering

concern, "it's another." He was a little piqued that the "missus" should go and have some accident just when he had all the limelight for once.

"She was holding on to the bread-knife," the white-faced Jordan explained to the doctor, "and I was holding on to it . . . and I never knew it cut her when she let go."

The woman opened her eyes. "It was an accident," she whispered hoarsely. "He didn't do it."

"Millie," Jordan True said desperately, "you was always square to me. I know you wouldn't go back on me. Speak to me."

"Get out of here," the old doctor ordered. "You're damn lucky the girl found her when she did. Another ten minutes and she'd have bled to death. Even now it'll be close. Get out. I can't have you jammering underfoot."

True backed blindly into the hall and almost tripped over Daisy.

"How is she?" Daisy whispered. "I can't believe it. One minute she's in the bar as large as life and the next. . . ."

"You'd best go back, Daisy," True said dully. "There's nothing you can do. She'll live," he added.

Another five minutes, he was thinking. If Elsie hadn't run upstairs when the rumpus started. If she'd only. . . . Oh well . . . it was just his luck.

"I've never had anything but trouble, Daise," he said in a strained voice. "A man of my elocutory ability ought to have gone far. A damn sight farther than this pub. But she's held me back. It doesn't seem right to say it now . . . but she's held me back like — like an anchor. It doesn't seem right to say it. After all, I'm married to her."

They stood silent. Each knew what the other was thinking.

George was already clearing the bar. Daisy sat down beside the cash register and dried her eyes with a dish-cloth. The canary hopped to the corner of his cage and cocked his head sideways to look at her. Then he gave a preliminary chirrup and prepared to sing again.

"For Gawd's sake shut up," Daisy screamed at him.

George turned and looked at her with bovine disapproval. "What's up?" he asked.

"That damn bird. It's got me crazy. I can't stand it. Everything's gone wrong." She pulled herself together. "There's the missus lyin' upstairs near dead and that little wretch singin' his head off. He ain't got no heart." She stood on tiptoe to unhitch the cage.

"What're y're goin' to do?" George asked. "The boss'll raise Hell." He was not feeling particularly well disposed towards the boss.

"I'm giving the orders now," Daisy said grimly. If she could not have Curly, there was always Jordan. "Here, Jim," she said, holding out the canary's cage purposefully to Jim Kleist. "Take it and get out, quick."

"All alone," Jim Kleist was murmuring, as he let himself and the canary carefully down the steps. "Only the little lambs to love me."

"Anyway," Daisy sniffed. "I've got rid of that damn bird." Then she sat down and burst into tears. She had lost Curly and she couldn't marry Jordan. It didn't seem fair.

George lumbered back into the bar and began to put away the glasses. "They reckon the missus'll be all right again in a couple of days," he mentioned.

"What d' you expect me to do." Daisy said tearfully. "Sing?"

## II

"Where to now?" Hamp remarked as he stood on the corner outside the Rose of Denmark.

"You can do wot you like," Bob Noblett announced truculently, "but I'm goin' to find that blasted flat-footed Hannam an' polish his buttons wiv 'is teeth."

Bob Noblett always went looking for policemen when he was drunk. His father had been a policeman and had begun his loving son's career by running him in. Bob never forgot and transferred his dislike of his father to all other policemen. "Once a policeman, never a man" was his favourite motto.

"Ye come along with us, old chap. We'll see you're all right," Jock Jamieson said soothingly.

"Lemme alone." Bob shook off his friends' grip. "I'm goin'

to fix 'im this time if I swing for it. 'E got me three munce. I'll break 'is bloody neck."

Jock Jamieson and Hamp between them led him down the steps into Plug Alley and half dragged, half supported him along the narrow pavement. From the secretive blank of the mean terrace cautious heads protruded slowly like limpets from their shells. A sound in Plug Alley after dark would bring the unseen dwellers to their narrow doors, so many sets of fixed attentive eyes. Those who did not emerge from the slits in the wall might be seen lifting a corner of the front window curtain as carefully as if a shower of bullets might reward their interest.

Hamp rapped at one of the black, coffin-like entrances and a dim light showed for a minute as Mrs Noblett opened the door.

"Is that you, Bob?" she asked in a frightened tone.

"We've brought him home, Mrs Noblett," Hamp said politely.

"Oh!" The door opened wider. They led the still pugnacious Bob into the sitting-room where a group of wide-eyed children clustered round their mother and watched in silence as Bob slumped in a chair.

"Well," he said defiantly, "whata y' lookin' at?"

The woman said nothing. She wiped her eyes on the end of the baby's night-gown. Bob's fighting mood began to melt.

"I done it again, Mamie," he said thickly. "I promised I wouldn't an' I done it again. I don't deserve to live. I'll go and drown meself."

"Well, I guess we'd better be goin'," Hamp remarked. "Bob always squares her," he explained to Jamieson as they reached the street. Hamp got his living in ways more ingenious than respectable but this did not affect the friendship between him and the sober Jamieson. "He'll be down at the markets to-morrow as right as rain. Puts 'is 'ead under the tap, that fixes him."

They paused at the corner where Plug Alley turned into Ogham Street. At this point Ogham Street broke into a rash of leprous little houses. One side of the street was dead black in shadow, while the other showed greyish white, with balconies along the wall like pouches under the eyes of a dead man.

"We might go up to Nora's," Hamp suggested. Joe, one of Nora's friends, had won at the races and, by all logic, the beer would be flowing at Nora's.

"No," said Jock grimly. "I dinna mind a drink — only one drink — but yon's anither matter. Fun's fun, Hamp, but Nora's pepul dinna know where to stop."

"Ar," Hamp looked disgusted. "Can't you have a night out once in a while?" His companion was silent. "Come on, Scotty."

"I'll be away," Jamieson said stubbornly. He liked Hamp; he had definitely decided to bring Hamp to a different manner of life; but he was certain Hamp was not going to do the same by him.

"Elsie'll be up at Nora's," Hamp said casually and grinned.

Jock set his jaw. It was one of those jaws made for setting purposes and it never looked quite at home when merely eating or talking. Having been formed from granite, it was happier set. He strode up the street in the direction of Nora's at a pace that left Hamp chuckling.

Elsie opened the door to them. "Oh, it's you," she said nastily. "The little white-'ead 'ero."

"I wish tae speak tae ye," Jamieson challenged. They eyed each other like enemies.

"Garn. Cut it out," Hamp protested. "Always roarin' each other up."

"Come on in, love," Nora, the lady of the house, welcomed cheerily from the front room. " 'Tisn't often we have any booze about the place, but when we have, the more the merrier, eh Joe? Come on in, Scotty, an' make your miserable life happy."

"Make up your mind," Elsie said impatiently. "Come or go."

The Scotsman still stood on the doorstep.

"I want a word with ye."

"Not here."

"Come out a minute."

"No," Elsie said defiantly; and almost immediately called to Nora: "I'll be back in a minute, love."

They walked round the corner into lower Lennox Street in silence. Then Jock turned on her sternly.

"I won't have ye goin' round with that crowd."

"You won't, won't you. Who the hell are you anyway?" Elsie's eyes blazed with anger. "Anyone'd think I was married to you. Come kickin' up a row at the hotel just cos I'm having one with a friend. Then you come looking like black thunder to Nora's so's I have to get you out of the way to save trouble. I'm sick of the sight of you. You leave me alone. D' y' hear?"

With her hair an aureole about her white forehead, her firm chin uplifted from the fair column of her throat, she looked like the carved figurehead of a ship, one of those women whose painted eyes stare through the salt spray at unknown coasts. Jock eyed her admiringly.

"Maybe it's only that ye've been drinkin'," he said, "but ye look grand."

Elsie almost stuttered with rage. "You think you've only to crook your finger an' any woman'll come running. Well you're wrong, see? I'm earning good money at the shirtmaking and I don't have to take orders outside working hours. Not yours, anyway. So you let me alone, or I'll get your ribs kicked in for you."

The future secretary of the Amalgamated Stove and Boiler-makers' Union was no whit disturbed. "Orright," he said quietly, "but I'm going to marry ye just the same."

"You! I wouldn't pick you up with a clothes-prop. No, not if it had insecticide on the end of it. And get out of my way. I'm going back to the party."

"A man," he said reflectively, "needs a home. Otherwise he goes drinking."

"Half the best boozers in Foveaux are married."

"I said Man. It's lonely for a man by himself."

Elsie hesitated. "I don't mind you coming round friendly like. But marrying's off. What does it get you except a mob of kids and a lot of worry? Look at Mamie Noblett!"

"The worker—" Jock drew out the word, "the worker is expected to live without pleasure or security. But, Else, lass, 'tisn't all as bad. . . ."

"Now don't you start that stuff about revolutions and that.

Gawd knows you ain't no catch without your looney ideas, but with 'em you're as much fun as a wet Sunday."

"I live respectable," Jock defended himself.

"If you're throwin' off," the girl said dangerously, "let me tell you I do what I like, and if you want to preach a sermon, get a soap box."

"But Else, I wasna saying. . . ."

But she had turned her back on him and was marching towards Nora's, contempt in every line of her. Jock watched her go with, Elsie told herself, a face as long as a laundry bill.

The girl was not feeling happy either. She found the party quarrelling over the reported demise of Mrs True as though their own lives hung on the issue.

"Oh let's have some music," she cried angrily. "Sittin' there gassin' all the evening."

So presently the gramophone was shivering the air with "Take Me Back to Mother Lulu". Elsie sang and tangoed and drank beer and screamed with laughter at Hamp's imitation of a world-famous Jewish comedian holding up his own race to Gentile contempt.

"Gosh, I could die laughin'," she gasped, but she was feeling very far from laughter. Jock's face kept rising in her mind, boyishly stern and miserable. "I'll be going, love," she told Nora. "No, it isn't that I ain't havin' a good time. But the beer don't seem to agree with me."

She refused all offers of escort. She would look after herself, she said.

"An' if that sour-lookin' bloke with the chin comes round," one of her friends offered gallantly, "you just let me know an' I'll fix him."

"Thanks, Sid," Elsie said mechanically. She was very glad she had not brought Sid with her when she reached the front of the three-storey residential where she slept. The entrance was in darkness and on the front step she almost stumbled over a seated figure.

"Oh it's you again," she said wearily. "Didn't I tell you to git."

"I'm sorry, Else," he said humbly.

"So you ought to be. I s'pose you come hanging about here

to pick a row with whoever brought me home." No answer. "Is that it?"

She tried to lash her anger but it was no use. Suddenly she sat down beside him and put her arms around his shoulders. He turned and kissed her fiercely.

"You silly mug," she whispered. "You oughtn't to be let out by yerself."

"Ah'm that lonely," Jamieson said desperately.

"Shut up." Her voice was tender. "It's all right. I was a pig to you."

They continued their conversation in a murmur of endearments until Elsie said in a louder tone: "Struth, it's cold sitting on this step."

"Is that you, Else?" a voice croaked overhead; and the landlady's steel curlpins glimmered faintly. "Don't be sittin' there like a good girl, you'll wake all the neighbours."

Elsie got up and stretched herself.

"I guess I'd better be goin' in," she said casually.

"Elsie," Jock pleaded, "Ah'm that lonely."

She looked undecided.

"All right, Scotty," she said, holding out her hand. "Mind, I'm not promising I'll marry you or anything. Look out for the bottom stair and be careful of the turn on the landing."

He followed her into the narrow, mouldy-smelling darkness of the hallway.

"Hold my hand," she whispered. "You're that helpless!"

It was Elsie's way of accepting his proposal of marriage, though she would have been the last to admit it.

# CHAPTER 4

## I

It was the visit of the charitable ladies that finally decided Bramley that he was going to work if he died for it.

The Cornish family had been getting tea ready when an authoritative knock came at the front door. Mrs Cornish hesitated. She was timid with strangers.

"I'll go," the Captain said, sensing her reluctance.

He crossed the threshold of the french window and stared at the two shapes in the doorstep.

"Good evening," he said politely.

The nearer of the two ladies was a formidable figure. She had sandy hair scraped back under a black straw hat from which the shiny black heads and barbs of two crossed hatpins protruded like antennae. Her black silk dress with a high boned lace collar was stiff with respectability. Her shiny black shoes with round turn-up toes were planted on the mat as though indicating that they were not going to allow the mat to impose upon them.

"Mr Cornish?" she said rapidly, her shiny little black eyes glittering as they fixed themselves on the plimsoll line where the Captain's waistcoat and trousers failed to meet over a bulge of shirt. "We are from the Ladies' Benevolent Society, Mr Cornish."

She seized the basket behind which her companion had been sheltering and pushed it into the Captain's hand.

"We understand that you are in . . . ah . . . needy circumstances and the society has made it its business to investigate you."

Her eyes glittered disapprovingly at the Captain's beard as though they would not leave even that fastness without investigation.

"I am happy to say the results have been very favourable,"

she nodded more affably. "Very favourable. So we decided that immediate relief should be given. All the ladies agree that it is a most worthy case. I understand you have no other means beside the invalid pension? Your wife goes to church regularly?"

"She goes," said the Captain grimly. A less authoritative lady might have perceived a simmering in the dusk such as the air betrays when something is red hot.

"Yes, yes. Of course you are debarred by your infirmity — but I trust the rector has called to pray with you?"

"No, he hasn't," said the Captain through his teeth.

"And why is that?" The lady's tone was sharper.

The Captain's was a good clear carrying voice even when he spoke in a whisper.

"Because," he said softly, "he doesn't come sticking his nose in where he isn't wanted."

The lady stiffened.

"Kindly tell your wife to return the basket," she snapped. "In future she may apply on Tuesday mornings at the side door of the church hall. Make a note of it, Janet, four in the family."

"Yes, Mrs Cooper."

They moved towards the gate.

"The kind of man," said Mrs Cooper audibly, "to whom I take an instant dislike."

"Here, hold hard a minute," the Captain said, stumbling after them. He thrust the basket through the gate so that a bag of sugar and some potatoes fell on the footpath. "Here, take it. Take your charity and your patronage out of here. It's enough to poison the air. What right have you. . . ."

"You won't get yourself anywhere by behaving like this, my man."

"What right have you to come investigating me, you buck-toothed worker of mercy? You go back to your flea-bitten society and tell them to keep their investigations to themselves and their charity too. . . ."

The ladies fled up the footpath but the Captain's voice followed them.

"Go home," he called. "Go home. Charity begins at home."

Stooping down he picked up the brown paper bag of sugar which he flung with uncertain ferocity. "Go to hell," he muttered. He searched for the potatoes but not being able to find them made his way indoors to comfort his wife who was almost in tears.

"Oh, dear," she said, "what will everyone think. They must have heard." The disgrace of being visited by a charitable society cut her to the quick.

"Go out with some newspaper, Tommy, and clean up the sugar," she said, touching her eyes with her handkerchief. "We can't leave it lying there. Pick up the potatoes too."

Chuckling heartily, the Captain made his way to the fire-place and placed over the embers the little pot of stew that had been standing to one side. Cooking was the Captain's job. Mrs Cornish, although she would go out to help relatives with the washing and ironing and scrubbing, never regarded the pots as having anything to do with her. The Captain liked cooking and under his ministrations the fireplace had long ago given up the idea of imitating marble. It had resigned itself to a soot-blackened domesticity.

From the hearth to the meat-safe the Captain steered his course as cleverly as he had ever done through treacherous archipelagos. Not that there was much furniture to obstruct him. They had nothing worth selling now, nothing that Isenberg, the pawnbroker, would give more than half a crown on.

On one side of the fireplace was a dilapidated rocking-chair which was also Tommy's bed; on the other a sofa, only the shadow of its former self, having lost three legs and the seat. Slats from fruit boxes were nailed across to make up the deficiency of springs and horse-hair. An ever handy box supported the head, while a brick propped up the foot. The sofa by night was Bramley's bed, by day it was both seat and cover for the woodbox. Across the window usually stood a great cedar sea-chest; but as that was both wardrobe and seat it could not be sold.

At the moment this chest was making its way across the floor in a series of drunken bumps and lurches under charge of the panting Tommy. He tugged first at one end, and then at the other until he had it safely alongside the table where it served as a seat for his father and mother with two boxes for himself and Bramley.

"Bob Noblett gave me some oranges," he said cheerfully. "Here they are."

From his pocket, which had a curiously swollen and distended appearance, he produced two rather damaged oranges.

"You shouldn't accept things," his mother said. "The Nobletts aren't nice people, and I've told you not to go down there."

Tommy's lower lip stuck out. "Jim Noblett has a guinea pig," he said in extenuation.

Tommy could not understand his mother's attitude towards the Nobletts. Mr Noblett, being a hawker of fruit and vegetables, had a fascinating backyard full of boxes. He was kind to little boys and let them help him sort out the rotten fruit from his stock. He never beat his wife and children when he was drunk as the other men did. He treated Tommy as though he were just one of his numerous offspring. Having so many of his own, he said, a few strays didn't matter.

Tommy was slow in his table setting. He took extraordinary pains to make sure the cloth was even, and that only an inch of table showed at each end. He walked round and round, his eye level with the table edge, moving the cloth, first a fraction one way, and then another. Settled at last to his liking, he produced two china plates and two chipped enamel ones, two cups and two enamel mugs, a little tin knife and fork with a twisted prong for himself and a similar one for Bramley, and a horn-handled knife and fork for each of his parents. A small piece of twisted loaf and a cup half full of treacle crowned the feast.

He stood back to eye the general effect.

"Well," he said plaintively. "I'm ready."

The rest of the family roused itself from a depressed silence, and gathered round the table. They bent their heads.

"For what we are about to receive," Tommy said in a rapid monotone, "the Lord make us truly thankful."

He seized his spoon and attacked the stew as though he were eating against time.

## I I

Bramley was only waiting until tea should be over. He would
ask Jimmy Rolfe how people got jobs. If anyone knew about
jobs, Bram thought, Jimmy should. He knew so many things.

"What are those creatures, half-bird and half-fish?" Jimmy
Rolfe used to say. "That's me. A pseudo-boarder living in a
scullery, half outcast, half lodger and a quarter platypus."

Jimmy, during a period of particular overcrowding, when
Mrs Webb's relatives had come to spend Christmas, had been
temporarily moved into the lodgers' kitchen and there he had
remained. His petition to sleep on the veranda was countered
with the explanation that as the lodgers usually cooked in
their rooms they would not miss the kitchen. Mrs Webb felt
she must be stern with Jimmy who owed rent from absence
of mind more than lack of money.

"But people do sleep out," the young man had protested
plaintively. "Believe me, Mrs Webb, it is done."

"There's a lot of things done, Mr Rolfe," Mrs Webb said
sternly, "that I wouldn't put up with. There's not going to be
any of that sort of behaviour in my house."

Rolfe had moaned and returned to his stone-flagged kitchen
where he dwelt, as he said, "like a kind of Buffer State", alien
from the lodgers because he was a boarder and from the
boarders because he lived in lodger's quarters.

It was in the kitchen that Bramley found him when, on the
way back from throwing the washing-up water on the peach-
tree, he knocked tentatively on the door. Jimmy, as a form of
protest against Mrs Webb's hint that his board was consider-
ably overdue, was eating a solitary tea off a piece of newspaper. He held a saveloy in one hand and peeled it with the
other, much as if it were a banana. dipping it from time to time
in a matchbox full of salt. On the gas ring a can of water
bubbled merrily. On Jimmy's bed, Bill, one of Mrs Webb's
cats, lay with his paws tucked in, purring hoarsely.

There was a fellow feeling between Rolfe and Bill because
whatever they did, they never received full credit for the

beauty of their souls and the nobility of their motives. Bill's trouble was scars. He came home with scars; and no one would believe that he got them defending his home against other cats. At the moment one eye was painfully shut and swollen, but the other was fixed in love and homage on Rolfe's saveloy.

"Our Socialist pal, Duncan," Jimmy said, looking up from a heavy book propped against a jam tin, "has just been trying to seduce me from the paths of liberalism." He bit his saveloy severely. "And how's school, Bramley? Have a saveloy?"

"No thank you." Bramley was still hungry but polite. "I've had tea."

He sat down on the end of the bed with Bill and regarded his friend respectfully. It must be wonderful to work in an architect's office as Jimmy did. Jimmy Rolfe was an untidy creature; his room was a muddle of books, old boots, ash trays and pipe cleaners. He would have dwelt content in the litter if he did not feel that Bramley looked forward to the shilling a fortnight he was paid for tidying and cleaning.

"And don't you do it any oftener," Jimmy had warned. "Mind I trust you not to burn things or sweep them away, a woman's trick that."

Jimmy's cleaning had been a godsend to Bramley who was by nature as neat and fastidious as any living soul. There were times when Jimmy Rolfe's shaggy mop of hair, his unpolished boots and flyaway tie really distressed Bram. He had been known to purloin Jimmy's shiny other suit, press it and remove the grease stains. Jimmy would never have noticed the difference if a lady friend had not commented on the odour of benzene. Whereupon Jimmy himself had sniffed, investigated and tracked down the offender.

"And I believe you have polished my boots," he said sternly. "They look different. Let me tell you that my friends love me not for my attire but for my brains and beauty. Don't do it again."

He had to smile at the crestfallen Bramley. There was a fine friendliness between the erratic, talkative Jimmy and the steady big boy.

Above the mantelpiece the wavering flame of the gas jet, like a ghostly blue finger with yellow nails, moved slowly in the draught. Jimmy rose, went to the cupboard and produced a frowsy muffler of knitted wool in shades of crimson and grey.

"I'm just going down to Bud's," he said. "What's on your mind tonight? You look as though you were attending your own funeral and someone had mislaid the coffin."

"Mr Rolfe," the boy said seriously, "do you know how I could get a job?"

Rolfe became serious too.

"Well, that's a problem." He rubbed his long chin thoughtfully. "What sort of a job were you contemplating?"

"Oh, anything. But you see I'm only thirteen."

"Oh! Fake your age."

"I couldn't do that," Bram said flushing.

"No, I suppose you'd have to get a special permit to leave school or something," Jimmy said carelessly. "Look here, I'll tell you what. Come down with me to Bud's. He's bound to know something."

"I'm not let out."

"Rot, wait till I see your mother."

"Don't tell her why," Bramley urged.

Jimmy, with a reassuring shake of the head, disappeared to perform the miracle.

"You can come for ten minutes," he announced on his return, "if you wrap yourself up. Go and do it."

"It's easy enough to get a job, son," Jimmy remarked as they shut the gate behind them, "but it takes a lot of courage to step out of one. Take the firm of tomb robbers whose head office I adorn." He shook his head woefully. "For a year I've been telling myself that next payday will be the last. When I went there I saw myself designing palaces and museums and God knows what. Huh! I've been a kind of under assistant to their clerk of works ever since." He eyed Bramley sternly. "I'm going to leave. And do you know what I'm going to do when I go? I'm going to take off my shoes in the general office (exposing that darn in purple wool so kindly contributed by your mother) and I'm going to shake the dust out of them. Then, *dammit*, I'll really start to be an architect even if I have to build pig pens. And you, sonny," he gripped Bram kindly by the shoulder, "shall be my head chief office boy helping me to remould this city nearer to what a city should be."

Bramley had heard it all before but it never failed to warm his heart. He muttered his thanks.

"Looka' that," Rolfe gesticulated towards the turreted residence of the respectable Mrs Agnew. "Blasted hut. And that one too. All of them. When you see the dumps the rich live in you realize they're hardly a step above Plug Alley."

His usual monologue on the houses of Foveaux carried them across Dennison Square to the door of Bud Pellager's Newsagency.

"Plug Alley," Jimmy was saying as they entered, "would not be tolerated by a sane civilization."

Bud Pellager's shop was officially a newsagency. It was also a house-letting agency and an employment agency, these two functions being discharged by a blackboard either side of the door. At the back of the shop were a set of shelves that Bud proudly referred to as "the li'bry". Ask Bud for anything from fish-hooks to scent and he was certain to have it somewhere stowed under the counter. The shop window also had more junk in it than any other shop window in Foveaux. There were fireworks, tobacco, chocolate mice, bootlaces, plaster statuettes, ink-bottles, novelties and hair-pins, all jumbled together with skipping ropes or tin whistles.

Bud's place was a newsagency in a different sense from his sale of papers. If ever there was a happy home for rumours, it was Pellager's. Bud knew everything that happened in Foveaux from a baby cutting its teeth to somebody cutting his throat. He would perch on his high stool, hopping down like a droll brown bird to overwhelm the customer with courtesies and inquiries after her cold, and hop back again to tell her life story as soon as she left the shop. Every night his own particular cronies would stroll down, buy a threepenny cigar, and stay perhaps for hours, leaning on the counter and yarning to Bud. The thing that brought customers to his shop he did not sell, but gave freely; that was his conversation.

Bud Pellager, with his wavy black hair, his happy smile and pink cheeks, looked such a dear little boy. Old ladies invited him to sit on their knees in the tram. It was only after he had been up night after night for weeks that his face went the colour of the nicotine on his fingers and his innocent choir-boy smile began to look a bit tight about the ears. Then it would be plain that Bud Pellager was no choir-boy for all his fluting voice. He was just a very tired man who had the misfortune to be permanently small.

Tonight Bud was looking as yellow and wrinkled as a dried apricot under his rows of coloured magazines hung from racks, his pictures of heavy pugilists, his flaring yellow and green and blue and red tobacco signs. The shop was empty.

"Well, well," he said, dropping his lids over his eyes. "Haven't seen you, Jimmy, since the goldfish died. What's noo?"

"Behold!" Jimmy pointed grandiloquently. "We come for advice." Bud loved giving advice. "We have a problem."

"Is zat so?" Pellager trilled. "Let it drip on the floor."

He listened and grunted.

"About the third job I've been asked about today. Bob Noblett wants to get young Jim into the ironmongery and Ossie Seber wants to find his wife some washing to do. Well, well." He tapped his teeth with a pencil. "How bad do you want a job?" he asked after a thoughtful pause. "Bad enough to work for Bross?"

"That's the chap who owns all those houses round the Foot?"

"That's him." Bud nodded. "I can write you a letter, kid, that would get you anything with young Bross but money."

"It's money I'm after."

"It might get you a job," Bud continued, "but I doubt if there's much money attached to it."

In after years Bramley was often puzzled by the venomous regard that existed between Bross and the newsagent. He could only deduce that one of Bud's shady deals had been Bross's shady deal also.

"Wait." The little man darted off for pen and paper, wrote a few lines, signed it with a scrawling flourish and licked down the envelope. "There you are, kid, give that to young Bross and if that doesn't get you anything, I'll see what next."

He loved to make a lordly gesture and sat there purring

while Bramley stuttered his thanks.

"Great man, Bud," Jimmy drawled. "See! I couldn't do that if you paid me."

"You couldn't do anything if they paid you," Bud retorted with friendly scorn. "All you can do is talk about tearing down houses people like to live in and putting up other houses that even the rats 'ud declare black."

Bram moved uneasily. He was anxious to get home and avoid questions and he knew that if anyone started on houses, it meant hours of oratory.

"Houses," Jimmy began. "You don't call these hovels by that name, do you?"

"Well," Bud drawled with a wink at Bramley. "Foveaux's been inhabited a good long time now and no one complains except the rent man. I s'pose you're going to try to shift Granny Deeps out of her cottage her grandfather built in the bush when he came out with the first white ship. Forget it. On'y an earthquake could move one little brick out of Plug Alley unless one of the lads threw it at a cop."

Long afterwards Bramley was to remember that memorable night before he got his first job and the way the two dismissed the job from their conversation.

"Listen Pellager," Rolfe said fiercely. "Foveaux isn't a place. It's something that even God would prefer to forget. Bram and I," he laid his hand grandiloquently on Bramley's shoulder, "are preparing to rebuild it. At present it doesn't deserve a minute's thought. It's a hole."

"It's a 'salubrious locality'," Bud shrilled in defence of his beloved Foveaux. "Maybe going down a bit in the world but still a nice place f'rall that. Real dyed in the wool conservative gents' houses."

"Overseas," Jimmy said sonorously, "they're really *building*. They'd tear down the whole of Foveaux for a chicken run."

"All right," Bud hopped down to serve a customer. "You find a foot of Foveaux that isn't built on already, and let's see you build."

Jimmy indignantly pulled his hat at an angle over one eye. "Pellager," he said fiercely, "I'll show you yet. I'll be putting eight-storey buildings over this hole of yours one day. Bramley and I." He courteously included his restive friend.

"Mr Pellager," Bramley managed to force the words out, "how much money would I get if I worked for Mr Bross?"

"I'd hold out for ten bob," Mr Pellager advised with a wink at Jimmy. "I hope you get it."

"I hope," Bramley gulped, "I hope I do."

## III

Young Bramley's entrance into the firm of Bross was marked by one unhappy incident. He had been deeply impressed by young Mr Bross, Bill Bross! Big Bill, who, as everyone knew who read the sporting page, was not only a great football back but a "cert" for the single sculls championship. Bramley eyed him almost with adoration, as young Bross outlined the duties, which he gathered were mostly concerned with keeping people out and going messages.

Young Bross was a big pink healthy creature who looked like an advertisement for bath soap. He accepted the homage of the new office boy as a matter of course.

"Now you understand," he ended his discourse on The Whole Duty of Office Boys, "if anyone comes in you are to go up to them and ask them to state their business. Have them write it out and bring it in to me. You're not to let anyone in without I say so."

"No, Mr Bross," his admirer said fervently. "Mr Bross," he plucked up courage, "would you mind signing my autograph album."

"Hey?" Bross said, and then, "Oh I suppose so." He scribbled. "Got everyone's autograph in this thing, eh?"

"Oh no, Mr Bross," his office boy replied with simple cunning. "Only the famous ones."

Bill Bross endeavoured to preserve his dignity.

"Remember," he said, "I don't want to see anyone."

Hence it was that Bramley retired determinedly into the gloomy dark outer office and prepared to defend his employer if need be with his life. The elderly typist regarded him with sour disgust and snapped at him. But when she went into young Bross's office to take dictation Bramley had the outer office gloriously to himself. He was sitting revelling in the pleasure of having a real job when a small untidy looking man came stamping in and without by your leave brushed through the swing door that hedged off the sacred portion of the outer office.

"Bill in?" he growled.

"Mr Bross," Bramley said with emphasis, "wishes you to state your business. You can't go in."

The shabby old man said in an annoyed tone, "Well, damn it, I've met some cheeky brats in me day, but as old Sam Wilkes said (he's gone now, God-rest-his-soul), you're never too old to learn. Get out of me road."

"If you will state your business," Bramley said coldly, "I will see if Mr Bross can see you."

"Like hell you will," the old man said vigorously. "I give the orders and you can take 'em from me, see? I'm paying your wages, not my son." He hung up his umbrella.

"Hey Bill," he shouted, "what's this you've wished on me?"

Bramley stood aghast. "I'm sorry Mr Bross," he said humbly, "I didn't know who you were."

Bramley could hear the old man saying as the door closed behind him: "Well you ain't got no taste in office boys anyway. Don't see what we need an office boy *for*." He returned to his stool in deep dejection.

"You've got to remember, Bill," old Bross wheezed at the darling of the sporting page, "that I on'y took you in me business 'cos I couldn't think what else to do with you. Don't you get any idea you're giving the orders."

Bill Bross chewed his lip.

"I give yer an expensive education," his parent continued, "and where does it get yer? Playing round with football teams. Where does it get yer? Nowhere."

Ever since he had gone into his father's office Bill Bross had had a dull lurking resentment against the old man. The very look of his father irritated him, the way he shuffled from the inner office, his bulging stomach carried carefully before, his mouth pouted under that grey moustache that so resembled a growth of barnacles. Old Bross had an unhealthy jelly-like pinkness. He gave the impression that, if you squashed him, he would spurt between your hands.

His son, on the other hand, was at least determined to look like a business man. On his big shiny desk he had a notice: "I am SUCCESS", and all round the office he had hung mottoes about having just a pleasant smile and thinking of the other fellow and caring for the Greater Things of Life. Bill Bross had a fondness for soulful and polite quotations graved in brass. He gazed piercingly into people's eyes to see if they were shifty. His father, with his shrewd, ramshackle way of doing things, his lack of business methods, drove Bill to the point of frenzy. The old man knew every one of his nine hundred slum houses individually and would not part with one of them. If any showed signs of crumbling, he would give them a coat of paint and raise the rent.

His slow, wheezy anecdotes nearly drove his son mad. "D'y' think I'm scared of tenants after years of 'avin' them try to put it over?" he sneered when Bill tried to introduce some much needed office reform. "Not on yer life. Old Bluey Samuel whose father used to own the greengrocer's opposite where you was born, me boy, he used to say to me: 'Sid, never take lip from any woman. Remember when you put 'er in 'er place, you're doin' some other poor cove a good turn.' Ah, a great chap was Bluey Samuel."

He started on another tack.

"It was you wanted this office," he said accusingly. "It didn't suit you . . . Oh no . . . to 'ave a father that drove round collectin' the rents in a buggy."

"Efficiency," his son said firmly. "It's a first principle."

"Oh, and I suppose it's more efficient to pay other people for doing what you've always done yourself."

It was a relief to young Bross that at this point the office boy knocked uncertainly to say that a gentleman wanted to inquire about a house.

"What place is it he wants?"

"He says it's in Ogham Street."

Old Bross nodded. "That'll be Number Ten."

"Give him this form to fill in," young Bross said magisterially.

It was a neat form beginning, "Are you employed?" "Where?" "Where were you living last?" and ending up "Married or Single?" "Number of Children?" with the place for the tenant's signature.

The office boy appeared again.

"He wants to see you," he said. "He won't fill in the form."

"Tell him if he doesn't fill in the form and produce his rent receipts we can't consider the application."

Bramley returned with the completed form, and Bross gave it a contemptuous glance. "I thought so. Not working. Tell him the house is taken."

He eyed the old man speculatively, "I don't know why you mess about with these old houses. Ought to be doing things in a Big Way. If you were to go in for some of those estates on the North Shore and open them up. . . ." He made a large gesture. "Vision, that's what's needed."

"You can have it," his parent growled. "Bit by bit and 'ouse by 'ouse I've got what I own together. I know when I'm well off. You can go and open things or shut them or do what you like. If you think this place isn't good enough," he said heatedly. "you can always get out and," he added as an afterthought, "take your damn cheeky office boy with you."

His son took no notice.

"What about those places in Anne Street that have been condemned?"

"Well, what about 'em?"

"I'm asking you."

"While I can get twenty-five shillings a week for them places," old Bross said, "it'll do me. No sanitary inspector ain't going to scare me into wasting money when I don't have to." He leant back contentedly.

"You've got to remember that things are changing," his son said impatiently. "What with all this outcry in the paper about slums it might be just as well. . . ."

Bross winked one wrinkled eyelid like a lizard lying on a rock. "Anne Street," he announced "is in Foveaux and Foveaux don't change. At least my houses don't. You was born in Ogham Street, boy, in one of them very houses you're talkin' about. The end one that was a barber's shop just off Plug Alley."

"I tell you the place is changing," his son argued. "The boom, the housing shortage, the influx of immigrants, it's turning the Government's attention to housing. Things must change."

Bross winked the other eye. It was a wink of tremendous disbelief.

"Go hon!" he said with a grin.

# CHAPTER 5

## I

Between the Eight-Hour Day excitement and the municipal elections nothing really happened except that an old woman in Plug Alley was missed by the neighbours who four days later decided to break down the door of her house. She had been dead some time and what the rats had left of her was so uninviting that no one in Foveaux who heard the details ate meat for a week.

All other interests were eclipsed by the municipal elections. The parliamentary elections were always tame, Foveaux having affectionately returned the same old gentleman to Parliament for fifteen years. It was felt that after all you couldn't deprive an old man of his livelihood. The idea prevailed that it would be a mean thing not to vote for him and so he was returned year after year with a thumping majority.

Honest John Hutchison was in the same enviable position as far as the municipal elections were concerned. He was a tradition. He had held the balance of power on the Council for so many years that he considered it his right; and Foveaux agreed with him. This year, the Labour Party was for the first time putting up candidates; but that did not in the least disturb Honest John who called himself a "Labour Independent" and voted how it suited him. As the Labour group were pledged to the Greater Foveaux scheme which Honest John had been advocating, there was little reason for him to fear any loss of prestige.

His prestige was enormous. He radiated benevolence and statesmanship. He patted children on the head and asked their names. Women said he was "a lovely man" and admired his beautiful beard. That famous beard, like the oriflamme of Navarre, had waved in the thick of many a battle.

"No breath," Honest John would shout, "no breath has ever

sullied my reputation."

And he would stroke his beard as much as to say: "Here it is. You can see for yourself. Unsullied."

Honest John's election policy was sound enough. He could point to the beautification scheme whereby Lennox and Mark Streets had suddenly found themselves graced by hundreds of round piles of earth and wood, each enclosing one seedling plane-tree. He and his faction had been battling to widen Upper Lennox Street and extend it through the church grounds, pull down the rectory and make Lennox Street a real main road instead of a Niagara spouting up into a beer bottle.

The rector had lost favour even with his own flock over his opposition to the idea. He had preached a sermon on the text: "And he opened the bottomless pit and there arose a smoke out of the pit as the smoke of a great furnace, and the sun and air were darkened by the smoke of the pit." The horrors that would follow in the train of driving Lennox Street through to Errol Street included (according to the rector) "noisome and repugnant sights and sounds, the din of industry, the roar of factories and workshops in the midst of a quiet area of Christian homes, and all those manifestations of man's greed and malpractice concealed under the name of commerce and at cross-purposes with both Christian teaching and Divine Law."

"I say," Honest John had boomed in reply from his wagon drawn up outside the church hall, "I say that the foot of progress cannot be halted by the old, the rich, nor the rustic in our midst."

The main election campaigns were waged outside the church hall, where a special polling booth was erected to contain the voters, and in Dennison Square. The wooden booth in Lennox Street was a joy to Tommy Cornish who with other urchins, their sisters, brothers, dogs and billy carts, hovered round to swoop on stray pieces of wood for the family fire. And the carpenters were liberal with it. After all it wasn't their wood. The Council paid.

In Dennison Square there were always meetings even without the elections. On Friday nights returning shoppers would pause, laden with bundles, and listen mildly to attacks on the

Christian religion, the White Australia policy, the Capitalist system, the eating of meat, or any other of half a dozen of their interests.

There was one old gentleman with a little stand, an old brown macintosh and a pair of spectacles who had occupied the same post three nights a week for years without anyone finding out whether he was attacking or defending the Bible. He would be greeted with joyous howls from his audience who would cluster round him lovingly, look over his shoulder at his notes, fight with each other as to who should ask him the first question, tug at his macintosh to attract his attention when he was answering someone else, and generally behave like a kindergarten when the teacher has lost control. There was always a babel of noise around him.

"Eh, Bertie, listen, Bertie. What did the archbishop say to the chorus girl?"

"Leave him alone. He's mine. I got him first. Listen, Bertie, you was sayin' the other night that you didn't believe in marriage. Now isn't that so?"

"One minute, my friends. One minute. . . ."

And the old gentleman would raise one pale hand to adjust his spectacles while repelling with the other the more aggressive questioners who sought to breathe down his neck and disarrange his necktie. He was invariably good-humoured. He was used to his crowds and knew they meant no harm. They liked him and he liked them and it would have gone badly with anyone who really molested him.

"One minute, my friends, and if the gentleman who is so interested in my notes will kindly return them — Thank you. We will proceed. . . ."

Above his thin voice rose the drone of the harmonium under the opposite lamp and the pleas of an earnest body of evangelists to "Come and know the Blessings of the Lord." The crowd always gathered for the music for the harmonium player was no mean performer. A little further down you might come across Duncan, as he thumped socialism into the crowd.

"Well right-o, you say how we can see our way clear to take over the industries since it takes so much capital to finance them. Well, right-o, I'm coming to that in a minute. . . ."

Beside his soap box young Jock Jamieson would stand handing out pamphlets with the fierce efficiency of a devotee. From the far corner of Dennison Square the monotonous thud-thud of the big drum bespoke the presence of the Salvation Army.

The Salvation Army met outside Bud Pellager's door and he was fiercely annoyed by them. The rest of the citizenry might enjoy free entertainment, whether it was afforded by the League of Friends of Freedom or the Come to Heaven Pilgrims, but Bud hated anything that drowned his conversation.

The elections, however, were the times of greatest joy for pre-war Foveaux. Everyone brought their own stale eggs and tomatoes. The hotels and shops diplomatically hung out flaring posters for the "greater Foveaux Scheme", the "Rates First, Streets Later" minority and, in fact, anyone who wanted to hang out a poster. The lads of Plug Alley, mingling with the crowds at the meetings, were apt to fling themselves on a rival push under the cover of patriotism, and with small boys darting about and policemen hewing their way into the churning mob and arresting any old enemies who happened to be handy, there was always something doing at election time. Men who on other occasions would peacefully agree, "Maybe so", if someone hinted that it would be a good thing to spend money widening the streets, would black the speaker's eyes during an election.

Willie Hannell who had put up for every Federal, State and municipal election that anyone could remember, and was supposed to be slightly daft, had got himself ducked in the horse trough when he went too far and hinted that Honest John's enthusiasm for giving Foveaux wood-blocked streets and little trees with fences round them was due to his shares in a certain timber company rather than to municipal patriotism. Stroking an imaginary beard Willie had concluded with a grin:

"And as for me reputation it ain't got a splash on it! No, sir!"

"Well, it's going to have," said an ominous voice and Willie, amid a rush of Hutchison's supporters and a roar of laughter, found himself dumped spluttering in the handy trough. He was a brave man to venture out again but he needed the money from the collection. If he could put the crowd in a good humour, he could whip round the hat on the plea of election expenses. Willie always apologized as he did so for not wearing his spats — a hit at Mr Sutton.

"Me grey ones bein' at the laundry, I says to Emma this evenin', 'Emma, where's me white spats? You know I'm goin' out to tell the boys why I should be elected to the Council an' you don't want me to be seen nakid.' 'Your spats,' she says. 'Yes, me spats,' I says. 'I remember hangin' them be'ind the laundry door last Toosday.' 'Them,' she says, 'why, I sent them away to be studded wiv diamonds.' "

Any reference to spats always put the crowd in a good humour. Willie proceeded to amuse them further with the anecdote of the lady who went out in a motor-car. "An' he says: 'Are ye still there?' " Willie took on the Scotch brogue of Mr McErchin. " 'Are ye still there?' he says." The answer came pat from fourteen different places in the crowd.

The crowd might swarm round Willie Hannell for diversion but the big lorry with the flaring blue and white poster, "Vote for Hutchison and the Greater Foveaux Plan", was the main attraction. In 1912 there was little solid opposition to the Labour candidates and Hutchison. The old Ratepayer group were certain of defeat. Even the knotty problem of the lodger vote receded into the background, though there was always someone to ask: "How about the lodger vote?"

Honest John, as usual, was pat with the popular answer:

"I say, ladies and gentlemen, that in a municipality such as ours the lodger vote is a necessity. I say that advisedly. It must come. Under the present conditions, with the housing shortage so very much in our midst, people who would be only too glad to rent houses under normal circumstances, are forced to live in rooms. You know yourselves of cases in which unfortunate families have been forced to sleep as many as six in a room on the floor." (Murmurs of sympathy.) "*But*, you will say, Foveaux has a tradition to maintain — a tradition of better-class houses and a genteel community. I reply that this tradition need not be abandoned. Let us give every facility to the rich man to live in our municipality, but are three-fourths of the population to be neglected? The working men who must live near their work because they cannot afford fares? No, I say."

He paused for breath and was handed a glass of water.

"The City of Sydney," he continued, "this queen metropolis on whose borders Foveaux is set——"

"Draw it mild," expostulated a voice.

"This queen metropolis," Hutchison repeated, "must expand. And it is to Foveaux she looks for those important business sites for shops and offices. We must look to the future. A man's home must lie near his work and with important industries arising we have seen more and more fine working men's families settling in Foveaux. Men whose interest is in their work, who have come to seek opportunities in this new land."

"A fat lot of opportunities there are," from someone in the crowd.

"I say there are opportunities for the man who is not afraid of work. I say that it is with the building of Australian secondary industries that the future of this municipality should and must lie and that it is the Council's work to see that they have living conditions worthy of them, good light, water supply, wide streets. . . ."

"He's going to start about running Lennox Street through to Errol Street," Rolfe murmured to Bramley Cornish. "You see."

"So that I stand firm by the principle of the lodger vote. I think that answers your question, sir. And now I would direct your attention to the third point of my policy. That of continuing the struggle against the native sloth and prejudice of our legal system which has for years been stifling the natural progress of Foveaux. I am referring to the prejudiced, the jaundiced policy, which has prevented the main road from the city, the thoroughfare on which we now stand, from being carried through to Errol Street. You can all see that it was for such a main thoroughfare Lennox Street was originally intended. Lennox and Murchison streets were to be the two main lines from the city markets to the outer suburbs when Foveaux was only farm land occupied mostly by market

gardeners. You can see what happened. Certain influences.
. . ." He paused significantly. "Certain influences were brought
to bear to end the roadway in this twist of lane, this footway."
He turned to the section of the crowd to his left. "And if, ladies
and gentlemen, you should see fit to give me again that representative power with which you have for so long loyally
trusted me, I shall rally every effort to see Lennox Street
extended to its rightful juncture."

"Not only Lennox Street," pursued the Independent, after
a suitable pause. "The widening of other streets is a vital
necessity in view of the increasing body of traffic, the danger
of motor accidents. . . ."

"What about Plug Alley?" It was the voice of Mr Melston,
the church warden.

"Well, what about Plug Alley?" demanded Honest John
truculently.

"When is it going to be pulled down?" retorted Mr Melston.
"You know the Lord Mayor is asking the councils to co-
operate in the eradication of slum areas and, if Plug Alley isn't
a slum, I don't know what is. There's houses down there that
were built in 1840. It's a disgrace sir. If there's any first task the
Council should have a go at, it's pulling down Plug Alley and
putting up decent houses fit for people to live in. Help to end
the housing shortage, help to give employment." Mr Melston
was a ceiling manufacturer. "People are moving away, respectable people, because Foveaux is getting to be a slum
neighbourhood."

There was a murmur of approval from the crowd. Honest
John realized that a change of tactics was necessary.

"I agree with my friend that there are areas within the
municipality which fall below the standard we would like to
set." He smiled. "But, I would remind my questioner that
the problem of resumption is by no means a simple one. At a
time when people are unable to get houses our friend is asking
us to condemn those houses, not only obtainable, but going at
a cheap enough rental for the working man to afford. I assure
you that everything will be done to maintain our housing
standards. . . ."

"At rents nobody can pay," from someone in the crowd.

"I will challenge anyone — anyone — to go into the same houses I could name in this debatable area and say they are not as clean and pleasant as any in Upper Foveaux. I see no reason —" he looked for support to the Plug Alley and Ogham Lane faction. "I see no reason because a man's dwelling is humble to deprive him of it. The Australian character. . . ."

"He must be getting near the end," Rolfe remarked to Bramley.

"The Australian character is notable above all for a love of liberty, liberty to live and act and think how a man pleases. To what do we attribute this love of liberty, this hatred of interference? To three things. Firstly, to the immigration of the boldest and most liberty-loving Englishmen, the Chartists, the rebels——"

"The convicts," put in a voice sarcastically.

"Yes, the convicts. The men who were transported because they refused to starve in silence. To those liberty-loving men, Irish rebels, Scotch tenant farmers evicted so my lord could turn his land into grouse moors, the rebels of all nations whose blood runs in our veins, it is to them that we must turn for inspiration when place or party attempt to subjugate free judgment. It is for this reason I call myself a Labour man. It is for this reason I shall live and die a Labour man, endeavouring to serve the interests of my fellow men and women."

"He used to be just independent," someone murmured audibly.

"Oh, come along," Rolfe muttered, "That sort of thing always makes me tired."

Bramley had been standing with his mouth open listening to Honest John. He roused himself and followed obediently.

"Anyone," Rolfe said bitterly, "can gull these mugs by talking to them about liberty and rebellion. They've no more independence than a goldfish in a bowl."

## I I

There were worse things being said in Hutchison's own home.

"I hope the old wretch gets hit with a bad egg," Marjorie Hutchison remarked viciously.

Her elder sister sniffed.

"That's no way to speak about your father," she said with an undercurrent of approval in her voice.

She had just had her request for a new summer frock refused, her father furiously maintaining that his daughters' extravagance would ruin him. He liked to have them ask for things but he hated to pay. He grudged even the money for the household bills and always made a scene over them.

Honest John did not believe in women handling money and refused to allow his daughters to work. "It would look pretty funny if I couldn't support my family," he grumbled. "A woman's place is in the home. And while I keep a roof over your heads you're going to stay under it."

It would have cut him to the quick if he could have realized the ingratitude bordering on hate with which his three daughters regarded him. It was true, he would have admitted, that he was a saving man but that was because he had worked up "practically from the gutter". Having been left a half interest in a small furniture factory he had transformed it and added an important and flourishing timber yard. The haunting fear of never having enough money was the main pivot round which his life revolved. If Honest John could see a chance of making money he would chase it down a drain if there was no other way of grabbing it.

"Independence," he would say. "There's nothing like independence." And to be independent he would have to have money, large sums of money.

His house in Jasper Street had a special porch to shelter all the people who came to see Honest John on business. If you wanted a signature for a petition, a subscription for a home for retired rent-collectors, free legal advice or the wangling of a job or someone to sit on a committee, Hutchison was the first man who sprang to mind. He was tirelessly courteous and helpful even if he couldn't do anything. But being pleasant to so many people made it all the more difficult for him to be pleasant to his family.

"God damn it," he would roar. "You've got nothing to do but sit round all day and dress yourselves. Why isn't dinner ready?"

Having upset himself over some such domestic tragedy as
the soup, he would rush off to a meeting with indigestion. After
the meeting he would stand a few drinks to influential person-
ages and drown his family's lack of understanding and his
indigestion. The result would be a headache next morning and
an increased irritability. His home life was a succession of
scenes and silences. He let it be known among sympathetic
friends that his wife didn't understand him.

"Poor man," they would murmur. "And he's so fine and
generous. It does seem a shame."

" 'E was that good about Alf," Mrs Hamp remarked sentimentally as she waited outside the polling booth to hear the
results read out on the Saturday of the elections. "I done what
I could, Mrs Hamp, 'e says, little though it be."

"And how is Alf?" Mrs Blore inquired. "I 'ear you've been
havin' trouble with 'im."

Mrs Blore had not bothered to take down her curlpins
because even though it was election night it was dark and no
one would see her.

"I wish they'd put 'im in jail and keep 'im there," Mrs Hamp
said lugubriously. "Instead of lettin' 'im out every now and
then to be a nuisance about the place."

"Well, we all got something," Mrs Deeps's daughter, Florrie,
put in. She was a woman so enormously stout that she looked
as though her clothes had been forced on. "Ever since the baby
was born I been sneezing like as if I had a cold. The doctor
says it's the effect of the baby."

"They do say," Mrs Blore sympathized, "that it affects you
in yer weakest part. I knew a woman and after the baby was
born 'er 'ead went wrong. She was never the same again."

"Well, I fixed the sneezin'," Florrie responded. "Went to
a herbulist. Chong Wah down the end of the street. He give me
something that took it away. Wonderful them Chinks are."

"Yes, they're wonderful orright."

"Mother wants to wait and 'ear the polls read," Florrie
continued. "I hope I'm as active at her age."

Mrs Deeps, realizing that she was the subject of the conversation, immediately put up a spirited defence.

"I can hear you," she snapped, "every word you say."

"I do 'ope Mr Hutch'son gets in," Mrs Blore chorused. "It's only right 'e should."

The little groups waiting outside the Sunday School hall for the returning officer to read the results made it quite a social occasion. Some of them sat on the steps of the hall, some of them amiably along the gutter, others stood round the lamp post and along the church fence, watching the children running frantically to and fro picking up the hundreds of pink and blue election leaflets. The favourites were the white cards with the vivid blue photograph of Hutchison on the back. Some of the cards had been trodden into the roadway, some were damaged by immersion in puddles and a general barter system of six damaged for two undamaged had been instituted. Small boys were busy "swopping" each other as though the election leaflets were cigarette cards and young Tommy Cornish was doing a thriving business in Ratepayer Leagues, two for one Honest John.

As Mr Keyne came out on the steps from time to time to announce the results, the groups would break up and come crowding round the steps to listen. The final results were received amid a breathless hush succeeded by a burst of applause. Honest John was in with a thumping majority.

"Hutchison. Hutchison topped the poll."

"Labour's in."

"Shut up. I can't hear."

"Old King's beaten."

"Hannell got two votes."

Honest John amid a surge of handshaking and cheering made his way towards a waiting car. A man with a megaphone jumped up in the back of the car and roared an intimation that Mr Hutchison would return thanks from the Prince of Wales Hotel. The car thundered away with the crowd running after it, men, women and children, all rushing towards Dennison Square.

## I I I

The election had tired Hutchison. In Bill Bross's car he let himself slump.

"Well," he said with a grunt. "That's that. How did it go, son?" Hutchison and Bross had been friends for years and Hutchison saved money by borrowing Bross's car instead of hiring one for himself. "How's your father?"

"He's not too good."

"I could do with a drink," Hutchison said meditatively as the car whirled up to the hotel entrance. "You know, I think I'm getting old." He shut his eyes. "I'll be glad when all this is over." But on the hotel balcony he was magnificent. "The waves of progress," he concluded, "will sweep away the wreckage which for years has cumbered Foveaux. The high tide of progress surges in upon us and that you have seen fit to place your trust in me at this critical time makes me the more sincerely pledge myself not only to be proud but, to the best of my endeavours, worthy of your regard."

There was almost a huskiness in his voice as he finished and they cheered him. He bowed right and left before turning to enter the lighted window behind him, a firm erect figure.

"Don't go, Billy," Hutchison said, shaking hands with his committee. "I want to see you."

It was some time before he had discussed everything with everybody, slapped his friends on the back, shaken hands once again, and ushered them all out without giving the impression that he wanted to get rid of them.

"This is more like it," he said at last, lying back with his eyes shut. His legs stretched straight out in front of him, the black pointed boots upturned, his head thrown back and his greying, pointed beard upturned, he looked noble and at the same time slightly ridiculous. Bill Bross studied him through his glasses.

"It's the beard that does it," he said, sipping his whisky.

Hutchison opened his eyes.

"Eh, what's that? Does what?"

"Gives you that holier than thou touch."

Hutchison sat up straight and raised his glass.

"Warms you in winter and cools you in summer."

"The beard?"

"No. The booze." He shook himself and was again the efficient far-sighted citizen.

"Well, let's get down to tin tacks. You naturally want to know how this will affect you, Billy?"

"You bet I do."

From his pocket Hutchison drew a pencil and one of the leaflets with his photograph on it. He began to sketch a map of the streets of Foveaux.

"This is going to be a big thing, Billy," he said in a low voice. "A big thing for both of us. If I pull it off, I ought to make enough out of this to retire."

"You've been saying that for the past five years," Bill Bross remarked.

"Never have enough money, son. My damn family keeps me poor. Well," he began to fill in little black squares beside the pencil lines that marked the streets. "I know all the arguments your dad would have against it. He's a conservative. He sticks to his pokey little houses as if they were chunks of gold."

"You've no hope of getting him to leave the damn ruins," Bill Bross said resentfully.

"If only he'd put his money into something else but these antiques. You take these blocks of flats. You can run them cheap, get a good rental and a fair class of tenant that wouldn't even look at the dad's place."

"That's true, Bill," Hutchison said. "Now listen here. This is where you get your chance to show the old man a few points. Collins, the inspector — I've got his report somewhere." He fished in his inside pocket. "Here it is. Now. . . ." They bent over the report. "He recommends that Lennox Street be extended through the church grounds into Errol Street. That means resuming the church land and throwing open two corner blocks here and", he pointed, "there. Then there's this side of Errol Street. . . ."

"I can see the idea of the corner blocks," Bross interrupted. "Flats, eh?"

Honest John almost sighed.

"You must get out of the idea of thinking only in terms of residentials, Billy," he rebuked patiently. "Now let me get this clear. Errol Street has to be widened. After the widening there's going to be land left over. What's it good for? Houses? Too narrow and noisy. Not factories. Too expensive. Shops couldn't compete with Murchison Street. All that resumed land will go dead cheap."

"Well then?"

Honest John leant over and solemnly tapped him with a pencil.

"Motor-car sales-rooms, my son. City blocks are prohibitive. This is the nearest place to the city where they can afford to buy. Just outside the city area. Right on what is going to be a main motor road. In four years' time, Billy, all along Errol Street you'll see motor-car show-rooms, motor garages, motor accessory and repair joints — motor everything."

Bross rubbed his chin, unconvinced. "I can see flats as a progressive move," he said, "but I'm damned if I can see any sense in buying up all those odd lengths along Errol Street."

"You wait and see." Honest John returned to his little map.

"All I ask you to do is to get the firm to do the buying from the Council and I'll see you get your cut. I can't go openly myself and buy them. Not my place as an alderman. You can see that? By the way, when you feel like branching out for yourself, there's those two old stone cottages in Lennox Street — that's a site for flats, if you like."

Bross nodded. A waiter approached.

"A Mr Bishop would like to see you, sir."

No one would have recognized in the wooden correct figure of the waiter that jovial blade, Fred Doust. "I'll tell him, Bish," he promised his friend. "Not that I think you have any chance."

"Tell him I'm busy," Hutchison said impatiently. "What's he want?"

"He wants to cast your horoscope, sir. Tell you your future."

"Ha, ha!" Mr Hutchison tapped Fred familiarly on the lapel of his coat. "You go back and tell him that I know exactly what's going to happen in the future, and maybe I could predict him a few things. Nothing doing."

He strolled restlessly across the lounge to the balcony and looked over Dennison Square. The square had wakened again with the chatter and laughter of people returning from the picture shows, the flow of theatre traffic, the noise of trams, cabs and cars. Through the patches of gaslight they moved below him as brilliant fish move underwater, crossing and recrossing, all busy and seemingly purposeless.

"You couldn't do better, Billy, than come in with me," Hutchison said absently. "You can see for yourself the city's brimming up and flowing over and the obvious outlet's through Foveaux. We can count on at least six years of a big boom and it's up to us to be on the crest of the wave."

He looked down on the square again. It was his oyster and, by Peter, he was going to open it. Let all those fools whose fathers and grandfathers had lived in stuffy, iron-railed, tall houses in Upper Foveaux sneer at the idea of his breaking their tranquil preserves. Foveaux was going to go ahead and he was going to push it. He felt the same contempt for the Agnews, the Suttons, the Misses Dimiter, the Wilbrams and Lawyer Foxteth that he would feel for a stone in his path. Clear them all out and let the road run through. Silly old fossils.

# CHAPTER 6

## I

Any interference with the normal life of Foveaux was always traced to one's neighbours. If the police swooped down on Plug Alley, the neighbours of the arrested were to blame. If some-one's cat died in Lennox Street, the neighbours would be sus-pected of having poisoned it. If flowers withered in the back-yard, it was surely due to the malefic influence of the woman next door. Then, eighteen months after that memorable election of 1912, when the people had grown used to work-men with picks tearing up the pavement at the top of Lennox Street, on the very day the boys and dogs had such fun killing the rabbit in the church grounds, something happened which could not be blamed on the neighbours or even on the council. A war broke out.

At first the war in Europe was just exciting. The only other chance people from Foveaux had had of being killed on a large scale was when some Dutch farmers in Africa had refused to play the game according to British rules. The pros-pects of the teams in this new war were discussed with all the serious consideration that might be given to a Test Match. Foveaux felt it was backing a winner. The young men, falling over themselves to enlist, were only afraid the war might be declared off before they had their innings. Even those who, with many misgivings, agreed to let them go felt that Fate would surely be satisfied by the sending of a team on the definite understanding that its members were not to be killed or hurt in any way.

Honest John during the war had his first real chance to exercise that gift he possessed in common with Julius Caesar of doing five things at once. He did not neglect his private duties or his interest in the land resumptions in Errol Street even in the midst of organizing a tremendous campaign for volunteers and money. As chairman of the Foveaux Canteen Fund he strained every effort to send his fellow citizens overseas in comfort, whilst he encouraged the home dwellers to put their money into war loans and generally showed that unfailing cheerfulness and public spirit that made him an inspiration to innumerable committees.

Patriotism such as Honest John's was almost universal in those early months. It was a grim contrast to the bewilderment and despair of the later years when the bereaved found out that they had sent their men to a game that had no rules.

One of the first effects of the war upon Foveaux was the sudden disappearance of the German band. As much a part of the landscape as Mr Keyne's palm-tree, the band had come up Murchison Street, round Dennison Square and down Mark and Lennox streets every Monday morning for as far back as could be remembered. Most people saved a penny for the band and the baby would stagger out with it tightly clutched in a hot sticky fist. Little boys followed the musicians respectfully from street to street listening to the medley of ragtime and classics and helping to pick up the pennies that clinked down on the pavement from windows overhead. The first morning the band failed to appear women watching for it could not believe its disappearance was due to the war. Later on they would blame everything to that cause from the shortage of sugar and the high prices to the bold way girls behaved. What became of the band no one knows. Its members might have gone with the wealthy owners of the piano shops to brew their own beer in a concentration camp. They might merely have decided that it was not wise to be a German band any longer.

There had begun to be spy scares galore. It was taken for granted that the terrible Hun, having over-run poor little Belgium, torturing and mutilating the inhabitants, was preparing to do the same by Foveaux. German warships were sighted off the Heads every foggy morning and rumours of plots to burn down Foveaux and even the city itself found many frightened believers. Anyone who "looked like a German" was an object of suspicion and most people knew what Germans looked like from studying the caricatures of the Kaiser in the daily papers. Small boys played at soldiers in the streets by day and trembled in their beds by night.

To Plug Alley and Ogham Street the war at first meant adventure and change. "Cripes, it'll do me," Curly Thompson remarked to Hamp. It meant bugles instead of factory whistles in the morning, cigarettes and cards and new mates instead of the same old round, the same dirty terrace, the same job year after year. It meant a free sea trip, a glorious if somewhat restricted holiday, the only drawbacks being the drill, sergeants, and the unnecessarily early hours.

The first to go from Mrs Webb's place was Mr Webb himself. In one of his wandering fits he found himself keeping pace with a band and a sergeant with a gimlet eye pounced on him and enlisted him before he could stammer out a protest. Fred Doust's only excuse for having volunteered was, as he feebly explained to Duncan, that old Bishie had predicted change and travel for him. Duncan's greatest disappointment was Jimmy Rolfe who had at first declared that he belonged to the B Brigade and would *be* home when they left and when they came back. But the fever got him.

"I'm not like Duncan or young Jamieson," he explained to Bramley. "I can't see myself on a soap-box telling the truth about the business to enraged hordes of mugs. You've got to fight harder to stay out of this war than you would if you were in it. Anything for peace. I'm going to be a damn coward and join up."

Jimmy Rolfe didn't really enjoy the war. He spent most of it either confined to barracks or on sanitary fatigue. His slipshod methods with his puttees nearly broke the sergeant's heart and he was never on time even for food. Jimmy got the reputation of being the second biggest liar in his battalion and that was all he did get except some shrapnel.

Bramley Cornish was one of those boy conscripts called for service with the naval reserve. He spent the war years chugging round the harbour all night in a motor launch. Some of Bramley's best memories were of those nights, of the lap of the water, the cautious put-put of the launch, the harbour like a dark bowl rimmed with fire and all the shadows and moods that stir across sea-water. They were wonderful years to him. He filled out, lost that worried fretted expression. He was being

paid more than his wildest dreams and when young Tommy
began to earn bits of money, it seemed that the war was going
to be a godsend to the Cornish family.

The bugles were blowing every morning in Foveaux Park.
Faintly through the mist they sounded a call to those whom
formerly the factory whistles had summoned. All along the
grey roads through Foveaux in the early light there would be
processions going to the docks. Foveaux never missed one of
them. Old men and women shivering in the cold, young girls
and children, they all turned out to watch the soldiers go off.

"G'bye," they called in their harsh, shrill voices. "G'bye."
It did not matter whether the lad they farewelled came from
the next street or four hundred miles inland. He had to have "a
good send-off".

"Don't they look lovely?" Mrs Blore would shout to a
friend. "I just love to see 'em marchin'."

You might, indeed, have thought that some of these men
were going to a wedding, they were so carefree, so glad to be
released from the tangle of their lives and those of other
people, from the useless, the old, those who must be left ashore
stuck in the mud. A far tide was carrying off the best, the freest
and strongest to a different life and a different death. "G'bye,"
the voices called bravely. People stood on the stones of the
demolished houses in Errol Street and craned their necks after
the procession. "G'bye."

## I I

The trouble with patriotism, as with religious fervour, is that
it is easy to arouse and hard to sustain over a long period.
Foveaux would have been enthusiastic all through a war that
lasted six months. A war that lasted year after year was a
different matter.

"I don't like the way things are at all," thundered Honest
John. "There are too many slackers and rotters leaning against
lamp posts while the boys in the trenches are crying out in vain
for reinforcements. These mongrels will tell you that if they
leave their jobs, industry will fall to pieces. But what do they
do? Hold out for higher pay. Is that the way to help the gallant

fellows who are holding back the menace of the Hun? Go slow. Sabotage. Is that helping to win the war? They don't go slow in the trenches. Not they. Let these loafers get out there and try their go-slow tactics and see where it gets them. These men, I tell you. . . ."

Then something happened that had never happened before at Honest John's meetings. An egg landed on the railing in front of him, burst and dripped down ominously on the platform. Honest John went purple in the face but controlled himself.

"You see," he said nastily. "There's one of them here. One of them who's so go-slow he can't even throw an egg straight. Easy to tell that came from a go-slow wobblie."

The audience laughed and Honest John managed to get through the meeting without more than an occasional heckling. But it was just as much a blow to his pride as if the egg had struck him. It was quite in order to throw eggs at anti-conscriptionist meetings, overturn their platforms, and chase them out of the Domain if you liked. But that he, Honest John Hutchison, M.L.C., should provide a target was a different matter. "Simply gone to the pack," he growled privately. "Over-run with wobblies and reds."

The egg, the ominous egg, had come from the hand of Joe Fulcher, once one of Honest John's most fervent admirers. He had been saving the egg for a gentleman who was trying to prove that the war was a judgment on Britain for not sending the Jews back to Palestine. But Honest John's remarks about high wages were just too much. Joe had a wife and three children to support and he had been asking for higher wages himself. On the specious plea that all other companies were paying two shillings, he and his mates had refused to load oil for one and ninepence and had patted themselves on the back when they got the rise. After the shipment was well and truly loaded, however, the company virtuously took the strikers to court and had them fined. Hence the egg. Hence the discontented and nasty frame of mind exhibited by Joe as he lounged away to listen to a fiery-tongued Scotsman explaining the War Precautions' Act. Patriotism, Joe considered, was all right as long as it did not consist of passing laws preventing men from asking higher wages. The cost of living had risen enormously and wages had not; but if you grumbled about it you were likely to be labelled a "wobblie" or a pro-German.

Foveaux grumbled, at the top of its voice. Its prophet was Duncan, the veteran of police raids, and the loyal Foveauxians swore by him. His furious protests in court when a beefy policeman laboriously read extracts from his book of "Republican Songs" were more against the policeman's pronunciation than the charge. Duncan was a pacifist; at least he started as a pacifist. Before the war was out he was red hot I.W.W.; and if he could have found anything more violent, he would have joined it.

Mrs Webb began to grow accustomed to Mr Duncan's being raided. She didn't like it of course; but after all it was war time, and one must expect hardships in war time, and if policemen tramping through the place did not constitute a hardship, she would like to know what did.

Mr Duncan paid no attention to jail sentences. He would be down in the old corn and fodder store, the anti-conscription headquarters, as soon as he got out. His face, as he bent over his dirty little printing press, was as stern as that of any Prussian field marshal. Leaflets, he demanded of his perspiring squad, and more leaflets. There were leaflets blowing along the streets of Foveaux, almost as though it were election time, leaflets in the gutter, like the leaves of the plane-trees in Lennox Street. Every now and then a man would lounge against a fence as all men did in Foveaux, and when he moved away, there would be a little sticker on the palings: "Capitalists, landlords, parsons," the sticker exhorted, "your country needs you. Workers, follow your masters."

Miss Dimiter was horrified when she noticed one of these yellow slips on the front fence. She went out herself and scraped at it with a table knife.

"It's disgraceful," she said, "disfiguring people's places. The police should do something about it."

Her sister was rearranging the crowded ornaments in their sitting-room, looking older and frailer than even the china.

"I don't suppose it matters," she murmured. "I am afraid the place is becoming impossible. Such low people! Every day it seems the tone of Foveaux gets lower and lower. I can't blame the de Russets' moving. We should move ourselves."

"But where are we to go, my dear?"

They looked at each other, quite frightened, two pale old ladies, dried like pressed flowers that had been kept between the leaves of a book.

"People don't like sending their daughters to a . . . a . . . slum!"

"Antonia!"

"But it is becoming a very low part."

Again they looked at each other dismayed at having come face to face with such a fact.

"Great horrid men lounging about the streets. All these strikes and things. . . ."

"No place," Miss Patricia Dimiter said firmly, "is low if there are better class people living in it, and while we remain Foveaux is not low class. No, it is not low class."

But the little flock the Misses Dimiter led up the hill to St Matthew's Church on Sundays had dwindled to a third of its former numbers. The working people who lounged in their doorways to see the peaceful procession go by would stream down to the Domain in the afternoon to listen to Duncan, heckle the speakers, throw flour and join in free fights.

To young Tommy Cornish it seemed that Mr Duncan who used to make such admirable cakes, had sadly deteriorated. He did nothing but talk about "The Twelve Men" in the same fervent tone the rector used for the apostles. These twelve men, Tommy gathered, had been sent to jail. At first he thought the twelve had been boiled in oil or something sensational and interesting and when he discovered it was only jail, he said, "Oh" in a disappointed tone. Mr Duncan himself was always going to jail, so why worry about twelve men doing the same?

"Tell me a bloke like Harry tried to set Sydney on fire," Duncan snorted energetically at Tommy. "Do you know what he was doing when the police saw him shake something out of a bottle? That wasn't phosphorus. He had a cold and he was sniffing friar's balsam. And another thing. The cotton wool they said he used for starting fires was down on the mantelpiece in Central a fortnight before. A frame-up, I tell you, Tommy."

Tommy nodded sympathetically. He took a fearful delight in Mr Duncan's society these days because he had been forbidden it. Mrs Cornish radiating pride, with her eldest son in a navy uniform, was determined that Tommy should not associate with a pacifist and an I.W.W. Tommy was just as determined that he would.

The temper of Foveaux grew ever more savage. Mr Montague was seriously considering moving his family out of such a plebeian atmosphere. He was now a commercial traveller for a button firm and comparatively prosperous. His horror when he discovered that Mrs Montague had good-naturedly signed a form making her a member of the Pacifist society brought on a glorious scene.

"Good God, woman," he raved, "you're mad! Do you want to ruin me? Have us all put in jail? You're mad . . . mad . . . mad."

"But I didn't like to offend Mr Duncan," his lady wife pleaded. "You used to say he was a very talented man."

"I tell you that he's a lunatic and a traitor and worse. You'll have the police down on us."

"Oh, dear, I hope not," Mrs Montague murmured. "After all I hadn't any idea I was joining anything. I though it was just another subscription for getting someone out of jail — twelve men or thirteen or something."

By a horrid chance the Montagues really were raided. The police searched the whole house. No one was home in the Montague room except Linnie who composedly followed the police officer about.

"What's that?" he said, snuffing suspiciously round the outhouse in the back yard. He pointed.

"It's a bath," Linnie said coldly.

"No, the thing behind it."

"That's a peanut roaster."

The policeman scratched his head. He had hopes the strange object was an infernal machine.

"Father took it for debt," Linnie piped. "It belongs to us."

They returned together inside where the policeman thumbed

through the household literature and closed determinedly over a thin paper-covered book.

"All right," he said with a nod to Linnie, and departed.

Mrs Montague, when she discovered what the police had taken, was nearly beside herself.

"But it's your father's family tree," she wailed tearfully. "He sent all the way to England for it. Oh! what will he say?"

Without waiting to find out she started feverishly for the police station insisting that she must see the chief of police.

The local sergeant tried vainly to soothe her.

"It isn't that Mr Bishop minds your men taking his books on astrology," Mrs Montague said firmly. "It isn't that I mind them taking the family tree. It isn't my family tree; but it's my husband's, sergeant, and he's very proud of it. I'm sorry but I must have it back."

The bewildered sergeant was able to assure her that they had no trees of any description.

"But this is a family tree," Mrs Montague went on insisting. "And Mr Bishop will be wanting his books on astrology. I simply must have that family tree. It was covered with grey paper with a crest on it. Now please, do find it for me before Mr Montague comes home. You know how you'd feel yourself," Mrs Montague said confidently, "if it was your family tree and you lost it."

Old Duncan, quietly checking over the literature under his floor boards, was undecided whether he should go down and interfere in the epic row that Mr Montague staged.

"I do wish there never had been a war," Mrs Montague was saying tearfully. "I'm sorry about your old family tree and I wish the war would stop — so there!"

Not only the I.W.W. members went to jail. In August 1917 the transport strike broke out and the popular song round Foveaux went to the tune of "The Wearing of the Green".

> *Just for going out on strike;*
> *Just for going out on strike,*
> *They're putting men in prison,*
> *Just for going out on strike.*

It was hardly a month before the great strike collapsed, leaving behind it a wreckage of broken unions, a chaos of unemployment, semi-starvation and misery. If you were on the black list with the ominous word "Red" against your name, it was almost impossible to get a job.

Old Nosey Owen's son did not march among the ranks of the tramway men in the Eight-Hour Day procession that year. There were many others absent too, who a few years before had swung along briskly. Children with collection boxes wandered among the crowds lining the march and cried: "Relief for the women and children." There was hardly any attempt at decoration. The very banners seemed to know they figured in a grim defeat, the very horses to toss their heads with an abject defiance: "Just for going out on strike . . . just for going out on strike . . . they're putting men in prison . . . just for going out on strike. . . ."

At the end of the procession came a V.C. winner with a banner proclaiming: "Join the One Big Union — the Khaki." To many it rubbed in the salt. They had dreamed of forming one big union themselves; but the crowd gave the banner a warm reception for the sake of the man who carried it. That was all. Patriotism among the people of Foveaux was at a discount.

"What did you say this place was called?" Old Duncan heard a girl in a motor car inquire of a man in uniform.

"Oh, Foveaux; it's a working-class district."

"Dear me," the young lady said gaily beneath her parasol. "What a weird place!"

Old Duncan looked thoughtfully round Dennison Square. It was drab with all the piano shops being pulled down and the leprous posters peeling off the corrugated iron fence round the new bank building. Errol Street, with its devastated area where Lennox Street burst into it like a bomb, was hardly any improvement. He wondered what Hildebrand Sutton would have said hearing his great-grandfather's farm so maligned. But Sutton had moved. Everything was changing, moving, shifting. He felt an old man, an old beaten man. Tommy Cornish, padding along beside him, would continue to ask questions.

"When will there be another strike, Mr Duncan?" he asked eagerly.

"Not for a long time," Duncan said heavily. He hesitated, then moistened his lips. He had not even enough money to pay his rent. "Strike's finished. Foveaux's finished. Everything's finished," he said savagely. "Here, Tommy, you go ahead. I want to see a man." He plunged into the swing doors of the hotel.

On the front veranda Tommy found Mr Bishop waiting.

"Where's Dunc?" he said anxiously.

"He went in the hotel."

Mr Bishop worked his false teeth about dubiously. "I'd better go up and get him," he said at length. "He's in a mood for anything."

Late that night Tommy lay awake and listened to the approach of Mr Bishop and Mr Duncan. Mr Duncan seemed to be singing "The Workers' Flag" but it had got so mixed up with Mr Bishop's rendering of "Sweet Mary of Argyle" that you could hardly tell one from the other.

" 'Sno good," Mr Duncan was saying lugubriously. " 'Sno good at all. Finished —'pletely finished."

They fell up the stairs exhorting and encouraging each other.

# CHAPTER 7

More than anyone else left behind the Captain chafed at his moorings.

"If I could only get a ship," he would mutter. "The sailing ship has its chance again, and I'd have one with it."

But before the Captain regained his sight the war was in its fourth year and there was throughout Foveaux that sullen hatred and defiance against those processions, the route marching and the campaigns for volunteers. From the other side of the world the wrecks of war, the maimed, blinded and ruined, the flotsam and jetsam that had been men, were being flung back to the place that sent them forth. Then, in that time of despair and disillusionment, the Captain underwent his operation. He lay without anaesthetic, without a quiver, while a famous surgeon cut the cataracts from his eyes.

"There's not another man I know," the surgeon said admiringly, "who would have stood that."

The Captain lay in the darkened room at the public hospital and his wife brought him jelly and held his hand in her neatly gloved little hand. He smiled as he lay there.

"Cheer up, lass," he said gently. "Things are going to be all right now."

The surgeon pronounced the eyes a magnificent success.

"The very best of luck," he said heartily. "The very best."

But a month after he came out of hospital the Captain was in bed again. This time with a whole list of ailments arising from that old attack of beri-beri. It was as though he fell to pieces all at once.

"Like a hulk," he said to himself. "Just like an old hulk."

Tommy sat on the bedside with the shiny black notebook in which they recorded their bets and "What's for Saturday?" the Captain would ask cheerfully. He knew he was dying but there was no need to mope about it. He might as well have a flutter.

They were reckoning up profit and loss the day the rector paid his last visit. He appeared so quietly at the open french window that Tommy, curled up on the bed, had barely time to close the notebook.

Dr Wilbram stood in the window, a tall old gentleman, somewhat stooped, and said: "Peace be to this house." The effort of facing the war, of facing a situation completely unknown and outside his grasp, seemed to have broken him as surely as the workmen's picks had demolished his church wall. He strove not to mention the war in his sermons. As a concession to his parishioners he prayed in church for their soldier sons and husbands; but his petition, "May they not be taken in their sin, in their warring and striving in war", was not exactly comforting.

More and more Dr Wilbram had come to perform his tasks with painstaking misery. That very morning when he went to break the news of one of the usual killed in action, the woman had run round the other side of the table and screamed at him to "get out of the damned house".

"Peace," she shrieked. "Peace to this house! I know what you're going to say. What peace is there where you go? Get out. Get out." He could not comfort her crying.

As he stood in the Cornish room he was thinking of that woman. Always when he came to visit the Captain he would recite the Fourteenth Chapter of St John; and after a few remarks leave as quietly as he came. The Captain accepted these visits as courteously as they were offered since no charity accompanied them. Between him and the rector these days there was a friendly understanding, although the Captain had been wont to attend church only once a year on Good Friday.

"Let not your heart be troubled," Dr Wilbram began, sitting down on the old rocking-chair, "neither let it be afraid."

And then he could not remember the rest of his chapter. I'm getting old, he thought, too old. But the only verse he could remember was from his favourite Revelation. "And God shall wipe away all tears from their eyes and there shall be no more death, neither sorrow nor crying, neither shall there be any more pain."

He noticed the Captain's little boy looking at him in a curious manner. Perhaps the lad noticed his hesitation. The rector's pause had set Tommy's heart bumping guiltily for he felt it was an accusation. Then the rector remembered his chapter and Tommy's troubled conscience began to be reassured.

"In my Father's house there are many mansions," said Dr Wilbram. "If it were not so, I would have told you."

Tommy's mind roved restlessly up and down a celestial Lennox Street with little gold balconies hanging out over the blue void of heaven.

"I go to prepare a place for you," Dr Wilbram continued.

Tommy's heart began to bump again for Dr Wilbram, as he spoke, was absent-mindedly fingering that black notebook on the bed. He took it up without noticing what he was doing. Tommy wondered desperately how his mother would bear the disgrace. Visions rose in his mind of the rector thundering anathema upon the family and denouncing the Captain's betting from the pulpit.

With a cry he darted forward, tore the book from Dr Wilbram's hand, and flung it in the fire. He faced the rector defiantly. There was a moment's silence. Then Dr Wilbram continued his recitation as though nothing had happened.

"I will not leave you comfortless. I will come to you. Peace, I leave with you, my peace I give unto you. Not as the world giveth, give I unto you. Let not your heart be troubled. . . ."

When the rector had bowed his head in silence for a few minutes and left, the Captain smiled approvingly at Tommy.

"Tight corner, Tommy," he said approvingly. "Don't know what your mother would have said."

A few days later the Captain died. He beckoned his wife to his side and pressed her hand.

"I've been very happy, Al," he said. "Happier than I deserve." He looked at Bramley, tall in his naval uniform.

"Look after your mother for me, boy."

"I will, dad."

"That's all right then."

The Captain drowsed into unconsciousness. He had had a

good life and he knew it was over.

They laid the Captain among the innumerable headstones perched like a flock of white gulls on the cliffs at Waverley. It was a dreary, rainy day; and the grave was in a depressingly semi-liquid state. Even in such circumstances his eldest son hoped that if the Captain was anywhere about he would notice how close he was to the cliffs and that far out on the grey edge of the sea a dirty little coaster contributed a smudge of smoke to the horizon and its vicarious presence to the funeral.

# BOOK II

---

# FULL TIDE

# CHAPTER 1

I

The lights were coming on in Dennison Square. In the confusion of buses, cars, horses, carts, people pushing their way on to overcrowded trams, newsboys yelling their papers, men noisily crashing into the hotels for a last drink, all stirring up the dregs of the day's energy with the dregs of daylight, the square had become a war of lights. The windows of the shops flared against the wet pavement and the headlights of the cars slashed across the rain in a powdering of silver dust.

The tremendous monotonous uproar over Dennison Square blended the thousand surgings of small noises as the one roar of the surf combines the confusion of a million broken bubbles. Shrill groups of girls chattering together as they clicked along with their quick step, men's voices and the tramp of big working boots, the ringing of the tram bells, the sputtering repetition of car exhausts and the overpowering purring of the big buses; all this noise, this swift preoccupied movement gave a certain stranger the feeling of a shepherd on a mountain peak.

Not one of the shut, intent faces was familiar to him. Their eyes passed over his as over a stone that is noticed in the same place year after year. Strangers standing on a corner of Dennison Square aroused no interest. Thousands of strangers besides Jimmy Rolfe had stood there for a time before they plunged again into the chequering of lights and darkness to become strangers on some other street corner.

It was almost a comfort to turn from the contemplation of the crowd to the fish-shop window behind him, blazing with light, lined with white tiles and green fern on which oysters were tumbled in a heap of mossy shells or appeared succulent on a plate as chubby satin pillows frilled with green lace. There were mullet in crisp overcoats of yellow batter, their tails

turned up in an inviting stiff curl. Pink and scarlet prawns
rioted on the fern in great heaps of colour and lobsters hung
from a rail above like a flock of flamingoes or lay split in
pearly halves adorned with lemon slices and parsley. The
scales of the schnapper shone, their round eyes fastened glassily
on the customer through the misty window down which
trickles of water enhanced their voluptuous invitation as that
of nymphs beneath a waterfall. Something of ancient poetry
and bloodstained romance lay in the ferns in the reddened
armour of the lobster. From within, the warm waft of frying
fish and drying humanity reinforced the urgings of the window.
But Rolfe with a hungry glance hesitated and turned up the
footpath towards the ordered confusion of magazines, toys,
books and tobacco, sweets and sundries which none but Bud
Pellager could have contrived. They proclaimed his presence
as surely as the news placard outside the door announced:
"Tragic Death. Actress Tells."

Inside, however, the picturesque disorder of Bud's domain
had suffered a transfiguration. It had altered as much in the
twelve years of Rolfe's absence as Dennison Square. The
shop certainly appeared to be selling more things than before
but they were all in separate compartments. A little office
had been partitioned off just inside the door and labelled,
"House and Employment Agency". There was a glass case
full of cakes and groceries. The library books had been
covered and numbered and put on shelves. There was a special
table massed with marigolds and daffodils for sale. Rolfe had
never associated Bud Pellager with daffodils. Tobacco and
revolver silencers, but scarcely daffodils. He began to wonder
whether Bud still owned the place. He was nowhere to be seen
and this had been his busiest time. He waited while the girl
behind the counter dashed up and down serving customers
and giving orders to the slow adenoidal boy who was busy
counting papers. She had stiff white cuffs and a neat white
collar and a nervous abrupt manner.

"Yes?" she asked at last.

"Is Mr Pellager still here?"

"Be in any minute. Anything I can do?" Her tone was cool
and official.

"I wanted to see him," Rolfe muttered hesitantly. Suddenly he felt sick again and it didn't seem worth while. No, he wouldn't even wait to see Bud. After all Foveaux was only a dirty suburb. Silly to do this returned mariner stunt.

"You can wait in the office, if you like," the girl said in a more friendly tone. Rolfe realized that he must be looking even worse than he felt.

"Thanks," he said with an effort. After all it was such a long time. Bud Pellager had probably altered. He might regard twelve years as too long a time to remember what had been really only a casual acquaintance.

The girl had darted before him into the office and pulled out a chair.

"I won't wait, thanks all the same," he said.

She was regarding him keenly.

"But aren't you Mr Rolfe?" she said gravely. "You must be Mr Rolfe."

It was Rolfe's turn to look surprised.

"Remember me?" she asked.

He shook his head.

"You had the kitchen at Mrs Webb's place. We lived across the hall. The clan Montague. I'm Linnie."

He gripped her hand. "Of course," he exclaimed. "Linnie all white socks and frills. With your hair curled."

She looked annoyed. "That was mother's fault. I hate frills." Then withdrawing into her business manner. "Bud'll be pleased. Always mourning over your loss. Seen Bramley Cornish?"

"No."

"He'll kill the fatted calf," she said with a quick smile. "Half a minute."

She darted back to the counter and served a couple of customers with quick dispatch. It was the rush hour and she had only time to call scraps of news to him as she dashed to and fro.

"Mrs Webb's gone. She went years and years ago. That's two and fivepence Mr Keyne. Know any good tips for Saturday? Right. I'll remember to tell Bud. Old Bishie's still there and Dunc and the Cornishes."

Rolfe had slumped down in the chair just inside the office but he felt he must keep up a polite interest.

"We've moved next door. We've got what used to be the boarding side. Mother's a terribly slack landlady. Too kind. Loses money. Mrs Cornish's much better."

Rolfe sorted out the information. "Then Mrs Cornish is running the old place and your mother's next door."

Linda nodded. "That's it. Mind the change, Danny. I say, you're sick, aren't you?"

Rolfe pulled himself together. "I'm all right," he said. A lucky rush of customers saved him further sympathy.

It was just as well that Miss Montague used a snappy and efficient manner for work in the same way that she used her glasses. She was unduly sympathetic. Her face had normally as much reticence as Bud's window. It was one of those faces which display a confusing and piquant variation of emotions by the chance that the features are not well assorted. While her chin was obviously in the Montague tradition and might have done credit to any predacious and haughty ancestor her nose had taken to Christian Science and decided not to worry about anything but an upward trend. Between the two Linnie's mouth was a nervous compromise, uncertain whether to be grim with her chin or airy with her nose. Above these incongruities her eyes had a separate tendency to disagree with whatever the rest of her face might be saying and be hostile when her other features were welcoming, and kindly when they looked grim.

"How is your mother?" Rolfe asked in a lull of business. More and more he had begun to wonder if he could slip out and have the meal his interior craved and then return later — perhaps.

"Angelique? She's still on the Christian Science."

Mrs Montague's daughter made it sound like some obscure disease.

"You're not going, are you?"

"I think I will. Tell Bud when he comes that——"

"Well is zat so?" A cracked voice called from the doorway. "You old son of a bitch."

There was an answering roar of welcome from Rolfe.

"Bud," he yelled. "You little dried-up ball of misery."

Bud Pellager fell on him and thumped him with his fist, talking and laughing and swearing. Rolfe lifted the little man up and dumped him on the counter where he sat oblivious of customers with his arm round Jimmy's neck and his head against his shoulder.

"Jimmy, darlin'," he crooned, "where the hell have ya been? Come on, tell us where y've been? You never wrote, you swine. You never let us know. Let's look at yuh." He patted Jimmy on the chest. "Where's yuh medals, son?"

"Bud, you know me. What gave you the idea I'd have medals?"

"I dunno. Just got an idea you may have got a medal for wife beatin' or sumpin'. Christ! It's good to see you. We gotta celebrate. Where you stayin'."

"I don't know — yet."

Bud glanced at him sharply. Jimmy Rolfe had never been handsome but now he was looking ghostly.

"What's wrong with yer?"

"Stomach and lungs," Rolfe answered ungraciously.

"Lightning," Bud called sharply to Linnie who was serving a customer.

"You leave this to me, Jimmy." He assumed his Napoleonic manner. "How about taking in a lodger, Lightning? Got room?"

Linnie nodded competently. "I'll fix it."

It would mean sleeping with her mother but she was just as determined as Bud that the protesting Rolfe was not going to vanish again. She put on her hat and coat.

"But look here, Bud . . . I mean to say. I just dropped in for a yarn. Only got off the boat this morning. I'll be all right if I have some food. Come out to dinner with me."

"You're goin' right along with Linnie," Bud commanded. "She'll find you something to eat. I gotta mind the shop. Soon as I shut I'm coming round to sit on your bed. An' if you ain't in bed, I'll knock you unconscious an' put you there." He growled like a puppy defending a precious old shoe. "Damn fool you are, wandering about in weather lookin' like something the tide washed up. Take 'im away." He waved a gran-

108

diloquent hand. "I'll be round later."

He followed them to the door with injunctions that drowned Rolfe's protests. "Look out for Lightning, she's a man-killer. Never say I didn't warn you they put arsenic in the soup. They'll tear you apart at Beggary Barn."

"What does he mean by Beggary Barn?" Rolfe asked.

"Just kidding," Linda responded. She was striding ahead. "They always call our place Beggary Barn now."

## II

Beggary Barn, or "Mrs Montague's Place", as it was now known to the polite, was no boon to the neighbours. The Beggary Barn lodgers believed in hilarity and late parties. They were not quiet, as Mrs Cornish complained. You could do anything in Foveaux if you were quiet. You could beat your wife, strangle your mother-in-law and set fire to the children; provided there was none of the noise usually associated with such proceedings. In that close-packed, nerve-racked area sound and sin had become almost synonymous. When Mike Shelley, the bank robber, was arrested, his landlady summed up the moral attitude of Foveaux when she exclaimed: "Oh, what a pity! Such a nice quiet man he was too."

Beggary Barn was a constant source of interest and acrimony to the rest of Lennox Street. The neighbours could have forgiven Mrs Montague's lodgers their loud discipleship of radical views, sandals, coloured shirts, psycho-analysis and free love. They could have overlooked being referred to as "the natives" and having their pet views retailed with roars of laughter and a chorus of "How primitive. How too divinely barbarian!" They enjoyed the view of Teddy Stewart modestly taking his sun-bath in what he regarded as privacy and an attic. But they did not like the Beggary Barn parties. Particularly when Angus McErchin would bring over his bagpipes, for, on sight of him, all the lady lodgers would shriek with joy and roll up the carpet in the sitting-room and push the furniture against the walls. Amid the lamentations of Mrs Montague and the preliminary keenings of Angus you would have thought a fight was about to take place rather than a dance. Even old Bishie, coaxed in from next door, had been taught to foot a reel; and he would whirl round his partner, shouting "Hoo!" at the correct intervals and snapping his fingers, a sight from which his stars might well have turned away their faces. The muffled thudding of the dancers' feet and the bray of Angus's pibroch would be broken by periods of loud and energetic drinking or songs in parts. Some of the lodgers had good voices, some had not, but they all sang. The noise would continue until the neighbours thundered on the door or the lodgers fell into a coma and ceased from sheer exhaustion.

"I don't mind a little fun," Mrs Cornish complained gently through the fence to Mrs Montague after one of these parties, "but not after two in the morning. I feel sure Mrs Webb would never have allowed it."

Mrs Cornish recalled the dances of her own girlhood. The gleaming dark floor of the ballroom, the palms, the white gloves, the little white fan and the white satin dress.

"I used to go to dances before I was married," she said a little wistfully. "But I gave it up because my husband didn't like it."

Tears came into her eyes when she spoke of her husband. The Captain still ruled the Cornish household with Mrs Cornish as his priestess. "Your father wouldn't have liked that", or "Mr Cornish always objected to drink", was the last ruling she would give on a subject. Every year Mrs Cornish seemed to grow smaller, more frail and more timid. She only went out to do the shopping now or occasionally to visit relatives.

"Your father would have wished me to keep in touch with poor Aunt Eileen," she would remind Bramley. "Not that there's anything anyone can do for her."

But even if she was shrinking and frail, little Mrs Cornish had her proper pride. Her grey hair was still crisped in little frizzles round her forehead. Her black dress was well cut.

"Your father liked me to dress well," she reminded the boys.

"You must come in some night," Mrs Montague urged for at least the tenth time. "There's no harm in them. They're just young. I like to have young people about. I like to enjoy myself as much as they do."

Mrs Montague was still blonde. It was a discreet, fluffy blondness out of a bottle. Her complexion owed much to science, but it remained pink and youthful. Her smile was gayer than ever though she secretly mourned the loss of her teeth. She wore glasses only when no one was about. In the morning Mrs Montague trotted round singing like a lark in a beautiful pink padded kimono and coy little slippers trimmed with pink feathers. Her chin was upheld by a patent chin-strap and every Tuesday she was invisible owing to her preoccupation with a green plaster which smeared and set on her features, completely obliterating every landmark but her eyes. The amount she spent on beauty preparations and frills occasioned her more practical daughter some anxiety.

"You'll have to cut down a bit, Angelique," Linda would remonstrate.

"Why should I, dear? Oscar has a good position at McErchin's. You seem to be quite happy with that queer Mr Pellager. Your father writes for money occasionally, I know, but I always manage to send him some."

"But we can't save anything," Linda would point out desperately.

Then Mrs Montague would break away with a triumphant little laugh. "My dear, that's just where wrong thinking comes in. What does it say? Take no thought for tomorrow. Even the sparrows of the field are provided for. There is never any lack in Divine Love."

So Mrs Montague, chirruping sweetly, would sympathize with Teddy Stewart and Wilfred Wilston when they told her a tale of woe.

"Don't worry about the rent until you get on your feet," she would coo. "I quite understand."

All her young men made love to her gallantly and she thought they were "sweet boys". She was having the time of her life as a landlady and it was she who often as not instigated the parties.

"I like people who enjoy themselves," she remarked to Mrs Cornish. "I never had much fun when the children were growing up."

Mrs Cornish's only connection with Beggary Barn was her

morning conversation through the fence with Mrs Montague. They discussed the chances of a fine day, the behaviour of Darkie, Mrs Cornish's cat, the price of groceries and the occasional misdemeanour of Joe, the postman. Mrs Cornish's little stock of interests had been narrowed down. Her lodgers were all well behaved. There was nothing to be expected from Mr Bishop, Mr Duncan, Miss Laurel, the deaconess, the two lads from the brush factory, or the young couple with a baby. They hardly made a sound.

Bramley just went to work, came home and studied and went back again. Tommy was never to be seen. He dashed in to tea and dashed off on mysterious jaunts of his own. So Beggary Barn was a secret diversion to Mrs Cornish. She followed its romances as closely as possible. She even tried to look up the word "inhibited" in the dictionary. She would cautiously draw aside the blind to watch the young man who wore short trousers like a boy scout, stamp up from the gate with a knap-sack on his back and a big stick in his hand. That was the one she wanted to marry Linnie Montague, not Wilfred, the artist. She had them all paired off. The tall dark young man with the frown who was studying law, sometimes brought "his young lady", as Mrs Cornish politely called her, and the short broad one with the moustache seemed to have two young ladies or even three. Mrs Cornish had little bets with herself as to which was his real love, quite unaware that Forster Brown considered polygamy a first rule of nature and loudly discussed with all or any of the three ladies the psychological benefits accruing to such a Solomon. Sitting at her open window (she didn't really regard it as wrong to listen seeing there were so few of the words she understood — besides, if they talked at the top of their voices, who could help hearing?) Mrs Cornish thanked her stars that Tommy and Bram were not given to such conver-sations. Even if Tommy was always losing jobs, even if he was a little wild, he was a dear boy. And everybody admitted that Bramley could hardly avoid making a name for himself, he studied accountancy so hard he might even become Prime Minister. Mrs Cornish felt she had much to be thankful for.

"Every morning," she confided shyly to Mrs Montague, "when they go off to work, I say a prayer that they may be preserved through the day."

"Well, I do think that's nice," Mrs Montague said encouragingly, "and it couldn't do any harm, could it?"

On that wet rainy day when Rolfe returned everything had gone badly. It was a Friday, and, as Mrs Cornish sniffed, "Friday never was a good day." The trouble had started with Darkie having kittens on Bramley's bed. This catastrophe was followed at lunch by Mr Bishop announcing that his roof was leaking. Mrs Cornish could feel herself developing a bad cold in the head and then the agent came with someone to look over the cottages. Periodic scares that the cottages were going to be sold had tightened the bond between Mrs Cornish and Mrs Montague for the past eleven years. The sale of the cottages meant almost the end of the world to both of them.

This gloomy event was followed by something infinitely worse. Bramley sent her a telegram. She opened it trembling and read: "Do not wait tea. Home late. Tommy got married this morning."

Mrs Cornish sat down and cried. It was really too much.

"First Darkie," she sobbed to Mrs Montague. "Then Tommy. Oh, dear dear!"

Mrs Montague's assurance that Divine Love was looking after Tommy married or not had no effect on his mother. She preferred him single.

"Perhaps there's some mistake," she repeated, clinging to an unsubstantial hope. The recollection of Neicie, Tommy's girl friend, with her red lips and short curls did not comfort her.

"I did hope he'd grow out of it," she wailed. "She's such a vulgar girl. And so loud spoken."

It was with trepidation that she opened the door that evening hoping it might be Bramley with better news.

"Oh dear me," she sobbed, her eyes streaming. "It's Mr Rolfe come back. Oh, oh!" Rolfe looked concerned. "Oh, Mr Rolfe, the agent's trying to sell the cottages again and Tommy's gone off and got married and the cat's had kittens." It all poured out. "I'm so glad to see you, Mr Rolfe. Mr Cornish always regarded you highly — but it's been such a terrible day."

Rolfe made soothing noises. "I just came in for five minutes," he explained. "I'm staying next door."

The limp frame of Mrs Cornish stiffened.

"Your place is here," she said. "We could at least give you a sofa." Then she dissolved again. "I know she'll treat him bad. He's so young, poor boy. His father wouldn't have wished it."

It was while she was going over the story of the telegram that Bramley let himself in all dripping and was immediately divided between worry over his mother and delight at seeing Rolfe.

"We'll just have to make the best of things," he told his mother. "There's nothing can be done."

"And Darkie's had kittens on your bed," Mrs Cornish wept.

"I'll drown them in the morning," Bramley promised. To Rolfe: "Where are you staying?"

"Next door."

Bramley grinned. "Look out one of the yearning females doesn't get her claws on you."

"Do they yearn?"

"Do they what? One came up and yearned all over me once. 'Don't you think, Mr Cornish,' she said, 'that more women should have affairs with more men?' "

"She didn't."

"It's a fact."

"Thanks for the tip."

Mrs Cornish regarded Bramley with terrified eyes. "Don't you," she mourned, "Don't you go getting married too, Brammy."

Bram patted her shoulder.

"Cheer up, old lady," he said affectionately. "I've got better things to do with my time."

He led Rolfe out into the hall.

"What beats me is how the little devil thinks he's going to support a wife."

"Why on earth did he get married anyway?"

"Don't tell mums but I believe I am about to become an uncle."

He dismissed the matter with a shrug of the shoulders.

"Funny, isn't it. Here I couldn't afford to get married myself, even if I wanted to, and my young brother on practically nothing a week is already provided with a wife and family." He hesitated. "I've got to get mum to bed and then, if you feel up to it," he had not failed to notice Rolfe's unnatural look, "I'd like to drop in and have a yarn."

"It seems to be a habit. Bud's coming too."

"Good. I'm glad you're back, Jimmy," he said half shyly. It was the first time Bramley Cornish had called Rolfe by that name.

"Bramley," Mrs Cornish called, "your tea will be all cold."

"All right, old lady."

He turned back into the damp and tearful atmosphere of Mrs Cornish's grief.

### III

The advent of a new lodger in Beggary Barn made as much stir as the falling of a feather. There seemed to be some kind of party in progress when Rolfe returned, for from the front room came the blare of a gramophone, shouts and laughter that almost drowned Mrs Montague's welcome. Someone had pinned a notice on the door, "Mangling Done Day and Night. We Never Sleep", and the noise certainly seemed to bear out the truth of the statement.

"Oh there you are, Mr Rolfe," Mrs Montague greeted him. "Linnie has tea ready in the kitchen."

Mrs Montague was a little ruffled because Linda had hissed in her ear: "He's having my room. Understand? And you're charging him five bob a week rent. Otherwise I'll get Oscar to collect Teddy Stewart's back rent with his boot."

"You must tell me all about your travels sometime," Mrs Montague continued, "I hope you don't mind a little noise. We don't often have a social evening. Hugh — excuse me, Mr Rolfe — tell them not to stand their beer mugs on the piano, like a darling." Her mind was obviously running on the party. "Linnie will fix you up." There was a crash from the front room and Mrs Montague with a smothered "Excuse me" turned and rushed inside.

"Just look at it," Rolfe could hear her saying as he groped his way to the kitchen. "You have no idea how to behave. I don't care. The least you can do is clean it up. Go and get a cloth, Bill."

In the kitchen Oscar Montague and his friend Angus, with their feet up on the stove, were in deep discussion of what seemed to be a technical problem. They merely nodded to the newcomer.

"I went over her," Oscar was saying, "and as far as I can see it's a short."

"Did ye test the generator?" Angus asked.

Oscar frowned and shook his head. "It couldn't be the generator. It isn't a month ago I went over the armatures and they were all right."

"Might be the timing," Angus suggested.

"Couldn't be the timing."

"Well, we'll get old Ian to have a look at her."

"Kelly put a roughie over Charlie today," Oscar put in. "Chap came in — you know the sort — wants free air and water in his radiator, then buys half a pint of petrol and gives you a bad two bob to change. Well, Kelly's standing down near Charlie's bench. . . ."

"Milk and sugar, Mr Rolfe?" Linda said loudly.

"Charlie was working on that four-cylinder job your father brought in. They're practically putting a new engine in her. By the time she gets a battery and some brakes she'll be fit to take out on the road, if they don't push her above thirty. Well, Kelly's standing there by Charlie's bench. . . ."

"Will you get out of this, Okker," Miss Montague requested irritably. "Bad enough having mother's gang in the front room. Can't hear myself eat. Pretty tough on Mr Rolfe having to listen to you."

Oscar responded in brotherly fashion. "Oh, yes. I suppose you think your line of conversation's a cut above us. Books and looney pictures. Or about dear Wilfred. Wait till you meet Wilfred, Mr Rolfe." He began to affect a high-pitched voice. "Dear Wilfred. So far above all this. Dear sweet Wilfred. Let me stroke your noble brow, Wilfred darling." He wiped the grinning Angus's hair into his eyes. "So full of sweetness. . . ."

Oscar was continuing when he looked towards his sister. "Come on, Gus," he said hastily. "We'll go up to my room and let her have it."

Safely outside the door he stuck his head in again. "Tell little Wilfred from me to shave once in a while and he'll be more of an ornament."

With this final shot he departed, leaving Linnie red in the face and breathing through her nose.

"More bread?" she said with an effort.

Rolfe did not dare to smile. "Families are like that," he nodded sympathetically. "Always butting in."

A battered-looking object damp and with its fur bristling appeared in the doorway.

"Why, good old Bill!" Rolfe said joyously. "Here Bill, here."

The cat disregarded him and miaowed towards Linnie whom he obviously regarded as the giver of charity.

"Stuggy, Bill's son," Linda corrected Rolfe. "Couldn't have fed him again," she said in an annoyed tone. "Always forgetting him. Here Stuggy."

She poured milk into a saucer and Stuggy advanced and lapped noisily. He was getting grey about the whiskers and rheumatic in the joints.

"Still a good mouser," Linnie observed. "He does try to get a job."

"Eh?" Rolfe looked up from Stuggy.

"He makes money now and then drawing advertisements. And a few weeks ago he had a joke published. I'll show you some of his stuff."

From the pride of her tone Rolfe gathered that she was referring to Wilfred. He managed to turn the conversation into more pleasant channels by offering to help with the washing-up. Linnie looked surprised. His suggestion was apparently unprecedented.

Over the washing-up she almost confided in him. "Must be someone to keep things going." she remarked. "Got to be a bit short sometimes. Angelique's too decent. They impose. Borrow money off her. Get her to mend their shirts. Press their clothes. That sort of thing. Got to be hard."

"Lightning," said Rolfe, "if you'd drop trying to be snappy, you'd have dimples."

For a minute he did not know whether she was going to be angry.

"Haven't got time to be fat. Too busy."

She might almost have smiled if the door had not opened suddenly.

" 'S Mr Rolfe," she explained to the young man in the doorway.

Obviously the new lodger was expected to recognize Wilfred by the mere glory of his presence.

"Well, well," Rolfe said, attempting the role of the old family friend. "Pleased to meet you."

Wilfred, whom Rolfe immediately classified as a long, pale worm, extended a reluctant hand and Rolfe did his best to break it.

"It's enough to make one sick," Wilfred said fretfully, pressing his uninjured hand to his brow. "Linnie, can't you do something about that noise in the front room?"

Linda looked distressed. "It's Margot's birthday. They wouldn't take any notice."

"A man comes in with his head splitting." Wilfred slumped into a chair and closed his eyes. "I haven't had anything to eat since midday, and this — this. . . ."

Linda hastened to the cupboard. Wilfred opened his eye and regarded the new lodger attentively.

"You remind me of someone, Rolfe. Your face. Particularly in profile."

Wilfred became very much the boy artist. Linda also regarded the new lodger attentively.

"I know," Wilfred cried, suddenly radiant. "You remember the banner I painted for the Socialist Club in the May Day Procession — the one the police tore up — the chap who carried it — that's who I'm thinking of. The same high cheekbones and the drawn pallor.

"A little group of Us," Wilfred addressed himself to Rolfe, "decided to form a movement for the Advancement of Proletarian Art." He paused and sipped the tea as though it was hemlock. "Linnie, my other coat. You'll find it in the wardrobe. I don't like to trouble you, but this one's damp. That's a dear girl, Linnie.

"A little group of Us feel that the claims of proletarian art are not being given real consideration. In fact I gave a lecture on the lack — the callous indifference — the complete absence of proletarian art in this part of the world. Are you interested in proletarian art at all, old man?"

It set Rolfe's teeth on edge to called old man by anything as picturesque as Wilfred.

"Can't say I know much about it." He remained the gruff old family friend.

Wilfred, hearing Linda returning, lapsed impressively, his hand to his head.

"Here's your coat, Wilf," she said gently.

He flung out his arm. "I don't want it now. For Christ's sake don't worry me."

"Does he often get like this, Lightning?" Rolfe asked with a nasty sympathy.

"It's one of his headaches." Linda was genuinely concerned.

Wilfred regarded Rolfe indignantly.

"It's nothing," he said. "Nothing, Nothing, Nothing."

He rushed towards the door.

"How about your dinner?" Linnie called. "Where are you going?"

Wilfred turned with a wan smile. "Who knows?" he said dramatically. "Anywhere, out of this." And then in a more casual tone, "I think I'll go round to Fred's."

"If you get drunk," Linnie reverted sharply to her every-day manner, "you can stay there."

She began to clear the untouched food from the table. "He worries," she explained. "He's a genius. Can't even afford to buy his paints and brushes. It's terrible."

"The world is all cluttered up with geniuses, Lightning," Rolfe remarked.

Linda ignored the inference. "Y'ought to go to bed," she snapped. "Bud'll be round any minute."

The attic to which Linnie led Rolfe looked out over the Cornish yard. It was obviously Linnie's room. Not that it was a feminine room. The walls were an unhealthy pale blue that looked like nothing so much as starch on washing day, the floor was stained black, the bed had the severe white look of a pall.

Rolfe sat down on the bed and regarded his landlady's daughter rather dazedly.

"I'm not certain how I got here yet," he said half to himself. "It's extraordinary how the habit of drifting gets you. Never settling down. Always going on. And all the time — all these years — this place has been just the same. Changes of course, but only surface changes. Same old house, same old stairs. Look." He pointed out the window. "The same blasted little peach-tree. The place smells the same. It's queer coming back to something you've forgotten."

Linnie was getting out some clean towels.

"That sounds like Bud," she said in the tones of a hospital nurse reproving a patient for getting the coverlet untidy.

Bud glowered at them from the doorway.

"Had to fight me way through a pack of beer-hounds," he croaked. "How is it, Jimmy? Not so good?"

Rolfe waited until Linda got out of the room. "You're a damn fine friend, you are," he reproached Bud. "Letting me get in among a mob of proletarian paint splashers."

"You can get into bed while you say it. What's all this?"

"Beggary Barn. Your help's home. You pushed me in here, didn't you? You knew all about little Nancy, the headache sufferer."

Bud was hurt though he tried to treat the matter as a joke.

Rolfe gave an exaggerated description of Wilfred dashing out into the night.

"At the end of the week," Rolfe concluded, "I will manufacture a proletarian aunt who wants me to live with her. Otherwise a little group of Us will organize something choice for Wilfred in the murder line. Wonder what the hell she sees in him."

"He's only one of a series. I've watched 'em come and go. Get a bit sicker. Say, the newborn-kitten stage, and you can cut Wilfred right out — just like that. She likes clinging vines."

Rolfe grinned feebly.

"What's up with yuh?" Bud asked abruptly.

"Various things. You don't want me to go spitting out

symptoms, do you?"

The little man perched on a chair and rolled a cigarette.

"Want a jab, Jimmy?" he inquired. He always pronounced the word as though it were on the end of a bayonet.

"Dunno. Still got some money. Had an idea I'd like to see this place. Get ground into the mud with the other wrecks. Hey!" He half raised himself. "I'm beginning to talk like your help. Is that Bram tipping out the washing-up water? Give him a hail, will you, Bud?"

"For Gawd's sake come up and jam some sense into this cripple," Bud yelled. He turned back into the room.

"Here I go hauling your carcase in an' offering yuh a jab an' all and you begin to give an imitation of the happiest corpse in the mortuary."

He sat down sulkily on the end of the bed until the sound of voices on the landing sent him leaping to fling the door open for Bramley and old Duncan.

"It feels like the relief of Lucknow," he croaked. "I been shut up with 'im for ten minutes and I didn't know how much longer I'd last."

Duncan drowned his words in a burst of welcome that sounded like the woofing of an old sheep-dog.

"Rolfe, begob," he bellowed. "You young scallywag, where've you sprung from?"

Twelve years had made a notable difference in Duncan. He had been a sturdy, hale, bull-voiced old battler in the days of war but of that Duncan there remained only an echo. It was a rather sad echo, striving for old times' sake to be louder and heartier than ever. He had lost his beard but his moustache remained, white as the quilt but no longer bristling and belligerent. He was still a fighter, but a fighter unmanned by too long a period of defeat, a fighter who had given up being indignant. His old hands were gnarled with knotted veins, but if he left them still, they might tremble, not with age, but with a kind of exhaustion, the exhaustion of a man worn down to his last resources of energy. He was trying hard to be jovial. From his hip pocket he produced a flask.

"Whisky," he announced unnecessarily. "Pour it out, Bram, and don't you dare tell your mother. Not that you would, lad, but — well — right-o. Did you bring the glasses? Good boy. Now, young Jimmy, you put your hand round this glass. Raise the other hand. Right-o. I, Jimmy Rolfe, hereby swear," Mr Duncan mumbled rapidly, "that I will henceforth stay in Foveaux and do the right thing by those who brought me up by hand. . . ."

"Don't make such a row, Dunc," Bramley urged. "You'll have them all up here."

"Row? Row? Who's making a row? I'm whispering."

"Whisky's no good to me, Dunc," Jimmy protested. "I've got an ulcer of the stomach among other things."

"You always were a black-hearted coot," the crestfallen Duncan said reproachfully. He had gone out and spent the last of his money on that whisky. "Talk about your fool stomach when a man offers you a drink. There's nothing whisky isn't good for."

"All right." Jimmy reached out for the glass, but Bramley carefully removed it.

"My need is greater than yours," he pointed out.

Duncan's eyes bulged out of his head. "Begob," he whispered. "I can just hear the old lady saying that your father's last wish was that you should never touch liquor."

"They tell me y' brother got married?" Pellager struck in. "Congratulations."

Bramley looked at him admiringly. "How'd you do it, Bud?" he asked. "The family only knew at lunch-time."

Bud's vanity swelled visibly. "I could tell you a few other things," he said.

"Come on, Jimmy," Duncan interrupted, "tell us what you've been up to? When I heard you'd landed this morning, I looked up the shipping list and said to meself: 'It must've been an Italian boat.' "

"You're right. I came down from Vienna. But look — I'll let you have it some other time. You talk."

Duncan was obviously disappointed. "First-hand information of the political situation of Central Europe," he mumbled, "is just what I'm after. I've got to give a lecture. . . ."

Rolfe's eyes were fixed on the black slab of the window as though it were the past.

"I've done nothing much," he said tonelessly. "Married. Left home by special request. Did a bit of surveying. . . ."

It was strange how faded those hot crowded years seemed now, as though they had passed like a fever, leaving him again with the only reality, which was these shabby houses in this shabby Foveaux. These men lounging about the room might have been ghosts or shadows gathered into reality, invoked by the old surroundings to the unaltered eternity of existence between the walls of Mrs Webb's place. It was as though from floating over experiences that left him untouched he had suddenly struck sharply against a rock of something tangible, hard and familiar. Something he could grip and hold. The smell of the place, the familiar landing, the mean streets, and dirty old houses that he had once reviled, now seemed more solid than any of the new great cities he had passed through. He had, he realized, ties to this place. He had not been such a sentimental fool to come back. "Eels," he thought illogically, "eels go back to the Sargasso Sea where they are born." A vision rose before his eyes of the weed-bound waters where they said the wrecks of the old buccaneers' ships still rotted among the tangled kelp. A waste of shallows and broken hulks.

"I've never seen the Sargasso," he said absently. "I always meant to. That comes of reading pirate stories."

The three men looked at each other in consternation. He must be pretty sick. Bramley was feeling gloomy himself over the fate of Tommy but he suddenly became more cheerful than anyone. They began to talk, cutting in on each other's reminiscences of this or that worthy of Foveaux.

"Remember old Isenberg?"

"Many a time I pawned the dad's binoculars there. . . ."

"He's shifted to a big place in Slazenger Street. They pulled the old shop down in nineteen-twenty-two."

"No, it couldn't have been as late as that."

"It was before they put Lennox Street through that the swanky people began to move."

"No, it was after. The de Russets didn't move till near the end of the war. Remember how they wanted to cart away the fern-house and the buyer went to law about it?"

"Isenberg moved just a bit after Willie Hannell hanged himself."

"This place is finished." Duncan reverted gloomily to the whisky. "I've been saying that for years."

They began to argue the matter. Bud Pellager claimed the change was due to flats and motor garages.

"I don't like to see them," he piped. "One more old place coming down each week. Land's too valuable to leave them up and let families grow in them. Pull 'em down and build something that'll give more rents than just houses. That's their game." He glanced appealingly at the inanimate Rolfe. "Remember when you used to tell me there'd be flats all over where the old houses were, and I laughed. Well, I ain't laughin' now."

"You came back just in time," Bramley put in helpfully. "The building boom's just about at its best. Our firm, Bross, Twyford and Massingham (I left old Bross when Bill Bross started out on his own), they're getting record prices for land everywhere. Bill Bross wants to put up some flats in Foveaux himself."

They were trying to reassure him, to encourage him, but Rolfe felt too tired to say he didn't care a twopenny damn if they were building straw huts.

"Foveaux is finished," Duncan reiterated. "When the factories began to come up the hill, the people went out. There's the die-stamping works in the lane at the back of Foveaux House. All the old places where Lawyer Foxteth and the Miss Dimiters used to live are cheap residentials — all letting rooms."

"It's a place for wrecks," Rolfe said suddenly. "All the wrecks cast up on the shore-line of the city. Who worries about the littoral or where the barnacles build? All the waves sweep over it, all the tides of factories and slum terraces and cheap shoddy shops and flats and makeshift dugouts. We're drift, just drift, left-overs. You, Dunc, me, Buddy, all lying on the lee shore. I used to think that, watching the Captain. Nobody lives in Foveaux unless they're wrecked someway, finished."

"Go join the gravediggers' union," Bud blazed at him. "This place is a good place, an interesting place. I've made a lot of money here and when I go travellin'— an' believe me, I'll be leaving next year. . . ." He stopped. "Snap out of it, Jimmy," he said, "You were the man who was going to pull down Plug Alley."

"Plug Alley still there?" Jimmy asked without interest.

"It is," Duncan boomed. "It stands as an indictment of capitalist economy — a burning indictment. . . ."

"Too bad," Rolfe said carelessly. "It's no use pulling down slums unless you do it on a big scale. They did that in Vienna. By gosh, you ought to see the joints they put up there. Parks round them. Little places for the kids to play. Plenty of sunlight. Workers' flats. But what flats." He almost roused himself, then said quietly: "What's the use?"

"Go on," said Bramley, watching him like a cat. "Suppose you could get something like that here in Foveaux. Wouldn't it be a starting point for others? I mean if you could put a bomb under the council and get them to knock down Plug Alley and build these. . . ."

"Personal philanthropy is all wrong,' declared Duncan. "You've got to change the system, not patch it up."

Bramley was not going to be put off. "I've got all the facts about slums. No one could work for old Bross for years as I did without learning all the ins and outs. Here's Jimmy full of overseas facts and figures—"

"And gastric ulcers."

"Shut up. We'll start a slum abolition league. We'll make Foveaux sit up."

"Bramley," Rolfe said with a glint of amusement, "you've altered a lot. Dunc, you're elected. So are you, Bud."

"Fine, fine," Bud crowed with spurious heartiness. Anything to buck old Jimmy up, he thought.

The room was thick with cigarette smoke and argument when Miss Montague entered with a glass of milk.

"Slum abolition meeting," Rolfe informed her gravely. "I take it you're joining."

Linnie laughed scornfully. "You couldn't abolish a barn," she said. "Of course I'm joining. Here, drink this up."

"This isn't a sudden thing," Bramley protested. "I've been thinking about it . . . a long time."

How long a time he did not mention. He had meant to be more cautious but it had burst out of him. He had not meant to let them know he was impetuous about the scheme. How he had planned and figured! It had been his hobby. Foveaux to him was no hill of solid mortared houses. It was something abstract, something continually brightening into dream, into the memory of Hildebrand Sutton's gracious house and the white doves on the convent roof. He had lost his heart to a dream that had never been anything more at the most than a well-drained solidity. Bramley didn't care. He was busy in his sedate mind picturing the crumbling of the dirty old places below the steps. He saw the grey steps twisting up the cliff beside the towering white houses, above gardens and great sunny buildings that would once more make the name of Foveaux something to respect. It would no longer be: "Foveaux, oh that's a slum isn't it?" It would be: "Foveaux — the place where they're experimenting with those big concrete flats? Most interesting."

"It isn't impractical," he said fiercely. "Not a bit."

But he knew in his heart it was. Even if those great places were built in Plug Alley, they would never come up to the fairy glitter of his vision.

"Enthusiasm," Rolfe murmured wearily. "What it is to have enthusiasm."

# CHAPTER 2

## I

There was something about Plug Alley that made it unique. People maintained that those mean stone houses, narrow and verminous and dark, had been built by convicts, and if so, some of the convict tradition had soaked into them. Of course they were not the same as they were, say in 1850. Reluctantly old Mr Bross had moved with the times and put in gas rings with penny-in-the-slot meters. There were even taps in the backyards. These formed the only water supply, but it was not so inconvenient as one might suppose, because you could span the backyard with your two arms, it being possible to touch both the kitchen wall and the back fence by standing sideways. The yards were paved with brick and all the drainage and rubbish ran cheerfully down a grating in the middle. This usually stank to heaven and gave rise to the belief that the drainage also dated from the convict days. Beside the tap were the copper, woodpile, dustbins, lavatory and washing. The yard was the only place for the children besides the street. They preferred the street.

All the houses had at least two rooms, some three. Of course there were no baths, but anyone who wanted a bath could always rig a screen round the copper in the backyard. The bathing and sanitary facilities gave rise to the kind of crude jokes that Plug Alley most enjoyed. The inhabitants would sit on their front doorsteps in the evening and crack shameless and ribald jokes about their neighbours. Plug Alley had no secrets.

The front room was in many cases bedroom and kitchen both, with another family living in the back room. In summer the houses were only tolerable with the front doors left open, and as the doors gave directly on to the footpath, anyone passing could see in. It didn't matter much at night, for few families in Plug Alley could afford more than a kerosene lamp. Many of them did without that.

"I like to be private meself," Mrs Sampson confided to Mrs Blore. "What with the men trampin' through the room, I always like to have a screen round me when I'm in bed."

"When y'r married daughter and her husband and four children's livin' with you, there's no use in bein' fussy," was Mrs Blore's response. Mrs Blore considered that Mrs Sampson "put on dog".

Quarrels were frequent in Claribel Lane. For one thing, there was Mrs Metting who enjoyed a fight more than anyone and would go out of her way to start one. Mrs Metting was a thin grey woman with tiny deep-set grey eyes peeping out under her bushy eyebrows. She sprouted grey hairs mysteriously around her cheeks and chin. Her hair was coarse grey and cut short and she looked as though she had walked through cob-webs and forgotten to brush them away. The fierce peering of her long nose from under those eyebrows gave her a look that did not belie her real nature. Millie Metting had poison on her tongue. "There's times I think she must uv been reared for a scorping," her husband, Joe Metting, used to declare. "But even the scorpings draw the line somewhere." Nobody blamed Joe for beating her and occasionally locking her out. He only had the courage to do it when he got drunk, so he got drunk fairly often.

Joe was not the only sufferer from Millie's oratory. She blackened the neighbourhood like a bushfire, and people had been known to move out of places on either side of her even during the housing shortage. She had fought with everyone in the street until the possible supply of material for battles was exhausted. Then she tried to rouse other fights between the neighbours. "If you could hear what they say about you behind your back," she would tell Mamie Noblett, "you'd never talk to anyone in the street."

"People will talk," Mamie had responded quietly. "You can't stop talking an' I don't mind long as they're polite to my face."

Then again, people were always moving in or out; and the older inhabitants, the Nobletts, the Sampsons and the Blores, and a sturdy group of old-age pensioners, naturally looked down on the newcomers.

"You have to be careful who you know," was one of Mrs Sampson's sayings.

The fourth house from the end, for instance, had been rented by two ladies who invited their friends. One night the police arrived by car without invitation and roped in a well-known razor-slasher and two gentlemen wanted for possessing other people's property. Immediately following their exodus the house was taken by a gentleman who kept two wives. They occasionally fought like cats and like cats he would put them out in the street with the admonition that they could either "Get out or get to bed." Apart from this failing they were quite nice women.

Next to them lived Joe Hicks who had an optimistic outlook and seven children. His wife was older than he was and her outlook was not so optimistic. She was always worrying about food, a commodity that the rest of Plug Alley regarded as something to be borrowed from the neighbours or "ticked up" at the shop. Not that Plug Alley was unmindful of the importance of eating. A certain minority discredited its necessity but even they took counter lunch with their beer. From old Uncle Herb who lived with two friends on a pension and whisky to Hamp peddling artificial flowers, they all ate, if infrequently; and the ways they went about getting a feed differed from the mysterious bumping sounds when they dragged the bodies out of Ma Brown's and laid them a careful distance down the lane to Darky Andrews singing outside hotels about his mother's silver hair.

All feuds by mutual agreement terminated if any of the opposing families fell ill. Then erstwhile enemies would immediately bring in food and lend old coats to act as blankets and wait on the invalid. There was any amount of sickness in the lane. The women spent most of their time waiting at the hospitals on out-patients' day with either one or other child sick. The drainage of the hill seeped down and lay under the houses in Claribel Lane just as it had lain in the original swamp over which the houses were built. But the old-age pensioners, even though they were laid up all the winter with rheumatism, and the damp rotted the floor-boards, would cling to the little two-room houses that, to them, represented independence, home, freedom.

"Anyone can become inoored to anything," Bob Noblett explained. "That's what Boney Miles said to an old girl that came back with a bag of grapes an' said they'd made her kiddie sick. 'E says that the harsenic they sprayed 'em with hadn't been inoored to little boys an' it was a pity but 'e couldn't change the grapes. Look 'ow mosquitoes get inoored to the idea that if they land on a bloke, 'e's goin' to have a crack at them. You can 'ear the little fellers 'umming to themselves an' saying 'Ah, missed me, see!' They don't mind. Inoored to it, they are."

Bob's place was the best in the street seeing that he had a little patch of yard just in the angle of the steps where he kept his boxes and odds and ends and the horse and cart.

"It'd be suicide me leavin' Foveaux," old Bob would say gravely when he discussed it with Tommy Cornish. "I ain't goin' to say what the goodwill means to me. I been sellin' round Foveaux for over twenty years and I'm just about roonin' meself if I quit an' go somewhere where I'm not known."

Bob need not have worried. There was no one who ever met him who had not liked him, even his old enemies the police. Bob was one of those people whom it is impossible not to love even when he periodically drank every penny he had, got himself converted by the Salvation Army once again, and came home broken-hearted but redeemed with his old announcement: "I've done it again, Mamie. Look, I'll go out and drown meself. You on'y got to say the word."

Now that the children were grown up Mamie didn't mind so much. She was getting stout and contented, though the marks of fear and worry that years of Bob's way had engraved could never be smoothed out. If Bob was not getting drunk, he was so wastefully generous that often he might as well have given away his fruit and vegetables as sold them. He would drive a shrewd bargain at the markets but he could never resist presenting an old lady with a basket of apples or children with a handful of plums, letting them eat up his profits while he enjoyed the feeling of being lordly and gracious.

"Don't mention it," he would say, raising one hand. "If a bloke can't help 'is fellow men what's strugglin', what's the good of it, eh?"

Tommy had played truant many a day to go round with Bob. One of his jobs was to try to collect the worst outstanding debts. Bob would have been ashamed to remind his customers that they owed him money. "I 'ates bein' reminded uv such things meself an' why shud I go an' do to others what I 'ates done to me?" he argued.

"The old man," Jimmy Noblett told Tommy, "is completely dippy."

But the Old Man had always been good to Tommy. He had made him his first billycart and painted on the side of it "Cornish and Noblett, Contractors", to the great joy of the small boys who proudly tugged it out to pick up sticks together on the understanding that alternate loads went to the Cornish and Noblett households.

Tommy was aware that while he loved and respected Bram and was fond of his mother, he had not the same feeling of being happy in their company that he had with the Nobletts. Frankly, since the death of the Captain, his family had seemed increasingly narrow and chilling like a room into which sunlight never came. Bramley was always working or reading for some kind of accountancy examination and he seemed to expect Tommy to do the same. Tommy was far too interested in a great many things to tie himself down to books. He could learn brilliantly when he wanted to but he hardly ever wanted to. He felt restless if he had to sit down.

Then there was his mother. Bramley might not realize it, for Bramley was too kind to realize anything that might disturb him, but Tommy had never recovered from the discovery he had made when he was quite small. It was neither himself nor Bram that mattered to his mother; it was the Captain and only the Captain. She would say as often as she liked that it "was her sons she lived for", in that quiet obedient tone that made her sound as though she were repeating a lesson; but she wanted the Captain, she would never cease wanting the Captain, and whilst she might be kind to himself and Bramley, might love them even, it was the Captain she wanted. For him she would gladly have left them both at a minute's notice. Her principles kept her alive. The Captain would have wished it, and therefore she stayed cooking dinners quietly and dusting the knick-knacks.

Bramley just didn't realize. He thought Tommy was wild because the Captain had been wild, and he smiled tolerantly, but it wasn't so. It was Tommy's mother. The wildness of her under that quiet black dress and disguising curls was incredible. It was like something gagged down and bound trying to call for help, and the very house seemed to Tommy plangent with that muffled struggle. Here was his mother, that baffled mariner, crying after the Captain on the black seas he had gone voyaging, crying like something left on the shore of a foreign land. She might be talking about the rise in the price of butter or the naughty way pussy had stayed out all night, but underneath the real essence of her was shouting in the dark in a strange language for the Captain, ready to answer the word or sign that never came. Every now and then it seemed as though she would brighten, would light a secret beacon fire, but no answer came. There was nothing but silence. No answer would ever come.

The silence in the old cottage was to Tommy intolerable. With Bramley studying under the central light in the sitting-room, his mother sitting mending so patiently by the window, thinking about things that had happened before he was born, he felt like getting up and shouting, "Stop it. Stop it, I tell you. Shout, sing, scream if you like, but don't sit there letting the silence get you."

So Tommy would adjust his tie and say with an air of fine casualness, "I think I'll just go out for an hour, mums. I've got to see Jimmy Noblett about the football practice on Saturday."

He knew his mother disapproved of his playing football. She would become sniffily human at the mention of it.

"They've got ghosts up at our place," he remarked to Neicie Noblett, lounging with the rest of the family on the footpath. "It's much more life down here."

He squeezed Neicie's arm and she giggled. But it wasn't

Neicie he wanted really. He liked the Noblett family. He liked big, stupid Jim and Fred, and dear old Bob, and Mamie always busy about something and wiping the hair out of her eyes and complaining about getting fat and her varicose veins.

He could sit and kid Neicie or yarn with Bob or talk to Freddy about Tarnhams' and piecework rates. Freddy had got on at Tarnhams' as a floor boy and later the manager noticed him and made him an apprentice. Freddy was mad about being a joiner. He would come home at night and take out the tools he had managed to gather together, and lay them out lovingly before he would set to work on whatever he was making for his mother. There was the long keen edge of the tryon plane for shoot joists. He liked using that, and his smoothing plane for traversing surfaces, his dovetail saw, his spiral screw-driver (a beauty), his ratchet, and hammers and ratchet brace, his mitre square, his bevel and all the other squares. His thumb-screws, his hacksaw and mortise gauge, his marking gauge and spokeshave, his wood-file and oilstone that Bob had picked up cheap, his bits and chisels and brads.

"Says his bloody prayers to them," Freddy's brother, Jim, used to tell everyone. Jimmy was working as an S.P. book-maker's clerk and hoped to be a real bookmaker some day by a weird stroke of luck he was always trying to coax.

It was probably from old Bob that Freddy inherited his love of tools. Bob would have been a foreman in the engineering works if, in his young days, he had not acquired a habit of reproving the boss for lack of courtesy. For many years he had lost jobs because either the owner would try to sell a faulty job to a customer and Bob would insist on explaining where it was faulty, or else he would feel his dignity was not being sufficiently regarded.

"I used to say, 'There ain't no 'arm in politeness, Mr Jackson'," he would explain to Tommy. " 'You expect me to treat you polite, an' I do, 'cause why? Not 'cause you're payin' me. I ain't ever crawled to anyone for that. But because you're a fellow man, see? Well, an' I'm a fellow man too an' it's laid down that you ought to treat your fellow men decent. So in future, Mr Jackson, when I says: "Good mornin' and 'ow is it?" to you, I'll expect you to do the same by me.' "

Tommy would rather have sat on the footpath smoking and listening to old Bob's queer stories, but the Noblett family, feeling that he was Neicie's "young man", had begun to efface itself. Mamie had obviously given Bob instructions that when Tommy suggested that they go round and have a lemonade (for Bob was periodically teetotal) Bob should refrain from accepting. Tommy was to be allowed to take Neicie out without feeling that he had to ask the whole family. He had grinned to overhear Mamie's whisper of admonition and Bob's grumbling protest that, if young Tommy was going for a walk in the park, he didn't see why he shouldn't go too.

Any time Tommy tried to shout the family to the picture show there was a unanimous firm refusal. Neicie was allowed to accept even though it was Mamie's company and Bob's that Tommy liked. He liked going out with Neicie but he would just as soon put his feet up on the kitchen mantelpiece and talk to Mamie while she did her ironing. He didn't really want to go walking with Neicie. It was much more fun sitting on the footpath enjoying the simple pleasures of Plug Alley. There was usually something doing. If a fight didn't break or somebody start to beat his wife, there was always Mrs Metting.

He formed the habit of dropping in to lunch or tea with the Nobletts on his way home from work.

"Brought you a couple of cakes, ma," he would say lounging into the kitchen and taking the family towel down from its nail. "Where's the soap?"

"You shouldn't a done that," Mamie would always protest. " 'Tisn't much you earn on them buses to go wasting it."

Tommy liked being a bus conductor. Bramley wanted him to "stay on and finish his schooling", but Tommy restlessly resented the idea of poling on Bramley. Even when he got a job he was not happy. He hated being in an office all day as much as he hated school. He tried factories but found that game lacked activity.

"Well, what are you going to do with yourself now?" Bramley had asked him when he heard the news that the tanneries were putting off hands and they had started with Tommy.

"Bus conducting," Tommy said shortly. "Ian McErchin says he can get me in if I fake my age."

It was no use trying to stop Tommy. If he decided he was going to ride a bus, clad in a white coat and peaked cap, he would do it. Within a few weeks he was prowling round the garages where the great buses lived, learning the routes and eyeing with awe a fat apoplectic little man, reputedly richer than Rockefeller, who stooped every now and then to pick up stray nuts and bolts off the floor and stow them in his pocket. This, Tommy learnt, was how he had grown rich enough to own all these buses.

Tommy really never worked out why it was that he felt so attracted to the Noblett family; but, if he had been asked, he would have said: "Because they aren't a bit like mums or Bram." He didn't like that crowd at Montague's. They did nothing but gas all the time. But there weren't any frills on old Bob and Mamie. That was the main thing. The way they saw things was simple. They didn't have anything hidden or baffling secrets about them like his mother and Bramley. There was none of this sitting and acting as if they were straight-forward ordinary people when all the time their thoughts were far away thinking something else. He liked people he could understand — vulgar, common, low people. People his mother wouldn't like and who would make old Bramley draw into his shell like a tortoise.

You only had to say something a bit offside to Bramley and he would blush like a girl. While Tommy did not look down on him for it, he could not really understand it. Bramley had a nice mind, he supposed; his mother had a nice mind. Tommy's mind was as hard as his face and, if he didn't like anyone else's face he was ready to improve it with his fists. It was unthinkable that Bramley would "mix it" with a couple of chaps on a street corner. He would simply stare at them coldly and walk away. As for kissing a girl, had old Bram ever really kissed a girl? Tommy doubted it. Tommy always kissed the gigglesome Neicie as a matter of course, but then he knew he was not the only chap who kissed Neicie. Neicie was pretty and she knew it. The one thing she was interested in was boys and still more boys. Everyone kissed Neicie. But Bramley! It really made Tommy wonder what would happen if Bramley fell in love. Not that he ever would. "Probably go into a blasted monastery or something," he muttered rebelliously. "A girl'd scare him sick."

He turned from the contemplation of his brother's failing to an argument with Jimmy on the chances of East Sydney getting into the semi-finals, a subject which ranked with beer, the dogs and test-matches as among the really important subjects in Plug Alley.

It did not shock Tommy when Bob went "on the beer", as Plug Alley termed it. He would good-humouredly assist the staggering Bob home with Jimmy Noblett propping up the other shoulder.

Jimmy usually cursed his father loudly and with acrimony.

"You go and get converted, I don't think! Fellow men, me eye. It would serve you right, if we let you loose, and you did stoush a copper and get pinched, you old. . . ." And so on and so forth.

But Tommy merely murmured with a grin: "Struth, I wonder what would happen if I ran into mum?"

He never did and Mrs Cornish preserved her little picture of Tommy as a boy too upright for this world.

"Such good boys," she would murmur. "Such good boys, both of them."

## I I

"If I had my way," Kingston, the Child Welfare Inspector, would proclaim bitterly, "I'd have all the grass and trees removed from Foveaux Park. The place could then be paved with cobblestones and nice steel spikes. . . ."

Most of Kingston's "affiliation" cases came from Foveaux Park. Even the pigeons there had loose morals. In other parks pigeons might live in sedate domesticity, pair by pair, but in Foveaux Park they were indiscriminate in their love, and casual in their lives. When a lady pigeon found reason for desiring a nest, she singled out one of her admirers and reminded him that, if he wished to be officially recognized as the father, it was his job to go out and get straw. The chosen pigeon thereupon puffed his chest feathers proudly and settled down to hard work as a provider. The Foveaux male pigeons might regard love-making as a gay pursuit but their parental instincts were, if anything, overdeveloped. They weren't fussy on matters of paternity but they were crazy about nest-building. They seemed to have caught the Foveaux interest in houses.

As for the sparrows, every September there was a housing shortage in the top of the park's one palm-tree, their favourite nesting place. It shook with the uproar of their chirruping and fighting. There were hundreds of them, gossiping, encouraging or insulting each other, like neighbours living in flats, floor above floor, frond above frond, forming a defence corps against the bigger and heavier starlings, going off with each other's wives, fluttering down to bring back a pigeon feather with great triumph and labour. You could almost see the sparrow dust his hands when he landed the feather safe.

The oak-trees, drab as factory girls in black overalls during the winter, were taking their new greenery out of tissue paper. The crumpled tender foliage spread out along the branches like the damp wings of pale butterflies. Just to see the new leaves with a green light of their own made you want to get off the asphalt path and roll in the clover patch that the gardener had left unmowed. So Tommy felt whenever he took a short cut to his bus route. He had on a starched white coat and a peaked cap, but the idea pleased him all the same.

The flower-shop windows were metaphorically rolling in clover. The blaze of gold that was August had passed in a fanfare of daffodils, marigolds, wattle blossoms and iceland poppies, and now with September the windows were delicate with branches of pink and white peach blossom, apple blossom, the frail azaleas, and all flowers with loose, cool petals, sweet of scent and swift to fall. The very streets and lanes smelt of spring in a renewed pungency of dustbins. Dogs went about in packs, barking, and cats hunted and made love in the park. Many a pussy came home with a little ball of blood and feathers to show some sparrow had forgone domesticity for good. They even hunted pigeons cooing and bowing and courting in the shadowy branches of the big Moreton Bay figs.

How Foveaux Park had managed to cling to those great

Moreton Bay figs when almost every other park had dug them out for flowerbeds is a problem that only the decrepit Peter Harkness who ruled the place could have solved. The Moreton Bay figs were a godsend to Foveaux. Old women, bent and hobbling, came to collect sticks under their great shadows, as old women, their ancestresses, had done in primeval forests under the shadow of just such trees. By day there were generally some down-and-outs lying under them or sitting hunched on the benches, mere sacks, emptied of energy, hope or any touch of spring, merely a drowsy hunger, a stolid bitterness, remaining.

By night those lying under the Moreton Bays would not be lying alone. No stringency of by-laws would make Foveaux immune to the hint of new leaves and new loves and the smell of mown grass. By night you could forget the asphalt paths, the wired-in area of the children's playground that had to be padlocked because otherwise it would be torn down by roughs for sport. The old band rotunda became a friendly shadow for murmuring couples whence the mother cats who reared stray broods there would lead their young on shadowy hunts and scuttlings.

"Puss, puss, puss," Tommy called to the wild little kittens.

"Aw, let them alone," Neicie protested.

They were sitting as they often did beside the pond because the grass there was thick and soft and it grew round the base of the Moreton Bay figs. In their own private shadow they could, secluded, watch the glow in the sky over the city, the flash of the cars racing along Errol Street. There was a sense of companionship with other couples, invisible and sympathetically indifferent, round the blackness of the lake — that two-foot mixture of mud and old tin cans. Over them the leaves cut dark arabesques on the pale sky and one could lie and look into the intricacy of the branches framing little sparks of stars.

Neicie was rather bored by Tommy. Any chap who would look up from kissing a girl to call stray cats was just a waste of time. She sat up against the twisted roots of the tree and fretfully plucked a small twig out of her hair.

"They must be hunting frogs," Tommy went on. "Or

crickets. When I was a kid and had the toothache my mother
would say, 'Don't cry. Listen and you can hear the crickets.'
Always think of toothache when I hear them. Listen."

Neicie yawned.

"Or it's frogs croaking." Tommy mused. "Just think! Not to
know a frog from a cricket."

"Why? Who cares?"

"Then there's the names of things. When I see the blue
flowers coming out, I often wish I knew what they were called.
Gee, someone's sitting on our old seat with the broken back.
Serve 'em right if it lets them down. Remember when we were
kids we used to come getting sticks and we'd fight about who
owned the seat? We scooted all the others off and kept it to
ourselves."

"You wouldn't let me come," she reminded him. "You
threw stones at me."

"Well," he grinned. "I let you come now, don't I?"

"I wish we'd gone to the pitchers," Neicie muttered. Tommy
was all right to dance with. He was, in fact, the kind of dancer
who could make a girl in love with him by swinging her once
round a dance floor. But he was more exciting as a dancing
partner than as a lover. This was not the first time Neicie had
watched the sky from the friendly shadows of the Moreton
Bay fig-trees and she had had more responsive youths to make
her forget a certain nobbliness where the stones asserted their
edges through the grass.

"It's a bit hard here," she complained.

"Here, have my coat."

If Neicie was not holding the full focus of attention, she
would quickly do something to re-assert herself. She was not
interested in stars or the smell of clover. She was interested in
just how attractive she might be. She had a well-founded
belief that she could make any man mad about her if she tried,
and it was her favourite pursuit to collect proof of this interesting fact. Not a man came within range but she sized him up,
hair and hoof, in terms of just how much he would be worth
if kissed in the dark. In such circumstances she often wondered
at her own forbearance in maintaining Tommy, in spite of their
quarrels, as her "regular boy". He was always handy about the

place, ready to take her to dances if she wanted to go, and he had just drifted into the position.

"What are you thinking about?" he asked suddenly.

Neicie considered it was a silly question. "I dunno. What're you?"

"I dunno." He realized that Neicie wouldn't understand if he told her. He had been thinking about cats and fur coats and rabbits and God and the old church when Dr Wilbram had it and he had gone as a small boy to sit under the cool green window-pane that he regarded as his own. The ivy outside the pane swayed like seaweed and he had drowned in drowsiness and the cool green colour so that the prayers were only a far-away murmuring in his ears. He could see the people in the church like nameless sea creatures against the stone pillars. They seemed melted out of their everyday shape by the dimness and out of their everyday mind by prayers. Only the admonitory steel fingers of the organ pipes lifted towards the light, their shining columns like the warnings of the law: "Thou shalt have no other gods before me." As a small boy he had shocked his mother by asking if the organ was God. He could not divorce the idea of those cold steel fingers, mathematical and shining, from his concept of an impersonal, steely God, even after he learnt that God was good and warm and loving. He immediately associated this God with his mother's sealskin coat which he continued to stroke with religious veneration until it vanished in a time of dearth never to return.

In the same way he had discovered with a shock that the mythical beast Dr Wilbram referred to in his sermons was not the bunny rabbit in the churchyard grounds. Like many other small boys in Foveaux he had dreamt of setting a little trap for the mythical beast and catching it. Many a night he had visions of coming out in the early dewy morning and finding the bunny in a cage in the backyard. He would then be able to stroke its fur, like his mother's coat, and give it grass.

"I wish we'd gone to the pitchers," Neicie repeated.

"It's too hot inside on a night like this."

"Well, it's not much fun here."

"Let's go home."

"Not on your life. It'll be like a furnace down there. We

could have gone to one of the beaches."

"We'll go tomorrow night."

"No, we won't," Neicie said shortly, "I'm going out with Bill."

"Who's he?" Tommy asked resentfully.

"A chap I know at work."

"Where're you going?"

"Never you mind. It's none of your business."

"It is my business." Tommy caught her by the wrist. "You're not going out with him, do you hear? I'll take you anywhere you want to go."

"You," Neicie sneered. "All you're good for is playing football and talking to dad. Fat lot you care about me."

"I do," Tommy muttered. "I do."

"Now Bill's different," Neicie said provokingly. "And he can kiss. . . ." Tommy suddenly hated her. It was common, he thought, of her to try to madden him. He knew she was doing it purposely, but that did not make it any the less painful. "He's one of those big fair chaps," Neicie drawled, "with muscles on him like — like. . . ." She giggled. "You ought to see him in a bathing costume."

Tommy's lips tightened. He no longer felt towards Neicie as he had to the wild kittens. He felt hot and cruel. He wanted to shake her, choke her.

"That's the kind you like, is it?" he said grimly. "You think I couldn't kiss you differently, if I want to."

Neicie felt a secret triumph. She was getting him wild all right. She maintained her pose of indifference. "When I come out with you," she yawned, "it's a bit of a change from going out with other chaps. Kind of restful."

Tommy clenched his teeth. "Is that so?" he said with emphasis. "Is that so?"

". . . If the place were only planted with steel spikes," Kingston maintained to his fellow inspectors, "the work would be cut just about in half and think what it would save the Government."

# CHAPTER 3

---

## I

"Well, if you don't do as you're told, you're not only a damn fool, you're a suicide," the doctor snarled at him.

"Honest John" Hutchison was shakily buttoning his shirt. There was almost a whine in his voice. "But look here, Harry, you can't go asking impossibilities."

"I'm telling you to quit."

Hutchison shook his head. "I can't, old man."

"Why not?"

"Money. You don't think I wouldn't get out, if I had enough money to live on? I'm a poor man."

"Money!" Hutchison's doctor laughed vulgarly. "You're rotten with it. That's your trouble. You people can afford to sit round and drink whisky and ruin your arteries and then you can afford to come here and wallow in the luxury of being sorry for yourself." He relented slightly. "How about that pig farm or rabbit farm or whatever it was you were going to buy?"

Hutchison brightened up. "I've bought it. Good paying concern, too. Got a manager and three men running it. Truth is, every time I go up there there's so much business to attend to, I'd just as soon be back in Sydney."

"Well, take a holiday," Dr Geraldton snarled. He never believed in being pleasant to rich patients, reserving his kindlier manner for the free wards. His kindlier manner had got him the nickname of the "cranky cow". "This is your diet list. No drink. No cigars. No rushing about. Get away to the country and loaf."

Hutchison almost crept to the door. He felt like a dying man as he fumbled in his pocket-book for the two guineas and received his receipt from the white-clad receptionist. Waiting for the lift he tried the experiment of throwing out his chest and straightening his coat.

"Damn robbers," he growled. "Take your last penny for nothing." He remembered wistfully that there had been times when he himself had wanted to be a doctor. "Sit back and tell people to go away for holidays when they're up to their eyes in work."

Hutchison brooded over the idea of a holiday. Go up to a mountain hotel, maybe, and have all the people he knew saying: "Well, what the hell are you doing here? Come and have a drink." And then telling them his doctor wouldn't let him. What a life! The sea made him sick. He couldn't even stay at home because his wife was having an architect in to remodel the place. Dammit!

Trout fishing! He had seen pictures of trout fishing. You wore an old felt hat with hooks on it and stood in the water up to your knees. It looked good. Mountain streams. Sunny days in the open. Good fellows to meet. Some little pub somewhere and a drink or so at night before turning in. No. No drinks. Still trout fishing might be an idea. Get away from the damn city and the committees and the speech-making and that little blighter of a secretary who laughed at him behind his back. Wouldn't keep him if he wasn't cheap.

The confounded god-damned worry of it all! May always wanting money. Sawyer pressing for a decision about the timber-yard. Marjorie wanting a trip to England. No thought of her old father's arteries. Everyone trying to bite him for something, and what with the bore of having to sit and listen to old Bullnose's speech in the House tomorrow, he felt depressed enough to take a holiday without any doctor to back him.

Outside a policeman was standing eyeing his car with suspicion and a notebook and Honest John immediately forgot he was a dying man in his haste to dodge the possible fine for parking his car where parking was forbidden.

"Oh, is that your game, young man?" he said jubilantly. "Been arresting any more bicycle thieves lately?"

The policeman's face relaxed in a grin. "Oh, it's you, Mr Hutchison. It's a long time since I've seen you. I was shifted, you know, a month after the bicycle was stolen."

He put his notebook away and leant on the car to talk for a

minute or so before Hutchison drove off. Honest John never forgot a face and he used his memory as one of his best business assets.

He did not like driving through the traffic. It made him nervous. He had been known to drive round and round for ten minutes trying to find a place to put his car. He never ventured to pass anyone on the road, and his manner of crossing intersections was reminiscent of an old lady looking for burglars. More than ever today did he dislike driving. He should have brought one of his daughters but, as usual, they were wanting to go somewhere else; never a thought for their poor sick father.

The headline on a newsboard caught his eye and turning to look he nearly bumped the car in front which had stopped for a traffic signal. This did horrible things to his arteries. So much that, whirling up Murchison Street into Dennison Square, he felt that he must pull into the kerb. Luckily he was outside the paper shop, so he stopped to buy a paper and investigate that headline: "Red Menace", it ran, "Europe Stirred by Disclosures." This was meat and drink to Honest John. If there was one thing he was interested in at the moment, it was the Red Menace. He preached the Red Menace loyally, just as previously he had preached the Yellow Peril. It looked as though the Red Menace was going to be the best card in the pack for the coming election, and Honest John felt it was an infinitely better line than, say, the Creeping Influence of Popery. For one thing, Honest John had too many Catholics in his electorate. He also had far too many adherents of the Red Menace to make it a comfortable electorate; but still no politician's life is a bed of roses. If Bill Bross's idea of building flats was sound, Honest John felt a better kind of people would be voting for him next year. Good class of people lived in flats. Good old Bill. Without realizing what he was doing he bought a cigar and lit it. He was feeling more benevolent and his nerves were soothing down.

As he picked up his change he noticed it was lying on a leaflet. There was a bundle of them on the counter. Honest John never could resist a leaflet, even if it were only advertising soap. He read:

## PUBLIC MEETING

Lockrow Hall, Tuesday, 8 p.m.

*Subject*: HOUSING REFORM

Speakers:

Rev. Adam Atwater ; Clive Saunders, M.A., LL.B.

"Claribel Lane has obtained for Foveaux the name of the worst
slum area in Sydney. Only a few streets away one may find the
peak of luxury in the most modern flat buildings and below them
a region of narrow, filthy lanes with houses overcrowded and
unsightly." (*Daily News.*)

> Help us to do something about this disgrace.
> Join the Slum Abolition League.

> Rev. Adam Atwater, *President,*
> James Rolfe, *Secretary.*

John Hutchison read the leaflet through twice. He had no
difficulty in placing Atwater. That would be the new Congre-
gational Minister. But who was James Rolfe? Any connection
with Barney Rolfe? Why hadn't they come to him before
forming a Slum Abolition League? What was behind the move
anyway? Who was behind it and what did they think they
were going to get out of it? Possibly the Anderson crowd had
decided that with the boom on they might get better terms if
they bought direct from the council rather than from Bross.
They had had their eyes on that Plug Alley district for factory
sites. Young Graves had let that out by accident. But what was
their game? Maybe old man Bross was holding them up and
wouldn't sell. Anyway sooner or later it had to come to the
council and he would be mayor next year for a dead cert.

Still, the business had a nasty sound. After all, Foveaux was
his oyster. No one else was allowed to sprinkle salt on it.
Worrying about his health, he hadn't been able to keep an eye
on things. Bud Pellager ought to know the strength of it. Sly
devil, Pellager.

"Is Mr Pellager anywhere about?" he asked the girl behind
the counter.

"He's upstairs. Just a minute and I'll call him."

That was the way Honest John liked things done. Service.

There was nothing really serviceable about Bud. The way he lounged through the doorway like a disreputable little cat, hopped up on his stool and rolled a cigarette, almost all in the one move, was so casual as to be almost insulting. He looked more than ever like a dissipated choir-boy.

"Well, Jawn," he croaked. "What's noo?"

Honest John was undecided whether to be the bluff beaming old mayor or a sorely tried and sick man.

"I don't suppose you've got a drink of water, Bud," he said hoarsely, deciding on the second role.

"Water?" Bud's voice was incredulous. "Hey, Lightning, glass of water. . . . Since when did you take to water, Jawn?"

Honest John thanked the young lady who brought the water and looked pathetic.

"Just been seeing my doctor, Bud. Getting old. Got to retire. It's the arteries." He shut his eyes and a mood of self-pity deepened over him. "Been working too hard, he tells me. Wish I were like you, son. You never. . . ." He was going to say "look a day older", but he remembered that Pellager hated to be reminded of his boyish appearance. "You never seem to get less spry. No 'retire to the country' for you."

"Jawn," Bud chirruped, "you could no more retire to the country than I could grow daffodils."

The mention of daffodils was a signal to Linnie to betake herself elsewhere. More and more these days Bud was leaving the shop to her while he spent his time in mysterious business of his own. Honest John was glad to see Linnie recede.

"Do you know where I can get in touch with a couple of good men, Bud? Fellows I can trust?"

Bud rubbed his chin. "Curly Thompson's out of jail—"

"No, no," Hutchison interrupted hastily. "You don't get what I mean. There's someone I want to keep an eye on."

Hutchison had long ago learnt never to put anything in writing, and to do his hiring through a third party.

"Oh, I get you." Bud nodded his head wisely. They discussed the terms.

"I see there's been some sort of a league or committee or

something on the move," Honest John picked up a leaflet casually as he was going. "What's the strength of it? Any idea?"

"Oh," Bud waved his hand. "Just amatoors. If they like to muck about, what's the harm? Young Linnie here's one of the committee."

"Well, well." Honest John became the beaming old mayor. "Very pleased to see such a charming young lady bothering her pretty head over these important matters, eh, Bud? Well, well. If there's anything I can ever do for your people, you'll let me know, won't you, Miss. . . ?"

"Montague." The Norman chin of the descendant of the Montagues remained unfriendly.

"Ah, yes, Miss Montague. Of course you have my every sympathy. Unofficially I may say that I feel those little hovels should have come down years ago. 'S a matter of fact, I've many a time said to myself: 'They must come down.' But you know how it is. One man alone — and I'm a sick man now, Miss Montague — a sick man — still." He pulled himself together bravely. "If I can do anything at any time. . . ." He talked himself out of the shop.

"Blasted old dodderer," Miss Montague remarked venomously as he turned the corner.

"Now, now," Bud reproved, "you mustn't be hard on him, honey. You mustn't be hard on Honest John. He's a sick man."

Honest John having disentangled his car from the perilous Scylla and Charybdis of two trucks parked behind and in front, drove round to McErchin's to tell him he thought the plans for McErchin's new garage were approved. For reasons of his own he had no desire for McErchin to be seen looking for him. Then, on the way home, he stopped opposite the skeleton structure that was going up in what had been the garden of Foveaux House. They had chopped down all the Moreton Bay figs so that the best use could be made of the corner and there were still great rounds of green timber lying about. Work had only just begun but Honest John had seen the plans and, in any case, his practised eye could discern how they were going to fit the new block of flats onto Foveaux House. By the time the stone had been given a coating of roughcast it would be uniform with the cheaper and newer building in front and no one would really know where the old Foveaux House ended and the new flats began.

"Good boy, Billy," Honest John murmured approvingly. Bross had a good investment there. He glanced across the lane and frowned. They ought to have pulled down those old warders' cottages by now. What did old Bross want for that land?

"Would you like to see over the job, Mr Hutchison?" It was young Bramley Cornish, Bill Bross's right-hand man. "Mr Bross would like your opinion."

"No thanks, I'm not feeling in top gear. Why doesn't Bill get those cottages out of his father? Disgrace to have places like that in this part of Foveaux." He waved his hand at the Cornish and Montague residences.

Poor Bramley flushed.

"See there's a campaign starting to pull down Plug Alley. High time."

"I'm on the committee," Bramley could not help replying.

Honest John looked at him with a queer expression. "The deuce you are." That was the worst of these young men. Wouldn't be a bit surprised to find that secretary of his was part of the Red Menace. Never knew when you had them.

"Well, well," Honest John said heavily. "Tell Bill I think the job's doing fine."

"You're sure you won't look over it?"

"Got to be going home, son. I'm a sick man." He climbed back into the car.

His first move when he reached home was to telephone Bill Bross.

"Listen, Billy. Don't think I'm kicking but don't you think it's a bit low-down to start campaigns all over Foveaux without giving me the tip?"

There was a surprised grunt from the other end.

"You heard what I said. There's been a slum clearance campaign started and every second person I meet's on the thing including your bright lad Cornish."

"Oh, Cornish is, is he?"

"Well, what's the idea?"

"No idea of mine. If he wants to join a slum clearance campaign I can't stop him."

"See here, Billy, are you trying to put something over me?"

"Not a bit of it, John. Cornish is a smart young chap. I tell you frankly I've nothing to do with it. I take it that they are after dad's bacon again. He should worry. How much would he get if the council resumed that Plug Alley place?"

Hutchison sucked his teeth. He mustn't let young Billy pump him. Shrewd man, Billy.

"Well, I couldn't say, Billy. Naturally I'd do my best for him but the land's going up in value and he'd be wise to hang on. Had an offer from the Anderson crowd, didn't he?"

There was a minute's silence at the other end. "I have an idea he did, Hutch. But you know what he's like. He won't part with any information, even to me, now I'm out of the firm."

"By the way," Hutchison said, "aren't those two old dumps yours — you know the ones I mean — two old stone cottages below the new flats. There's a good site going to waste, Billy."

"Yes, they're mine, Hutchison. When the dad and I split I took them over. But I can't see my way clear to do anything with them yet."

There was another silence. "Well, g'bye Hutch, look after yourself. It's going to put the value of those flats up if they wipe out some of those Lower Foveaux dumps, and you're right about those cottages. Down they come."

Hutchison hung up and sat by the telephone drumming his fingers on the table. A vision of Lower Foveaux as he considered it ought to be had come into his mind. Broad straight streets cutting through to the railway. Factories, warehouses, neat grey cement. He turned to the telephone again as his wife came out of the drawing-room.

"What did the doctor say?" she demanded. "I've been waiting for ever so long. What on earth became of you? Did the doctor. . . ."

"For heaven's sake stop babbling about the doctor. I'm all right." He addressed the telephone. "Is that Levering and Jones? I'd like to speak to Mr Levering. Tell him it's Mr Hutchison. . . . That you Levering? You were right about

Andersons. But listen, I can fix it. You see, it's like this. . . ."

A happy smile stole over his face and his wife with a sigh turned back to the drawing-room.

## II

The Slum Abolition League, as any of the Committee would have admitted, produced a great deal more thunder and lightning than its size warranted. It attracted attention and sympathy but few members or active helpers.

"That in itself is an asset," Rolfe argued. "Look at the trouble we had with that confounded Mrs Agnew." Bramley and Linda nodded agreement. "She doesn't even write letters."

The main occupation of the committee was writing articles and letters. Its biggest job was getting them published. Any time an article appeared headed: "Sydney's Slums, American Housing Expert Interviewed", you could bet Rolfe had put in something startling that whoever he interviewed had left out. They even managed to wangle into the headlines, "Slums are Disgrace, Says Overseas Visitor", with the visitor's photograph underneath. This had raised quite a tempest among the proud citizens.

Then there was the other type for the women's magazines headed: "Welfare Club Tours Slums" or "What Women are Doing to Better Housing Conditions among the Poor." These came from Linnie's typewriter with bright little comedy sketches, such as "Claribel Lane's Sunday Morning", "Mrs Morris Moves", which sometimes brought in welcome additions to the funds.

Bramley was naturally stronger on facts and statistics than literary style. He did turn out a number of laborious articles embodying a wealth of research on sickness, infant mortality, comparative cost to the State of clean suburbs and slums, maternal mortality in slum areas, crime and juvenile delinquency, some of which were muffled up in a couple of trade journals.

The one on the "Stonework of the Gold Boom" found a home in the *Mason and Plasterer* and his effort on the decayed and sagging roofs of Plug Alley, with notes on weathering in general, found its way into the *Roofer and Tuckpointer.*

"The great thing," Rolfe admonished them, from the heights of his job as under-publicity agent for a soap company, "is to know what these little magazines want, and give it to them. You can do anything if your publicity is right."

Rolfe had decided eventually that Bramley's painstaking mass of facts be kept as a base for the others to work on and Bramley be transferred to the controversy section. The Reverend Adam Atwater was an old hand at writing letters to the newspapers but he had become so formidable on the subject of slums that there were few dared to stand against him. It therefore became Bramley's job to watch when interest flagged and revive it again.

To the Editor,
Dear Sir,
  [he wrote wearily on innumerable occasions]

I would once again crave the indulgence of your columns while I put before your readers some important facts which your correspondent, Rev. A. Atwater, in his letter (Church and Slums, 20/4/28) has seen fit to omit. It is not, as he suggests, either the fault of the landlord or the municipal council that the houses to which he refers are in the alleged bad condition. Mr Atwater has conveniently forgotten that people of the worst type, the very dregs of humanity, will always get into these cheap houses and wreck them under the owners' very eyes and leave them without paying rent to carry on their filthy habits and destructive tendencies to some other so-called "slum area". It is the people who make the slum, not the landlord. Let the Rev. Atwater change the attitude of the slum people towards other people's property and we will soon hear less of the deplorable condition of such houses.

     Yours etc.,
      "FAIR PLAY."

Poor Bramley was also "Taxpayer", complaining of the waste of public time and money pampering "the unemployed and other undesirable elements" while the average taxpayer found his burdens increased by the resumption costs undertaken by philanthropic councils. As "Father of Six" he carried on a heated controversy with the Reverend Adam Atwater on the iniquity of tearing down the only cheap houses that poor people could find to live in.

But it was the Reverend who was the real literary light. He flooded the letter columns with surging denunciations. He had articles (with his photograph) in any number of weeklies under such headings as "Parks for the Children", "Evangelist Leads Stirring Reform".

The Reverend Adam Atwater regarded the Slum Abolition League as a direct answer to prayer. He was one of those men who would have been happier in the days when it was possible for a prelate to don armour and lead the parishioners out to battle on a war-horse. Born in the wrong age, he was much addicted to social reform and discovered sadly that he did not have opportunity for organizing anything more complicated than a church social. He had suffered on committees for the good of his soul before now; but he had never known any committee so compact and determined as this "little band of helpers" who had gathered round him just when he had decided to give up the unequal struggle to direct public attention to what it would rather not see. They had appeared out of nowhere and elected him their chief in a rather bewildering way.

"Makes a damn fine figurehead," Rolfe had declared, and the others accepted Rolfe's verdict.

Rolfe was again "a ball of muscle", as he termed it, working on the Slum Abolition League and giving desultory attention to brightening the sale of soap.

"I can always get a job when I'm fit," he told Linnie. "But I can't when my interior starts to act like a circus."

He considered the slum abolition campaign a tremendous jest. "Not that it'll do any good," he remarked. "But there's always the chance that if you shout loud enough you may bring down the walls of Jericho."

Across the milk-blue wall of Rolfe's attic there now hung: "The Plan: Front Elevation, Side Elevation, Rear Elevation" of what all the new blocks of flats in the "Claribel Area" ought to look like when it had been remodelled. There was the view from the steps to Lennox Street looking down, view from North Street looking south, view from Ogham Street looking west, views from every conceivable angle of the great white square chunks of buildings that the committee intended to submit to the council with costs, specifications and all the rest of it, if the council ever got to the stage of calling for tenders.

The plan was known as "The Porpoise", and a tiny porpoise had been sketched in the corner of the sheet on Rolfe's wall. The Reverend Adam was a little perplexed by the levity with which his "little band" was apt to regard serious matters, but he was certainly learning things about organizing that he never thought possible.

For instance, take the calling of a conference of all bodies likely to be interested in slum clearance. Undoubtedly very efficient, very. He had not even been bothered by the printing, and though all the letters had gone out in his name, he had only to sign them. As for funds, the manner in which they had seized on his little following of fashionable old ladies and rich widows and "milked" them, as they rudely expressed it, had astounded him.

"Well, if she can contribute to dogs' homes, Mr Atwater," Miss Montague had protested, "why shouldn't you send a letter to Lady Kensington Phillips asking for support in what is a much more laudable endeavour? You know how she admires you."

When Linnie Montague wanted to make a good impression she used pronouns. Privately, she expressed it as "grabbing a couple of tail feathers out of the tough old fowl".

Occasionally doubts of his committee's real Christian sincerity occurred to Adam Atwater. He was most at home with Bramley Cornish whom he pronounced to be a fine upright young fellow. However, whatever their private morals, as long as they worked, he was willing to welcome their activities and praise the mysterious Purpose which sent them.

And they certainly worked.

"The initial drive must be for publicity," Rolfe declared. "Then we will call a conference and see who there is with influence that we can use. Remember it isn't just Claribel Lane we want pulled down. That's only the start."

They were working in Rolfe's attic which had become a kind of office. To go anywhere in the room it was necessary to step over old Duncan prostrate beside his dirty little duplicator. For a week he had monopolized the floor with piles of smudgy circulars and notices of meetings on which no one was allowed to lay a foot or a finger. Linnie was doing an interview with the Reverend Adam Atwater much in the manner of a lion-tamer drawing teeth, the Reverend Atwater protesting from the side of the bed where he was meekly helping to address envelopes.

"Sydney's Slum Crusader," Linnie said relentlessly, "asks: 'Do the Rich Realize?' How's that, Rolfe?"

"Good stuff," Rolfe responded absently. He was checking over a list of charitable organizations which might be expected to co-operate in the campaign.

"I don't want to disparage your efforts, Miss Linnie, not really," the Reverend said with great distress, "but I feel such an . . . idiot. Yes," he repeated defiantly, "a confounded idiot when I read all your fine, yes indeed, your very fine and carefully worded efforts. . . ."

He was politely ignored as Linnie read on: " 'We must have a new outlook,' the Reverend Adam Atwater told me, pacing up and down the narrow book-lined office from which this great campaign is being directed. His leonine head was thrown back and the sunlight streamed through and caught his uplifted face as he looked from the window on that crowded area whose people love him."

There were sounds of distress from the leonine one.

"All right so far," Rolfe commented. "Work that profile stuff for all it's worth. They eat it up."

"I protest. . . ."

"Protest recorded." Rolfe grinned. "Carry on, Lightning."

" 'Can we,' the Crusader asked, 'do we dare pray for the souls of the poor while their surroundings are such that they pray for bread and shelter and both are denied them? The very air the poor breathe is inferior to the air we breathe ourselves. That is why the Slum Abolition League is urging the resumption of all such neighbourhoods as the Claribel Lane Area which is intended for a model housing scheme.' "

"The council will be peased to hear that," observed Bramley.

"It'll be the first they know."

"No harm getting their minds used to the idea."

"How about pathos?" Rolfe asked. "There isn't any of the real stirring, soul-wringing sob in it yet."

"I'm coming to that," the interviewer continued, unmindful of the weighty creaking by which Rolfe's bedstead betokened an ecclesiastic uneasiness. "Remember that Higgins case? Well, this'll be the end of the second column:

> " 'Why don't you go and play in your backyard?' I asked one little fellow who was playing in the gutter.
>
> " ' 'Cos I ain't got no backyard,' he responded. 'We live in a room.'
>
> "I took him by the hand and he led me to a house—no, I will not call it a house—say rather, a den, around the door of which lounged a group of slatternly women. They drew aside for me to enter and I asked to see the lad's father and mother. The mother was sick upstairs and the father out looking for work. They had paid no rent, the old woman who kept the house told me, for several weeks, but she could not turn them out as there was nowhere for them to go. In the room upstairs lay the sick mother on a heap of old tattered coats. The five little children slept on heaps of dirty clothes on the floor. The little chap who had led me there pointed to a heap in the middle of the floor.
>
> " 'That's my bed,' he said. 'The Sunday School teacher give me a pitcher and tol' me to hang it over me bed. But I ain't got no wall of me own. I ain't got nowhere to hang it'."

"It's a bit extreme picking out the Higginses, isn't it?" Bramley grunted. "You know you and Rolfe make everything sound so much worse. . . ."

Linnie looked at him scornfully. "Got to caricature," she snapped. "Don't think I like writing this bilge, do you?"

"The public like human interest stuff," Rolfe maintained. "Might even be able to get a slogan out of it: 'Give him a wall to hang his picture on.' How's that?"

Bramley groaned. His was the modifying influence.

But Rolfe was following up his brain-wave. "How about

getting Wilfred to turn out some posters showing the family asleep on the floor? Spread them round for the conference?"

Linnie looked confused. "Rather you didn't ask him," she said quickly. "He's pretty busy." She could just imagine how outraged Wilfred would be at the idea of his turning his skill to what he called "Petty bourgeois reformist ends".

"All right, I'll have a go at it myself," Rolfe volunteered. "That kid with no wall to hang his picture on could be worked up into a big drawcard."

### III

The infant with no wall to hang his picture on nearly wrecked the public meeting; for a stout lady delegate from the Methodist Mothers' Guild rose in the body of the hall to say that she had been so touched by the Reverend Atwater's story of the dear little child with no wall to hang his text on and she felt that if such little children had somewhere to play it would very much relieve their poor sick mothers at home. At the same time she did think that it would be better to provide a park rather than an expensive set of buildings, but if a park were opened very strong measures should be taken to prevent children damaging fences and destroying property. She was thinking in particular of the recent case with which the council had had to deal of people uprooting pickets from the fence round the cricket ground and taking them home for firewood. And the committee should also remember the occasion when certain children had broken into the grounds of Foveaux House and stolen the goldfish out of the fish pond, taking them home in tins. She would therefore move a motion that if a park were decided on, no pond or ornamental water or pool containing goldfish should be recommended as part of the scheme of the grounds.

In spite of the motion being ruled out of order as there was another before the chair, a number of people rose to inform the lady that the park had not been decided upon, but if it were opened there was no reason why there should not be a pond in it. By the time the meeting was called to order and a vote taken that a deputation be sent to interview the Foveaux Council regarding the demolition of Claribel Lane, many in the audience were not sure whether they were voting against the park or in favour of the goldfish.

Throughout the meeting, Linnie, who had persuaded Wilfred to come, was getting hotter and hotter, partly because the chairman, that distinguished old muddler Senator Kentham Cousins, was letting the meeting get out of control and partly because Wilfred would insist on talking and keeping her from listening to the discussion.

"You really are getting too wrapped up in this tin-pot committee," Wilfred argued in what was scarcely a whisper.

"Shhh."

"It's just humanitarianism. If you would only wait until after the revolution instead of trying to bolster up the system. Footling around with housing schemes!" Wilfred's tone assumed the correct note of contempt. "I don't know why you want to be mixed up with this crew of petty bourgeois reformists."

"Ssshh!" Linnie remonstrated again. "Be all reported upside down," she fretted. "I know they'll get in the damned goldfish and leave out the stuff about the building proposals."

Wilfred relapsed into a fidgeting silence and began to draw on his agenda paper. He nudged Linnie to direct her attention to a quite clever sketch of Bramley taking notes at the minute secretary's table. Linnie gave it a brief glance and a nod and continued to listen attentively. Wilfred began to feel savage. Either she would have to cut out this good-angel-going-to-meetings stuff or he'd leave her. It wasn't fair when he wanted to take her out and show her the lights on a certain wharf reflected in the harbour that she should drag him to this wretched meeting. She was probably in love with that unspeakable Rolfe.

"You'll have to take a pull," he said sternly as the meeting ended. "I've told you before, Linnie, you'll really have to take a pull."

"What do you mean?"

"About this abominable suburban respectability of yours. Messing about with parks and houses." Wilfred waved a bony hand. "All right in Soviet Russia, but not here. Not under the guidance of your dear friends, Cornish and Pellager and Rolfe. Not a nice thing to see you making a trend to the Right."

"Not trending to the Right."

"You can't go dabbling with all this reformism. I've told you time and again that our duty is to expose it. What did Lenin say in his—"

"What did Lenin say in eighteen-eight?" Linnie retorted.

Wilfred thought deeply for a moment and then muttered: "Don't be a fool." He lapsed into an injured silence and then remarked: "I suppose you're going to wait for your beloved friend, the Reverend Atwater, the right Holy Rolfe and dear respectable Bramley."

Linnie turned on him suddenly.

"Seem to expect me to take anything you say," she exclaimed fiercely, the Montague chin taking the lead and the Christian Scientist nose for once in agreement. "Look here. I'll see who I like, do what I like, and, if you don't like it, you can go back to Clare or Jean or any of the others hanging round Luke's Club. You go and find someone else who isn't so bourgeois and middle class and respectable and tainted. You won't be," she concluded, "any real loss."

Wilfred was taken aback. He had been planning to move when the Montagues moved and to move with them. His quarters had always been comfortable. He was never bothered in regard to his rent. The mother and brother were unfortunate. So were Linda's other connections. Nevertheless. . . .

"Linda, my dear girl," he said gravely, "you do take everything in such a wrong spirit." He assumed the wounded air of a strong man suffering. "Of course, if that's the way you really feel, I have nothing to say." He waited. "Nothing to say," he repeated.

"All right," Linda snapped. "Shut up."

This was worse and worse, Wilfred felt. They had quarrelled before, but this time she didn't look as though she would come round easily. He decided to try another tack and laughed sardonically.

"Oh, that's it?" he said fiercely. "You've decided that I'm too poor to give you all the comforts that your bourgeois upbringing demands. So you've decided to attach yourself to a rich lover, you little—"

"Be quiet," Linnie hissed.

"I won't be quiet. I'll shout at the top of my voice if I want to. Listen to me."

It was one of Linda's weaknesses that she hated a scene in public. Wilfred knew that she would do anything rather than look conspicuous.

"Having an argument on the chances of success," she flung at Rolfe and Bramley, who were approaching in a tactful manner. "Wilfred thinks we're heading for trouble."

"I don't see what you can do," Wilfred muttered. "Not under the capitalist system."

"It keeps us amused," Rolfe said with a grin. "We must do something with our spare time."

The Reverend Atwater boomed down upon the group:

"Ah, there you are, Miss Montague. Well, well, what did you think of the meeting? Great work, eh? Thanks to our young friends here, and, of course, yourself. The response was a little disappointing, but that couldn't be helped. Very representative on the whole, wasn't it?" He beamed. "Especially dear old Mrs Palmer, poor soul, and her goldfish." He started to chuckle, then checked himself. "Dear, dear. Yes, yes. I've just had some news, Rolfe. I consider most important news. It may have a bearing, a direct bearing—"

"Why? What's up?" Rolfe said quickly.

"Most distressing really. There's been a shooting in the Alley."

"A shooting!"

"I fear so. I very much fear so. You saw the lad who came up and spoke to me as I left the platform? It appears — I couldn't get it quite straight — that it has something to do with a man called Hamp."

"Hamp!" Rolfe said and whistled reflectively. "It sounds likely." His brain began to flash headlines: "Murder in Plague Spot of Slums. Tragedy in Claribel Area. Agitation for Resumption."

Wilfred was yawning. He had a beautiful pillow of red silk made for him by one of the girls who understood him better than Linnie, and on it she had embroidered a hammer and sickle in gold thread. Admittedly the thing had got a little greasy and dishevelled from being overmuch occupied; but nevertheless whenever Wilfred longed for a rest a vision of it rose in his mind.

"Got to be going," he muttered rudely. "Come along, Linda."

But Linda took no notice. She was busy discussing with Bramley what this new development might mean to the campaign. Wilfred shrugged, after all, he thought wearily, why should he fetter his soul? It really looked as though Linda were lost to the Movement.

# CHAPTER 4

## I

"The trouble with Curly Thompson," Jordan True pronounced, delicately crooking his little finger around the wineglass, "is an accentuation of intolerance."

Jordan True was seated at a table in his resplendent new wine bar in Dennison Square; himself more resplendent than ever, gold seals, gold rings, diamond tiepin and studs complete. His hair was the same mousy old-rope colour, his eyes the same boiled blue, his language decked like a millionaire garbage contractor.

"Curly," he repeated with a frown that belied the unruffled tone of his remarks, "had a refined and alleviating line of conversation with skirts. He could always string the feminine."

A certain dark night many years ago when Curly Thompson had narrowly missed murdering his barman occurred to Mr True. His brow grew darker as he pondered the amount of money Daisy had cost him since. Perhaps if he had encouraged Daisy to forgive Curly, that dallier with ladies' hearts might now be suffering the effects of Daisy's temper rather than himself.

"I never had any luck with the fair," Mr True said sentimentally. "They kid you along, and what does it all amount to, these blandishments?" He drank sadly. "In the end, I mean. Bull, it's all bull."

His wife, he thought, taking it all in all, had treated him as well as Daisy. She had at least agreed to a separation; but Daisy resolutely refused to be separated from anything so profitable as Jordan, pointing out with great logic that you couldn't separate from a man if you weren't married to him.

Black Charlie, the cook of the *Poilu*, who always came ashore with at least seventeen pairs of smuggled silk stockings around his waist, raised his voice in voluble praise of the wares he was pulling from under his green silk shirt. The gold rings in his ears twinkled and jerked above the flood of broken English. Jordan raised his eyebrows at Sid the barman.

"I move up here," he complained to his friend McDonald the bookmaker, "to get away from the old crowd, and that's the kind of thing I get. Drags 'em right out in the open, lowering the tone of the place. A man ought to heave the bastard out on his ear."

"What was wrong with the Rose?" McDonald asked, sprawling back in his chair. He did not drink wine for preference. He came to True's wine bar mainly to talk with Mr True.

"The place was going to the pack. You'd turn a man down with inflexible determination and you'd get your head split open with a pint mug."

"Any rate, it's a nice place you've got here," McDonald offered. "Any of the crowd round the Foot drop in?"

"Not more than I can help it," Mr True said firmly. "Reverting to Curly — if it wasn't for the skirts. . . ."

"He's a game cove," McDonald agreed. "Got a bullet in him a month ago. Not a squeak out of him."

"Woman," True sighed. "Always Woman. Reminds me of that beautiful song. You know it, Bardy? I heard it twenty years ago, and I've never heard it since. I once offered a man a quid to get the words for me." He shook his head despondently. "I've even been to the Public Library, and the Librarian — as courteous a man as you're likely to meet, Bardy — he went to no end of trouble, no end. He searched about till he found out it had been published in America. 'A Hundred Choice Slices of Melody', I think it was. The man used to sing it — he lives on the North Shore Line still. . . ."

"Why don't you get it off him?"

"We had a disagreement," Jordan said sadly. "It all started over young Johnny Conner and the big grey Manders was training at the time. At any rate, it made me ineligible to receive from his lips the full version of that very beautiful song. Sid, wake up that woman, she can't go to sleep here."

Sid, in response to this admonition, went over and gently shook the customer, who woke, ordered another sweet sherry, and went to sleep again.

"Well, what was the song?" McDonald was beginning to get impatient.

"It began, 'It was in a cabman's shelter. . . .' I can't remember it all, but it was a beautiful thing. The seventh — no, the sixth verse goes something like this:

> *"The cabman looked down through the roof of his cab*
> *And he uttered no sound or cry.*
> *It was his dear young wife who sat there,*
> *Her lover sat close by.*

"Then the lover kisses her and . . . tra la . . . something else, and then Bob, the cabman, raises his whip to heaven and urging his horse onward, he cries: ' 'Tis the last time you deceive me. . . .' " Jordan broke into song:

> *"Of that you may be sure.*
> *Never again shall you ride in a cab*
> *With your cursed paramour.*
>
> *I am driving towards the river,*
> *Now, pray Heaven, in your fright;*
> *'Tis the last time you deceive:*
> *You are driving to Hell tonight.*
>
> *The horse galloped on to the river. . . ."*

"Now, Jordan, old man," Bardy McDonald protested, "you can't tell me that a cab-horse galloped."

"Well, he's urging it on with his whip, see, Bardy, and it's frightened, what with the woman shrieking and them trying to jump out. It was a lovely ballad. I was going to obtain the words and have them beautifully bound. You know Nosey Bob, the only real survival of the old-time cabby, I was going to present a bound copy of the song to him on his birthday. Nothing offensive, you know. I just wanted something he'd really appreciate. The chorus goes like this:

> *"And whenever a man goes right or wrong,*
>   *There's always a woman to blame. . . ."*

He noticed that McDonald was staring behind him. Usually Jordan sat with his eyes on the door, but he had moved round to keep watch over Black Charlie, and so had not seen Curly Thompson until McDonald's expression indicated that something was wrong. When Thompson came up to the table Jordan did not turn his head and Bardy's face froze in an unwelcoming glare.

"Hey, I want to see you, Bardy," Curly announced genially.

"The song to which I was referring. . . ." Jordan's many years in a bar had given him a perfect technique in dealing with ear-biters and trouble-makers.

But McDonald defeated his purpose by growling, "I don't know you and I don't want to know what you want."

"I want three quid," Curly responded blandly.

The eyes of the bookmaker were frosty. "You go and see Hamp," he snapped. "I'm slinging it to him."

Curly, still smiling, leant over and tapped McDonald on the shoulder.

"You remember me, Bardy," he said. "We was boys together. You used to stand in the corner of the playground and snivel if anyone spoke to you. You wouldn't turn down an old friend for three lousy quid, especially when he needs it." Again he slapped the bookmaker on the shoulder cheerily. "I knew you'd be only too glad to know that your old pal Curly was round looking after you."

"I'm slinging it to Hamp," Bardy said sullenly, but he fumbled in his vest pocket. Both he and Jordan knew it was pay up and look pleasant.

"You'll excuse me," Jordan said, and he rose and left them.

"What's up?" Sid asked in a low tone when Jordan returned to the bar.

"Curly just stood over Bardy for three quid."

Sid gave a low whistle. To "stand over" McDonald meant somebody collecting bullets. "Lay off Bardy," Hamp had said to one would-be claimant on the golden bags of the bookmaker. "Lay off Bardy, he's my meat." The standover refused to take the warning and later received a shot through the lung as he was coming home from a friendly game of billiards.

"Here, what's up with you?" the bookmaker snarled at Hamp when he strolled in well pleased with himself about an hour after Curly's visit.

"Anyone been kickin' up a stink?" Hamp inquired inelegantly.

"I just had Thompson in here and he stood over me for three quid."

An expression that might almost have been regret twisted Hamp's leathery face.

"I thought he was a friend of mine," he said. "It just shows you that yer best friend will put it on you cold. . . ."

"What are you going to do about it?" McDonald growled.

"He won't come back for more," Hamp responded.

He sat down at the table and thought out his plans, the others watching him in silence.

"Curly's interested in Elsie Jamieson," Jordan True almost read Hamp's thoughts.

"Who's Elsie Jamieson?" Bardy asked.

"Wife of the dark chap who walks on stumps. They've been in Newcastle for some time. She's a waitress in that café across the square."

Hamp rose. He took his battered hat off the table. "Well, I'll be seein' you."

He limped towards the door. Hamp had always moved like that since the shooting affair with Tommy Jones when he had taken a bullet in his spine. They watched him go in silence.

"Curly," said Jordan, accepting McDonald's offer of a drink, "is becoming a nuisance."

"There's always someone trying to get on top of you," the bookmaker replied. "If it wasn't Curly, it'd be someone else."

If Curly won the affair with Hamp, he would stand over Bardy from that time on. But it was a state of affairs to be accepted philosophically. If Curly Thompson preyed on Bardy, he would see that no one else did.

# I I

The fact that Hamp would be waiting to get him troubled Curly very little. He had a large contempt for Hamp, who was growing old and slow. He didn't deserve to be a "standover man" if he couldn't move quicker. He had better go back to selling artificial flowers.

Tilted back on his heels Curly surveyed Dennison Square in the hot late-afternoon sunlight and lazily considered his next move. He might go back to Maisie's place and get his gun, but it wouldn't be worth it with the police only looking for a chance to pounce on him. He knew the slow deliberate mind of Hamp, and was certain he would take a long time to fix his plans. Therefore, Curly strolled into the International Café where what looked like the same seductive mullet lay in naked abandon in the window as they had done on the night of Rolfe's return. Elsie, Curly calculated, would just be coming on duty and it was still too early for many customers. He would have a good chance to talk to her.

"Hullo, George," he greeted the smiling Greek behind the cash register. "How's the boy?" He passed on with a self-satisfied swagger, conscious of his pearl-grey suit, neatly striped, his general air of opulence. Curly always bought good clothes. They brought more when you pawned them.

Elsie Jamieson watched him advancing with a slight tightening of the lip. "Here comes that big swank again," was her inward comment. She held out the menu unemotionally, acknowledging his boisterous greetings with a nod.

"I don't really wanta eat," Curly explained. "All I'm lookin' for is a chance to have a yarn with you, Else. Never seem to be able to get a word in edgeways if I don't come an' eat something. Well, well, bring us a coupla oysters so's George'll love me. He seems to be the only one that does these days."

When Elsie returned with the oysters he said quickly, "Don't go away. George is a friend of mine, and he mightn't like you to discourage the customers." There was a hidden threat under the friendly words. "What you been doing with yourself lately?"

"Nothin' much," Elsie said indifferently, touching her hair.

She had grown handsome in a broad, rather heavy style. She had always been big. "Come here and work. Go home and see to the kids. Go out to meetings sometimes."

Curly made contemptuous noises above his oysters. "Meetin's," he said, "meetin's. A lot of mugs gassing their heads off." Elsie stayed silent. "Jock still out of work, I s'pose." No answer. "I was thinkin', Else, you and me bein' the friends we are, that I might put in a word to get him a job." The necessity to boast was to Curly as urgent as breathing. "Y'know I've got a lot of influence one way an' another. If you say the word, there's a friend of mine, Jimmy Durell, down at the Empress Button Factory. He'd probably find something if I made a special point of it."

"My husband's working," Elsie cut in. It gave her a vicious pleasure to say it. Inwardly she wondered what would happen if she ever told Jock that she had endured these attentions from Curly. She dismissed the idea of worrying Jock. He had enough to worry him, building up the Party unit in Foveaux and trying to make his union take a more militant stand. The recurrence of Curly would upset him as much as if one of the children had measles.

"Well, is that so?" Curly said with spurious interest. He changed his tack. "Y' know, Else, the only people who work are the mugs."

Elsie fanned herself with a paper serviette. She could see nothing for it but to listen to Curly boasting and philosophizing and hinting all the great things he could do for her until a rush of customers should signal release.

"Everybody bludges and robs. They got to, to make a living. Now, if I was to break in your front door and lift a couple of quid off you," Curly worked up a show of righteous indignation, "I'd be branded outside decent society. Wouldn't I, now? But if I'm a lawyer or a doctor and I take a couple of hundred off you for a court case that turns out a flop or an operation that kills you, what am I? A good citizen." He prodded the last oyster. "It's all a standover. You go into one of them big stores. The owner knows the stuff he sells isn't worth what he's getting. They take it away from you as sure as if they was dips and put their hand in your pocket to get it out. Now, take a man like me. . . ." Elsie knew this was coming. "Everybody likes to move in good company. Everyone wants to be seen with a high-up feller. When I pass the time of day to a cove he feels that's a rap for him, see? If I take a girl out, she can be pretty sure she's going to get the best. She'll be with a gay, not just a bunny anyone would pick up." Elsie prevented herself from yawning with an obvious effort. "You know, Elsie, if you was really dressed up in swish clothes, there wouldn't be a girl anywhere to come up to you. What you need is a chap who's free with his dough. Splashes it around. Give you anything you want."

"Curly," Elsie said deliberately, "you remind me of my kid, Hughie." She collected the oyster shells that Curly had distributed round the table. "When he was little, he wanted everything in the shop window." She almost smiled. "He heard his father talkin' about capitalists one night and he wanted me to buy him one right away."

"How about some more oysters?" Curly said sulkily.

Elsie strolled towards the kitchen. "Like to buy a copy of *Failure of Social Democracy in Austria*? I've still got a few copies left." Every time Curly enjoyed Elsie's society she fined him something even if it was only the price of a *Workers' Weekly*.

"How much?" he asked.

"Threepence to you."

He took the pamphlet up and turned it over distastefully.

"Always wanting money, Else," he said expansively. "I ain't forgotten you wanted to put me down on some subscription list. Here." He drew from his pocket three crumpled pound notes and threw them on the table. "Send that to the starving children of the bloody miners."

Elsie eyed the money distrustfully. "What's the game?" she asked.

"I'm giving it to the starvin' miners or whatever-it-is this time." Curly looked pained. "What's wrong? They're good notes."

Elsie shook her head. "You can hand it in at the office," she said slowly. "But not three quid." Her strong white dimpled chin set hard. "Three quid might buy a coupla miners, Curly, but you'd need a helluva lot more for me."

"Now, Else," Curly said in an injured tone. "You got me wrong. All this second act stuff. We're old friends, kid. Snap out of it. Why," he was pained, "when I realized how those miners' kiddies in Whatsisname wanted sugar, I went right out an'. . . ." He suddenly realized that Hamp was standing beside the cash register talking to George. "Take it," he said harshly. "There's a back gate, isn't there?" He had slipped round the screen and through the cookhouse before Elsie knew it. Hamp wasn't so slow after all. If Curly hadn't nicked round that screen it might easily have been a case of an "unknown man who came into the shop and shot another man who was eating oysters".

Back at Maisie's place Curly found her just returned from a shopping expedition. She was unwrapping brown paper parcels on the bed.

"Where you been?" she asked. "I get here and find Hamp waiting for you. Said he couldn't wait any longer."

Curly's expression was unpleasant. "How the hell did he get in?"

"He knows where the key is. Why shouldn't he come in and wait?"

But Curly was rummaging in the drawer where he kept his gun. "It's gone," he said. "I thought as much."

Maisie turned a sickly yellow. "He didn't — he couldn't have taken it. My God! I thought you and him was friends."

Curly sat down heavily and thought. "I must go and see ma," he said.

Curly Thompson never visited his mother unless he had to, because she held unkind views about work. Curly had not worked since he learnt to use a gun during the war. He had simply carried over the tactics of the trenches into private life. His mother was apt to harp on what Father O'Malley had said in a way wearying if you had heard it before. She was a truculent stout old lady, with the air of a prize-fighter and one blind eye. All her life Mrs Thompson had been what she called "battling for a crust", and although in this epic battle she had never been quite knocked out, many a time she had only been saved by the gong. When Curly arrived at her house she opened the door to him suspiciously.

"Well, what do *you* want?" she asked pessimistically. Trouble and Curly usually sought her doorstep together.

"Gosh, you're hard, mum." Curly looked apprehensively behind him. "Here I thinks to meself I'll call in an' see the old woman an' this is the way you treat me." He shut the door behind him and eyed the street through the window.

"You can't stay here," Mrs Thompson said decidedly. "This is a respectable place, and I don't want no shame and disgrace and the neighbours watching for the police like last time."

"I just wanta go upstairs a minute," Curly said persuasively. "Is Frank still sleepin' in the back room?"

"Yes, he is, but he won't like you messing about with his things."

"I'm not going to touch his things. You sit down and keep your eye on the door."

"Why?" Mrs Thompson asked truculently.

"Because there's a man dwelling on me. That's why." Curly was grim now. "You keep that door shut and keep your mouth shut."

From the window of the upper back room he looked down on the alley way behind. He could not be sure but there seemed to be someone watching in the shadow of the fence. Curly pulled down the blind, dived under the bed and carefully worked a board out of its place in the corner. The object he sought was still there. With a sigh of relief he slipped the revolver into his pocket. Now he could meet the world on equal terms. He felt quite well dressed with that comforting weight on his hip.

"O.K., mum," he called down the stairs.

"You've never been a comfort to me, Herbert," his mother snapped. "What're you doing?"

Curly had slipped through the window on to the noisy tin roof of a neighbour's shed and into the next door backyard, quickly scaling the fence into the alley. He had been mistaken. There was no watcher. The sickly yellow light where the alley opened into Claribel Lane seemed fainter for the heat. The loud voices of people in the houses on either side came to Curly.

"Give the dog something, Amy," a man said close to him in the lit doorway of a kitchen.

" 'E 'ad something this mornin'," a woman's voice objected. "Can't always be feedin' the damn dog."

Curly edged round the corner and broke into a trot. Hamp would be somewhere about watching like a cat at an empty mousehole. At the top of the steps leading from Plug Alley to Lennox Street he turned and caught his breath, crouching close to the wall of the Rose of Denmark. Hamp was below him, limping along with his queer hoppy stride. Curly drew a deep breath. The sweat was running down his armpits. It stood out in little beads on the fleshy wrinkles of his forehead. He waited till Hamp reached the foot of the steps and then he fired.

He saw Hamp drop and heard his scream. He fired four shots in succession at the writhing figure, then turned and walked up Lennox Street. He made himself walk. There is nothing more noticeable than a man running on a hot night. He had covered three streets and was heading for Maisie's flat to establish an alibi when the idea occurred to him that Hamp might have been carrying his, Curly's, gun. What a put-away! He paused, half deciding to go back, and then his reason assured him that Hamp would have hidden it or thrown it away. He wouldn't keep it about him. The thumping of Curly's heart eased down. He'd have to watch the papers. Hamp himself would never tell anything, that is if he ever recovered consciousness.

Curly sighed. " 'Struth, you earn your money on a stand over," he told himself. "I ain't so sure sometimes that a man's such a mug to work. Times when I almost feel like giving it a go meself."

# CHAPTER 5

## I

It seemed to Mr Bishop that lately everything had been changing with bewildering rapidity. Mrs Cornish kept on telling him that she feared he really would have to look for new lodgings, as the cottages were to be pulled down for certain next week. After nineteen years in the same attic the thought of moving made him feel quite lost and helpless. In addition he had dropped the upper plate of his false teeth and broken it, and heaven alone knew where he could borrow the money to pay for a new set. Duncan was no help. There was no chance of borrowing anything from Duncan these days, and you could hardly see him for leaflets.

"It comes of being born under Cancer," Mr Bishop mumbled. "Me fortunes move like a crab, Dunc, sideways. Forward and backward, maybe, but always oblique."

"If you move your foot off those papers," Mr Duncan reported from the floor, "I could get at them better. And anyway what's all this about moving? I've got to shift too, haven't I? Right-o. Think I like it?"

Mr Duncan had already done most of his moving. He had a great deal of trouble borrowing enough suitcases to carry away all his books. They were mostly old, paper-covered, inflammatory pamphlets about everything from sewage to trade ratios. There was also his cherished collection of paper clippings dating back to 1888. This he had inherited and added to with the jealousy of a connoisseur. There was his oil stove and his cookery book, though he hardly ever used that now. Quite a little procession carrying old cardboard hat boxes, piles of newspapers tied with string and all kinds of oddments had helped transfer him to the bleak dim room looking over the backyards of Slazenger Street, which was all his small pension could afford. Jock Jamieson's eldest boy, Gordon, carried the duplicator, and his smallest brother the ink and paper. Linnie, Rolfe and Bramley followed with a couple of suitcases each, and Duncan puffed along in the rear with four volumes of Karl Marx in his arms.

"No marble palace," he breathed, dumping them finally on the narrow dingy bed. "I only need a place to sleep." He looked round forlornly. "Haven't got anything to give you boys, but I'll tell you what. If you like to come back to the cottage, you can have the empty bottles. Ought to fetch in a bit. There's two years' collection under the bed. Right-o?"

"That's all right comrade," the eldest Jamieson responded complacently.

"Fair day's work, fair day's pay," puffed Mr Duncan. "Right-o. If you don't want it, you can give it to some fund."

So now, feeling that he, an old gnarled tree, had taken his uprooting from his beloved attic well, Mr Duncan was aggrieved by Mr Bishop's complaints.

"What'samatterwithyou?" he growled. "Anyone would think you were the only pebble on the beach."

This unconsoling retort silenced Mr Bishop. "It comes of being born under Cancer," he mumbled, and drifted away.

Perhaps if Mr Bishop had not complained to Duncan that night, he might have gathered credit for the extraordinary and miraculous transfiguration that befell him just when things seemed darkest. It was by many links of chance that he was eventually drawn into the magic circle of the Seekers After the Sacred Light, into the position of a gold and crimson robed Elder of the Tenth Order, living in respectability and comparative opulence in a cottage at Roseville. After veiling her face with a dirty sneer for so many years, Fate, the Stars, or what you will, decided that something was definitely owing to Aloysius Bishop, Seer, and proceeded to pay up with interest.

It all began with a lady who had visited one of Bishie's classes calling on a sick friend. The friend was no less a personage than Dillys Delaine who, having had a palatial flat newly decorated by a new husband, had returned from her honeymoon to find the husband an inconsiderate low creature who made a scene about the decorator's bill. He made another scene when the great Delaine had made a scene about his making a scene. The new decorations suffered from splashes of priceless broken crystal and the new husband went forth to seek a lawyer and the expensive safety of divorce exactly three months after his expensive marriage.

The great Delaine, surrounded by an entourage consisting of her mother-in-law, her secretary, her last husband, two lawyers, a beauty expert and seventeen adoring friends, immediately went to bed and stayed there, refusing all food except eggs beaten up in brandy. She succeeded in weeping herself into a state where she had to be restrained from suicide.

"Poor girl, how you have suffered," her closest friend murmured, reverently laying on the bed an enormous bunch of red roses. "Oh, what a beast that man is!"

Dillys Delaine smiled her famous smile rather wanly. Her eyes filled with tears. Sympathy is so catching.

"I've gotta that state," the Delaine's golden voice was a mere whisper, "when I don't give a hoot in hell."

Her friend looked concerned. She was a motherly lady with a big sentimental nose, a string of false pearls and an income too large for her. "What do the doctors say?" she asked.

Miss Delaine rolled her bronze head feebly on the pillow. "What good are doctors? I'm all in."

The friend patted the white hand on the green taffeta coverlet. "What you need, darling," she said reassuringly, "is Advice." She could see the protest rising. "Yes, I know you've got lawyers, but what good are they? Can they really *do* anything? That's what I want to know. Can they *really do* anything? Not a thing. Now what you want to do is to see the really marvellous man Marjorie Brown dug up from somewhere. I went to one of his classes and, my dear. . . ." The lady broke off impressively. "You've no idea the things he told me. For instance, he said Fred would be back in November and sure enough he was. Not only that. He told me what was really causing all those little pains down my back. He gave me something to take for it. And I feel a new woman. He really is marvellous."

Dillys Delaine looked impressed. "What kind of a guy is he?"

"Oh, he's quite ordinary and old to look at, but his horoscopes are simply astounding. And as for predicting things! You know when the papers were printing stuff about that murder in that slum place — you know the name — dear, dear, how silly of me. Anyhow, the night before this murder I was at his class and he was looking very gloomy and he said something terrible was about to happen in — ah, I've got it — in Foveaux. Oh, he's marvellous."

In the midst of the flowing stream of praise Miss Delaine sat up in bed, a thing she had not done for three days, and shouted for her secretary.

"Julie!"

"What is it honey?"

"Get them to send round a taxi. Quick!"

The secretary, a tired woman, cast one venomous glance at the complacent friend behind the roses. "But you can't go out," she wailed. "Please! To please me!"

"Get a taxi, Julie, and don't stand there drivelling and bring me another brandy and egg."

She was helped out of bed, and with the air of a martyr much enfeebled by the dungeon and rack began weakly to clip her corsets.

"I gotta go to him," she said soulfully. "Somehow I feel he's what I been looking for."

## II

It was a dirty, wet grey afternoon and the taxi spanked up in the puddles at Mrs Cornish's front gate as if contemptuous of the puddles, the rain, the place, the very street.

"Does Mr Bishop live here?" a stout lady with pearls inquired as Mrs Cornish opened the door. Little Mrs Cornish, overpowered, merely nodded humbly.

The stout lady rushed back to the cab to assist out another lady, very feeble, very much in the fashion, who gave Mrs Cornish a wan smile and then turned to the taxi-driver.

"I guess you can wait," she said in a delicious drawl.

Between them they half carried her to the front veranda.

"Where is he?" she asked, and the dumbfounded Mrs Cornish indicated that Mr Bishop was upstairs.

"I'll go up," the lady said royally, and she did so, clinging to her stout companion.

"What could I do?" Mrs Cornish asked Bramley later. "I thought they might be relatives." Though why Mr Bishop should have relatives in furs that might have cost a fortune Mrs Cornish could not imagine.

Mr Bishop was eating toast as he hunched over the table in a dirty faded dressing gown. His egg boiled merrily on the gas ring and he bent forward to read the folded newspaper propped in front of him, munching the spare piece of toast and waiting for the egg to boil. Toast had been the staple of Mr Bishop's diet lately, and he found it a painful one without his teeth.

He said "Come in" to the knock on his door because it would be either Bramley or Duncan. Even seers who read the future like an open book are occasionally caught in their dressing gowns. But he rose nobly. Or rather he didn't rise. Bishie was too old an astrologer to treat rich ladies with anything but a becoming insolence.

"Come in," he snapped, "and shut the door behind you. You should have come to see me long ago. No, I don't want to see *you*." He waved the stout lady away. "I have something important to say to your friend." He fixed Dillys with a piercing black eye. "Haven't I?"

"You can wait in the car, Dora," Miss Delaine murmured. She sank into the only chair, her hypnotized gaze fixed on this rude, extremely shabby individual.

Bishie waved a benign farewell to Dora. "Be careful on the tenth of the month," he said, much in the manner of one warning Caesar of the Ides of March. "Don't say I didn't tell yer."

He turned chuckling and lifted his egg from the boiling water. "You was born under Venus," he croaked at the overawed Delaine. "And you're in trouble. Don't tell me about it. I know. You would be at this time of the year. Everything against you." He muttered to himself under his breath. "What date?" he snapped. She shook her head. "What date were yer born?"

"September the thirtieth," she murmured.

"I thought so," Bishie grunted above his egg. "Always the way. You find a mystic at grips with the Material, vanquished by it. You're definitely mystic," he announced, reaching for the salt. "It's all due to you warping your true nature."

"Yes," the lady breathed. "Yes, you're right. I am mystic. By gee!"

Dillys Delaine was not only impressed, she was thrilled. She had been told a number of things about herself by male persons, some of them highly complimentary, some the reverse, but she had never, never been told she was mystic.

"That's just what Cyril wouldn't realize." Her chin quivered. She was weak from lack of food and very near tears. "He goes off talking about a divorce and leaves me without a cent, and never even lets me know where he is, so I can send the bills, and — oh, I guess you're right — I'm at grips with the Material." She sniffed. "He's so material himself. Not a bit spiritual." She dried her eyes. "What am I to do?" Already her tone implied that Bishie had only to speak and she would hear. "He's wonderful all right," she said later. "Impressive. That's it."

"On no account—" Mr Bishop's tone was solemn. He drew his terrible dressing gown about him. "On no account are you to move — from the place you are living in at the moment. Go home. Stop worrying. Everything will be all right. You must wait in patience. Your husband will return. But on no account go away from where you are at present. That will be all," he finished. "Leave me your address and get in touch with me a week from today."

He returned to his egg. He did not even offer to see Miss Delaine down the stairs and, strange to say, without any assistance she managed quite well. One last adoring glance she cast from the doorway at the Seer.

"You know," she sighed. "you ought to be somewhere else beside this dump. Somewhere where your light can show."

"When the time comes," the Seer said majestically, "the vehicle will be provided."

Bishie had as yet no idea of the Sacred Light at so much a lesson or the circle of occult souls dressed in crimson velvet at so much subscription per month. It might have comforted him a little as he brooded over whether he should have charged her half a crown then while he had her or staked everything on getting her as what he called "a regular"

"Women like that," he mumbled disgustedly, "got everything, and still wanting to leave it. Don't know when they're well off." He thought wistfully of the kind of place the woman must have come from. Comfortable. She might be good for a meal sometimes.

"I've simply got to keep that man by me," Miss Delaine was repeating in the taxi. "I'm going to send the taxi back for him after tea. He may not come, of course, but I'd feel a darn sight better with him about the place. He's so disinterested. Austere, that's it."

In her mind's eye Dillys had already added Bishie to the two lawyers, the pomeranian, the secretary, the seventeen dear girlhood friends and the maid. She intended to have him, no matter what he cost. He was probably only living in that queer place because he was austere. He simply didn't care about material things. She sighed happily.

"Darling"— she pressed her friend's hand —"he says I'm mystic."

## III

Moving out of Mrs Webb's place was to Linnie Montague a horrible nightmare. The lodgers, and Wilfred in particular, seemed to regard it as her fault that the landlord had at last decided to pull down the cottages and build flats. Mrs Montague also quite failed to understand how anyone could be so unkind as to tear down the cottages when they were all so comfortable. "And where?" she demanded with mild indignation. "Where does he think we're to go?"

Her daughter responded with a kiss that Mr Bross probably thought there were plenty of other nice places. Linda always treated her mother as though she were a petulant but delightful small girl.

"Well, I do think it's very unjust," Mrs Montague announced. "Most unjust and unfair."

"You just pack your pretties, Angelique," her daughter

suggested. "We'll find a place somewhere."

"I'm not moving out of Foveaux," Mrs Montague said determinedly. "You can't get cheaper vegetables anywhere. And out at Bronte, Mrs Webb says they charge threepence more for frying steak than they do here. I know what you're going to say, Linnie — that's only Error. But even a Christian Scientist doesn't like to be imposed upon."

Linda herself had many misgivings. Oscar had announced that he was getting a new job through a friend of his in Maitland. He was very keen about it, as it entailed driving a tenton truck for a firm that paid good money.

"There'll be more opportunities than McErchins'," he summed up. "Of course I couldn't live in Sydney, sis, but now that you are breaking up this place, it won't matter, will it?"

Linnie had noted that even he unconsciously adopted the attitude that she was responsible for the change. "I'll look after Angelique," she said. "You go ahead."

Okker looked at her sideways. He felt a little guilty leaving his sister alone with their mother, but money was money, and a job was a job. Besides, a man had to branch out for himself some day, and mother would be sure to say that Divine Love would watch over him just as well in the country as in the city. She never made a fuss.

Mrs Montague was a little wistful at his going. She had not minded her husband, but Oscar was her favourite, her only son.

"You must do what you think best, dear," she said bravely. "Linnie and I will manage."

Oscar was only too glad to go to the new job before the actual removal took place. Linnie had hoped that with Okker's wages it would have been possible for their mother to give up letting lodgings. Their money was little enough, and the position was not made easier by Mrs Montague's reluctance to leave Foveaux. Finally by good luck in that time of high rents and boom prices Linnie discovered a roomy three-storey place near Nosey Bob's old dwelling.

"But, Linnie," her mother protested, "it isn't very nice down there, quite near all those terrible people round the Foot." Living in Upper Foveaux was one thing; the Foot was quite another matter.

"Only place you can get," Linnie argued. "Good letting. View from the balcony."

It was the view from the back balcony that had made Linnie decide that if she lived longer in Foveaux, this was where she was going to live. It made her giddy to stand on that shady little balcony above the black gulf and the far-flung lights. It was an exhilarating, mountaineering giddiness that her mother did not by any means share. She complained about the stairs.

"You find something better," was Linnie's answer. "and I'll go there."

But it was hard to find something they could afford that would really suit Mrs Montague's taste.

"If only we could afford one of these new flats," Mrs Montague said ruefully, "I could have a canary in the window and you know, Linnie, I saw such a cheap blue curtain material in Murchison Street for one and nine a yard."

"Beloved," Linnie said kissing her fiercely, "when I am rich you shall have pretty little flats and window curtains all to yourself. But just for now — try and like it."

"Very well, dear," Mrs Montague said submissively, although she knew she wouldn't. Her religion did not allow grumbling.

The Montague lodgers had manifested all the premonitory uneasiness of bees about to swarm. There was a general desire that Mrs Montague should set up a new lodging house in Foveaux and they should go with her in accordance with Foveaux tradition. When Mrs Webb had moved to Darling-hurst her boarders went with her. When she moved to Rand-wick, the boarders also moved. They all had to be shifted again when she transferred her household to Bronte. Only Mrs Webb's death would part them.

And so, Mrs Montague's boarders felt, it should be with themselves and their landlady. There was great rejoicing over Linnie's discovery; whilst the destruction of their late home gave the excuse for a wake that lasted until they were well installed in the new establishment.

"I'm glad I survived that farewell party," Rolfe observed to Linnie. "I stayed out as long as I could, but I had to creep in about two o'clock. I'm afraid my advent might have sent some of the visitors home early."

"Sorry," Linnie said shortly. "Angelique might as well enjoy herself when she gets the chance."

Rolfe and Linnie were supposed to be working on a pamphlet, "Sydney's Slums — A Protest"; but the irritating glare of the naked light in the kitchen of the new residence and the flapping moths through the door were enough to try any nerves. The moths plunged from the darkness at the light globe and flopped on the table where they whirred in demented circles on the papers. Overhead, a persistent, irregular bumping indicated that Mrs Montague was in no less aimless fashion moving furniture round the new rooms. Linnie and Rolfe had excuse for drifting on to the dark back veranda, a ricketty structure, from which wooden steps plunged down towards the gloomy backyard and a spread of street lights.

The attitude of the stiff and austere Linnie towards her mother both amused Rolfe and made him feel queerly sorry for her. It seemed a pity that Linnie should spoil herself by posing at being efficient and capable and middle-aged, wrapping her stiff manner round her like a horny shell and drawing quickly inside when anyone touched her. As he leant over the rail he realized that he could never remember Linnie's face. If anyone mentioned her, there flashed up the bowl of daffodils in Bud's shop mingled with an impression of her quick brown hands on a typewriter.

"Where has Wilfred gone?" he asked idly.

Linnie cast him a suspicious glance. She could never be sure whether this elderly man was making fun of her. She always thought of Rolfe as old, interesting, but old.

"Wilf has an aunt," she said sedately. "He's living with her."

"Is she of the proletariat?" Rolfe teased.

"Has a cake shop." Linnie would not commit herself. It was not poor Wilfred's fault, she thought, that his father had been an auctioneer instead of a wharf-labourer or engine-driver. She often felt guilty about her own origin. She did not come from a working-class family. She had never suffered the distinction of being one of the down-trodden workers, but while she lived in Foveaux no one was likely to question her bourgeois ancestry. The people who really mattered in the revolutionary organizations all accepted her as one of themselves. "I wish you wouldn't laugh at Wilf," she said. "If it hadn't been for him, I might still be just. . . ." She paused to think of the right word. "He taught me what books to read and how to think and how to try to write. . . ." She paused again. "He was kind to me."

Wilfred had been the first man to realize the possibilities of that angular, fierce, brown girl. The fact that he had also tried to seduce her had not mattered. A number of people had tried to do that, but Linnie took it as a matter of course, however firmly she might decline the honour.

"Wilf has his faults," she said defensively. "Everyone has. But he's been decent. A friend. I'm fond of him."

"It was like that with my wife," Rolfe responded. "She made such admirable omelettes that it made you forget the rest." He sighed half regretfully. "No one really understands the importance of omelettes in this country."

"Was she very pretty?" Linnie asked curiously; and then cursed herself for an inquisitive fool and drew back into her shell.

"Very pretty," Rolfe agreed judicially. "But she didn't like me." Linnie waited. "She said I got on her nerves. She accused me of — that was the term — laughing up my sleeve." His long face twisted unhumorously. "It was better to laugh than to kill her. I suppose we'd better do some work."

Linnie would have preferred to hear more about Rolfe's wife, but turned to take up the task of translating Bramley's figures into prose when Rolfe mutinied.

"I quit," he declared. "Let's go for a walk. It's hot."

Linnie shook her head. "Ought to go and help Angelique. She'll bust herself." But she did not go.

"Queer," Rolfe said, regarding the lights of Ogham Street. "It's queer the way people are washed together again after so many years and washed apart. I can't ever get out of my head when I'm in Foveaux that it's a kind of seashore with flotsam and jetsam tumbled together in the strangest heaps. Dark tides. . . ." He paused. "Strange tides, washing people about."

"Corpses," Linnie said bitterly.

"Why?"

"They're all dead here." She spoke fiercely. "I've been here all my life, choking in it. The apathy — the sodden acceptance . . . the always-has-been and always-will-be stuff. That's why I'm keen to see Plug Alley come down. Like the hole in the dyke, a start."

"I see. Let the city flow out this way and break the place to bits as it flows. But how about our garden houses?"

"We'll never get them."

"God and the council, alias John Hutchison, alone know that. But it will be something to break up that stinking, festering warren. It's not fit for rats."

Linda nodded. They had been all over that before. A silence descended upon them.

"D'y' ever feel," she said queerly, "that you've got a pain inside you in the middle of your chest and that it's almost tearing you to pieces?"

"Growing pains?" Rolfe queried, half lightly.

She nodded. "Perhaps. I got it standing on the balcony outside my room last night. It's glorious to see the lights and to feel you're on a level with the clock in the tower." She broke off and glanced to see if he was laughing, but he was serious. "It's possibly the thought of all those people, all those lights, like phosphorescence on the surface. And you can hear it roar — the city, I mean — at night. Just like a surf with the tide rising. . . ." She stammered, almost inarticulate with nervousness, but forced to say it. "You can stand up there and feel that if you fell, if your hands slipped off the rock, and you drowned and the pain drowned with you. . . ."

"Mustn't be morbid, Lightning."

"I'm not." She was back in her hard shell immediately. Something had broken between them, some light invisible current was broken. "I've got to go and help Angelique. She insisted on bringing all her old junk and she doesn't know where to put it." Linnie shook her head hopelessly. "I tried to smuggle some of it over the fence to Bramley, but it was no use."

"Bramley would do anything for you," Rolfe said pointedly. "Anything you'd let him."

Linnie grinned at him from the doorway as she went in.

"Bramley," she said. "One of my oldest admirers. Gave me a dead butterfly when I was ten."

A few minutes later Rolfe could hear her arguing with her mother about a hall-stand which Mrs Montague wished to keep at the head of the stairs.

"You can't have it there," Linnie declared. "There's no room."

Rolfe, slumped in an old cane chair, was thinking of all the people in all the streets spread out below him. All being battered into sand for other people to build into useless shapes that would be smashed again. Even himself was being pounded slowly into smaller disintegrating particles under invisible waves. He wondered how long he could keep his job if he had another of those sick spells of his.

"But why put it *there*?" Linnie was asking with grim patience. "Jimmy, would you come and tell Angelique she can't leave things in the dark for people to fall over."

Rolfe ascended to add his weight to the process by which the small but tenacious Mrs Montague had to be reconciled to the final placement of each separate article of furniture.

"Now, what's the use of your moving this old lounge suite round again, Mrs Montague," he was presently saying persuasively, "when you and Linnie will be buying all new things? Here is your daughter planning to marry a millionaire and furnish a palatial flat with everything the heart could desire and you try to alter about a lounge suite that won't match the wallpaper anyway. Look at it in a sensible light."

It was no use trying to joke with Mrs Montague. She always took everything in good faith, unless it was labelled joke on all four sides.

"Perhaps you're right," she agreed. "It would never really match."

And she gleamed at Linnie questioningly. Not that she believed Rolfe's assertion as to the millionaire suitor; but lately Linnie had been seeing less of Wilfred and much more of Mr Rolfe. Mrs Montague knew nothing of Rolfe's financial position except that he paid his rent regularly. She did not believe that he was a millionaire, but he seemed a very respectable man, even if he did wear terrible ties and baggy old suits. She began to look arch. Linnie realized it and moaned inwardly.

"Come on, Angelique," she said impatiently. "We'll have it over here." Her mother always clung as tenaciously to her hopes of Linnie's suitors as she did to her bits of furniture.

# CHAPTER 6

## I

Mrs Cornish had put on a brave air about moving. "I was so long at sea I got used to changing," she declared proudly to Mrs Montague. But the thought of leaving her room, that cheery front room, where in more troublesome though happier days the whole family had lived and the Captain had cooked his now fabulous stews, disconcerted and frightened her. It looked so permanent, with pussy basking on the cedar chest under the window, the big old bed in the same corner it had always occupied and the smoke-blackened mantelpiece brightened by the two hand-painted vases that Aunt Eileen had sent from Melbourne. How was she to know she would like a new place? And how would poor pussy take it? They said if you put butter on a cat's paws, it would not go back to the old house or stray away; but Darkie was so independent.

Anyway, Mrs Cornish reminded herself, if everything else changed, there was always Bramley, her sheet anchor in any storm, her sure rock of refuge. Then she felt a little sinking of the heart, for nowadays when she thought of Bramley there was the association of that Montague girl, dark, long-legged and determined. Not that Bramley had ever had any time for young women before; but there must be some reason why he stayed out at so many meetings and took such an interest in making the council pull down old houses, Surely, knowing how it upset his mother to have their own old cottage pulled down, he would not seriously want to take away from old Mr Bross the little houses to which he must be very greatly attached. No, this scheme thing must be only an excuse for seeing that Montague girl. Mrs Cornish was not jealous, but she wondered sadly what would become of her.

She was not, she felt, parasitic on Bramley. Her old independence revolted at the idea. She darned and washed and mended and kept house for him. But if she did not have him, if she could not cling to him, the city, she felt, would roll over her and engulf her; the savage noises and the big buildings and the new things she did not understand after so long at sea, so long also in the lotus tranquillity of the old cottage. If Bramley married, she would not come and live with him. She had her principles. A man and his wife should leave family and friends and cleave only to each other. That was right, and she would abide by what was right; but, oh what would happen to her if Bramley did marry?

"Linda Montague came up today to say the little house next door to Mr Budin's will be empty shortly," she mentioned to Bramley one evening about a week after the Montagues left. "The people would want us to pay fifteen pounds for the furniture."

Bramley put down his fork and considered the proposal. They would be lucky to get a house even if they had to buy unwanted furniture with it. Most outgoing tenants were accustomed to demand five pounds for the keys. It was a profitable industry at the time to move into a series of houses putting into each a few old sticks and then demanding anything from twenty pounds upwards for a furnished house.

"Would you like that?" he asked.

"It's for you to say, boy. If you were to get married—"

Bramley laughed. "Don't be silly. Who would I marry?"

Mrs Cornish felt she had to know the worst if it killed her. Her eyes pleaded with him and then they dimmed with uncontrollable tears. Bramley came over and put his arm round her shoulders.

"Don't you worry, little lady."

"There's Linda Montague," she said bravely. "Your father always liked dark girls. So did your Uncle Charles."

"As far as she's concerned," Bramley said quietly, "I wouldn't stand a chance. I'm not proletarian." He patted her hand. "Let's drop it. Finished. Nothing doing, little lady."

Mrs Cornish, however, kneeling beside the big bed in which she had slept for so many years, that night included in her petitions that Brammy would not go marrying like poor

Tommy, and that if he did, she would please be guided what to do.

## II

The possible new residence was next in the terrace to Mr Budin's place and on the other side was Mr Keyne's of the famous palm-tree, but beside the brave free front of that gentleman's abode it looked pitifully shrinking, having grown a green beard of creepers all over its face, like a disguised bigamist. So long had the greenery waved that it had managed to suck all the colour out of the house, leaving it sullen and aggrieved. Perhaps it was Linnie's recommendation that prejudiced Mrs Cornish against the place from the start; perhaps it was that the house deliberately stuck out its elbows and its projecting shelves just to bump your head or a couple of steps where they would trip you.

"Your Uncle Herbert," Mrs Cornish commented, rather daunted by a turn in the landing, "fell down just such a flight of steps."

The two upstairs rooms were painted the usual sickly blue green and the downstairs a uniform dead brown.

It was Tommy who really decided that the house would do. He pointed out that the big tool-shed at the back was just the place he was looking for to keep his old motor-bike. With improvements it might even let as a garage.

The garden, by accident of the street's angle, was bigger than the average. Over the fence wistaria was throwing a mauve mist of flowers. It was probably the wistaria together with Tommy's strong recommendations that reconciled Mrs Cornish to the narrow, gloomy little house.

"We'll take it for the time being and when something better turns up we'll move," Bramley declared. "Sure you'd sooner not rather move out of Foveaux, mummy? You're only to say the word."

"It's for you to decide, Bramley," she repeated like a good child. All her life someone had made her decisions for her. Her husband, Brammy, or Tommy, before he was married, had dictated what she should wear or do. Secretly, she felt it would be interesting to move somewhere else, but she knew Bram. She knew that Foveaux meant more to him than it did to her. This idea that she was wedded to Foveaux was only something he used to disguise his own wishes. Because she left the decisions to her sons did not mean that she abandoned the art of thinking.

"You'll be able to take one or two lodgers," Tommy pointed out. In Foveaux, if you had a "place" of more than one room, it was almost blasphemy not to take lodgers.

"I don't think mummy's quite up to it," Bramley said gravely. "She has a nasty cough, and we don't want her to be overdoing it, do we, little lady?" He patted her gently on the shoulder.

Mrs Cornish did not reply. No lodgers! She saw another of her little interests whittled away. Just as it had at first seemed incredible to have a room to herself, so now it seemed improper to have a house lodgerless.

Sad to say, Mrs Cornish justified Bramley's concern and celebrated the removal by getting really sick. For a long time she could only sit in the sunny little backyard with a rug over her knees. Sometimes she darned or crocheted a purple and pink tea-cosy or outsize woollies as a present for her daughter-in-law who, she discreetly informed Mrs Montague, was "expecting". All the major housework fell to Bramley, who had in the space of a couple of months become an expert washer, if a trifle inclined to wring the buttons off his shirts. If the Sunday were fine, Mrs Cornish would go to morning service, always with an umbrella in case the weather should stealthily change its mind while she was in church. As the weeks lengthened into months she became quite accustomed to her new routine of diets and doctors' visits, taking care not to strain herself unduly.

"I have my boys to live for," she would sometimes say to Mr Budin through a crack in the back fence. "And there's the bird for company. Oh, I'm not lonely."

To the Cornish ménage there had been added by the enterprise of Tommy a pink and grey galah, a bad-tempered selfish bird, which did not even appear to advantage when hungry. Mrs Cornish cherished a hope that with encouragement it might be tempted to say: "Pretty Cocky". This seemed to her an eminently fitting thing for a parrot to say, but Cocky fluffed out his little pink side-whiskers and hunched on his perch making cursing noises. He occasionally hung upside down shrieking, to the delight of Mrs Cornish who regarded such behaviour as a mark of affection. She preferred to sit in the backyard with Cocky, for while the house frowned more and more as winter approached, the garden smiled. A man had sold her some broad bean seeds at the door, and with the simple trust of those long at sea she had planted them and been quite pleased when they came up nasturtiums.

Mr Budin next door knew all about plants and ordered the changes in her garden and was very annoyed with Bramley when he weeded out the seedlings Mr Budin donated. They had trained pussy not to dig in the garden, so now she stalked fiercely up and down, keeping pigeons from settling on the little plot of lawn. "An over-developed property sense," Mr Rolfe called it.

Mrs Cornish never tried to improve the house. The furniture stood just where Bramley had placed it when they moved in. The picture of Queen Victoria left by the last tenant still sneered disapprovingly in the dining-room, though Tommy agitated for its removal every time he visited them. Mrs Cornish thought it rather disloyal to take down the picture of a British sovereign; she also had a superstition that if you lifted anything heavy your inside would drop out. Besides, what was the use of improving a place that Bramley said they had only taken for the time being?

"I see there's more houses to let in the paper," she remarked to him one evening. "I was wondering. . . ."

"What's wrong with this?" her son demanded with the startled air of a stag roused from its native haunts. "It's close to work and handy for you to do your shopping." He frowned thoughtfully. "I'll tell you what, little lady, you wait until we've saved up enough pennies and we'll buy a house of our own. How would that do?" He brightened as he thought of some more good excuses. "Besides, look at the furniture. It's all full of horrors. If we go into a new place, we'd have to have new furniture, and we can't afford it. At least not just now."

He forebore to mention that it was her illness that had eaten into the savings so that they could not afford another move, and Mrs Cornish for her part did not like to say that she thought the damp forbidding house made her ill.

So Mrs Cornish continued to sit in the little back garden, doing her fancy work or reading the books Bramley brought home from the library, mostly novels about rather foolish young women and their love affairs. Bramley cherished a delusion that his mother was debarred by her age from reading anything except the sloppier romances, although the only book in which she expressed any real interest was one by a Mr Masefield which Bramley had brought home for himself. It was a story about a ship just like the one dear John used to have. Tears started into Mrs Cornish's eyes as she read. He described it all so well, the noises the water made slapping against the ship, the wind, the creak of the sails, the sunrise, everything as she knew it. Oh, if only she could be at sea again! It was wrong and ungrateful of her when she had Bramley lapping her in little comforts. She had not had any comforts on those voyages, not even good food sometimes.

"Still, it's different if it's your own man," her wild heart said inside the sedate black dress. "It's different." And her day dreams flared up in a picture of them standing, just she and John Cornish together, as the *Falada* sailed into Valparaiso. "Oh God, give us new things. Let us not rot on the shore," she prayed, without knowing she prayed. But the next minute her hands had mechanically taken up the purple and pink tea-cosy. We must be grateful, she told herself. Look at Emily's girl. Esme had never been grateful, and now the doctors said she was incurable.

"Isn't it a beautiful morning?" she said gently through the fence to Mr Budin when he came out to tend his little garden. "Those little plants you gave me are coming up very nicely indeed."

"I got them rose cuttin's," Mr Budin growled amiably over the fence. "I'll give some to your son if you remind him. Good cuttin's they are, too."

Mr Budin liked to talk over the fence to Mrs Cornish about any news there might be. Her timid deference was welcome.

Now his children were grown up and gone things were dull for Mr Budin. He liked racing himself, but he gave it up because his wife thought it was low. He hardly ever went out at all because she didn't like it. Connie didn't like his talking over the fence much either, so the only real distraction he could legitimately claim was one night a week at his lodge and a few minutes in the evening at the Rose of Denmark.

With these limited opportunities it was amazing how popular Mr Budin was in Foveaux. Of course, he had been living there for any number of years, but his popularity was really due to his untiring good nature. If your roof leaked, he would go out in the middle of a howling gale and replace the slates. He was a builder by trade, but he could doctor dogs and cats, yes, even horses; and his two parrots could talk, as he expressed it, "like angels". He had only one vice. He insisted on making cement flower-pots. "And goodness knows, we got enough of them pots about the place already," Connie Budin, his stout wife, would complain.

There were pots imitating old tree stumps and pots smooth: rough flower-pots, and flower-pots with minor auxiliary flower-pots sprouting like buds out of the side of the large one. The proudest day of Mr Budin's life was when he actually received a commission to make a cement lawn-roller for a private tennis-court. He told Mrs Cornish all about it with a suppressed enthusiasm and one eye on the kitchen for his wife who was, as he reminded Mrs Cornish, "terrible jealous. Why, if she as much as sees me talking to me shadder, she wants to know all about it." Mr Budin winked one eye kindly under its bushy white eyebrow. "Terrible jealous of me, she is."

Mrs Cornish had not known quite what to say so she said nothing.

"I see they're putting up another factory building in Connor Street." Mr Budin continued his monologue. "It's a thing I don't like to see." His tone became more severe. "This is a resident'al district. Always has been. The way they build these factories, too. Putting in steel frames on the winders, cutting everything down as fine as they can. It takes all the good out of a man's trade. There ain't much work going nowadays for all they say things is so prosperous."

"Dear me."

"That's why you see me 'ome 'ere, Mrs Cornish, on a fine sunny day when I ought to be out on a job. Good time, they say. Buildin' trade boom. And 'ere I am. They think I'm too old to work. Work! I've worked with a poisoned hand when I could've screamed every time I touched anythin' and I've laid bricks better an' faster than any of them. I've worked when I could hardly see in dust and heat that'd burn your eyebrows off, and I've laid bricks when the mortar was freezin'. One time — it was the slump about 1907 — and things were terrible tough, Mrs Cornish — I says to Connie, 'Well, I'll have to try me luck, old girl.' She didn't want me to go. The kids was only little, you see, but I 'ad to go where the work was an' they said it was in West Orstralia. So I books me passage and leaves Connie here and goes over with what money I 'ad. And the first thing I does when I gets off the boat is break me leg."

"Oh, how dreadful!"

"I suppose," Mr Budin picked a blade of grass and nibbled it, "I suppose, Mrs Cornish, you ain't never lain and wondered and wondered what'd happen if you died?"

"Yes," Mrs Cornish said, nodding, "I have, Mr Budin."

"Well," Bob Budin shook his head as if to deny her the right, "you ain't laid and felt your hair turnin' grey wonderin' what 'ud happen to your wife and kids if you pegged out, have you? That's what I done. I got to the stage where I says: 'Bob, it won't do no good, you worryin',' but I'd worry just the same, 'cause I 'adn't any money and I knew Connie 'adn't none. I was out before me leg's 'alf right. 'You're a damned fool,' the doctor says. But I 'ad to 'ave work. . . ."

"Bob, I want you," Mrs Budin demanded from the kitchen.

Mr Budin hastily brought his monologue to a close. "So you see, Mrs Cornish, just bein' out of work don't worry me. I've known worse. Of course, we did think one time with a bit of luck we'd get out of 'ere into a place with more fresh air where we could 'ave a real garden. Our own home somewhere up the line. But you know how it is? There's a lot of things you can't have in this world." He disappeared suddenly. "Well, don't forget those cuttin's." He popped his head back over the

fence. "But cement work — making flower-pots — there's nobody can touch me on that," he said, and was gone.

"You want to watch out," Bramley teased his mother, "or
you'll get a summons for alienating the old boy's affections."

Mrs Cornish thoughtfully stirred the sauce she was making
over her little gas griller. "His wife's terrible jealous," she said
gravely. "And he's such a nice man."

Even a grey-haired old lady can appreciate the flattery of
being noticed by an expert in cement flower-pots.

### III

Mrs Cornish had a horror of visitors. They affected her much
as a bright light might affect a small moth. She went round in
bewildered circles wondering what she should do.

"You will explain," Mrs Cornish had counselled Tommy
anxiously when he was first married, "that it isn't because I
bear any ill-will but it's just that I'm flustered by a stranger."

"That's all right," Tommy assured her. "Neicie isn't keen
on visiting either."

It didn't occur to him to warn his mother-in-law. Not that
Mrs Noblett would ever have summoned up enough courage
for a ceremonial visit had she not heard that Mrs Cornish was
ill. Even then it took repeated urging from Bob to make her see
her duty.

"We don't want 'er to think we don't know what's right,"
that grey-haired smiter of police announced. "You get into
your best clo'es an' go up an' see 'er."

Poor Mamie, dubiously reviewing the few shabby old dresses
behind the piece of calico that served as her wardrobe, realized
not for the first time that she had no best clothes. There was,
however, the old brown skirt given her by a lady whose
cleaning she used to do and a brown woollen knitted jacket. She
had only her old black shoes and stockings, but there was the
black lace hat Neicie had given her when she took a dislike to it
herself. This, brightened by a blue bow, would certainly
smarten her ensemble. She had never worn it before and, as she
wistfully reviewed her kindly brown face in the little scrap of

mirror, she remembered the time when she had been as pert
and pretty as Neicie. Her hair was growing grey and her ill-
fitting false teeth made her look older than her age. It was a
wonder, she thought, that Bob, who was still a handsome man,
had not taken up with some smart young girl long ago. A wave
of gratitude to him for only getting drunk flooded over her.
She went downstairs again quite happy and confident.

"Well now, Mamie," Bob said, looking up from the racing
news, "you do take the shine out of these young tabbies all
right."

Mrs Noblett beamed. If she were well enough dressed for
Bob, what did it matter about Tommy's mother?

"I get that red in the face climbing 'ills," she explained, "I
thought I'd start early and take it slow."

"Don't you forget them bananas," Bob reminded her. "Real
tops they are an' you can tell 'er they're good for 'er, whatever
she's got." Bob never asked for details when a lady took to
her bed. He had been embarrassed too often.

"I ain't anxious to go," Mrs Noblett hesitated; but after due
persuasions and what Bob called "smoogings", she found herself setting out, misgivings, bananas and lace hat complete.

When Mrs Cornish heard the doorbell she no more expected
to see Mrs Noblett, as she said afterwards, than "an angel
with wings". She nearly fainted on the mat with terror.

"I come," Mrs Noblett said with an effort, "because I heard
you was sick."

"Won't you come in?" Mrs Cornish said faintly.

She crept ahead of Mamie into the front room and sat down
on the cedar chest like a little black cat. She folded her hands
one inside the other as a kitten folds its paws and waited
quietly.

Mrs Noblett, letting herself down with a creaking of stays
onto the new cane chair which had replaced the one in which
the Captain used to sit, glanced around her humbly. It was a
lovely place, she thought. Some people had all the luck. There
was a vase of artificial flowers over the mantelpiece that particularly caught her eye.

"Well now, you must excuse me," she said in a genteel tone,
"but them flowers certainly is pretty."

"Yes, aren't they?" Mrs Cornish said timidly.

"And that box on the mantelpiece, I bet Tommy got that from my boy Freddy," Mamie continued with a beam of motherly pride. She was feeling more at her ease. "He made me one like that, too. I keep me sewin' things in it. 'E's in the joinery and real clever with bits of wood. Always was even when 'e was little."

"Like Tommy with motor-cars," Mrs Cornish put in, feeling she must keep her end up; and then at the mention of Tommy, her eyes began to fill with tears and brim over so that she had to get out her little white handkerchief.

"There, there," Mrs Noblett said gently. "Don't you fret about them. I didn't feel none too happy meself but after all when you're young, you've got to get what you can out of life. It's little enough you get when you're old."

"I do hope she's good to him, Mrs Noblett," Mrs Cornish sniffed. "It isn't that I've got any objections to her but it was all so sudden. He shouldn't have been so sudden. It wasn't fair to me." She looked up, her eyes streaming. "I've had a lot of trouble. First, my husband, Captain Cornish, losing his sight. . . ."

"I know," Mrs Noblett nodded sympathetically.

Mrs Cornish was beginning to feel glad Mrs Noblett had come. It was good to talk things over with another woman, even if she was an uneducated stout woman in broken shoes and a grotesque lace hat.

"Bob says you mustn't ever think we tried for Tommy to marry Neicie," continued Mrs Noblett. "He says to tell you not to think we'll ever be a drag on him. The boys are bringin' in good money and Tommy'll 'ave enough to look after Neicie and the baby when it comes. We'll never be, Bob says, the ones to make calls on 'im. And it's only right, he says, that Tommy should look after you a bit an' if there's any trouble from Neicie — she's a high'n mighty little puss, if she is me own daughter — that. . . ."

"Oh, no," Mrs Cornish said quickly, her pride touched. "I never want to interfere. When a man marries, he must go with his wife. His mother shouldn't ever interfere." She sniffed. "When I married my husband, it was always just the two of us, and that's the way I'd like it to be with Tommy."

"Still," Mrs Noblett said, settling herself with sundry creaks back in the cane chair, "boys are different from girls. I near cried me eyes out when Harry got married and I s'pose it'll be the same with Freddy and Joe and Bill. A mother misses a boy."

"You see there's my other son, Bramley," Mrs Cornish said with pride. "The last thing his father said to him was: 'Take care of your mother, boy,' and I must say there's never been a better son, and as for taking care of me—" she threw up her little hands —"no one will ever know, Mrs Noblett, how good that boy has been."

"No young lady?" Mrs Noblett asked.

"No," said Mrs Cornish firmly. " 'I'm not the marrying kind, mum,' he often says. 'It's different with Tommy.' "

"Ah, Tommy's that quick on the uptake," Mrs Noblett agreed.

"His father was like that. His father married young, too. But not Bramley." Mrs Cornish gave a little decided nod. "He takes after my side. The Hatfields were not really marrying people. Lawyers, my father's family were."

"Mr Noblett's people," Mamie responded, "were in the wood an' coal line. But Bob was a third son and, of course, he had to shift for himself."

"Won't you have a cup of tea?" invited Mrs Cornish.

"Well, I could do with some," Mrs Noblett brightened visibly. "It's that tirin' walkin' up'ill. And you see I'm fat. It's harder on me than the thin ones."

Over their tea Mrs Cornish and Mrs Noblett developed a kind of guarded friendship and Mrs Cornish found Mrs Noblett's interest in her illness both stimulating and acceptable. She was not afraid of Mrs Noblett because Mrs Noblett dropped her aitches.

"Brammy won't let me do much now," she confided to Mrs Noblett. "The doctor says it's bad for my blood pressure."

To look at tiny Mrs Cornish you would hardly think she had any blood at all, much less that it would inconvenience her.

"Well, deary me," Mrs Noblett exclaimed, "you must be like me with me veins."

"I have a diet," Mrs Cornish went on, like a small girl with a skipping rope. "I have to be careful what I eat. 'No meat,' the doctor said. 'To touch meat, Mrs Cornish,' "— her voice was firm and proud —" 'to touch meat means certain death.' "

"Did 'e now?" Mrs Noblett gasped admiringly.

"It runs in our family," Mrs Cornish added. "I remember my Aunt Ada when I was a little girl. She was forbidden to touch meat. But I think that had something to do with her skin complaint rather than her blood pressure."

"Very likely," Mrs Noblett agreed.

From illness in general they plunged into the fascinating topic of how they had felt at each of their confinements and all the trouble Mrs Cornish had with her inside after Tommy arrived.

"I never thought he'd live," she found herself saying earnestly. "We bought a goat in Hong Kong, but the Chinaman cheated us. He had given it something to make it look fat and milky. It all fell away to skin and bone, Mrs Noblett, and jumped overboard when we were three days out."

"Fancy now. I 'ad the same trouble with Freddy. Seems to be getting the wrong things to eat does it."

"We were right in the middle of the Pacific on Christmas Day, Mrs Noblett," Mrs Cornish went on. "Look, I can show you a chart." She produced it from within the great cedar chest. "See the cross and where my husband wrote, 'Pea Soup'? That was all we had to eat because the stevedore had cheated about the stores. I had to go on feeding Tommy myself all the way to America."

"My 'usband," Mrs Noblett said, "if 'e 'as one fault, it's that 'e never could look after 'imself. Anyone can take 'im in."

A look of understanding passed between them.

"Won't you have another cup of tea?" Mrs Cornish said presently.

"Well, thank you, but I must be gettin' along." Mamie heaved herself out of the cane chair with some final farewell creakings. "I'd ask you down, Mrs Cornish, but the place is that small, I. . . . Of course it's clean," she said in an embarrassed defence. "But you know what it's like with boys trampin' in and out?"

"Of course," Mrs Cornish agreed, equally embarrassed. "I do hope when you're passing this way you'll drop in and see me."

"I will. Indeed I will."

They farewelled each other thus cordially as far as the gate and then Mrs Cornish pattered inside and shut the door with a sigh of relief.

"Thank 'eaven," muttered Mrs Noblett, hastening downhill to the familiar ease of home. "That's over. I believe in doing the right thing but once is enough."

# CHAPTER 7

## I

Lennox Street, even before the boom years and the building of the flats, had justified Honest John's prophecy by developing into a roaring spate of through traffic from the city. It was no longer "the street in which Foveaux House stood"; it was "the direct route to the Eastern suburbs". As such it gave tongue all day in a thunder of trucks and lorries, laden with everything from cement to beer, and between them slipped the shining, sleek taxis and small craft of every build and breed.

The motor-car fever hit Foveaux hard. Almost everyone who could borrow or buy on time payment a rattling, old-fashioned model, set up as a motorist; and there were, owing to the undoubted prosperity of the times, a number of families ready to mortgage father's wages in return for the joy of packing the dogs and children and swimming costumes and lunches and bidding farewell to Foveaux for at least one day out of seven.

Most of the Foveaux cars were a mongrel mixture of parts, patched together by a friend of one of the boys who had once worked in a garage. If they fell to pieces, the family sat by the roadside and waited for rescue or tied the model together again with bits of wire. Bob Noblett was in great demand as an unpaid consulting specialist in such cases and only as a last resort would he advise a visit to a garage, much as a surgeon would advise an operation. Times might be good and everything in the garden lovely, but Bob considered that McErchin and his fellow pirates whose blue, red and yellow signs were beginning to flare along Errol Street, were clutching too large a percentage of the loose money.

"These garages," he was wont to say, "charge you for the smell of oil on the grease boys' overalls."

Bob himself sometimes wistfully contemplated buying a ninth-hand utility truck, but decided against it on the grounds that you couldn't teach a car to know the run as well as a horse.

Down lanes whence it seemed impossible that anything bigger than a cat could come, the trucks would shunt out in the bleak early mornings to join the spate down Lennox Street. Every back street was honeycombed with garages, ranging from large important cement structures to tiny sheds at the end of a backyard full of clothes-props which must all be removed before the family pride could enter or depart. Those car-owners who did not boast a garage cut a hole in the back fence and backed their purchase through it.

During one of the strikes at the Iredale Engineering Works the directors drove up to attend a conciliation conference and found, so they alleged, that it was impossible to park their cars because the strikers' cars were ranked nose to tail round several blocks. This may have been managerial exaggeration, but it is certainly true that the expenditure on old cars, new furniture, toys and outings was never higher. A general air of careless generosity pervaded all except the shopkeepers, for, if the basic wage was a record, prices were commensurately high.

To the motor-car epidemic none were more subject than the busmen, Tommy Cornish among their number. They would spend their hours off duty taking their families for runs in crazy side-cars; and on the occasion of the busmen's picnic, although the companies provided buses for the drivers and their families, many preferred to go in their own cars. Those on motor-bicycles enlivened the drive by circling gaily round and round the buses and shouting rude remarks to those inside. As the buses stopped at every hotel en route and all the cars and motor-cycles stopped with them, this racing and circling became rather a dangerous proceeding after the sixteenth hotel.

Tommy's motor-bicycle was a modest effort compared with those of his mates. One driver, the notorious "Coalie", supported both a motor-car and bicycle as a result of his economical use of the company's petrol. In one of the shops on his run he kept a big oil drum, and when occasion offered he would refill this without expense by the simple expedient of crawling under his bus and "milking" her. He excused this habit on the ground that the Chief was so mean that although he might put a five-pound note in the plate at church, if you asked him for a sixpenny rise, "he'd shoot you". Busmen claimed that "Old Jeff" was so sabbatarian that he locked his hens away by themselves on Sundays — and as for drink — there was no second chance for a driver he saw coming out of a hotel.

"He sees we don't get anything to waste on booze," Coalie would declare. "Any rate, I'd sooner have a red nose from beer than indigestion."

It was Coalie who instituted the custom whereby on the early morning run the conductor would take the fares and pull no tickets, the driver and the conductor afterwards sharing the takings between them. Tommy, in a fit of absentmindedness, once incurred the severe displeasure of his driver, "Head-lights", by forgetting this rule and issuing tickets to a whole busful of workmen.

Usually, however, Tommy enjoyed being first mate of a bucko bus; for those were the mad days of buses, as of house-building, land-selling, and company-promoting. He liked being offsider for Headlights, a wizened, bespectacled racing driver, whose mad speed as he swung his charge down a quiet subur-ban road in pursuit of a rival bus made old ladies hold on tight and call out to him to be careful.

"Right-o," Tommy would roar, as he heaved a stout lady and her children on board. "Let her go." And he shrilled his whistle as they lurched away.

Headlights raced rival buses for the love of it and, some-times, even Tommy was moved to protest that they would be killed.

Headlights, however, was always ready with his argument: "If you let the other company's bus get ahead, they'll scoop the pool and the Chief likes heavy bags. It's no use coming in with a light bag."

Headlights would stop to pick up passengers; but, if he was racing, he would not let them down until he got a lead again. On one occasion a furious passenger hit him over the head

202

with an umbrella. "Damn passengers, anyway," Headlights whined. "If it wasn't for the passengers wanting to get off all the time, this game would be all right." They could always get the next bus back if they happened to be carried too far past their stopping point.

Most passengers, indeed, had their favourite buses and would wait for them loyally. Staid businessmen nursing leather attaché cases would lean forward to urge their driver on as he swooped ahead to grab up passengers from under the very radiator of an opponent.

At night, Tommy might be seen lying full length over the front mudguard, with his cap held over one of the bus's lights to "disguise" her as she crept, with all inside lights out, upon the unconscious look-out in the back of the rival company's bus. Then with a blaring horn and a mocking howl they would tear past the open-mouthed crew of the enemy and rattle off at full speed.

"You ought to get something steadier," Bramley occasionally protested to Tommy. "It doesn't seem much of a job to me." But then, Tommy reflected, old Bramley was a cautious, saving old cuss who never really enjoyed himself.

A similar reputation was attached by Foveaux to Mr McErchin, though he, unlike Bramley, was pointed out as an example of what thrift could do for a man. His admirers deduced that Mr McErchin's rise from a humble start in a shed to his elaborate service station on the corner of Errol Street must have been due to that quality mainly, for no evidence was forthcoming that he was even a passable mechanic. He left the actual tinkering with engines to his sons, and the office was his chosen domain. There his thrift and skill at adding up accounts to be sent to those he termed "mugs" exercised the qualities for which he was justly noted. Not even his sons could extract an actual living wage from him; but as they all lived at home, he could protest that they took it out in board.

McErchin's, although the most ostentatious, was not the only big garage in Upper Foveaux; and more than McErchin looked with eyes of approval on those towering blocks of flats springing up in the locality. Expensive flats meant more car

owners who needed to garage their cars, to have petrol in their
tanks, batteries recharged, oil in their engines and differen-
tials, and grease in all their joints.

Flat owners were notoriously gay and lavish with their
money in contrast with the more penurious nature of the
average Foveaux lodger. They went to late parties and came
home swinging. They took taxis instead of walking, they ran up
bills, and could generously afford to pay them, if they could
afford to live in seven-guinea flats. The garage owners rejoiced,
the little shops where the flat dwellers could buy all the things
they forgot rejoiced, the flower-sellers rejoiced, the hotel and
café keepers all rejoiced at the prospect.

## I I

The walls of the old cottages came down stone by stone, the
dust blowing out like a thick choking smoke that set the
lorry drivers and demolishers' men coughing and swearing. A
pile of lumber, tossed at random to wait removal, had mas-
sacred the little peach-tree. The lower-floor windows were
blinded with sheets of corrugated iron, the upper ones knocked
out, the roof, ripped off like an Indian scalp, exposed the sore
and naked plaster of the dull blue walls which, in their turn,
would be more clouds of choking dust, so many more lorry-
loads of old rubble.

Mrs Cornish watched the tearing down of the cottages as
she went past to Dennison Square, doing her messages, getting
the liver for pussy and the brains the butcher always kept for
her. The men were ripping up the floor-boards, the old damp,
rotten floor-boards.

"I wonder," Mrs Cornish murmured, "if I could find that
sixpence that dropped through the kitchen floor."

She did not like to go and ask the workmen; they might
laugh to see a little old lady searching the desolation for that
long-lost sixpence. She stood there rebellious and grieving.
They were wronging the Captain, tearing down the place where
he had last lived. She didn't believe in ghosts. She and her
husband would meet again in a much more appropriate setting

than Foveaux; but it was wrong of people to tear down the place he had lived in. It was like pulling up tombstones, not proper. They did not realize how a house's personality was made up of the people who had lived in it. Surely an old house was as worthy of respect as an old living person.

Mr Bishop also watched the cheerful activities of the demolishers resentfully. "Tearing down and loosing Influences," he muttered, working a new set of false teeth about under his loose wrinkled face. "They wouldn't care if they built over a cemetery. Not like the Chinese." He shook his head. "I've been warning them all I dare. Never say I didn't warn them."

His mysterious and dreadful warnings quite frightened Mrs Cornish. She had a greatly increased respect for Mr Bishop since that interview published in the paper with his photograph and his prediction; and now that he was doing predictions weekly for the papers she was faintly proud of him.

When in due time there rose the foundations of the flats she eyed them as though, like the walls of Jericho, they might crumble at the trump of Mr Bishop's disapproval. If it had not been for the night watchman, her feelings might have been justified. Foveaux regarded new buildings not only as a spectacle but as an opportunity. Joists and beams would float away mysteriously; bricks dissolved into thin air. A wheelbarrow, any night, might decide to take itself off with a bag of cement.

Little by little, however, Foveaux Flats struggled up to the stage where it was possible to ward off marauders. A smell of new paint and fibro, cement, putty and wood-shavings began to emanate from it. There were glass doors with a glimpse of imitation marble halls and newly painted letter-boxes demurely awaiting owners. All sorts of people from Mrs Montague to Mrs Blore had been over the flats investigating the fabulous possibility of their renting one, hot and cold water, private bathrooms and all. Soon someone had taken the fourth floor flat on which Mrs Montague had set her heart and hung their canary on the little balcony. Orange curtains fluttered from those windows where that lady had wished to hang blue ones.

"Still it's very interesting to see all those modern improvements and the cute kitchens," she reminded herself. "And such a nice man showed me over."

The landladies of Upper Foveaux, those select and deliberate women, who occupied all the tall, stalwart houses from which the glory of the Agnews and the Foxteths had departed, hailed the flats as an accolade of their gentility. The glory was returning to Israel, they felt; and, coming home from a tour round Foveaux Flats, they took from their front windows the signs: "Apartments", "Single Room to Let", and put out "Upstairs Flat", or "Self-contained Balcony Flat". It made them feel quite progressive. None of the Foveaux landladies ever patronized an agent while there was a chance of letting a room by means of a window sign. Agents wanted half the first week's rent.

A stranger, inquiring for rooms, could not realize how individual were these tall, once dignified old houses or these landladies, who at first glance seemed so much alike. They all emerged every morning to whitewash the path to the gate, black the doorsteps and wash down the pavement; and then retreated again to be seen scarcely all day. If their early-morning diversions ever served any useful purpose was hard to ascertain, but generations of landladies rigidly observed the tradition. All footpaths and doorsteps must be cleansed re-gardless of the state of the stairs or the bathroom. Rolfe had once advanced the theory that there was some kind of secret bureau to which landladies contributed the footprints of all moonlight flitters, non-rentpayers and persons who smoked in bed. This would explain the whitewash and blacking, but it failed to account for those who devoted their main attention to sweeping the grass plot in front of the house.

All the Foveaux landladies played a game known as "Keeping to Yourself", which consisted in finding out as much as you could about the women next door and their lodgers with-out giving any information in return.

By this means it became generally known that the Misses Susmilch, who occupied the topmost house of the row, were related to a millionaire. On the strength of this connection the Misses Susmilch kept their front path as well as their doorstep glossy with black varnish. It was so awe-inspiring that few feet dared the shiny expanse. The grocer's boy had worked a

206

detour through the pansy bed where his footprints did not show so much.

Next door to the Misses Susmilch the landlady lived in an odour of good deeds, disinfectant and furniture polish, while in Number Fourteen the landlady lurked under the stairs in a damp stone kitchen and gave the impression that if somebody sprinkled disinfectant she would scutter for the skirting board. But in one thing all the landladies agreed: they were irreproachably correct in their lives, manners, lodgers, surroundings and thoughts. It was only fitting that the flats should be erected as a tribute to the undoubted gentility they lent the neighbourhood. They never went out in the street when Bob Noblett or some other hawker passed bellowing: "Choice carrots, oranges, apples, bananas, twenty-four f'r sixpence. Here y'are. Best handout of potherbs in Sydney today for ninepence. Big cabbage, beetroot, cauliflower, turnips." They remained at the front door and bought. Similarly, should a bottle-o come crying mournfully up the street: "ANNNNy EMMMMPty BoLLS," they didn't take the bottles to the man. They made him come in and get them.

# CHAPTER 8

## I

The Slum Abolition League during the early months of its career had progressed from strength to strength and conference to conference, impoverishing the members of its committee and replenishing the general knowledge of painfully uninterested parliamentarians and others in high places. The Foveaux Council, according to plan, was to be presented with a petition only when the organization was at the height of its power. Unfortunately, the mass removals of the executive somewhat upset the general meetings and plans; and although the letter to the council requesting an interview was all in order, the actual accosting of the council was most wearisomely deferred.

This was rather the fault of the Reverend Adam Atwater, who had promised to head the deputation. Mr Atwater, with characteristic versatility, had been smitten by the idea that all this bothering about the unfortunate of Foveaux was well enough in its place, but he must not neglect his congregation. The focus of his attention, having once more been attracted to the actual congregation, he started, as was his habit, to do things thoroughly. Brighter services, he demanded. Yes, indeed, not only did the hymns, the prayers, the sidesmen, the church itself and the lights need brightening, his own sermons must be more startling, more thought-provoking. He began well enough by tackling the not-unthumbed topic: "What Have the Movies to Offer Jesus?" and continued on a series which concluded with: "Are Short Skirts Sinful?"

As Mr Atwater's sermons naturally lengthened, it was only humane to demand that his church committee raised enough money to provide more comfortable seats. Wireless services were his next move; and, to the joy of an overflowing church, mostly strangers to Foveaux, he announced that girl ushers would be introduced as a trial form of cheerful worship.

It was not that Mr Atwater meant to leave his social activities in the lurch; but he felt he did owe something to his congregation. Beside, if the slum dwellers were really appreciative of his efforts, they might well come and partake of the softer seats and other spiritual comforts, all carefully disinfected after every service.

Rolfe also had been unexpectedly preoccupied with a patent belonging to one of Bud Pellager's cronies. The patent Bud had recommended as a "real little gold mine". Rolfe, seeing a chance to escape from the monotony of soap advertising, was equally enthusiastic.

"If I can only interest enough capital in the thing," he exulted, "Teddy says I'm right for a third share. And, by heaven! I'm going to raise that capital, if I have to seize it with my teeth." He was almost affectionately disposed towards the patent, a new flexible sheeting for floors and ceiling, euphoniously titled "Tickolat". "I'll never use soap again, even in conversation, once we get the factory going," Rolfe declared.

Bramley and Linnie under difficulties strove to keep the campaign from going to pieces. When all the others failed, they would arrive at meetings and pass resolutions and argue between themselves.

As the possibility of a deputation to the council became more and more remote, a compromise was reached whereby the Reverend Adam Atwater and other representatives were to interview the mayor and request his personal assistance in placing the position before the council. The suggestion came from Mr Atwater and he was quite hurt by the lack of enthusiasm with which it was received by the executive.

"I don't suppose it can do much harm," Rolfe admitted. "If the old dingo intends to put one over us, we might just as well know in advance."

An interview with the mayor of Foveaux was always an uncertain proceeding. He might be back five minutes or five years hence. It was a matter of waiting, however firmly the hour of interview had been fixed. The deputation from the Slum Abolition League finally boiled down to Linnie, the

Reverend Mr Atwater and a vague female who represented the Conjoined Patriotic Women's Societies. Grimly they waited in the shabby plush and light-oak ante-room of the town hall with the prospect of being still there when the cleaner opened it next morning.

Three-quarters of an hour after the appointed time Honest John accidentally blew in, having remembered that he was to meet a man about some timber. Honest John never ignored a business engagement. When informed of the deputation's presence he was full of affability and fervent apologies.

"Just been out on a very sad case," he burbled, shaking the Reverend Adam warmly by the hand. "One you would thoroughly have appreciated. Yes, yes, much more in your line. Poor young woman. Husband in jail. Young baby. Very sad, very. But we have to do what we can, even if it's little enough. Come in, come in. Harry, fetch the lady a more comfortable chair. Disgraceful, the way the place is falling to pieces. No chairs, no nothing. But there — the money's wanted for better things. Better things."

It was a most effective entry, the kindly benevolent mayor, breathless from doing good, trying to give his best to everyone. Mr Atwater could not get out the little speech he had prepared. Every time he began to outline the requests of the Slum Abolition League he found himself so drowned by a flood of goodwill and eloquent assurances, that he could only come up gasping.

"Very kind of you to see me personally. Oh, I quite see your point. You can be certain that I will co-operate to the best of my powers. To the very utmost, if only as a mark of gratitude to you, Mr Atwater, for bringing these charming ladies to brighten my labours. Ha, ha. Quite lights up the old hall to have ladies about it. I know you won't mind if I ask you to leave the whatsisname, the model flat plans and so forth, for me to look over later. Sure to be lots of long bothering talks with the engineer and pow-wow on the council before we can get anything done. But let me assure you people that you have done wonderful work, marvellous work. Those dreadful pig-sties about the Foot must come down. Wouldn't keep a dog in them. Should have come down long ago. Always said so."

"Then, sir," the Reverend Atwater asked gladly, "we may gratefully leave the entire matter in your hands?"

"You may. You may, indeed. I'll bring the whole matter up at the next council meeting. You may be sure I'll do my best."

To tell the truth Honest John had been doing his best since the day he pounced on a leaflet in Bud Pellager's shop. On the Model Housing Scheme of the Slum Abolition League he bestowed the sympathy and pity that the mother of a football hero might give up to the mother of a boy pianist. This footling little scheme was all right for publicity purposes, but it needed business-men to see it through properly. Certainly tear down Plug Alley, but also tear down Anne Street, Little Torrent Street, Byswater Lane and all that stinking network round the Foot. Ogham Street — he paused at Ogham Street — there were too many lucrative factories in Ogham Street to go altering it; but, where possible, all those tiny streets must go. Why, the Foot was an ideal factory area! The council ought to be able to sell the land at its own price. Drive through wide roads, bring the place up to date, give every facility for heavy traffic through to Slazenger and Lennox streets. Drive another road to link up with Murchison Street. Pull all the houses down and slash roads through the void like Divine commands, direct, peremptory and unwavering. As for this potty idea of building some miserable blocks of workmen's flats, it couldn't be considered for a moment. Who would finance the thing? Upper Foveaux was the place for flats, away from the factories, yet handy to the city.

At the council meeting Honest John assumed his classic part of the far-sighted civic father:

"Admittedly, the valuation of certain sites appears excessive. That is a matter for further inquiry. But let us look at the whole question in a sensible light. If we resume the Claribel Area, where does it lead us? Nowhere. We are merely yielding to unthinking public sentimentality. Let us put the whole thing on a business basis. By carrying out the further resumptions that I suggest and by making the necessary improvements, we are looking to the future. We are making an investment — an investment which it behoves us as sound business-men to consider well. Don't let us be hasty in this matter. Let me give you

these figures in regard to factory sites in other parts of the city.
. . ."

He was so cautious and full of statistics that the council
began to regard the expensive resumptions as a bargain that
might slip through their fingers at any moment. In a magical
manner the Claribel Lane Resumption Proposal was amended
to include Anne Street, Little Torrent Street, Byswater Lane
and other areas essential for Honest John's replanning of
the streets. Two special meetings of the council were held but
the discussion was so favourable and the details passed so
rapidly that it seemed almost as though someone had been
oiling the wheels.

Naturally one or two old and crusted aldermen stood out
and denounced the whole scheme as a criminal waste of the
ratepayers' money, but little attention was paid to them. People
felt that Foveaux had got too much undesirable limelight over
the Plug Alley shooting. Landowners would be discouraged,
aldermen pointed out to each other, if they found they were
building expensive flats and shops in a place with a bad name.

The newspapers, which had only reluctantly given space to
the Slum Abolition League, now came out with headlines:
"Plug Alley To Go. Foveaux Council Leads Way In Slum
Abolition."

True to his promise, Honest John brought the scheme of the
Slum Abolition League before the council. It was at the end of
the second special meeting and the aldermen might be forgiven
for being tired and anxious to go home.

"The final business of the meeting," announced Honest
John blandly, "is the consideration of a plan submitted, I may
say, without invitation, by a group which calls itself the Slum
Abolition Committee. If any of you wish to go into the details
of this interesting proposition, I must remind you that the hour
is late and that the scheme has been aired, excessively aired, in
a section of the Press. I regret to say, after going into the
matter very closely, that I think too much attention has been
given to it. One of the leading schemers — ha, ha — not using
the term in any derogatory sense — is an architect who, I hear,
has recently returned from Europe very, very full of these
rather — h'rrm — European ideas. Possibly he thinks that he

212

would also be the best person to carry them into effect. In any case I will call for the engineer's report."

The council listened with bored impatience to the engineer's disparaging mutterings.

"Moved that no action be taken," chanted one of the more crusted aldermen. And added under his breath, "crack-brained bosh."

With a great deal of circumspection a reply was indited by the town clerk thanking the committee for the submitted (and returned herewith) tentative Housing Scheme which the council had neither the power nor the means at its disposal to carry out.

"One step at a time," Mr Atwater carolled, undismayed. "Surely, we cannot expect everything at once. We have stirred the conscience of the council at least. The demolition of the slum area is in itself a wonderful step."

But Jimmy Rolfe reached up and with one wrench swept down "The Porpoise" from the wall. Perhaps only Bramley had been deluded enough or cared enough for Foveaux to believe in the possibility of "The Porpoise" ever seeing the light.

II

The news of the council's decision to demolish Plug Alley was received by the residents with mixed feelings. The more militant viewpoint was expressed by Mr Noblett.

"All these years," he complained, "I been acting like a 'uman being, doin' me best for me feller man an' now I'm expected to lead the 'orse out into the street an' me fambly with it. Where we goin' to? An' who's to pay me the valoo of the trade I built up round 'ere? Damned if I'll get out."

This attitude, however, did not extend beyond the old pioneers, the Blores, the Sampsons and the Nobletts. The drifting population of the other houses took the thing more philosophically. One house was very much like the next to them. They could only afford the worst wherever they went, so it didn't really matter. On one thing they agreed. The places might be brought down about their ears any day. They weren't going to wait for that disaster, not they. Little versed in the procrastinating methods of councils but conscious of the possibility of keen competition for empty houses, they began hastily to move out, despite the assurances of rent collectors that they were perfectly safe. Besides, they felt, if the "nobs" on the council thought the place ought to be pulled down, it must be worse than they thought. "An awful smell there is," one lady confided over the fence to the next. "I thought it was only Mr Noblett's vegetables, but seems it must be somethin' real bad."

The exodus, in spite of the difficulty of finding other houses as cheap and bad as those they were leaving, was well under way a fortnight after the council's fateful decision. Old Mr Bross's office was besieged with persons seeking houses in other localities and the few strangers he did manage to get into the Plug Alley houses mostly moved again when the neighbours told them of the impending peril.

Besides, if a house were left untenanted for a week, it became a wreck. The enterprising in Ogham Lane, quick to seize their opportunity, went forth by night and began the demolition of Mr Bross's property in good earnest. Doors sold for half a crown, windows for six and six. The floor-boards were ripped up for firewood. They removed the lavatory doors, stair rails and every burnable adjunct. They knocked out bricks to pave their backyards. They took down the corrugated iron from the roofs and made themselves little fowl-runs with it. Soon the old settlers were able to point out to prospective tenants that it wasn't worth while moving in because there was nothing to move into. The houses were mere shells. Finally, in the interests of public safety, it became necessary to remove the tottering wreck of what had been three-quarters of Plug Alley. Only the inhabited houses remained whole.

"There ain't no need for the council to chip in," Bob Noblett remarked with a grin. "She's demolished all right."

Bob's horse now had a new shelter of rusty corrugated iron; iron that had once belonged to Mr Bross, Bob truly explaining that when a landlord couldn't stop a thing, he had no right to complain. Over the weed-green ruins of the erstwhile terrace the youth of the neighbourhood had laid out a

214

miniature golf course. The demolition of the terrace was most providential as the Foot had no "minny" golf links. Here was a heaven-sent opportunity to indulge in the sport of the moment. With home-made clubs and old balls the Minny Golf Club gleefully sallied forth on warm evenings. Lovers murmured among the ruins by night; small boys played bushrangers there when they should have been at school; cats sunned themselves on the remaining mounds and dogs sported across the terrain.

### III

On his way home Bramley sometimes paused at the top of the steps to look down into the devastation of Claribel Lane where small children, playing at war, were accustomed to crouch behind the broken brickwork and yell at each other in the way of small children. Where Rolfe's white towers should have caught the light there were only close-packed chimney tops and dirty backyards. In the distance, where stretched Anne Street, Byswater Lane and Little Torrent Street, bald patches indicated that the council's policy, grinding slowly but exceeding small, had munched down an undergrowth of small cottages, much as a sea-cow might demolish part of Rolfe's well-beloved Sargasso Sea for lunch. For the most part the jagged terraces still presented their dun-coloured coral reefs in dirty repetition. Of the two types of desolation, the built and the unbuilt, it seemed to the young man gazing down that the built was the less dispiriting. Lost like a silver ring in deep water, his foolish idealism lay below there, not broken, but encrusted and dull, never to be recovered.

It seemed there could be no cleanliness, in either the council's devastation or the stubborn masses of standing brick and mortar. Leprous they looked by day, and by night, flecked with the phosphorescence of the council's lighting, they were gathered into a darkness whence the chimneys loomed only as weed-tangled turrets, drowned and desperate. Around, the roar of the city's night-tide rose, the thundering of railway traffic, the faint scream of engines dragging their loads to the docks, all louder and lonelier as the other sounds of men's lives were stilled.

# BOOK III

---

# THE SURF

# I

Ogham Street was scarcely the haunt of blood-stained crime that the legends of Foveaux would have you believe. A narrow street that began in a cluster of Chinese eating houses and ended in the bulk of a brewery, it ran the gamut of the oldest, dreariest and most dilapidated set of shops, hovels and factories any district could possibly assemble. Ogham Street was the city's backyard and, like most backyards, it contained those things decently hidden from the eye of visitors. If there had to be bottle-yards, old rag and scrap-iron dumps, leaky verminous cottages and smelly, smoky workshops, they might just as well be in Ogham Street as somewhere where they would arouse more comment. After all, the inhabitants of the street had grown used to breathing air that was half smoke and a third part chemical fumes.

By day Ogham Street was a clamorous place, what with the whirr of machinery in the knitting mills, the click and stamp of the button factory, the tooting of whistles, the shouts of men loading drays, the hammering from the stove-works, the tramping and jangling of teams and the cheery conversations which were of necessity carried on in shouts. But there were peaceful little stretches of footpath past which the tide of commerce raced unregarded. There were whole terraces where old gentlemen sat on the front steps in the sunshine and their wives came out with buckets of water and carefully washed down the pavement as though it were the face of a favourite child.

When the days were fine, Old Granny Deeps would sit snoozing outside the minute stone house on the corner, her sagging old cane chair planted across the footpath, her scarlet shawl wrapped comfortably about her. She would let her lids fall and enjoy the sunlight through them, harbouring her

energies in a warm daze, the brown skin of her face like
wrinkled tissue paper with the bones showing around the
darker brown hollows below her eyes. Her black straw bonnet
with its bit of ostrich feather nodded forward. Her thin white
hair was drawn back behind her small fleshy ears: ears that
had been pierced and decorated with gold rings. Her toothless
mouth was a little open as she slept. Below the dusty hem of
her black skirt her elastic-sided boots projected, limp and
twisted as though her ankles were broken. Around her feet a
fat tribe of black-and-white cats basked insolently, heedless of
the noise of the street or the half-defiant sniffs of passing dogs.

There were hundreds of cats in Foveaux. They ran wild.
Households might lay claim to half a dozen as their own, but
the cats mostly cadged their food and lodging from door to
door and did not fare so badly.

Sitting with one of these strays in her lap on a hot February
afternoon in 1929 old Mrs Deeps blinked herself awake. She
called to one of her numerous daughters who had dropped in
to "clean up for ma":

"Beattie. . . ."

"What is it, ma?"

"The place doesn't seem to be as quiet as it used to be.
Spotty's kitten was run over yestiday by one of them motor-
cars."

Her daughter did not bother to reply, and Mrs Deeps
honoured the street with a reproachful inspection.

"All bush it was," she said in her cracked voice. "I can
remember when it was all bush."

The daughter, a stout red-faced woman with a four-year-old
urchin behind her, came and leant in the doorway.

"It's hot enough to sizzle the ashfelt," she observed, wiping
her brow. "I dunno how you sit out there, ma." The boy
ventured from the footpath and she turned her attention to
him. "Come on off that road, Stanley. I ain't got no money
for wreaths."

"What's all them men doin'?" Granny Deeps's attention
was attracted by a crowd farther up the street outside Hutchison's timber-yard and joinery. Granny was like that; she
would take no notice of her surroundings for a week at a time

and then glimmer out of her shell like some old mollusc on a wet rock. "They been hanging round all day," she observed. "What they doin'?"

"They're picketin'," her daughter announced importantly.

"Eh?"

"They're picketin' because of the timber strike an' they're changin' shifts. Don't you see the p'licemen?"

Mrs Deeps screwed up her rheumy old eyes.

"They're goin' to have a torchlight procession," her daughter continued with unction, "and they're goin' to burn a guy of the old judge whatsisname what's against them."

"The Foxteths' people had a judge among them," Granny Deeps ruminated. "William Foxteth, the third son. It ain't Billy Foxteth?"

"No, ma."

Apparently satisfied, Mrs Deeps settled back. "The Foxteths wouldn't uv been mixed up with no strikes," she announced. "In the tallow and hides, the Foxteths."

The afternoon sun simmered down drowsily. Around the high paling fence of Hutchison's yard the men talked in small groups. Other groups gathered to watch them. A hot wind full of little particles of grit swirled up from the baked desolation where a year or so before Plug Alley had sweltered.

Mrs Blore, stout veteran of the demolition, passed on her way to the hotel with a billy-can for the evening beer.

"Hot, ain't it, Beattie?" she greeted Mrs Deeps's daughter.

"It is that. Know anything for Saturday?"

Mrs Blore paused and mopped her forehead. "They say Huxter has a chance. Freddy, Ada's husband, he put all his strike pay on it last Saturday and it came home six to one. 'Tisn't often, though, you get a horse winning two big races runnin'. That's why I'm thinking twice about backing it."

"How's Fred's head?" Beattie asked. "It was a nasty cut."

"Oh, he's all right. Went off to his picketin' on time this mornin'. No picketin', no strike pay, as 'e says."

"Why are they picketin' Hutchison's yard? It's on'y a little place compared to some."

"It's got scabs in it, same as the rest of them," Mrs Blore returned virtuously. " 'E may say it's a joinery but they been sending the wood 'ere instead of to the big timber-yard. Bob Noblett's boy told the men." Noticing a friend hurrying up the street she called, "How's y'r bowels, May?"

The friend, a small aggrieved-looking woman in a salmon-pink silk jumper, joined the group on the doorstep.

"I didn't get a wink of sleep, dear," she said impressively. "I said to Joe this morning that if I don't get better soon, I'll have to go up and get something from the chemist."

Mrs Blore swung her billy-can and fanned herself. "Did you hear about Mrs Simons? They say the cyst has bust and the doctor 'olds out absolutely no 'ope."

"You can't tell me," Mrs Deeps's daughter put in with languid sympathy, "that it ain't all his doin'. Goes and takes a job as a volunteer and gets himself fractured. I don't wonder the woman's frightened herself into a cyst. And them four poor little children! What's to become of them, I don't know. Their father a scab and their mother in hospital. Afternoon, Mrs Sampson."

Mrs Sampson, having sighted Mrs Blore waddling slowly towards the hotel, had overtaken her. "I jus' seen you goin' up and I says, there goes Annie. I'm thinkin' of droppin' in for a wine meself and it'll be company if I go with 'er. How are you, love?"

"I was just tellin' May 'ere about poor Mrs Simons worry-ing 'erself into a cyst," Mrs Deeps's daughter explained.

"But you must remember, dear," the small aggrieved woman reminded them, "that the Foveaux Women's Commit-tee went to see her and asked as nice as could be for her to persuade her husband not to work. You can't blame the men when they're only doin' their duty." She looked important. "I'm late myself and we women on the committee are helpin' the men picket." She turned back to call: "Are you coming to the mass demonstration, Beattie?"

"I might," Mrs Deeps's daughter responded lazily. "Depends if there's going to be a row. I jus' love a good row."

"We're getting up a deputation to old Hutchison," May said, returning a few paces. "Will you come to that?"

"I dunno."

"You can count me in, May," Mrs Blore said massively. "I

got a few things I'd like to say to that rat meself."

"All right. And you can bring any others you can."

"That was a good turn out when we went down and interviewed the boss at Carlingford's," Mrs Blore said approvingly. "They tried to stop us an' we went through 'em like so much rhubarb. You should 'ave seen the look on the old crawler when we knocked 'is secretary outer the way an' bust in 'is office. We told 'im what we thought of 'im. I got a 'andful of the secretary's 'air and I got it yet."

"Yes, I was sorry I missed that," Mrs Deeps's daughter said regretfully. "It's little enough fun you get these days. I missed them chasin' the scabs on Monday too and the p'liceman gettin' 'it on the head."

"Come on, Flora," Mrs Sampson said impatiently. "We ain't got all day if you want a drink an' be back before they start to escort 'em 'ome."

Mrs Deeps's daughter looked disapprovingly at their retreating backs. "I wonder they let women like them on the committee," she exclaimed. "Drinkin' as they do. It's no thanks to them Foveaux's got a good committee."

"What's that?" her mother asked suddenly. "There's a lot of good in Foveaux."

"Yes, ma. You'd better be coming in now."

"I've seen 'em hung in chains." Mrs Deeps said with great satisfaction. "Ah, for less than strikes."

Her daughter helped Mrs Deeps creakingly out of her chair and supported her as she tottered in. As she did so a truck rumbled by towards the timber-yard to be welcomed with a shower of stones.

"Hurry up, ma," Beattie said impatiently. "You don't want me to miss it, do you? The whistl'll be blowin' in a minute."

"Hung in chains they were," Mrs Deeps said decisively. "It did them good, too. They needed it."

II

"I never seen such a mob in me life," the great McCullemy said in weary reproof. "The first job is to train the pickets. I seen one fellow the other day trying to break a scab's arm across his knee." He shook his head. "Willin' but raw. Now one blow with an iron bar would uv done the trick for him in a second."

"But you can break a chap's arm by twisting it under your knee," another of the picket captains contended. "You get his wrist like this and his arm so and that's that. Maybe the picket had heard of the trick and had just got it wrong, Mac."

"Well, he'd no right to get it wrong. By the time he'd finished bending the scab this way and that to see how he'd break best, he'd have half the coppers in Sydney on top of him."

They were sitting in the old hay and fodder store which had been converted into the Foveaux Strike Committee's headquarters. Legitimately speaking, the timber strike was not Foxeaux's fight, since most of the timber-yards were down by the waterside; but as a lot of the men from the Foot worked in the timber-yards when they could get a job, Foveaux felt it was involved. The cabinet works and the building trade, too, were held up for lack of timber and the joiners had plenty of time on their hands. The strikers and their sympathizers gathered in the old corn and fodder store nominally rented by Jock Jamieson and discussed ways and means of dealing with volunteer labour; and when not in the picket line it was here that the choicer spirits were to be found.

In the early days of the strike, when picketing was going on in an orderly, not to say sedate, manner, with a minimum of bloodshed, the leaders had seen the advisability of weeding out the more daring and active of the pickets for special duty. These, two hundred strong, were divided into little groups of five, quickly earning for themselves the unkind title of the "basher gangs". Of the basher gangs the great McCullemy was ringleader, head plotter and chief adviser.

The older men who could not picket would follow a volunteer home and find out his address for the gangs who would one night wait upon the volunteer and dissuade him from working at the timber-yards. After which the volunteer would be carried away in an ambulance with sundry fractures and his place would be vacant in the morning.

Jack Noblett, Bob's youngest son, was in the great McCullemy's own gang. Jack was a big, hulking youngster, a preliminary boxer for a time, but now, as he said, "scratching for a living", mostly round the docks or the timber-yards. The strike had been meat and drink to him. He regarded his brother Freddy's frettings as the wailings of a babe, not a unionist and a cabinet-maker. Jack had none of Freddy's love of his trade. In a choice between working and fighting he preferred to fight. His prowess as a basher had spread from his wife to the neighbours long before the strike started, Jack had been too young to go to the war, and the timber strike was his first real chance of massacre on a large scale.

It was he who, at the beginning of the strike, instructed the uninitiated in the making of black jacks and he would discuss with loving detail the claims of mahogany and the tipping of a truncheon with lead. Going to the police station one night to bail out a comrade, he had remarked to the rest of the gang, "I suppose I'd better do something with these. Don't want to get lumbered with them on me." And fishing out a vicious assortment of old bicycle-chain and chunks of lead from his pockets, he had dropped them in the shadow of the police grass plot to be resumed on his return.

He would relate with detail the grievous loss of his revolver when, being pursued by the police, he had thrown it into a clump of bushes in Foveaux Park. "And when I went back to get it," he mourned indignantly, "some cow had pinched it."

Jack was in and out of jail with the others of the basher gangs regularly; and although the committee publicly repudiated him, his strike pay rose to five pounds a week while in jail. As he left three pounds of it to his wife who also collected prisoner's aid and the dole, she did not mind his absence very much.

Old Noblett regarded his son's activities with disapproval. "Strikes," he would say, " 'ave to be won an' scabs 'ave to be knocked out. But even when bashin' a scab, Jack, you got to remember 'e's a 'uman bein' like yourself wiv a wife what'll mourn 'im if 'e pegs out."

This seemed to Jack a weak and unnecessarily sentimental attitude.

The other persons in the "Committee Hall" regarded the little group in the corner with respect. They were preparing the place for a dance and between sweeping and hanging coloured paper festoons along the rafters, they would shout cheerful remarks to the elect sitting in the corner with their heads together planning some coup. It made the members of the Foveaux Committee proud to have such reputable persons as McCullemy, Jock Jamieson and young Noblett doing their planning in a corner of the corn and fodder store. It lent lustre to the place. Men in dirty old sweaters would lounge in and give their reports and lounge out again; but the group in the corner sat interminably rolling cigarettes, interminably talking in low tones.

Jamieson, providentially out of work again, had been made chairman of the Foveaux Committee on the strength of his reputation, but he was regarded by the basher gang as too cold and cautious.

"I tell ye," he advised McCullemy, "that it's a bad move to burn the ballot papers. The thing is not to give them anything on ye."

"The orders are," McCullemy responded, "that the picket captains lead their men down to the Trades Hall and each man is to put his paper in the sacks. They'll be taken out and burned in the streets, after that the torchlight procession will form up and march to the park, where the judge's guy will be burnt."

"O.K.," said the deputy picket captain, trying to look nonchalant.

Only Jamieson scowled. "It's a bad move to give them anything . . ." he was beginning; but a sign from McCullemy stopped him.

"It's all right, Jock," McCullemy said. "We aren't really going to burn them. We'll ring the changes, see, and burn some sacks of old paper and mark the ballot papers and send 'em in afterwards ourselves. But no one'll know."

Jamieson rubbed his long chin, then nodded. "So long," he said, "as you don't go sending in more No votes than there's men."

"Leave that to us."

Later the judge was to remark that there was a strange similarity of handwriting noticeable in the votes recorded from the strikers of New South Wales.

"And now," McCullemy said in a low voice, "what're you doing Tuesday night?"

Again Jamieson rubbed his chin dubiously. "I'm being watched," he mentioned. "But I can shake them off. What's on?"

"Young Noblett says there's a consignment of timber in Black Wattle Bay. Tuesday should be a good night."

Jamieson nodded. It would not be the first punt loaded with timber that a few cautious men and a couple of auger holes at the water-line had sent canting on its side with the timber slipping down almost noislessly into the water to float harbourwards and be a danger to shipping. Later, when the owners, finding their volunteer labour was too scared to come to the yards by land, hired launches to bring them up the harbour, the same methods of holes, cautiously bored near the waterline of the launches on dark nights, produced embarrassing results for the volunteers.

"I'll be there," Jamieson said slowly. "The same place?" McCullemy nodded.

As Jamieson walked away the group in the corner was still sitting quietly discussing the process whereby a handful of Condy's crystals placed in a stack of timber would, with a little glycerine poured on it, presently smoulder and burst into flames. A slight frown creased Jamieson's forehead. The whole strike seemed to him to be very carelessly and crudely conducted. The Central Strike Committee was spending money like water just to bash up a few hundred volunteers and close down the yards. But where were they progressing? "No theory," he told himself. "No theory. They rush at a red rag like a bull." If the strike were a general strike, or if they could make it a general strike, he could see some sense in it, but these crude picketings and forays seemed to him to be lacking in finesse. No subtlety. Too much like children with their little plots and plans.

Going down the flight of steep wooden steps, he cannoned into old Duncan who was coming up them like a schoolboy.

"How's things, Jock?" he beamed.

Jamieson nodded solemnly. He had a respect for Duncan, not for his eternal enthusiasms, which Jock slightly disparaged, but for the real efficiency with which the veteran had cut out drink and was guiding round the suburbs an old car he hardly knew how to handle. Duncan was collecting nearly two hundred pounds a week for the strike fund and he was as honest as the day. His books and receipts were always in order. A man to be trusted, although Jamieson felt he had long outgrown the old socialist's tutelage.

"How's Elsie and the kids?" Duncan puffed.

"Fine," Jamieson said laconically. The shadow which hardly ever left his face deepened. Elsie, working all day in a café and part of the night with the Women's Auxiliary, was wearing herself out. And for what? The strike would be broken. That Jamieson could predict. He felt rather tired sometimes thinking of the waste of it all. The strike had to be fought out. That was all there was to it, and however much he might disapprove of the catch-as-catch-can methods of the fight, it was all training. Men who had never done anything except lean against a post, and discuss the chances of the entrants for the Melbourne Cup, were out in the picket line. Women, who had previously been content to help run stalls for St Brigid's Church Bazaar, found themselves dignified as vice-presidents of the relief committee, distributing vegetables to strikers' wives. They were learning, he coldly decided, they were being trained for the coming revolution.

"By the way, Jock, I think I've got another recruit for the Women's Auxiliary," Duncan called happily. "Remember young Linda Montague? I thought she could do some work for the *Militant Woman*."

Jamieson nodded abstractedly. He did not approve of the women who hung round the strike, the strikers' wives and female relatives. He admitted that it was the "right line", that they should be used, but Elsie was the only woman who seemed to be able to stay normal. All the rest got shrill and hysterical. Deep down in Jock Jamieson there was a contempt for all women except Elsie. Certainly the women had broken up the Industrial "Peace" Conference and done other good work, but they fought among themselves. They seemed to be either stout beefy old matrons who had been in every Labor battle since the split in the Foveaux branch in 1919, or small women with the manners of a piece of barbed wire, indefatigable in collecting, vociferous in grievance, shedding leaflets on all occasions.

Worse than the old battlers were the young muscular militants who, full of their own importance and determined to be the Florence Nightingale of the picket line, went out looking for jail sentences and newspaper notices and got them. Being frog-marched to a police station seemed to be their idea of sport, and clawing bits out of constables a legitimate pleasure. They were the spiritual descendants of the suffragettes and twice as virulent. The more elderly female warriors thought them unnecessarily red in politics and lips. They would go out all day raising money for the strike and distract the attention of the younger strikers all night. At dances, district meetings, house-to-house visits, or picketing, their malicious, uncontrollable and headstrong behaviour did more than any bashings of volunteers to create that atmosphere of excitement in which they delighted. When not engaged in mobbing policemen or tongue-lashing "scabs", they could always be depended upon to raise a fight among themselves.

"You'd better tell her to go and see Emily Anseer," Jamieson said in reply to Duncan's question. "That is, if you think she's useful."

One woman more or less made little difference as far as he could see; but it was his duty to draw everybody into the revolutionary movement, however much he might disapprove of them. More and more he found himself disapproving, not only of wealthy persons, bosses, their wives and families, office-workers who wouldn't be organized and preferred to play tennis, workers who were not class-conscious, and others of whom it was legitimate to disapprove. He found himself disapproving of and disliking even his own associates.

"Sometimes I get thinking, Elsie," he said a little wistfully to his wife who was just getting ready for work as he reached home, "that we'd be better off if I could get a job in the country and take you an' the kids out of this." He made an abrupt gesture. "Cut it all out. Foveaux, the committee, the union work — even the revolution. The whole issue."

Elsie looked at him in amazement.

"But, Scotty," she said, "you'd go mad in a week."

"I don't know," he said gloomily. "What's the use of it all? Maybe there'll never be a revolution. Maybe they'll just go muddling along."

She hugged him.

"I wish I'd never come back to Foveaux," he went on. "We were all right up north."

"And we're all right here," she said cheerfully. "Now you get these ideas out of your head. Of course there's going to be a revolution." Her manner of speaking was much that of giving a child a favourite toy. "And you'll be secretary of the union next year and Holbein promised you a job next month and Hugh's getting a job in the button factory."

His mouth was grim. "Times," he said slowly, "I wish I'd never married you."

The horror in Elsie's eyes caught him up. " 'Tisn't that you haven't been the best wife any man could have. I thank God for you, Else. I couldn't live without you and you know it." The fear died out of her eyes. "But I didn't treat ye fair. If ye hadn't married me—"

"If I hadn't married you," she said contemptuously, "I'd be a dirty, slatternly woman, standing at the door of one of the houses in a back street, idling and gossiping with the neighbours. With nothing in me life but work and scandal." She grinned. "I might have married Curly Thompson. Gosh, what a life!"

Jamieson was still sombre. "Has he been pesterin' ye again?"

She shook her head hastily. One of the basher gang would have gone out after Curly, and then it might have been the worse for Jock. "Don't worry, Scotty, me son," she said affectionately. "I've got you and you've got me and"— she smiled as though he were a small boy —"the revolution."

"Sometimes," Jamieson said suspiciously, "I believe you don't care tuppence about my worrrk and the revolution."

Elsie stuck on her hat with a careless pat. "Maybe you're

right, darlin'. Get yourself some tea and see the kids have some." And with a blown kiss she was off to her job.

Jamieson sat for a time tapping the table. It wasn't much of a life for Else, he thought; but then it wasn't much of a life for any of them. A vision rose in his mind's eye of some cottages he had seen on the northern coalfields. Blossomy places with little fields for a cow and some chickens behind. And immediately he began to despise himself for his weakness. He was not just a man, he was a member of the working class; he was a class-conscious militant with more to do than enjoy himself. The Presbyterian conscience of his Scotch ancestors rose within him and disapproved. What the working class needed was not muscle but determination and plans. Discipline, more discipline, and then more discipline. He had fought for discipline, for organized, sober planning and discipline all his life. And he could not discipline his own desires. Instead of looking forward to a glorious revolution, he was thinking in terms of private property, of a small cottage with Elsie no longer working in a hot café, but hanging out white sheets in a green paddock with trees around it. Of himself sitting on the doorstep with a pipe and a newspaper and, maybe, doing a bit of gardening. His mouth curled in contempt. No better than a petty bourgeois scab. He who prided himself on his discipline!

### III

"Of course we'll be awfully pleased to have you, love," Emily Anseer said in a patronizing and gracious condescension. "Although you don't really belong to the working class."

"I thought on my afternoon off . . ." Linda said, and halted. No one knew the amount of sacrifice needed to volunteer her afternoon off to help the timber workers. Bud was generous as far as pay went, but he expected her to put in overtime on the shop. Sundays and Wednesday afternoons were Linnie's only free times.

"We need everyone we can interest," Emily Anseer said in her throaty voice. "Everyone." A good contact, she thought, she can be used, even if she is only a narrow little petty bour-

geois. "I don't suppose you've seen anything of the actual
strike," she said, with a faint disparagement, as one cutting
away the bad part of a cabbage that is still cookable. "I mean
you don't learn much just frequenting these arty radical clubs.
You haven't seen anything of actual working-class tactics?"

"Have a job," Miss Montague explained. "Work pretty long
hours."

She sat neatly with her little patent leather shoes side by side,
as though she were answering questions at a Sunday School,
her eyes on Miss Anseer, who someone, probably Wilfred, had
once described glowingly as the "Madonna of Militants".
Rather too glowingly, Linda thought. Miss Anseer sprawled
across a bench, rolling cigarettes, her untidy black hair pushed
under a faded beret. The most noticeable thing about her was
her clothes. Jock Jamieson, when he took the soap-box, would
begin to get undressed, tearing off first his tie, then his collar,
his coat and waistcoat. Emily Anseer, in an emotional crisis,
became as disordered in her raiment as any ancient matron of
Israel. The other lady pickets could usually manage to arrive
at the police station in a fairly tidy condition; but Emily always
had her attire half ripped off her. This was less attributable to
police action than to the failure of an assortment of old safety
pins that held her together. Surely, Linnie thought in feminine
revolt, there was no need for Miss Anseer's legs, clad in brown
cotton stockings with the black elastic garters all too apparent,
to be crossed at quite such an angle. It wouldn't make her any
less militant to pull up those same stockings so that they
didn't wrinkle round her ankles.

"A lot of us," Miss Anseer was saying with the use of the
plural that had so irritated Linnie in Wilfred, "are going down
to encourage the pickets. They should be here now." Her tone
was tolerant.

"It's a wonder," an acid voice put in from behind her, "that
they've the strength left to get down to the picket line, the
way they stay up all night. Like a lot of cats."

The lady who had spoken was grey-haired and bespectacled.
She did not look up from her typewriter as she spoke, but
went on tapping busily. There was no Madonna of the working
class about her, Linnie thought. She was business-like. Her

clothes looked as though they had come out of the poor-box, but they were neat. She formed a striking contrast to the sprawling, leggy Emily Anseer.

"Now, comrade," that lady said almost reprovingly. "I don't think there's any necessity for that attitude." She turned to Linnie. "You knew Comrade Wilston, didn't you? I remember him mentioning you were on some slumming committee or something."

Her tone warmed at this mention of Wilfred. Linnie could see Emily cataloguing her as one of Wilfred's discarded loves. "Completely frigid," Wilfred's sour verdict had actually been on Linnie. "One of these born virgins. Likely to die like it." The same could not be said of Miss Anseer who distributed her favours so liberally that a meeting of protest had been called by the male members of the committee who, bringing Miss Anseer up for censure, had been discomfited by a fit of hysterics and the reminder that most of them had at one time or another seen fit to be much less censorious.

"But, comrade," one of them had protested, "we agree that you have a right to live your own life and enjoy your own freedom and anything else you may say, but we can't have the committee disrupted and people accusing us of loose morals. You know it alienates the working class if they think you have loose morals."

Whereupon Comrade Anseer, sobbing upon the table with an unecessary display of bosom, had been so abjectly penitent that the censors divided their time between embarrassment and enjoyment. Shortly afterwards Miss Anseer, speaking in a neighbourhood entirely inhabited by hard-working and godly soap-makers, had, in response to a question from the audience, launched into a glowing eulogy of free-love as exemplified in the Soviet Union. The soap-makers had been so incensed that they withdrew their support from the timber strike.

The lady at the typewriter, who answered to the name of Comrade Stanchen, rose, shook her papers together and began putting them into envelopes. It was she who presently rescued Linda from a catechism extending to her family life, her morals, her ancestors and other pertinent particulars.

"I'm going out to Herricks', the big timber-yards," Mrs

Stanchen said casually. "If the comrade would care to come with me, she'll get an idea of what's happening."

Emily Anseer, who had already decided that Miss Montague's brevity of speech indicated that she was a paid spy of the timber combine, endeavoured to caution Mrs Stanchen, but the would-be recruit was already gratefully accepting the offer.

"We'll walk," Mrs Stanchen said bluntly when they got outside. "I haven't the money for a tram."

Miss Montague walked beside her, wondering if it was bad form to offer to pay the fare.

The timber-yard did not look to Linda to be much out of the ordinary. A few policemen stood about in casual attitudes and a few stolid men lounged on the opposite pavement. A bleak gritty wind, smelling of salt and wood shavings, came up the narrow street from the flickering grey of the harbour and the great piles of yellow timber beyond the dirty grey paling fence with the faded notice, "G. Herricks, Timber Yard," upon it.

To be near the water at any time was to Linda Montague exhilarating, and this feeling was intensified by the heady and dangerous sense that she was there with people engaged in what old Mr Duncan would call "revolutionary activities".

"There should be eight thousand men here this afternoon," Mrs Stanchen said in a rather tired voice. "This is to be the response to the No-Picketing Act. The men won't be here much before five, but that won't be long now. The tram stop'll be the real centre of trouble."

They moved to the tram stop at the top of the narrow street leading to the yard. Here Mrs Stanchen introduced Linda to a group of young timber workers who showed great eagerness to be helpful and explanatory.

"Herricks is one of the biggest men in the timber combine," a young fellow with a dirty cap over one eye explained. "That's why the mass picket is concentrating on his yard. He's better at organizing his scab labour than the others."

There was a stream of people unostentatiously moving in on the area in which they were standing. They seemed to come from nowhere. One minute there were only a few men and women grouped under the shop verandas and shortly afterwards the pavement was crowded.

Up the road from the city came a procession, a long procession, carrying tiny placards on the end of extremely useful-looking garden stakes.

"Ten thousand of them stakes they bought," the young picket informed Linnie under his breath. "Hooray, here she comes!"

From the opposite direction the black maria lumbered up and decanted a sergeant and a squad of police before modestly backing down a handy alley. The sergeant glanced at the oncoming procession and the masses of people on the footpath and then gave rapid orders. A policeman on a motor-cycle roared away. Another went off to telephone for reinforcements.

Up the street from the yards a big timber lorry came grinding in second gear, the driver grimly honking his horn at the surge of hostile people. A storm of booing went up as the crowd and the police closed round the lorry. The head of the procession with McCullemy and company in the front rank arrived just as it crawled through to the hilltop. Being men of action they neither booed nor hurled insults at the driver. McCullemy and Noblett, their little placards no hindrance to their smiting power, leapt on the policeman beside the lorry driver and knocked him from his hold. Immediately a confused struggle began round the lorry, the police surging in from one direction, the procession closing in from the other. Strikers got in each other's way in their endeavours to smash up the lorry. Half a dozen eager huskies sprang up behind and began throwing down timber into the roadway while others tore at the spark plugs, the lorry sliding dangerously downhill until brought up with a jolt against the kerb.

In the midst Emily Anseer, all flying hair and garments, was busily hacking the ankles of two policemen painfully endeavouring to drag her to the black maria.

"To me, comrades," she called dramatically; and a body of young strikers, plunging to the rescue, found themselves outnumbered two to one, and were in their turn lugged away, the police working on the procession with the tenacity of ants attacking a wriggling caterpillar.

The excitement of the onlookers, the block in the traffic as they surged across the road, the ringing of tram-bells striving to get through, and the furious battles proceeding here and there made it difficult to tell friends from foes.

"They're taking the scabs to the other tram stop," someone shouted; and immediately a rush set in. But the volunteers were already loaded on the trams and on their way citywards amid howls of baffled fury. The policemen began to look less worried; but they counted too soon on outwitting the strike committee. The rearguard, waiting its chance, leapt on the tram; and one picket, clambering dangerously out on the swaying car, dragged at the rope holding the pole on the wire and cut it. With a clang and a shower of sparks the pole bounced from its moorings and the tram slowed down in an eddying mass of strikers who pounced into the tram compartments and began dealing out "stouch" to the terrified passengers.

"This is where you get off," roared Jack Noblett, lifting a writhing man bodily and throwing him out on the pavement.

"Give it to 'em! Put in the boot, boys!" the onlookers encouraged.

In the midst of cries, shouts and police orders, motor-cars hooting, tram-bells ringing, and the home-going traffic trying to fight its way through eight thousand strikers, the discouragement of volunteers proceeded with enthusiasm. As the non-combatants sorted themselves out at a safe distance, it became a matter of individual fights, with a group of pickets chasing a volunteer here, and there a policeman chasing a group of pickets. Little by little the police gathered their catch around the black maria which had roared up conveniently, and began to bundle them in.

"I say, have you seen my hat?" Jack Noblett was appealing to the crowd. "Here, mate. See if you can see my hat, will you? 'Tisn't mine, it's me brother's." His condition of arrest did not seem to worry him. "Pass the word along for my hat," he shouted. And then, with a desperate plunge, he was out of the grip of the policemen holding him and off into the thick of the crowd.

One of the police stooped down and picked up a dirty be-trampled object. "He left his hat," he said thoughtfully, "after all."

"Hang on to it," the sergeant advised. "It'll be useful evidence."

Suddenly, it seemed, the ferment died down. The trams were on their way again. The fight was over. The crowd, thinning down like mist, had recollected that it was tea-time. Policemen straightened their helmets. The traffic moved on. Linda, separated from her companions, moved off home alone.

"Well?" Rolfe said with a grin as she came into the kitchen. He was sitting with Bramley, their chairs tilted back, their feet on the back veranda rail. "How'd you get on? What-ho the girl militant!"

"Somehow," Linda said sadly, hanging up her hat, "I think they're doing very well without me. Any tea?"

# CHAPTER 2

## I

The Red Menace, it seemed to Honest John, had suddenly directed all the force of its insidious powers upon him. He went about explaining in a heart-broken voice that as part owner of Hutchison and Company, he was powerless to modify that company's policy. He had gone to church on Industrial Peace Sunday; he had worked hard and long hours trying to get the misguided strikers to go back to work. He had even adopted a conciliatory attitude to Duncan when that beastly old blister had the hide to buttonhole him in the street. Honest John had done everything, as he maintained, except agree to restore the old conditions of work. If the strikers held out against the owner's interests, he, as a timber merchant, could only approve of the justifiably severe sentences the magistracy was imposing.

"I am as anxious as anyone," Honest John declared, "that an agreement be reached as soon as possible. All the employers ask is reason and justice. We will not be cowed by truculence, terrorism or the snatch-and-grab policy of the unions."

In this noble British attitude Honest John persevered against odds. More and more of his volunteer labour was being carried into hospital on a stretcher. His old-time popularity in Foveaux was gone for ever. His manager rang up early in the strike to say that every window in the yard office was smashed. A group of shabby, angry women forced themselves into Honest John's private office screaming in the one breath for the reinstatement of their husbands and his blood. When he found that someone had set his car alight in its garage, he merely collected the insurance with a feeling of happy relief and a determination never to drive a car again. Some even contended that Honest John had set his own car on fire. But as the strike wore on, he began to live in a panic of plots and whisperings and hatred; all, he felt, the work of the Red Menace.

"Damn it," he roared at his wife, returning from one more day of business, mayoral and legislative responsibility, to trip over the watering can which the gardener had left in the path. "Isn't it enough to have every Tom, Dick and Harry in this blasted place trying to murder me without you sitting there like a stuffed mummy?" The gardener must be directly in the pay of the Red Menace and his wife didn't seem to care.

She merely said: "You'll worry yourself into a breakdown, John. You will, really." Which was not at all helpful.

Honest John thought of issuing revolvers to his workmen for their protection, but hastily decided against the idea when he remembered how one nervous volunteer had put a bullet through another volunteer's hat.

In the night Honest John lay awake, tossing and turning and cursing the bedclothes. Years ago, he brooded gloomily, when he had been a young enthusiastic socialist, confrère of that damn fool Duncan, he had firmly believed in the class struggle between employee and employer and had exulted in the idea of a society in which no one would own any of the means of production. This had seemed a glorious far-off scheme to be heralded with rejoicings; but as Honest John grew older and wiser, even as a Labor politician, he had seen a greater light. There was not only a class struggle; there was an individual struggle, to him a much more important affair. Recognition of this had returned him to the council as an independent candidate year after year, although Foveaux was strongly Labor in sympathy. He believed even old Duncan supported him as "a lesser evil". He was independent by nature and disposition, and they all admired him for it. But now he was afflicted by nightmares.

As soon as he shut his hot eyelids a vision would rise behind them of a great tidal wave surging up from the Foot of Foveaux. It towered higher and higher while he stood in that cold-rooted horror peculiar to dreams. The great grey wall of water rose until he had to crane his neck to see the curling foam on the crest. It seemed that the foam was a foam of faces — faces he had seen in the mob around the timber-yard — faces of those greasy swine who called themselves "leaders"; faces of the screaming women in his office, hard faces, fierce faces, ravaged faces, alien faces, some of them with slant eyes; and while he stood powerless and sweating, the great grey wave would crash down on him and on Foveaux. In the horror of it he woke up.

"Why the devil don't you do something about that grocer?" he snarled to his wife at breakfast. "The coffee's poisonous. Here, take it away. I can't drink it."

He snatched at the newspaper and devoured that rather than his breakfast. All this hot air denouncing the increase of four hours, reductions from three shillings to twenty-three shillings a week according to margins of skill, dismissals of twenty-five per cent adult labour and replacement with juveniles in proportion of one to three! The unions whining again!

"I suppose," he said bitterly, "that they're going to let these fiends go on hitting innocent people with bits of gas-pipe and get away with it. All in league. The police are as bad as the rest of them."

Only one item in the paper gave him real satisfaction and that was the report that a notorious basher called Fred Noblett had been identified by the police. A constable had picked up the man's hat and noticed that it had sweat stain on the front of the hat-band. The police had enlarged the Press photographs of the procession and there in the front row was the man in the sweat-stained hat. He was returned his headgear with six months' jail thrown in. His solicitor's plea that the Press photograph fitted any one of the four Noblett brothers was treated as waste of the court's time.

"Clever work, clever work," Honest John exulted to his secretary.

"They're putting over a roughie at Central," the secretary, a lounging, pimply ex great-public-school-boy, mentioned casually. It was astonishing the number of things the dull-looking fish picked up by associating with reporters. "When a cop brings in one of these strikers, a sympathetic bobby down at the court rings up the Trades Hall. The Trades Hall mob race down and ask how much to get him out. Even if the bail's a thousand, they've got it with them in notes. The police have to let him go. They can't refuse to take the money but they tell him to be back in a couple of hours for the line-up. As soon as his mates get him away, they dress him up in a bowler hat and a double-breasted grey suit with a carnation and send him back to the line-up looking like a feast of song." He giggled airily. "No end of a joke, when the poor volunteer comes to identify a guy in a dirty jersey and old cap who bashed him."

Honest John did not think it was funny. He told the youth so with some heat. There were times when he cursed the day he had expansively suggested to the rich and influential squatter who had sired the brat that young Braceford get "some experience" as his secretary. Honest John could not sack Braceford without alienating his old man, though Braceford's superior college airs, which Honest John termed "swank", made him boil. Between Braceford and the Red Menace he almost preferred the Red Menace.

Soon after the mass picketing effort outside Herricks's timber-yard Honest John was gladdened by the rumour that the Central Disputes Committee had been arrested.

"Now you'll see something at last," he boomed. "This is more like it." But again Braceford was there with confidential information concerning the arrest of the seven members. He joyfully told Honest John how the secretary of the committee, seeing the seven arrested chiefs sitting cheek by jowl with the detectives in the outer office, had quietly entered the inner office by another door, unlocked the safe, collected all books and accounts, handed them to a confederate to leave in some other union's room until the police departed and then returned to the office to await arrest.

"Where are the books?" the inspector had demanded.

"We don't keep any books," the secretary responded with a laconic lack of interest. "We're not as efficient as all that."

"Well, come on. Where are your accounts? You must keep some records."

"I keep them all in my head," the secretary responded dreamily. "A marvellous memory I have."

He went unarrested for lack of evidence while the police scraped through the waste-paper baskets and collected stray pieces of paper about the office floor.

"Disgraceful," Honest John boiled. "If I had them I'd show them!" The seven were committed for trial on "serious charges", and Honest John again brightened. But the unions, or the Red Menace, working in their usual stealthy way had a list of the jury panel three weeks before the trial. All the jurymen, it found, were to be drawn from a distant suburb of wealthy people unlikely to be favourably disposed towards the strikers. The Red Menace set to work sounding out a friend of a friend of a friend of the unconscious juryman to be. If the reply brought back was: "Yes, he thinks the timber workers are putting up a jolly good fight, more power to their elbow", that juryman went down on the list the union was preparing. The defence had fifty-six challenges, eight for each man. At the table in front of the court, sat a reverend, hoary old lawyer. When he raised his pencil the defence challenged the juryman; when he lowered it, the juryman was accepted. The fourteen days' examination was a lawyer's picnic at seventy-two guineas a day; but at the end the jury, composed of doctors, dentists, professional and business men of good standing, acquitted the seven representatives of the Red Menace without leaving the box.

Honest John went home and took to his bed.

"Cheer up, chief," Braceford offered coolly. "The strike's as good as broken. They can only stand on the bridges and throw stones on the roof of the steam tugs, or basket bombs through some poor devil's window. They're licked."

"I don't care," Honest John said feebly. "It's the injustice of it I can't stand. Lemme alone."

He was ordered, as usual, a long holiday. The strain of fighting the Red Menace had begun to tell on his weakened constitution. Everyone except himself had lost their heads.

"This diabolical thing, Communism," he declared in one of the last speeches before his breakdown, "menaces, pursues, and strangles its human prey, mangling the souls and branding the bodies of its victims with its own hell-fires."

A strange, unnatural light in which assets looked like so much waste paper was beginning to transfigure the business landscape. Weather prophets of commerce were predicting a cyclone and were spawning articles which explained away the depression together with the gold standard, exchange rates and currency. A willy-willy of words sprang up, a blown dust-spout in the path of an oncoming storm.

In his place of banishment Honest John leant over the beautifully hygienic pens, a dirty felt hat pulled over his eyes, and watched Eustachia II and her litter taking their morning nourishment. Beyond him the lucerne fields stretched to a line of willows by the creek. A hundred miles, he reflected, separated him from the smell of the city, from the whirlwind of trouble about inflation, rationalization of industry and equality of sacrifice. At first he had treated this depression as a slight trade fluctuation that would pass as quickly as it came; but, as his health began to improve, he bullied the assistant pig-walloper, whom he regarded as his only friend, into bringing him some newspapers. Then it appeared that the fall of Wall Street, over-production, the Red Menace and Saturn in the ascendant were all combining for further trouble.

"The way to forget about the depression," one of Honest John's fellow mayors was reported as saying, "is to own a bowl of goldfish." Naturally he was opening a goldfish exhibition. Cures for the depression were as rife as curses.

A few days later Honest John read that a mob of unemployed persons had marched to Parliament House, but were dissuaded from their intentions by police four deep. Obviously he must go back. He had an uneasy feeling that in his absence the Government had lost its grip. He would risk death by driving down with his speed fiend of a manager on the weekend. He would see for himself just how the Red Menace was shaping.

## I I

On the Monday morning Honest John's wife, terrified, was trying to dissuade Braceford from seeing him.

"He'll have a stroke," she kept repeating. "You mustn't tell him."

"But he'll murder me if he finds out when it's too late to do anything," the youth muttered sullenly. "He has to be told some time."

He entered the darkened room cautiously. "How is it, J.H.?" he whispered, all the superior airs gone out of him.

"Not so good, Brace, not so good. Pull up that damn blind and let's look at you."

Poor Honest John, in the light with which his secretary obligingly flooded the room, seemed to have shrunk. His look of puffy affability had collapsed into a system of lines and wrinkles and little waves of flesh. His white hair was standing up untidily, his beard was unkempt, his hands on the counterpane no longer looked powerful; they were small and slack with big veins standing out on the freckled horny skin.

"What's wrong?" he asked irritably. "What's in that paper?"

"Your wife wanted me to wait until you were better," his secretary said apologetically. "But I didn't see how I could. This is this morning's paper."

Honest John snatched it from his hand. "Where are my glasses? Blast it. This the article?" He mumbled under his breath. "Foveaux Council Muddle. Ratepapers Demand Inquiry. Questions in House." And further down a subheading announced: "Government To Appoint Commission."

John Hutchison flung the paper on the bed and sat for a minute in silence, his brilliantly striped pyjamas and pudgy figure at odds with the energy that suddenly revived in his face.

"I might have known that as soon as my back was turned," he said offensively, "some goat'd go talking. Reporters!" He snorted bitterly. "Someone's been having drinks with a reporter."

Braceford quailed and Honest John glared at him accusingly.

"I wouldn't be surprised," he said, "if—"

"You're wrong, J.H.," the secretary babbled. "I didn't open my mouth. But I know how they may have got at it. A couple of us met a chap I know down at the Metropole — runs a concern for making walls and roofings — and he introduced me to his partner. Well, I was just telling this chap how you sidetracked a mob of fools who wanted to build flats all over the resumptions and he was terribly amused. Asked a lot of questions and—"

"You bloody fool," Hutchison said. "Look in that cupboard and see if you can find my trousers. And so he tipped off a journalist friend of his, I know." Honest John was himself again, if shaky. "Let 'em all come." He swung his bare feet to the floor.

"You can't get up," his secretary protested.

Honest John eyed Braceford undecided whether to pity his lack of sense or to risk his important connections and throw him out. A man who would not only talk but come and tell you he'd been talking!

"Brace," he said sadly, "I predict for you a great parliamentary career." Then he brightened and rubbed his hands. "Well, well, they think they've got me, do they? Let 'em try."

This was much better. This was his own fight, an independent, individual fight. It had nothing to do with the Red Menace, or coal strikes, or timber stakes, international depressions or unexplainable gold standards and the Labor Party ruining the country. It might be his last fight, but, by golly, it was the kind of fight he enjoyed. He'd show them if they could hold commissions on him and his pet council.

"Get Mileston on the 'phone," he ordered. "Tell him he'd better brief a barrister. Ring Jessel and tell him to find out who the commissioners are. Then get my bank manager. Bring me the black-covered account book from the safe and tell Mrs Hutchison to have them send up some steak and onions."

It was as though Honest John had been given a new lease of life. His voice was firm; by holding on to the bedpost he drew himself erect.

"I'm not dead yet," he said. "Not by a long way. You just get that idea right out of your head."

## III

Honest John's memory was badly affected by his nervous breakdown. This became apparent a few weeks later when the Commission began its inquiries. The good old man's memory would brighten up amazingly when there was a clear opportunity to prove how upright had been his dealings, but where he felt any doubt existed, he refused to commit himself.

On occasion his counsel would call for an adjournment and plead his client's ill-health. Providentially, when the Commission again took up its inquiry, Honest John was able to recall a whole set of new facts which placed his dealings in a more favourable light. He feebly allowed himself to be asssisted into the witness box; and it was his habit, when heckled by the opposing counsel, to put his hand to his head and ask for a drink of water.

Public sympathy was aroused as much by Honest John's courage in sickness and undeserved misfortune as for his well-known good works. After all, it was due to his efforts that the first organized attempt had been made at slum clearance in Foveaux. He had pioneered the idea of wide through-streets for traffic; he had actively assisted returned soldiers; he had been on committees innumerable. And here was this commission actually suggesting, politely and without staining his character in any way, that from all these activities Honest John had obtained what one witness for the Crown vulgarly termed a "rake-off".

The Commissioner immediately inquired what was meant by the term and the counsel responded: "A rake-off, your honour, is the perquisite customarily attendant upon agreements involving the granting of concessions or contracts. A firm will either approach or be approached by persons having some influence on the granting of whatever concession is sought, and, in return for help in the matter, an agreed-upon sum of money changes hands."

Honest John fought every inch of the way. He had no intention of being the scapegoat for all the Brethren of the Oiled Palm who, sitting tight in their clubs, would be saying: "I see they've got a line on old J.H. at last." He wriggled; he played out the line of indictments, he ran round a log and chewed the hook off.

Those things that were well known and proven he cheerfully, even nobly, admitted. Certainly, he had taken transfers of war gratuity bonds below their true value. He had made false declarations and prepared the false declarations for the soldiers to make, too. He had done this, as far as his failing memory served him, about eight or nine times; but he had

245

done it as a favour only for certain friends who needed the cash at the time. His memory was a complete blank as far as the payments of certain amounts into his bank account went. He had lost all record of the transactions involved. He became quite upset over some of the questions. It was not a fact that he had received money from Mr Jasper Bross at the time of certain resumptions of land in which Mr Bross was interested.

"Had he not intended to make a rake-off — very well, if there was any objection to the term — personal gain from the council's lease of the resumed land as factory sites?"

To this question Honest John's counsel objected and the objection was upheld.

There was no limit to their ferretings. They even wanted to know what firm had supplied the wood blocks for the widening of Errol Street. They referred to his campaign for the planting of trees along the streets of Foveaux and asked whether his firm did not indirectly supply the timber used as fencing round the trees.

The choicest episode in the whole inquiry was that of McErchin's garage. Honest John admitted having received thirty pounds from McErchin. McErchin had seen him after interviewing the Superintendent of Traffic, the chief inspector of the Surveyor's Department and the Foveaux town clerk. All of these had objected that the erection of McErchin's garage at the corner of Errol Street would constitute a danger to traffic. An adverse report on McErchin's application was submitted to the Foveaux Council, but this mysteriously disappeared and was replaced by a recommendation that the application be approved. How the second report came on the business sheet and who drew it up Honest John could not remember. As for the thirty pounds, it was a gift. He had not made any antecedent agreement with McErchin to accept the money.

"He came into my office, your honour, and I naturally said: 'Well Mac, pleased to see everything went off all right. I told you that I'd do anything I could.' He put the cheque in front of me and I asked him what it was for. I naturally supposed it was for some charity in which I was interested. He explained that it was a personal recognition for my speech in favour of the application. I protested, sir. I told him that I had never inferred for a minute that I required payment, and he said: 'I know, John. That's all right. You've done me a good turn, and I wish to make you a little present, just as a memento.' "

Mr McErchin, in the witness box, corroborated Mr Hutchison's statement. Although McErchin had never been known to part with even an old bolt without a struggle, he was full of generosity and friendship. The money had been a gift.

"The whole business is a gift if you ask me," one of the solicitor's clerks said with a grin to Mr Hutchison's secretary.

Honest John, when he left the court, left it without a stain on his character, without a smirch on his purity; and it was decided that the Foveaux Council, not through any lack of honesty, but through the carelessness of the town clerk's assistant, had got its finances in such a mess that it was necessary to take over its functions without delay. For the rest of the depression a soulless commission administered the affairs of Foveaux. In the years to come it was found advisable to incorporate the municipality in the city of Sydney. There were no more council meetings and back-scratchings and secret agreements and financial juggling. No longer did the inhabitants stand lined up at Honest John's door with humble petitions for assistance which he always heard and sometimes heeded. Honest John and his little crew had gone down in a blaze of glory, the old flag flying, and their like as takers of baksheesh would be no more in the land.

"We gave 'em a run for their money," the unrepentant Hutchison was heard to remark. "And anyway, thank God, I've got rid of that damn Braceford."

Nor was Honest John in any way downcast. To be sure, he was no longer Mayor of Foveaux; but there was no Foveaux Council to have a mayor. Like Samson he had pulled the temple down with him. He sat cheerfully in the ruins, listening to Bill Bross who, as usual, was brimming over with plans for something "big", something that "would give scope".

"I don't know, Billy," Hutchison was saying. "I really ought to retire. Settle down in the mountains. But if you really think I can do anything. . . ."

"Hutch," Bill Bross said fervently, "we need you."

# CHAPTER 3

The uncertainty and frustration of the depression had had ill-effects upon Bill Bross. While things were going well he had flourished, a big, rather fleshy sportsman in a well-cut grey suit immaculately creased. His thinning hair was always carefully brilliantined above the pink, rather wrinkled forehead. He was breezy and cheerful and, at times, slightly beery. But when his business suddenly crashed about his ears and the new flats, his pride and joy, fulfilled every prediction that that cautious crab of a Cornish ever made, a sick feeling of uncertainty and panic overcame him, so that he filled the clubs with his curses and his office with wrath.

"The damn Government," he declared furiously, "is deliberately trying to drive this country to suicide. The whole lot of them ought to be towed a mile out to sea and the rope cut."

Bross said these things mechanically, not because he believed them, but because he gained a certain comfort by loading his trouble on something. "If one could only get at them," he breathed ferociously, "I'd eat them alive."

In this mood he embraced with joy Massingham's suggestion that he join a secret organization that was planning to do "something", whatever that mysterious something might be.

"You know, Billy," Massingham said earnestly, "most people simply don't know just how close we are to a revolution and bloodshed. I know for a fact, old boy, and I can show you the evidence, that there are twenty thousand paid Reds in this country aiming at revolution and absolutely prepared to murder everyone who isn't on their side. They've got lists." He waved his hand importantly. "As a matter of fact, according to our spies, I'm number twenty-seven to be shot." In his suppressed pride he was a small boy again. "Our mob's about the only thing that stands between this country and civil war."

"I'm with you," Bross said fervently. "Lead me to it, whatever it is."

A year before, if anyone had told him that he would be joining secret societies with knocks and passwords like a school kid, he would have roared with jolly laughter; but worry had driven him from panic to hysteria and hysteria was driving him savage.

"We're not the only ones," Massingham assured him. "There's hundreds and thousands of chaps absolutely desperate and at their wits' end."

Of the hundreds and thousands of chaps who went by numbers and signals and secret signs and oaths, there really were a few decided zealots who, in the blazing heat of their weekends, when they should have been surfing or playing golf, drove out and drilled on lonely country roads with stolen rifles and awkward office clerks as raw as themselves. It kept their minds off the slump in business. They felt they were really "doing something" to stop the depression at last. They would do away, in an as yet unexplained manner, with the Government which had brought this depression upon them and in the meantime they certainly were getting a good deal of excitement out of being secret and full of plans and rumours. Bill Bross's digestion, which had begun to trouble him after years of beer drinking, actually began to act cheerfully again. The marching did him good.

"You been doin' something for yer stomach, Billy?" croaked his abominable father with that Foveauvian frankness that his son deplored. "You look as though your bowels are working well."

"We're doing something for the whole country," Bill Bross responded sternly. "You wait."

His father cackled. "I been a Mason for fifty years," he said nastily, "and I was in the old militia and I let you be in the Boy Scouts, but every time I see the fat ole fools you get round with now, I 'ave to go away an' laugh because it gives me a pain in the guts to hold it in."

"Twenty-four hours after a cabinet meeting or an inner executive meeting of the Labor Party or a Trades Hall meeting or any meeting, we have a report on it," Bill Bross said in a lowered voice. "It's the most marvellous espionage system, they say, that has ever been put into action."

"And if three Chinese get together in the back room of a gambling den, I guess the third is you in disguise," his parent wheezed. "Look at me. Ain't I hit by the depression? Ain't half my houses empty and the others payin' no rent? But do I go gettin' dressed up and drillin'? Not on yer sweet life. Why?"

"Because you're an old man," his son said austerely.

"Because I got some sense," the old man retorted. "Anyway, if I did join anything, it wouldn't be your push."

There was plenty of other choice if old Mr Bross had really decided to offer his undoubted powers of strategy to any of the conspiratorial clubs. There were groups of anarchists meeting traditionally in cellars and proclaiming themselves an army with the help of a stub pencil and the back of an envelope. They would presently go forth and tell their friends about the stores of bombs and ammunition that they intended to accumulate vaguely for future use; and the friends, in great secrecy, would pass the story on until it unrolled its dreadful length in offices of the highly excited Bill Bross or one of his confrères. There were groups of sober unionists forming political guards or socialization units or constitutional clubs. If Mr Bross had returned to his native haunts, he would have found half the tougher and less cautious element round the Foot were members of a local army that had been got together by a highly excitable Swedish shoemaker in Slazenger Street. The officers of the Foveaux Army met in the back room of what had been Mr Isenberg's pawnshop amid the cobwebs and stored junk, and here also there were long talks about arming and fighting, but against what and when was all a little vague.

A member of one organization would often shadow a member of another organization and, finding on closer inspection that it was one of his best friends would adjourn to the nearest hotel for drinks where they would swap secrets from their respective organizations under pledges of confidence. Altogether the number of different armies was somewhat confusing; but they settled down as being either for or against the governments. If you were for the existing Labor Government, you were *ipso facto* against a revolution; and if you were against the Government, you alleged you were going to overthrow it in order to stop a revolution. Those persons officially not belonging to the separate armies were in no way averse to joining in a brawl when it started. Onlookers at meetings who did the most furious fighting had for the most part not taken an oath to maintain or overthrow anything. Good citizens would leave the picture shows at the rumour that the local branch of the Defence Army was encountering opposition from the Guard of Democracy and swarm out to smash the windscreens of the enemy's cars, slash the hoods and puncture the tyres. Even if you had no money to go to the pictures, there was always better entertainment to be had either fighting or watching the fights.

Whatever the armies were fighting for, the battle usually resolved itself into a row between business-men (anti-government) and "hooligans" (upholding the constitutionally elected Government). Foveaux was naturally a strong fortress of the Labor army, and the boldest of the Bross contingent thought twice before they invaded its labyrinths.

Tommy Cornish, who was strongly anti-government owing to the sudden stoppage of the buses which saw him without a job, inclined towards the anarchist point of view. Bramley attended all the street meetings and enjoyed them without being a member of anything. Rolfe was in the intelligence departments of both sides and had a busy time, as he said, shadowing himself. Bud Pellager was a warm Laborite but scornful of Linnie who was becoming an out-and-out Communist, which meant that she was a revolutionary without being for the Government, and was therefore unorthodox.

"You'll grow out of it," her boss said annoyingly, "if you don't get your head split open first."

Duncan was naturally a group leader for the Labor forces and, in spite of his increasing rheumatism, he was snowing leaflets in the winter of his life as gaily as ever.

"You spik 'ere tonight?" the Italian fruiterer at King's Cross would ask Mr Duncan anxiously; and on receiving the affirmative, he would chuckle and rub his hands. "Ver goot, ver goot. I sell all my eggs, I sell all my fruit, all my tomart.

You bloody good feller. You spik, eh?" And he would pat the grinning Duncan on the shoulder joyfully.

At Dennison Square one dull Thursday night about ten listeners and a dog had gathered round the rickety platform on which Emily Anseer was appealing for some obscure cause. Jock Jamieson stood sourly among the ten, disapproving of her silently and with patient intensity. A terrific wail of sirens was the first sign that the secret legion was about, and immediately after seventeen motor-cars swept into the Square and discharged their occupants around the meeting. News in Foveaux travels as fast as a small boy heading for ice-cream, and from the billiard saloon, the back of the shops, and the cafés in Mark Street the inhabitants of Foveaux emerged like angry hornets. The residents of Slazenger Street and Lennox Street came running with sticks and bits of old gas-pipe, a favourite weapon. They came with their nostrils spread to the battle and with a whoop of fury. The enemy had penetrated even unto the stronghold of Dennison Square.

The legion had arrived too early. The big meeting they had bargained on breaking up did not start until a quarter to nine. Nobody in Foveaux liked a meeting to start too soon. The vanguard of the legion came upon the scene of what might be called the preliminary round. Ten minutes after the arrival of the legion, however, there were thousands of people in the square all ready for battle. Police were telephoning for reinforcements, rotten fruit was flying. Emily Anseer, upset in the gutter and coming apart as usual like a rag doll, was busily kicking the shins of two beefy legionaries. Constable Murphy, a firm Labor supporter, who had time and again expressed his disapproval of Miss Anseer and all she stood for, charged down on Duncan undecided but boiling with excitement. "I don't know whether to lumber the beggars or knock 'em," he yelled. "Begorra, I'll knock 'em." And leaping forward on the largest of the legionaries, he sent that disturber to the ground with a beautiful right swing.

The sound of smashing windscreens and the sirens of motor-cars arriving, some of them police cars, made the endeavours of the Labor speakers as the rustling of grass in a tornado.

"Don't you think you'd better not speak?" the secretary of

the Labor Party branch howled in the ear of the distinguished Labor politician who, clad in a pearl-grey suit, presented a beautiful target. The secretary himself, an old hand at meetings, was covered by a dingy waterproof.

"Why not?" the distinguished visitor shouted back.

The secretary shrugged. He was not a coward. Springing up on the rim of the Sutton Memorial Fountain he endeavoured to make himself heard. Tomatoes, stones and rotten fruit showered in on him. Yells, boos and the discordant singing of "Rule Britannia" drowned his words. The distinguished speaker, leaping up in his place, received a flight of eggs that completely ruined his suit. He was taken down by the police, the sergeant shouting in his ear that it would be a favour to the police if he wouldn't speak. As he limped into the lobby of the hotel a friend rushed gladly to meet him. "Joe," he said, "I want you to meet a lady friend of mine. She thinks you're thrilling." Then he held his nose.

"Some other time," the politician said morosely. "Some other time."

Outside the battle raged on. It was hopeless to try to arrest more than a scattering of the persons attempting to break law and order. A group of hot-headed youths, sons of wealthy squatters sent down to Sydney to join the legion, chased Jock Jamieson down a side street; but did not know him again when they came upon him lounging in a doorway and asked him if he had seen himself go past. Jamieson courteously directed them down the street he had taken. Around the memorial fountain McCullemy and his fellow fighters armed with packing needles embedded in cork sunk them with effect into the opposition's flanks. The legionaries responded with knuckle dusters. To tell the truth the invaders were becoming alarmed. They were outnumbered and the damage that was being done to the parked cars made them anxious for their retreat.

They had certainly broken up the Labor meeting but when the recall sounded, many of the car-owners found that not only were their windscreens ruined and their tyres punctured but that some thoughtful member of the Foveaux Army had sweetened their petrol tanks with liberal handfuls of sugar. With a feeling that their carefully prepared plans had not been altogether successful the invaders retreated, leaving behind them a litter of stones, fruit and vegetables, broken glass, two of their number who had been trampled unconscious and a smell of rotten eggs that made even the police shiver.

"There's one thing about livin' in Foveaux," Mrs Blore said proudly. She had been in the midst of the fray and could instance for her prowess a legionary's collar which she had ripped off and was keeping as a memento. "You certainly don't miss much."

The council men spent most of Friday and Saturday trying to clean the memorial fountain. The fountain had hard luck ever since it was erected, having migrated from one end of Foveaux to the other several times. It started its career outside the old town hall, was moved to Foveaux Park and from that quiet retreat to a position outside the courthouse, where it had arrived just in time for the egg-throwing. Not all the efforts of the council men could wash the egg stain off it.

# CHAPTER 4

## I

Mrs Montague's sore throat did not seem to improve. This she explained by a peculiar homeopathic method of her own. "It's a hard lump, you see, dear," she told Linnie. "Well, I asked myself, what have I in my thought that would cause a hard lump. And I immediately realized that I have thought hardly, very hardly, about your father. I really have been at times quite resentful of his behaviour." She looked triumphant. "But of course, now that I know what's causing the lump, I will be able to change my thought and get rid of it."

Her haggard look and barely concealed pain, however, showed that either her hard thoughts were unaltered, or the lump had some other contributory cause. The time came when she had to stay in bed.

"It's just a matter of rest," she lied almost cheerfully. "I've been too busy to give time and attention to shaking it off."

Those cheerful souls who had been accustomed to holding parties at her expense began to find this change uncomfortable. Her gayer lodgers began to think of changing their place of abode.

The girl "who did the hands' illusion", expressed the general opinion. "The old lady's getting too far under the weather," she said. "Things aren't the same these days. There's always Linnie coming in the minute you begin to kick up a bit of a row and asking you to be quiet. You're expected to creep round the place as though you're deaf and dumb."

The departing lodgers were influenced by the fact that good lodgings were very much easier to obtain now so many people were unable to afford them. Little by little, Linnie realized, their source of income was diminishing. People moved in and out; mostly they did not pay. Two rooms remained vacant for over a month, and when Teddy Stewart departed, she was at her wits' end.

"Terribly sorry and all that, Lin, but where I'm going, I'll be nearer the office. And I'll have the chance of getting digs with a chap and so I—"

"Quite understand, Teddy. Thats all right." Their new lodging-house was not as convenient as the old cottage. The contiguity of the Rose of Denmark and Ogham Street gave an altogether different atmosphere from that of Mrs Webb's place.

"Don't know what I'm going to do," Linnie confided to Rolfe. "She's getting worse, she's been getting worse for months, but she won't let me get a doctor. Sits and reads her books." She shook her head gloomily.

"She must see a doctor," Rolfe demanded.

Linnie hesitated. The long fear of doctors bred in her by a Christian Science training made her nervous about the matter. "She hates the idea. Keeps saying she's feeling better, though she doesn't look it."

"But this is ridiculous," Rolfe said. They were sitting as usual in the kitchen, Rolfe having insisted on increasing his rent money on the excuse that he had tea with the Montagues almost every night. "She can't go on like this. I'm going to get a chap I know. I'll ring him now."

"But it's night-time. He wouldn't come." Linda's knowledge of doctors was vague. "I'll ask her tomorrow."

But Rolfe was already gone.

"Where is she?" he asked on his return.

"Lying down, poor lamb."

"Well, don't disturb her. And look here, Linnie, I'm paying for this."

"You're not."

"I am. Good Lord, your mother's done enough for me in my time. Don't grudge me the privilege."

He took off his coat and began to roll up his sleeves in preparation for the washing-up.

"He won't be here for some time, I expect. He's pretty busy but said he'd come as soon as he could."

Linnie was becoming more and more nervous. "Can't be anything but a sore throat," she said half fearfully. "But it's the way the thing keeps on and on." She began scraping the plates. "Angelique's getting worn to a shadow, just with a sore throat."

They completed the washing-up in silence. Rolfe was wondering absently why he should feel so happy just washing up dirty dishes in this kitchen with a rather tired-looking girl. He had not this feeling of home-coming at Mrs Montague's old lodging-house; it was a new growth, born of chance domestic intimacies over the dishes or sitting with their feet up on the back balcony rail as they watched the lights of the city below. It flashed in his mind that he had not really liked Linda when he met her; he had thought her hard until he realized her tremendous affection for her mother. Then he refused to accept her at her own valuation and had taken her rather at her mother's, as a stubborn little girl who could be pretty, if she would spend some money on clothes. She was willing enough to spend money on little dainties for the beloved Angelique. All in all, Rolfe decided, you would go a long day's journey before you met anyone half as sterling as young Linnie.

Suppose it had been Linnie who crossed his path when he was a young idealist full of plans. He smiled at the idea of that hard-working ability of hers in harness with his own young powers. They would have made a good working team. But what was the use of his imagining such things now? At any minute he might find himself among the job hunters or lining up in the queue outside a soup kitchen. Tickolat Preparations Limited, that struggling little company, was about to go under. The prospect did not alarm him for himself. How would it affect his relations with Linnie? He could not stay on, depending on Mrs Montague's charity, when she and her daughter were so desperately poor. He would have to go somewhere else. Their basis of meeting would be different. They had come to be his family; he had adopted them; but if the time came when he had no money and no prospect of any, he would have to leave them.

"Can't make out why you're so decent to us," Linnie said abruptly. She had been turning over without bitterness the many excuses Wilfred would make for his non-appearance.

Not since her mother had been taken ill had she seen him; and she began to feel she did not really want to.

Wilfred always had a sound excuse for keeping away from any of his friends who were in trouble and she had heard him say on other occasions: "For God's sake don't ask me to go near him! Bad luck's catching." But Rolfe had said nothing. He had merely gone on being kind and normal and friendly, cheering Mrs Montague, taking her out when she was well enough. He had never said a word about his Tickolat Preparations, which was a sure sign that they were in a bad way, except to joke about the millions he was going to make when the tide turned. All in all, there were qualities in Rolfe which made Wilfred look sickly by comparison.

"Been no end decent," she muttered. "Don't know why you should."

"I suppose," Rolfe said with a grin, "it's because I belong to what old Wilf would call the decayed bourgeoisie." He settled back talking idly, alert for the ringing of the door-bell.

"Take the old crowd at Mrs Webb's place when you were a kid. Remember the way they hung together? The people who've come down in the world, the people you and I come from, know they have no real friends. The class from which they sprang regards them only as courteous beggars, even though they may never actually beg, but their very existence implies a demand on the wealthy class to which they no longer belong. On the other hand they have nothing in common with the lower classes whose abandonment revolts them. The working class don't care. They're used to it."

"That's not an argument," Linda broke in.

"Well, anyway, they have their own solidarity. But your broken middle class have another tie, a tie of common memories. Memories of what they might have been." He walked restlessly to the door and back. "So they do one another little acts of kindness, acts that they would not accept from people below them and that they would regard as charity from people above." He was beginning to enjoy his own philosophizing. "They're all so wistful, particularly the old ones. They are the people who could have enjoyed life but are denied the opportunity. At the same time they are not prepared to enjoy it in a manner which they consider undignified. Drunk they may be, but it is gin, and in the privacy of their own rooms. . . ."

Linnie had scarcely been listening. "This is why you take Angelique to the pictures or trips to the beach?"

"No," he said quietly. "I've never had a family. Every time I've tried to settle down something has occurred to set me rolling again. There's a kind of taboo against my resting long in one place. And I think I'm in love with you," he added ruefully.

He had rather taken Linnie's breath away. She wanted to reply but there seemed nothing to say.

" 'S far as falling in love," she added slowly, "you'd better not."

"Why?"

She shook her head. "Spoils things. Look at Wilf. We had good times together. He starts making love and finds I don't like it. What happens? We aren't friends any longer."

"But Wilfred is a rat," Rolfe said deliberately. "He shows your lack of taste, though I must confess I in a measure wronged you. I used to think you were his mistress."

Linda blushed disconcertingly.

"Sorry," he apologized. "But you know how people spring to conclusions."

"That's all right." She was getting angry now. "You've been very condescending, haven't you? Falling in love with me? 'S a wonder you bother to tell me about it. Only spoil things."

"You've got me wrong. Give me a chance." He spoke urgently. "When I say I'm falling in love with you, I don't mean I'm going romantic like a passionate young lunatic." His tone became graver. "What I mean by love is that I'd like to spend the rest of my life, say, coming home and doing the washing up and telling you what happened at work like a — what is it Bud says? — a reg'lar guy? When you had toothache, I'd like to hold your head and fetch you stuff to stop it. I'd like to spend the rest of my life with you. That's about all I have to spend, God knows!" He cocked one eyebrow at her half humorously. "I'm beginning to love you."

Linnie frowned at the floor between her feet. "It's loneliness," she said. "Don't I know it? Love's different. I've been in love." She grunted contemptuously. "Couldn't eat for a week. Huh! What a fool! No, you're lonely. So'm I sometimes, but I have Angelique." It was as though she had dismissed the subject. "Gosh, I wish that doctor would come."

Rolfe also reverted to the worry of the moment. "Have you written to Oscar?"

"Yes. He's out of a job again. The coal lock-out. Ever notice how things come in spasms? You get a run of luck when nothing turns up and then everything happens at once. I'd better prepare Angelique. She'll never forgive me if she isn't wearing her peach satin night-dress with the lace. And she'll want to put her false teeth in."

The doctor rang as Linnie hustled her mother into bed and the peach-coloured satin. "If you don't tell him truthfully how you feel I'll murder you," she threatened.

The doctor did not need much telling. He was a rugged young man who looked as though he would be a useul football back and, after a cursory examination of Mrs Montague's sore throat, he flew into a passion which directed itself naturally enough at Linnie. He waited until he came downstairs before really letting fly.

"That woman should have had attention long ago," he raged. "How long has that lump been there? Nearly two years?"

Linnie shook her head. "She's had it for ages."

"Why didn't you *make* her go and have it seen to?"

"She doesn't believe—"

"What is it?" Rolfe broke in. "Is it serious?"

"Serious? She must be operated on at once. It's a growth, a malignant growth."

Linnie's face pinched with horror. She looked ten years older. "Can you cure it?" she whispered.

"I don't know. Tracheotomy. Have to cut it out. She may have a chance, but I doubt it."

He need not have been so brutal, Rolfe thought. "Is there no other way?" he asked.

"Well, there's ray treatments. Costly things. Specialist's job.

Cost you over fifty pounds at least. She may die under the operation and she may not, but left alone she'll die anyway. If you like, I'll make arrangements for her to go into hospital tomorrow."

"How long'll she live without the operation?" Linnie asked quietly.

"Maybe six months."

"And with?"

The doctor shrugged his shoulders. "It's a chance she'll recover."

"I'll let you know our decision," Linnie said stiffly. She was trembling despite her efforts to keep calm.

The doctor relented a little. He was tired and his nerves were frayed. "If you want another opinion. . . ." he said.

"It isn't that. I'll have to ask my mother. Thanks for not telling her."

As soon as the doctor was gone she turned to Rolfe. "What'll I do?" she asked.

He shook his head. "There must be another way out." He marvelled that Linnie stayed so calm.

"Linnie," Mrs Montague was calling from the stair-head in a husky whisper. "Linnie."

"Darling." Linnie rushed up to her. "You've been listening."

"Oh, Linnie," Mrs Montague was crying. "Don't let him send me to a hospital. Don't let him. I want to stay with you."

Linnie looked at Rolfe, who had followed her upstairs.

"Don't worry, Mrs Montague," he said, patting her shoulder. "We'll look after you. Young fool didn't know what he was talking about. You see. We'll take you to a good man."

Mrs Montague was not listening. "Get Mr Dale," she whispered. "Get Mr Dale."

"Yes, darling, yes. Just as soon as I put you to bed. I'll get him. Don't worry."

"Ring him up,' Mrs Montague's throaty, unnatural whispering went on. "Ring him up. Tell him to work for me. Tell him to work. He won't mind about money. . . ."

"We'll pay him, darling. As long as he gets you well." Linnie gathered her mother up as lightly as if she were a feather and walked with her into the bedroom.

"Tell him to work . . ." Rolfe heard the feverish guttural whispering die away.

He stood helpless, and the consciousness of his impotence was a quick pain, a twisting misery. He waited at the top of the stairs, striking the railing with his palm and frowning perplexedly.

"Linnie," he burst out as she came down the hall. "Linnie, can I do anything? You've got to let me help."

There were tears in her eyes now. "Blast it," she said, cramming on a hat. "Come with me while I ring this practitioner."

"What's a practitioner?" he asked, as they ran down the steps to the street level.

"A Christian Scientist who cures you when you're sick."

Mr Dale would certainly work for Mrs Montague. He would give her absent treatment. Yes, he would give her a thought through the night. Yes, he would come down tomorrow.

"Tell her not to be in any way disturbed," Mr Dale said in his beautifully modulated voice. "The good must triumph."

"Thanks." Linnie hung up. "I wish," she said bitterly, "that I believed this religious bunk."

Mrs Montague was strangely comforted. "I can sleep in peace now," she declared. "It's a great protection."

Down in the kitchen again Linnie pressed her hot head between her hands. "Don't," she said when Rolfe touched her. "Don't." Then she looked up, her eyes bright and feverish. "Fifty pounds." Her eyes narrowed. "I'll get it if I have to steal it."

"But will this ray treatment be any good?"

"It's got to be. Not going to have them cutting the poor little sweet up." She gulped down her tears again. "She didn't deserve it. Never done anything in her life to deserve such a thing."

Rolfe was silent. If I were a dog, he thought, I could lick her hand. Linnie began to laugh.

"Don't," he said in his turn. "We'll get the money somehow."

"I was thinking," her breath came in gasps. "In picture shows the good daughter goes on the streets to save her mother's life.

Damn it. I couldn't even do that. Wouldn't know how to lumber a man if my own life depended on it."

"Oh, shut up."

"Well, I couldn't. There's a technique to it. No, I'm damned, if I could get a bloke in the street and say—"

"Stop swearing and pull yourself together."

She began to cry. "Poor sweet," she repeated. "Poor Angelique."

Rolfe, as she sobbed with her head on the table, lit the gasring and boiled some water for tea. By the time he poured it out Linnie was beginning to wipe her swollen eyes. "Thanks," she said huskily. "I'd better go up and sit with Angelique."

"You drink that tea first." Obediently she gulped a few mouthfuls. "And you'd better do something about your face. Don't worry," he said tenderly. "It'll be all right, Linnie. We'll get ray treatments. We'll get her well. You take her to a specialist tomorrow and charge it to me. You will. Listen to me. Tell Bud you want the day off and take her in a taxi." His arm was round her shoulders protectingly as though she were a child. "I'm taking charge of this, d'you hear?"

For a moment she clung to him. "I don't know what to do," she whispered. "I'll wire dad." Already she knew her father's answer would be sincere condolences. The dreadful loneliness gripped her in which Rolfe seemed the only solid support. Then she pushed him away. "Good night," she said wearily. "Decent of you, Jimmy."

Rolfe bit his lip. Any other girl would have been more responsive, more willing to share her sorrows and cling to him. But Linnie, above the dark waters of life, clung to a straw and that straw was her small mother. Now if it had been big, staid Bramley, he thought, she might have acted differently. Even with Wilfred. A little spasm of envy struck him. Then he shrugged. What a beast he was to worry her!

Upstairs with Angelique's limp little hand lying in hers, Linnie was saying over and over monotonously the creed she had been taught as a child, the creed she no longer believed. It seemed to be comforting Mrs Montague:

"There is no life, truth, intelligence or substance in matter. All is Infinite Mind and its infinite manifestation. . . .Would you like some eau-de-Cologne on your forehead, Angelique?"

"Go on saying the Scientific Statement, dear. It's such a comfort to hear you."

Linnie cursed under her breath. She sat silent a minute.

"Why are you stopping?" Mrs Montague inquired.

"All is Infinite Mind and its infinite manifestation . . ." Linnie continued. "For God is All in All. . . ." Were the cells in Mrs Montague's throat that had started on an independent life of their own at her expense part of that All in All, Linnie asked herself. "Spirit is immortal truth," she continued aloud. "Matter is mortal error. Spirit is the Real and Eternal, matter is the unreal and temporal. . . ."

Mrs Montague lay still under the pink satin coverlet of which she was so proud. Linnie reminded herself that she must fold it carefully. It worried Angelique to have the cover creased. "Spirit is God and Man is His Image and Likeness. Therefore, Man is not material, he is Spiritual."

"I wonder if you would just pass me the Bible," Mrs Montague croaked. "It's over there on the sewing machine."

"You lie down," Linnie said hastily. "I'll read it to you."

As the night bore on and Mrs Montague lay so uncomplainingly, Linnie herself grew hoarse from reading, but she did not stop. Anything was better than sitting in silence, thinking. She read on desperately.

"I like to know Mr Dale is helping me," Mrs Montague whispered, a smile on her face.

I bet he's asleep long ago, Linnie thought. She was terribly tired. When her mother's eyes finally closed, Linnie lay down quietly on the floor, a pillow under her head and a rug to cover her. I must get my bed in tomorrow and sleep here, she thought, in case Angelique wakes in the night. Over and over in her mind the Scientific Statement of Being whirled its sentences like a dark gramophone record:

"God is All in All and Man is His Image and Likeness. Therefore Man is not material. He is Spiritual. . . ."

## I I

"How much did you say she wanted?" Bud asked incredulously when Jimmy called in to explain Linnie's absence.

"At least fifty."

Bud's yellow mask set hard. "I got no time for all the frills and trimmin's," he snarled. "The woman's got to die. Might as well get it over quick." He clicked his fingers. "Like that. Clean finish."

"They seem to think she might have a chance with this ray business. And by gosh she'll get it if I go to jail."

"No. She'll die. Damn cruel to keep her hanging on." Bud tapped the counter with end of a dirty nail reflectively. "When ma died, I give her a good funeral. Me three bothers up country never s'much as gave a red cent towards it. Okker doing anything? No, I thought not. He takes after pa. Well, hoo-ray, I'll be seeing you."

Bramley, on the other hand, was horrified when Rolfe told him the news. He had his own private worries, being engaged at the moment in following the cash account to the edge of a deficit where it was committing suicide like one of the Gadarene swine.

"If I knew where to raise the money, she'd have it," he said quietly, then he thought for a minute. "Look here, Jimmy. What with Tommy losing his job, we're pretty hard up, but I could manage a fiver, if you could find a way of using it." He blushed at the thought of Linnie trying to give his five pounds back. "But don't let her know who it's from. I wish I could do more." He clutched the fair lock of hair that came down on his forehead when he was excited. "I wish I could do something."

"You're not the only one," Rolfe said bitterly. "Here am I — practically flat broke. Don't know if I can scrape together enough to pay my rent next week. Anyway, Mrs Montague can't carry on. Linnie's going to take a room. She's hoping the furniture will raise fifty pounds, but I doubt she'll get fifteen."

Bramley nodded. "We're all in the soup together," he said with a twisted smile. "Have you met anyone today who isn't cursing?"

Rolfe felt a little resentful towards Bud Pellager for being so full of common sense. Admittedly, Mrs Montague was going to die, and there was no use in prolonging the business by treatments that even the specialists did not claim would cure the mysterious long-named thing that had camped in her throat. But, damn it, Bud need not be so callous!

Bud was just as abrupt to Linnie when she came into the shop the same night.

"I been taking your shift," he snarled. "And you know damn well I had to go out today to see about some other business. What'd the specialist say?"

"Seems to think his ray treatment might do some good," Linnie said wearily. "Wouldn't commit himself about an operation."

"You sending her to hospital?"

"No." Linnie was suddenly fierce. "She loathes the idea."

"Well, I'm not having any more nonsense," Pellager snarled. "You're goin' to do as *I* tell you. I'm takin' charge. Get that."

Linnie smiled. "So's Jimmy."

"Jimmy!" Bud snapped his fingers again. "Jimmy's idea is to owe the doctor the money and then go to jail. They're too shrewd for that. Now, listen. I been doin' a bit of ringin' up and I've fixed things. All right. But I've gotta have you here because I've trained you to the business almost as good as a man an' I ain't goin' to have it fallin' to ruin. Get that."

"Yes, Bud."

"And shut up till I finish, can't you?" His manner relaxed a little. "I'm taking a flat. Flats are cheaper now. Get a five-pound one for two-ten. That joint they built, Foveaux Flats — where you used to live — close handy. Three bedrooms. She can have the sunroom for the nurse. I'm having the bedroom where the maid's supposed to camp. Shut up, can't you. There'll be no maid. Get a girl in." He paused again, his eyes narrowed "This is how I figure it out. Send a taxi to collect yer ma tomorrow, move her in. Mind y're only gettin' the morning off. This nurse, Mrs Brierson, I knew her old man, she can take yer ma in to have these ray treatments, so you don't have to leave work." He was talking quickly so that she could not get a word in edgeways. "Be kinda company for me, you livin' there. I won't interfere or get in your way. Well, speak up. What's a matter with you? Think there's a catch in it?"

"But Bud, what's it going to cost?"

"Listen, I'm takin' a flat. I'm invitin' you and your ma for chaperone to come an' live there. If I wanta roon me reputation, I'm old enough and ugly enough to do it. An' as for the dough," he made a magnificent gesture, "if you want any amount of blue, purple and pink rays, you can have 'em. I'm the on'y man the depression ain't left a tooth-mark on." He turned away sharply. "All right, that's settled. And you see you're on the job tomorrow at one o'clock sharp."

"But, Bud. Look, I can't. How am I going to explain to Angelique?"

"You don't. Oh, I forgot the keys. Here." He tossed them on the counter. "One o'clock mind." His face relaxed into that peculiar sweet smile. "I got the top flat, honey," he said gently. "The one you said she wanted. And I've had 'em hang blue curtains."

All the way home Linnie's eyes dazzled so that the lights seemed shooting sparks through her tears. She was still crying when she reached the kitchen and an anxious Rolfe mopped her eyes for her.

"What is it, Lightning? Did the little devil sack you?"

"What do you think of this?" She poured out Bud's fantastic plan.

Rolfe looked puzzled. "It sounds mad," he frowned. He did not like to bring up all his objections. He could not stand in the way of something that would take a little of that load of worry off her shoulders. If he could have offered her security himself, it would have been different.

"Think I ought to accept, Jimmy?"

"You'll have to decide that yourself," he said slowly. Bud had been his friend for years, though Jimmy had never regarded him as a saint.

"I'll put it to Angelique. After all she's the only one that matters."

The glowing colours Linnie used in describing Bud's offer to her mother left little doubt of the issue. "Listen, darling. Wonderful thing's happened. Old Bud is going to look after everything till you're better. You know the little flat, the one at the top of Foveaux Flats. Well, when he heard you were sick, he took it for us, and he's going to fix up these ray treatments, and you'll have a trained nurse and everything. You see, darling, you'll be right in no time."

"But, Linnie," Mrs Montague whispered, "isn't it expensive?"

"Not a bit, dear. Could take it ourselves. Bud's lonely, you see, and he hasn't any people of his own. He'll take one room and it'll help pay the rent."

A smile spread over Mrs Montague's haggard face. Her throat worked convulsively. "Blue curtains," she whispered. "A light blue on the front windows."

"Yes, dear."

"And my pink satin bedspread. Pink and blue."

"Yes, dear."

"Mr Dale called." She lay back happily. "He gave me a healing. He says I am protected. It's wonderful to realize how right he is." She shut her eyes. "Everything is good, nothing is evil. There is no evil."

"No, dear. We'll move in tomorrow and I'll get this place settled up by degrees."

Mrs Montague opened her eyes again. "All due to Science," she whispered impressively. "I always wanted that flat." She did not notice that Linnie was crying.

Downstairs Rolfe paced slowly up and down the kitchen in his shirt sleeves. So this was the end of his little lapse into domesticity. He must go drifting again. Where? He did not know. Foveaux was an unlucky place. Everything he had started there had crashed. His career as an architect, his plans for Tickolat, the slum business. He had gone to the war from this place. He must make a clean break, get away from it for good. Away from Linnie, too, and the dangerous emotions she aroused of pity and pain. He could do her no good now. He must go.

In his pocket there touched his fingers the five pounds Bramley had brought in on his way home. He must give Linnie that, he thought. Perhaps he might be useful himself in helping to settle the affairs of Mrs Montague's home and disposing of the remaining lodgers, acting as an unofficial caretaker. However humiliating for him, it might be of some assistance to

Linnie. Bramley and I, he thought, no use either of us. Bramley tied too close to his mother and himself too much of a drifter. Neither with any money. Bud Pellager was a sportsman. He was doing what Rolfe and Bramley would have done in different circumstances. And he was doing it well, not meanly, but royally.

# CHAPTER 5

Jock Jamieson was in something of a dilemma over the matter of his eviction. "The Party line," he said gravely, "is to demand a rent allowance and they don't like these anarcho-syndicalist tendencies of the tenant barricading the houses and defying the landlord to evict him. Still, I don't see what else I can do." He rubbed his chin reflectively. "Naturally, the Party's right. But I'm damned if I'm going to sit down and let them chuck us out when Elsie's sick."

"I heard a good one the other day," McCullemy chuckled. "It was at the Unemployed Relief Picnic, and Joe said to old Flaherty: 'What'd you do if I fell overboard?' and the whole mob yelled, 'Throw out the Party line'." He laughed at his jest.

Jamieson was not impressed. "It looks," he said after deep thought, "as though I'll have to agree with the Party in theory and be anarcho-syndicalist in practice."

McCullemy eyed him expectantly.

"You can call out the boys," Jamieson smote his fist on the table. "We'll show 'em how to do it properly."

McCullemy nodded approvingly. "None of their couple of strands of barbed wire that a cop can walk through with a pair of clippers. We'll make it something like an eviction."

All this was decided on receipt of the notice to quit; and after a notice to quit there was always an interval, more or less prolonged, of court pleadings of impoverished circumstances, granting of time, application for extension and refusal or granting of the extension.

The walls of the hot, stuffy courthouse had heard more pitiful stories than any other place in Foveaux. Before the tired old magistrate filed a stream of women, women with babies in arms, women dragging small children marked with the dreadful sores of impetigo, that last extreme of malnutrition. It was the women who appeared in the court and faltered out their stories. The men were usually looking for work or sick or doing something to prevent them from that last humiliation of going into the box to testify to "impoverished circumstances". Also it was better policy to let the women go. The magistrates were easier on the women. Not that they were hard or cruel men; but they were so used to lies.

"Go out and put your coat on," one of them sharply ordered a hard, sullen-faced man who took the witness box in his shirt sleeves. "I can't," the man said shortly. "I've just pawned it." He met the magistrate's suspicious look defiantly. "And here's the pawn ticket," he added.

"I don't want to see it," the old man said handsomely. He made the defendant a little bow. "I'm sorry. I apologize."

"He wasn't such a bad old cow," the sullen-faced man said afterwards. Some of the magistrates were secretly very much in sympathy with the evicted tenants.

"You are the mother of this child?" one of the gentlest magistrates questioned a woman in the box who was holding a small baby. She was a thin girl, once good looking, but now worn and strained and shabby.

"Mother!" the girl said fiercely. "I'm ashamed to say I am a mother. I've sweated and worried and starved myself, I've starved these kids to pay the rent. There's two of them in the South Sydney Hospital, and last night the nurse said the doctor don't think they'll live. And the baby's sick, too. A mother! Me! I ought to be ashamed of myself." She burst out crying.

"I don't want to hear any more," the magistrate said, giving the full limit of three months to find a new home. "Keep those medical certificates," he ordered the clerk.

At lunch-time he walked down in the heat, an old thin man, to the house where the woman was living and gave her a pound note. "Keep in touch with me," he said, "and I'll see what I can do."

All the afternoon in the hot, stuffy courtroom the woman's face kept rising before him in all the procession of thin, worried faces. He was unusually liberal with extensions of time.

It was that afternoon that Elsie stepped into the box. Her explanation of how she fell sick and lost her job and had to spend the rent money on medicine was received. She was given six weeks in which to find another house. When the six weeks expired, she was back again before another magistrate, who issued the ultimatum that they were to be off the premises in a fortnight.

At the end of the fortnight two bailiffs appeared and Jamieson, at the front door, merely smiled at them so disconcertingly that they went away. The two policemen, who appeared later, took one look at the barricaded windows and the tough, nuggety-looking group of pickets on the balcony. They strolled round the back and noted the barbed wire ramparts along the back fence, the sandbags, the old iron plates from the dump, piled against the house like armour, the windows closed with sheets of corrugated iron. A light came into the younger policeman's eye.

"They've done it in style this time," he said, almost with reverence in his voice. "It's going to take a bit of time digging them out."

"I bet there's fifty of the flamin' cows in there, if there's one," his mate said disgustedly. "Come on."

There had always been evictions in Foveaux, but now it was nothing unusual to have ten in a day. The number of people who went out meekly on notice to quit exceeded those who waited to be taken to court; and the number of those who left on expiry of the time granted by the court was many more than the hardy battlers who stayed on and put up the slogan: "No Evictions for the Unemployed".

"But even when they do stay in," McCullemy would say disapprovingly, "they don't put up much of a fight."

The usual procedure was to wait fatalistically until your furniture was thrown out on the pavement and then to send up to borrow the tarpaulin kindly donated to the unemployed committee by Mr Hutchison.

"I have great pleasure in acceding to your request for a tarpaulin from the council's stores," he had written early in the depression, "and I trust that the gift may never be used in the manner you suggest."

It was often used. It was almost a commonplace to see the draped pile of somebody's furniture on the footpath with a sympathetic cluster of neighbours around it, while the owners went down to apply for their allowance from the Charities

Board, usually a pound to cover the cost of moving and perhaps a couple of pounds for the first fortnight's rent. The furniture stayed in the street until a house was found and it was just hard luck if it rained. The evicted family quartered itself on the neighbours, a child here and another there, and the parents with the people next door, until, by forged rent receipt and false names, they might find another dwelling. Some gave up the struggle and moved into rooms, as many as six children and their parents sharing the one room. Others flung themselves on the mercy of relatives as poor as themselves and moved "for the time being" into the already overcrowded, child-ridden, flea-ridden, bug-ridden residences, where they might be sharing a room, four in a bed, but being all related, it didn't matter.

On those rare occasions, however, when the tenant showed fight and gathered his mates on the principle that a Foveauvian's home was his castle and now was the time to fortify it, the landlord very often weakened. No one could blame him for weakening when he came down to find his little property turned into a barbed wire entanglement with hostile troops camped within the fortifications. It is hard to be considered a tyrant and usurper, a down-treader of the poor, when you are trying to collect what you have long regarded as your just dues. After a few weeks of mutual defiance a landlord often paid the tenant to get out, though sometimes he was driven nearly desperate by the terms the tenant demanded. It was not unusual to claim (and get) five pounds to move out, a clear rent receipt, a new home found before the move took place and two weeks' rent paid in advance. Thus was defeat turned to victory.

The feelings of Foveaux were always on the side of the evicted. Any person who refused to move had instant warm support and all assistance. Fatigue parties of pickets would make a tour of the shops collecting donations and supplies. Lorry loads of stores and barricades would pour in. During one famous case it took six pounds a week to feed the pickets who were working in three shifts, and all the money was raised by donations. One of the pickets superintended the cooking as a full-time job.

It was an elaborate business when the Foveaux Anti-Eviction Committee really moved out to battle. All the furniture had to be shifted to places of safety. The women and children were moved to the houses of friends out of harm's way and then the pickets moved in. Once in, only force or cunning would get them out. People would come from streets around to gaze in loud, approving groups at the dark and sinister-looking dwelling with its barricades and its posters.

Poor old Mr Budin, out of work and worried by debt, received his notice to quit long after the Jamiesons; but when Tommy enthusiastically suggested rallying the unemployed committee and defying the landlord, Mr Budin fairly bristled with indignation.

"Don't you think for a minute that I'm going to have my house turned into a stamping ground for a mob of hooligans." His white moustache quivered at the thought. "My place has always been a decent, respectable, quiet place, and I'm not going to have it any different now." He continued collecting the tools out of his little tool-shed. "The missus and me may have to move into a room, and if we got to, we will, but we ain't going to have a lot of young fellers come up here making trouble with the police. If we've got to go, that's all about it."

This attitude was one that the anti-eviction committee deplored. There were hundreds of Mr Budins proudly going away with their sad little bits of furniture, not wanting "any trouble". They were horrified at the lurid limelight playing about those tumbledown dwellings of the Foot where the unemployed really made their stand. The people of the Foot had a pride of a different kind; they gloried in the excitement of sharing an anti-eviction riot.

Of these was "Snowy" Sampson, a slack, loose-jawed, exciteable fellow with a gleaming eye that won him the reputation of being "nuts". It was he who cornered McCullemy and, breathing beer on him, announced that he was prepared to make a contribution to the defence fund.

"I got a bonza bottle of prussic acid," he said enthusiastically. "I thought if it was any use to you—"

"Of course it will be," McCullemy declared. "Give us it."

He bore the bottle back to the Jamieson residence almost

ostentatiously. Jamieson was perturbed.

"But you're not going to use that stuff."

McCullemy reassured him. "Of course we aren't. But we're going to spread it about that we've got it, see? We're going to tell everyone about that bottle of prussic acid. It won't take long to spread."

At dead of night McCullemy and Jamieson took the acid into the backyard, broke the bottle and buried it in the trodden patch of dirt which was once a tiny garden. But, as McCullemy had foreseen, the prussic acid had done its work.

"I 'ear you're goin' to get them chaps out in Paradise Street?" Joe Dacey, the barber hinted, as he settled the cloth round the neck of one of the police force.

"My oath, I'm not," was the response. "The goats are mad. D'you know, they've got prussic acid in there and they swear they're going to use it. They got mines under the house and God knows what."

Though the landlords, banded together with deputations and petitions for police protection, were insisting that the police force break in the doors of those who defied eviction, nobody at the Foveaux police station was too keen on the idea. They had met McCullemy and company before. When the landlord who owned the house in which these worthies were entrenched ordered the policeman on the beat to break down the door, the policeman responded that he had instructions to keep the street peaceful and law-abiding and there wasn't anything said about door-breaking. If the landlord wanted his door broken in, let him do it himself.

After a three-weeks' siege a raid on the Jamieson encampment was planned and carried out with efficiency, a force of police attacking the rear while two more closed in from either end of the narrow street in front. The beseiged tightened their grip on their weapons, realizing that retreat was impossible. The sergeant, braver or more foolish than his following, arrived at the window and thrust his head in. It was smitten resoundingly with a heavy piece of wood and the sergeant was of no more use. The difficulty of finding out who had done the smiting was never really cleared up; but as McCullemy was the most wanted man, he was naturally enough credited with the blow. No one accused Jamieson of hitting the police sergeant. It was generally recognized that planning and strategy were much more in his line. He had hung on to the house with a grim Scotch tenacity. He had organized its defences. He had fought his losing fight capably, quite certain that it was a losing fight; and when the dust of battle cleared away, he found himself in the dock on the charge of being in possession of barbed wire reasonably suspected of being stolen.

There was no chance of proving a charge of wilful damage of property. Everything was in apple-pie order. Apart from the fact that the house had sunk an inch and a half on its foundations with the weight of armaments and barricades, it was completely unharmed. The search for the bottle of prussic acid was a failure, though the police dug up what had been the little fowl-run. But the actual fight for possession was fruitful enough of charges, both sides suffering minor injuries, apart from the sergeant, who was a more serious case. One constable bore witness against Bob Noblett's son, Jack, that the same Jack had inflicted on his chin certain lacerations. Jack's defence was repeated around Foveaux for months.

"He's lying," Jack stated baldly. "I didn't lacerate his chin. I would ask yer honour to take a look at me. I stand six foot two and I weigh thirteen stone. If I 'it 'im, your honour, he wouldn't be talkin' about lacerations. 'E'd taken 'ome something more than a scrape on the lug."

"You admit you were on these premises to prevent the police evicting the defendant?"

"I do that. No eviction for the unemployed. I was there to see he wasn't evicted and I hit every copper except this one. And 'e was right at the back and I couldn't get at 'im."

"Jack, me lad," Old Bob said, farewelling his gallant son to jail, "you did noble. 'Tisn't often a chap'll stand up for 'is feller man the way you done. And to 'ear what you did to them Johns, sonny, it gladdened me 'eart. I can tell you that. I'm sorry you didn't give the razzer oo was lacerated a proper go in, Jack." Bob paused impressively. "Yer mother says to say you're to speak pleasant to the warders, and if you come across Joe Fleming oo married Betty Marks, to tell 'im she'd like 'is wife's address. 'E's a warder at one of these pens."

Jack listened to his sire's injunctions somewhat wearily.

"You won't find it so bad," Bob continued. "Yer brother Freddy says there's usually a track-in, some screw who's willin' to do his job warderin', to smuggle snout to the men so you won't go short of a smoke. And you can always get a bet 'cause there's sure to be some bloke wiv a life sentence an' a wireless. As long as you don't smack a bad blue, you ought to 'ave a 'appy time. Well," he shook hands, "I'm proud of you, Jack. Great boy," he murmured to himself as he walked out. "A great boy."

The day the case came on should have been made memorable by a mass demonstration outside the court, if the plans of the anti-eviction committee had worked out as they had been laid down. The crowds were there with the true Fouveau-vian expectancy of trouble; mothers had brought their children in push-carts, some had even brought their lunches in anticipation of a long court sitting, the unemployed were there with banners and shillelaghs; but there was no demonstration, no trouble. The police simply refused to let the mob into the court, and a handful of them kept over a thousand people from doing anything but walk about and look foolish. Everyone waited for everyone else to start something. It was a self-conscious mob. There was not even the chance to give an ovation to the prisoners who were smuggled in and out of court by a back way.

"If you put the energy into the rent campaign that you waste organizing mass demonstrations," Jamieson suggested frostily afterwards, "you'd do a darn sight more good." He was worried about what would happen to Elsie and the boys.

"But Comrade Jamieson," his interviewer protested plaintively, "surely it was an occasion for a mass demonstration."

"You should never call any public meeting or demonstration," Jamieson laid down the rule which was to guide his later successes, "unless you know in advance that ye're going to have things your own way and then don't call it unless ye're sure."

"How about the eviction? You got put out of the house didn't you?"

"Ay," Jamieson said simply. "But it was a success. What ye might call publicity. Ye don't think I'd do a thing like that for nothing." Jamieson had collected on aggregate charges what a more hardened jail-bird would call a "drag" or three months. "It was worth it," he said deliberately. "Front page in all the papers and an outcry, ye realize that, an outcry from liberal opinion against these evictions. An' the only real casualty Joe Perry cutting himself with an axe when he's chopping a bit of firewood."

"You forget the sergeant."

"Ay," Jamieson agreed, "I forgot him. Ah well," he sighed, "it was grand while it lasted."

Elsie was of a different opinion. "Burning the electric light day and night," she complained. "They don't seem to realize the electric light bill's in my name. Oh well, we just won't be able to pay it, that's all. And they may talk about collecting donations of food, but how about broken cups? I borrowed a dozen from Mrs Dent and I'm ashamed to look the woman in the face. Don't talk to me about eviction campaigns again. If Jock wants to get himself evicted in style next time, he can do it on his own."

Elsie was already settling in another house which the landlord had carelessly left unlocked. When he came down one morning, he found that Mrs Jamieson had moved in. There was no chance of charging her with breaking and entering because he had left the door open for another prospective tenant to view the place, and he knew it.

"So you're here," he growled.

"We are," Elsie said complacently. "You'd just better make the best of it. I've got the rent. So if you'll just hand over a receipt. . . ."

The landlord hesitated. To give a receipt meant admitting tenancy; and then there would be all the trouble of getting them out. He met Elsie's eye and realized that he would have to get her out anyway. He wilted and wrote out the receipt.

"I hope one of these days," he said, "that you move into one of old Bross's places. He'd be the man to show you."

She smiled at the landlord and before he knew it, he found himself smiling back.

278

"Good morning, Mrs Jamieson," he said, touching his hat.

Elsie shut the door. "It's all very well for your father to organize getting people out of houses," she remarked to her sons who whooped around her joyous with congratulations. "But it takes something like organizing to get them into another one afterwards."

# CHAPTER 6

I

Bramley Cornish always made out Bud Pellager's income-tax papers. Linda, from her mother's bedroom, could hear them in the living-room arguing over various details. Bramley was glad enough these days to make any money he could. He never knew from week to week whether he would have a job next pay-day.

When Linnie came in, he looked up from the scatter of papers on the central table and asked, "How is she?"

"Not so good," Linnie said shortly. She went through to the kitchen and returned with the set tray for her mother's nightly nourishment. It seemed to Bramley that the sternness she had cultivated was like a wall around her. He watched her out of the room before returning to the income tax and Bud watched him with wise black eyes.

"I don't know," Bramley said with a sigh, "how to make it look possible. If you'd only tell me, Bud, exactly how much you are getting and from where, I might be able to do a better job. It's hard to fake an income tax without leaving some loophole. According to your figures, you're running at a loss." He knew that Bud was making a profit and a heavy profit somewhere. "Wouldn't it be more feasible to balance the budget, even if you only just balanced it?"

"The Guv'ment ain't balancin' its budget, son, and I ain't either," Bud croaked. "If they think you've got a ha'penny in your kick, they'll thieve it off you."

Bramley sighed. "All right. Deductions for dependants? No legal dependants?" He smiled at Bud, who smiled mirthlessly back.

"Not legal," he said, narrowing his eyes. Bud knew that Bramley was one of the few who did not take his relations with Linnie for granted. Foveaux, with that human tolerance of failings that the tolerator also possesses, took it as a matter of course that the boss of the newspaper shop should be living with his "young lady". They knew her mother was ill and did not respect Bud for the bargain they believed him to have made.

"A hard-faced piece the girl is," Mrs Blore reminded Mrs Sampson. "That little Mr Pellager'll find he could 'ave done better, with 'er mother on 'is 'ands an' all."

"Ah, well, dear, there's no accountin' for tastes," Mrs Sampson had responded. And there Foveaux let it rest.

Of Linnie's old friends only Rolfe and Bramley remained; and they did not often come to the flat for fear of disturbing Mrs Montague. There had been a time when, under the new ray treatment, Mrs Montague revived and chirruped as gaily as ever.

"The trouble is that the treatments have less and less effect as time goes on," the doctor warned Linnie. "I'm afraid," he shrugged his shoulders helplessly, "it's only a matter of staving it off."

"But can't you really do anything?"

"My dear young lady, there is nothing fixed or final. She may recover." He patted her on the shoulder and Linnie hated him for his cheerful acceptance of fees, fees, and then more fees, while he knew all the time that Mrs Montague would benefit only temporarily, if at all, from his treatments. She had perhaps less faith in him than in Mr Dale, a fine saintly old man, who came and sat soothingly at her mother's bedside by the hour. At least Mr Dale did seem to calm Angelique; she could hold his hand in a spasm of pain. Angelique needed something to cling to, and Mr Dale supplied the need when Linnie was not there.

Mrs Cornish had offered timidly to help in the kitchen or mind the flat, but Mrs Montague and she had never had any real understanding. They were both relieved when Linnie sent word thanking her and politely refusing the offer.

It was on Linnie that the main charge of the nursing fell. Mrs Montague refused the trained nurse. She wanted Linnie with the selfish, appealing tenacity of the weak. Her gaze followed the girl about, and even when she could not speak,

Linnie knew what she wanted by her eyes.

Mrs Montague was terribly changed. She clung grimly to life as though to the oar of an overloaded boat that was rowing away leaving her struggling in the water. The terror in her eyes wrung Linnie's heart with a misery too deep for tears. It seemed at times that her mother's pain had lodged in her chest and was stopping her own breathing. Linnie had no religion to uphold her with any promise of reunion elsewhere. She was not a Christian Scientist to believe that death is an unpleasant transfiguration to something unimaginably better. She only knew that they were battling fatalistically against an enemy already seated in the throat of the sufferer and steadily choking the life out of her. Knowing that every fight might be her last, Mrs Montague did not fail to fight. In a paroxysm of pain she would fix her eyes on Linnie and struggle back to consciousness, to the sound of the voice that was soft to her.

"You'll be better, darling, sweetheart. You'll be well. We'll have such fun. Remember how Angus would bring his bagpipes and we'd dance? You shall make as much noise as you want to. You shall dance all night." And Mrs Montague would rest in her daughter's arms, gasping but safe.

Bud, a laconic and quiet person, Mrs Montague strangely enough did not mind. He would sit with his legs tucked in on a chair beside her, talking softly in his cracked voice, changing the wet bandages on her head, giving her drinks of water. He snarled at Linnie when she protested against his loss of sleep.

"Tryin' to drive me out, are you? Know damn well I can't sleep more than two hours a night. Always suffered from insomnia. Get out of it and get some rest."

He would come in with a soft croak of; "How's it now, ma?" and Mrs Montague, who had always thought Mr Pellager an "unspeakably vulgar man", smiled at him faintly and nodded to Linnie to go away.

Half Bud's attention, Bramley knew, was being given to his income-tax return and the other to the shaded room where what remained of Mrs Montague, the little skeleton figure, the fevered face that had become hundreds of years old, was lying, breathing almost imperceptibly. Bramley, realizing this, added and subtracted as rapidly as he could.

"There," he said at last. "I think that's as watertight as we can make it." He leant back.

"Bram," Bud Pellager croaked, "there ain't nobody except that godforsaken Jimmy that I could trust as I trust you. Jeeze, I wish I'd got your head."

Bramley smiled his rather tired smile and took off his glasses to polish them on the tablecloth. It was a soft cloth and soft cloth had an attraction for Bramley. He had once absent-mindedly polished his glasses on the edge of his typist's silk coat and the memory never failed to make him go red.

"There's as many accountants on the breadline as plumbers," he responded. "I'll probably be there myself next month."

"Then what?"

"God knows. I might be able to crawl back with old Bross."

Bud's mouth twisted. "Hell! Send you trudging round rent-collecting."

"That's possible," Bramley said steadily. "I'd be glad to get it. I'll probably have to eat dirt for it, too."

Under the electric light his face was no longer young, though that mysterious, invisible acid which seemed so to scar and twist the faces of the dwellers of Foveaux had tightened Bramley's skin, stretching instead of loosening it. Over some faces the invisible tide of bitterness washed, leaving them puffed and pallid; others it coarsened to red blubber, loosening the flesh, wrinkling the skin to dirty leather, flaked with grey stubble, like an encrusting salt on cheeks and chin, but always changing, distorting and disfiguring, as the sea water wears the grey rocks.

Bud roused himself. "I got something you might do well at," he said in a low voice, leaning forward. "Though don't ask me to put it in me income tax." He paused, then went on cautiously: "Ever heard of the Salamoa Lottery?"

"I believe I have. What about it?"

Bud tapped his chest. "I'm one of the guys what run it."

"One of these days," said Bramley, "you'll get caught and there won't be any."

Bud's voice rose in protest. "Why, compared with some of these rackets they run for charity, it's honest. We don't pretend to be in it for our health. So far the cops have kept out."

"Did you let Jimmy know about it?"

"Jimmy claims he don't want to spend half his life in slow. He wouldn't come in on it. How about 'self?"

Bramley shook his head. "You're sure to get caught sooner or later," he responded. "Honestly, Bud, why don't you get out of it?"

"Get out?" Bud's voice was angry. "Do you think I could live on what I get out of the shop? No chance."

Bramley's face became suddenly anxious. "Is Linnie in this?"

"What if she was?" Bud snarled; and then he changed his tone. "There's a diff'rence between livin' on ill-gotten gains and actually helpin' to get them," he said sardonically.

Linda opened the door. "Doesn't seem to be picking up, Bud," she said anxiously.

Bramley rose. "I'll be going," he said, "unless there's anything I can do?"

"No," Linda answered, her face averted. "There's nothing."

Years ago, when she was a shy, little kid, admiring him through a crack in the door, he had smiled at her, she remembered suddenly. He was standing with that same apologetic smile now. "There's nothing," she said again, tonelessly. "Thanks."

## II

Mrs Montague's eyes were open, but it was obvious to Bud that she could not see. She did not respond to any asking even with a movement of the eyes. Only her breath moved to and fro in her throat in a kind of low gurgle as though the tide that had torn at her so long was going in and out with a contented ripple.

Bud realized at once that nothing could be done. Even Mr Dale, sitting immobile by the bedside, realized that.

"Would you like me to give you a little help, Miss Montague?" he said kindly.

"No," Linnie said shortly, and then she added reluctantly, "Thank you."

"I will be in the sitting-room when you want me," he said quietly.

Bud followed him out and Linda could hear them making arrangements in an undertone.

"It may keep up for days," Mr Dale was saying. "It may last only a few hours."

To Linnie it seemed that her mother was already dead. That slow, deliberate ripple of breath was not part of her mother's life. It was part of the alien life in her, living in her body, after Angelique was dead. You could not believe in any after-life when you saw a woman die by inches and her body possessed after her by something else. Perhaps in an inmost, hunted recess something of Angelique was still unextinguished; but that slow, terrible gurgle was not her. Her body might go on breathing, but she did not.

Little visions of her mother flashed up in the girl's mind. Mrs Montague in her curl-pins and kimono arguing with the milkman about short measure. Mrs Montague trying on a new dress as pleased and excited as a girl or singing about the kitchen or telling some awful man that it didn't really matter about his rent with a pleased little smirk when he held her hand. Poor Angelique. She had wanted a blue and pink bedroom, she had so enjoyed this flat. And now, what had become of her?

Nothing altered in the room. The pink-shaded light and the pink bedspread and the vase of flowers on the dressing table, the glass of water and the medicine by the bedside, all stood in a timeless dream. The terrible, monotonous gurgling went on hour after hour. Bud came in again without saying anything and sat by the window. Mr Dale entered now and then and went out again. The clock's hands crept round and round. Bud went outside to smoke and came in again to find Linnie asleep.

She woke with a start to find the monotonous tide had ebbed fainter. It was almost imperceptible now. There was a grey light showing outside and the sound of the milkman clanking his cans came through the window. A truck rumbled past. The distant roar of the morning trams began their chorus of sound. Attending to these things, Linnie was only half aware that the harsh gurgling to which her ears had long grown accustomed, was not there any longer. Imperceptibly as she listened it had grown fainter and fainter and ceased.

"Go and lie down, hon," Bud said gently. "I'll see to things."

"How about the shop?" she asked faintly.

"I've fixed that up, too. Sammy'll take the papers round and open and Miss Gunner's coming in to hang about till I get there. Forget it. I'm lookin' after this."

"She'd like a Christian Science funeral," Linnie whispered. "I don't think they're expensive."

"That'll be all right. Dale's fixing it."

The weariness which had so long held Linnie's body seemed to have affected her mind, too. The whole thing seemed dreadfully unreal.

"Wake me in a couple of hours."

"Sure."

She did not wake until late in the afternoon when, wandering out to the living-room, she found Rolfe sitting on the sofa eating biscuits.

"Dunc's been here most of the day," he said. "Bud had to go out. Bram's mother wants to know if there's anything she can do. I've been trying to stop people ringing the bell all the afternoon."

Linnie's mouth was grim. "They didn't come while she was alive," she said, and began to cry. "It was only you and Dunc and Bram and Buddy. You—"

"Hush," he said, gently rocking her to and fro, his discarded biscuit incongruous on the leather arm of the sofa. "You can't blame people. They get worried by things they don't understand. It wasn't that they didn't like you any longer. They were afraid of Bud."

"As though anyone could be afraid of Bud. Where would we be without him?"

"Don't go blaming people, Linnie. Don't be hard."

She sat up straight, conscious of her swollen eyes.

"What am I going to do?" she said, her lip quivering.

"Have a hot bath. It'll make you feel better."

She jerked her head towards the door of the bedroom. "Angelique?" she whispered.

"The doctor's been and Mr Dale's sister fixed things and the men from the funeral place. We didn't wake you. It wasn't worth while. Look, Linnie," he urged as she began to sob again. "Don't, please don't."

"You needn't comfort me," she said thickly through her grief. "I'll have a hot bath."

There was no one, Rolfe thought, who took affection so casually as Linnie. He went to the kitchen and took down an apron from behind the door. All he ever seemed to be able to do, he told himself, was either wash up or cook for her. Oh, well, that was something. When Linda returned to the living-room, the table was set, not too neatly, with a large tin of jam as the central attraction, its ragged lid thrown back. Behind it hovered Rolfe, still in his apron, his look half deprecatory. For the first time for days Linda smiled, not so much at the rugged jam tin and the butter on an old saucer, but at the kindness that had gone into these things. "Behold!" Rolfe said, his old-time dramatic swoop a little subdued. "I, having consumed most of the biscuits, decided to invite myself to tea. All I could find was some eggs."

She did not want to eat. The food choked her, but she accepted the rather blackened toast and cup of tea because it pleased him. To break the silence Rolfe began to describe what he termed the "bachelor's residence", where he and five other men were living, a dilapidated house at the Foot.

"Oh, we're very severe and monastic, but little by little luxury is creeping in. When the landlord came in and found us there, he was going to call for the police to throw us out. We finally — I, most of all, with my persuasive tongue — convinced him that, as he has no chance of letting the place and he couldn't throw us out, he'd better let us act as caretakers. And now we have an official status, you've no idea the improvements we are putting in. Old Dunc's going to join us next week if he can sneak away without the landlady catching him. He's been bringing down his books little by little, but he doesn't really trust us. He's scared we'll pawn them."

For all Rolfe's gaiety he was, as Linnie knew, only trying to distract her attention.

"We put all our dole tickets into the common fund and

anything that Alf pinches goes in as well. You've no idea how handy Alf is. He arrived home the other night with a lorry he had borrowed with a bedstead on top. A whole bed, blankets, sheets and all. We don't like to ask where he got it for fear he tells us he lifted it off someone's back veranda. A marvellous man."

That was Rolfe all over, Linda thought. If he was dying, he would joke. And then the memory of Angelique caught her again, and her eyes blurred.

Rolfe ached to take her in his arms and tell her that he would care for her now and for ever and ever. But how could he? It would be like adopting a kitten when you had nothing to feed it on. Bud, he reflected, was the only one of them who could keep her.

"As soon as things are settled," Linnie said, drying her eyes, "I'll tell Bud I'm going. Do you think," she asked anxiously, "that he'll feel I'm an ungrateful beast?"

"Well. . . ." Rolfe looked thoughtful. "I s'pose it's your circus."

"I don't know what to do," Linnie said doubtfully. Her eyes brimmed again.

"You just get some rest," Rolfe said, "and you can argue it out later." He took off his apron and began putting on his shabby coat.

"Where are you going?" Linnie sobbed. Rolfe could see that she was working up to a fit of hysterics.

"I'll be back." When he returned he was tenderly carrying a large flask of whisky. "I remembered you didn't drink beer," he announced. She was too busy crying to take any notice. "Now come on," he soothed. "To please your uncle Rolfe. Drink this."

"I can't."

"Try."

She gulped it. "Have to pay you," she said huskily. "Can't have you using your money on me."

"It's all right. I've been selling silk stockings all the week. Marvellous what you can kid some women into buying. Have another drink."

"No."

"Come on. If you don't drink it, I can't."

"Jimmy," said Linnie piteously, "I will be drunk."

"Who cares?"

"That's true," Linnie said passionately. "Who cares?" She took another drink, looking very unbeautiful from her crying. "Haven't got anyone, except our mob. S-survivor, that's what I am."

"A survivor," Rolfe echoed, nodding. "True."

Linnie wailed. "I haven't got anything to hang on to now." She swung round on him. "You've got a sense of humour. Bud's got all his queer deals and a feeling of getting the best of people. Old Dunc's got his revolution. Bram," she swallowed hard, "he's got his mother." She took another drink. "I haven't anything."

"You can hang on," Rolfe was grave, "to any one of us. I'd advise you to stay by Bud."

Linnie stared at him. "Huh?"

"He's falling over himself to have you stay on here. Not only in the job." It came hard to say it. "You're a mug if you don't. He's a good chap. Look after you."

Linnie's head dropped in her hands. She began to laugh. " 'S funny," she said. Then she got shakily to her feet. "Help me get to my room, Jimmy. Room's going round."

He swung her off her feet, carried her into the next room, and laid her gently down on the bed, covering her with a rug.

When Bud came in, Rolfe was sitting on the sofa with a book, nibbling biscuits.

"How's she taking it?" Bud asked sharply. "Where is she?"

Rolfe jerked his head towards the door. "Drunk," he responded laconically.

"Didn't think you'd have that much sense," Bud remarked. He was looking worried. "Well, it's all fixed up, funeral an' everything. If anything happened to me, you'd keep an eye on the kid."

"Too right. But what would?"

The little man rolled a cigarette. "I may be spared for the fun'ral," he said. "But that don't say I'm goin' to get a break. The cops are after me."

Jimmy whistled. "What is it? The good old Salamoa Lottery?"

Pellager cackled with harsh laughter. "Wish you were right. No, me and a few pals have been doing a bit of printing. Just in our spare time. They wouldn't have got on to it," he said almost wistfully, "if it wasn't that the post-office has the only two-way perforator and we had had to perforate the stamps down, so, and then across, instead of both ways at once. Even so, it was a good job we turned out." He rapidly rolled another cigarette. "I bin neglecting business what with the kid an' ma going an' all. Oh, well, we've cleared everything out. They'll be up here any time now."

His mouth twisted bitterly. "Tell th' kid I'll try and fix it so me brothers don't get their claws on the shop."

There was a loud ring at the bell.

"That's them," Mr Pellager said, almost relieved. "One comfort, they can only put me in the library. I'm too little for hard labour. Bram's got the bail money for us. Here." He passed a roll of notes to Rolfe. "Give these to her. They're good ones."

On the mat was standing an elderly, rather stout man, unostentatiously attired and wearing a grey felt hat. Behind him stood another gentleman of the same pattern with a similar grey felt hat.

"Hullo, Mike," Mr Pellager said casually.

"Hullo, Bud," the police officer returned. "We been a long time coming, but we got here at last. How about a walk?"

His captive grinned mischievously. "With you, Mike," he said, "I'd go anywhere."

"And less of the Mike," his captor retorted. "You don't want me to get a bad name, do you?"

Mr Pellager shook hands with Rolfe. "Give me love to Lightning."

Mike's unobtrusive companion strolled in, hung up his hat and sat down on the sofa. The door shut on the small news-agent and the other detective.

"Nice evening," Mike's offsider said placidly, licking a cigarette.

"And a nice day for the funeral tomorrow," Rolfe responded.

"Eh?"

"I said, a nice day for the funeral. You must come," he assured his new acquaintance. "It would be nothing without you."

The detective's eye grew glassy. He almost decided to arrest the long-faced, impudent chap and then thought better of it.

"Where's his girl friend?" he asked.

"Oh, she's home."

"Where?"

"Lying dead drunk at the moment."

The detective nodded. "I'm not surprised," he responded.

"Neither am I," Rolfe hastened to agree; but he had other reasons than his companion. "Funny how things always happen at once," he remarked.

The detective eyed him coldly. "That's so," he replied; and then as Rolfe rose to retire, he added: "I wouldn't go. We may need you."

After all, Rolfe reflected, he might as well wait and break the news to Linnie.

"You wouldn't like a hard-boiled egg, would you?" he asked courteously.

"No, thanks," the plain-clothes officer explained. "Gets at me stummick."

"There's nothing like enjoying your health," Rolfe responded.

"That's so."

They sat in silence eyeing each other cautiously.

# CHAPTER 7

## I

Neicie, after the first flush of married life had worn off, was inclined to be bored. It was her habit to take young Robert John Cornish, otherwise known as Bunny, to stay with his grandmother for the day. Too much of him, Neicie said, got on her nerves. Neicie had neither any idea of caring for an infant nor any desire to learn. "His grannie thinks the sun shines out of Bunny" she would say tolerantly. "And his father likes Grannie to look after him."

For herself, Neicie was more interested in seeing methods of brightening life. These varied from quarrelling with Tommy on every possible and impossible occasion to buying clothes, vases, pictures, necklaces they could not afford and might never be able to pay for. Tommy never knew when he came home whether he would find her sulking over a burnt remnant of dinner or defiantly pleased with herself and a new gramophone.

Tommy's nerves were not particularly steady these days. His old job on the buses vanished automatically with the buses themselves. The overseas investors, who had lent the money for the trams, wanted their interest and an embarrassed Government offered up the competing buses during the depression as a smoking sacrifice. In any case Tommy had decided that with Neicie he needed more money and he would be able to make it as a taxi-driver. Having borrowed the five pounds deposit from Bramley, and started as a full-blown driver, Tommy found that it was possibly the worst time he could have chosen to go into a luxury trade. People were looking for ways to economize; and taxis are not the most economical means of transport. He could not too often disconnect the meter in a well-meant effort to deprive the company of its half-share of profit, but he tried the trick, like any other driver, as often as he thought it was safe. By sleeping in the car, eating in it, practically living in it, he could not satisfy Neicie or pay for all the new dresses and hats that Neicie bought.

"You don't give a damn," she stormed, "whether I have a rag to my back or anywhere to go. As though it wasn't bad enough you being out every night of your life, you've got to try starting this union business." This was a sore point.

"The union takes a couple of hours a week," Tommy said grimly. "How many do you spend up at Doris's flat?"

"I can't even see a girl now, can I?" Neicie raged. "I've got a good mind to clear out and see how you like that. Stuck away in a room with a whining kid all day. What kind of a life do you think this is?"

Any other man, Neicie thought, would have slung the sauce bottle at her and made it up fittingly afterwards, but Tommy merely tighened his thin mouth and rolled a cigarette.

"You," she sneered, enraged by his silence, "you don't think I would have married you, if it wasn't for the kid."

But he had heard it all before. It was a long time ago that the jibe hurt him. Tommy was very tired; he had enough traffic summonses to paper a room, and there was no real pleasure in anything.

"Go to hell!" he said with weary brevity, got up from his breakfast, and walked out.

"You been 'avin' another row with Tommy," Mamie said accusingly, when Neicie dumped Bunny roughly on her kitchen table.

"Here, take the little devil," Neicie retorted. "If I have a row with Tommy, it's my own look-out."

"It's those women you get about with," Mamie said indignantly. "You never used to be like this."

"Oh, shut up!" Neicie almost spat at her. "I'm fed up. Fed up with the lot of you." And she slammed out, leaving the wailing Bunny to be cuddled by his grandma.

"She's just got sick of me," Tommy remarked dejectedly late in the afternoon, when he strolled in to snatch a bite of tea. Tommy found his mother-in-law a comfort. He had to take his troubles to someone and he was certainly not going to let his own family know how true their unspoken predictions of disaster had proved. "She wants to chuck me and she's told me so a dozen times. Only waiting the chance."

"But what are you goin' to do?" Mamie asked.

"What can I do, mum? I can't stop her."

"Even if she's me own daughter," Mamie's lips were tight, "don't you think for a minute Bob and me ain't on your side."

He patted her on the shoulder. "Don't I know it? You've been a real pal. Looking after Bunny. I'd be nearly mad if I didn't know you had him." He stopped abruptly. "Come on, son. Home to mummy."

"Neicie's never satisfied. She doesn't know what she wants," Mamie said sadly. "Not even when she gets it."

## II

If Neicie did not know what she wanted when she quarrelled with Tommy, she found out shortly afterwards, definitely and permanently. She had gone to Dennison Square with her friend Doris, holding the leash of Doris's pomeranian while that lady purchased some household necessities. Doris, who had once been glad to wear her elder sister's cut-down dresses, was shrill and scornful concerning the furs displayed in the windows.

"Why, I wouldn't even wear them as a gift," she declared, pointing scornfully to a coat marked Fifteen Guineas. "I got a set out of Isey that'd make those look like something the cat brought in."

Neicie regarded her enviously. Doris was not really pretty. Her fair hair was elaborately curled about a carefully painted little face. She and the pomeranian had something in common in their high-stepping fluffiness and sharp, excited noise.

"I could do with a drink," Doris exclaimed. "Shout you a dose of paint at Jordie's."

Neicie shook her head. "Tommy'd lay me cold if he even thought I went there."

Doris shrilled. "You don't mean to tell me you take any notice of a blasted log of wood like him? C'mon."

Once they were within the discreetly swinging door of the wine bar and seated at a table, Neicie felt happier. She did not want to forfeit Doris's friendship over a foolish scruple, but old Bob's drunken fits had given her a horror of drink. She chose the most innocuous of the mixtures offered and sipped it cautiously.

"Yunno," Doris said, watching her, "you ought to chuck Tommy, Neicie. He's no good to you, the money he's raising. Pity you don't take a tumble to yourself." Her rather mean face was expansive. "You could easy make enough for yourself."

Neicie had thought of that, but the idea did not appeal to her.

"When my old man got on the dole," Doris was saying, "you can bet he tried to cash in on me. 'See here, Dorrie,' he said, 'we'll take a flat somewhere, and you're pretty, you can kid some of these old jokers into payin' the rent.' 'Not on your life,' I says. 'If I have to keep meself, I don't see keepin' you into the bargain.' " She nodded coolly to a couple of girls on the opposite side of the room who were grinning derisively in their direction. "And now look at me. Tell me there's a depression on. There's still enough mugs to go round, if you know where to look for them. Mugs!

"They say there's one born every minute. Well, now, they're being born twins. I can keep meself and me new bloke in the bargain. Bought him a new suit the other day."

The two girls had decided to stroll across. "Hullo, Bet; hullo, Vi," Doris greeted them. "How's things?"

"Pretty bloody," the girl called Violet responded as she sat down without invitation. "How's things with you, love?"

They were introduced. "I jes' been telling her," Doris mentioned, "that I bought George a new ten-guinea suit. I took a tenner off a old goat the other night and it came in handy."

"That's nothing," Vi struck in. "My boy's got half a dozen suits if it comes to that."

"You beggars talk a lot." Betty took her share in the conversation. She was a plump, gaudily dressed woman, older than the others. "But you ain't none of you bought your boy a car, 'ave you? Well, I 'ave. Big sedan, it is, closed in. Gee, you ought to see it."

"Too right I ought," Doris said jeeringly.

"Well, you can. 'E's out in it now and 'e's calling for me 'ere. Think I'm skiting, do you? I can skite if I want to. I earn the chaff. Why, if someone did a night with you and threw you a sein, you'd snatch it with both hands." Betty had had one drink too many.

"Now then, Bet," Jordan True said in a low voice over her shoulder as he drifted past, "you don't want the razzer in the street to know about it."

Doris was looking venomous. "Here, Woffles," she called ostentatiously to the pomeranian who was tying himself into knots round one of the table legs. "He's a pedigree miniature, he is," she said loftily. "Cost me twenty pounds."

" 'E isn't a car," Bet retorted, fairly swelling with pride. The car was unanswerable.

Neicie had come to recognize that among Doris's friends a man did not necessarily do the providing for the family. It was much more often the woman's job. Their men had nothing to do all day but hang round the billiard saloons, go to the races, or show off their clothes. They would growl if their meals were not ready on time, they expected to be waited on hand and foot. In return their women could boast about them much in the manner of a millionaire who presents his wife with a world-famous diamond necklace, not to show her off, but to show his own riches. The manner in which one kept one's man marked social standing. A shabbily dressed "boy friend" meant that a girl had lost caste. She could no longer provide for him properly. Her talents were on the wane.

Neicie listened silently to their boasting. To take ten pounds off one man one night and spend it on another the next pleased her flamboyant, somewhat shallow nature. She swung the yellow liquid round and round in her glass.

"I've got to be going," she said presently. It was getting close to six. As she spoke, the door swung open and a group of men lounged in.

"There, I told you," Betty said full of pride, " 'ere comes Harry and some of the boys 'e's picked up in the car. Now, you got to wait and see it. How are yer, Curly? How's she ride?"

"Some car," said Curly Thompson, foremost of the group, as he dropped into a chair at the next table. The minute Neicie set eyes on him, she decided what she wanted. She wanted Curly. Why she should do so is a mystery. Curly was not looking particularly opulent. He was going slightly grey about the temples. Down one side of his face was a long scar.

"Somebody been trying to do you up with a chivvy?" Doris asked, eyeing the scar. Curly fingered it and grinned. "Where you been lately, Curly? Haven't seen you in a dog's age."

"I got a drag," he said not too regretfully. Three months was a good deal less than he had expected. His eyes were resting on Neicie. In this crowd of low heels, quandongs and ripperty men, she looked at her ease and yet not of them.

"I ain't seen you about either," he said humorously to Neicie. "Been in smoke?"

"I got to be going," Neicie said again to Doris. "You coming, too?"

"Eh, wait on a minute," Curly protested. "Have a drink with me. Gee, I only just meet you and you start going."

Neicie's heart leapt; but she said casually: "Got to get home to the old man."

"Look, we all got to go. Wait a minute."

Sure enough Jordan and his henchmen were clearing the bar. "Come on everybody. Twenty past six."

Curly was beside her out in the open air whilst the mob clustered round the big, gleaming car that Betty had acquired.

"Doin' anything tonight?" Curly asked.

"Why?" Neicie said impudently.

"Jus' thought you might do a show with me." He squeezed her arm. "How about it?"

She gave him a slow, long look. "I can't tonight."

"Some other time."

"I'll think about it."

Both of them knew that theirs was more than a casual contact. Next time Neicie went to the wine bar with Doris, she was deliberately looking for Curly. He too had been waiting for her to reappear. Doris watched them with her eyes narrowed as they talked. She did not stay long.

Curly and Neicie, left to themselves, were not sorry.

"What's y'r old man do for a crust?" Curly asked.

"Works," Neicie answered shortly. "Drives a taxi."

Curly raised his eyebrows. "A squarehead." He must be careful. If Neicie's husband had been a "knockabout", Curly could have dealt with him according to the unwritten rules of his own circle. But "Never attack a squarehead" had always been Curly's motto. There was too much danger that a squarehead would top-off to the police in a jam. Still Neicie was worth a bit of trouble.

"I brassed a mug yesterday," he told her, "and everything's sweet again." He flashed a roll of notes as big has his fist. "Ask for it an' it's yours." Neicie looked at him admiringly. "How about a drive for a start?" he added. "Hey, Pete, call a taxi."

"No, don't," Neicie said quickly. It would be just like Tommy to swerve into the kerb.

"Whasa-matter?"

"Nothing," Neicie responded, flinging her last scruple overboard. Being Neicie she was not going to let anything stand in her way. Curly's profession of a standover was no deterrent to her liking. In fact, it made him all the more adventurous and glorious in her eyes. He was something like a man. Neicie had once thought that Tommy was like that. Exciting, dangerous, ready to cut her throat one minute and kiss her the next. Now that she had the chance of rectifying her mistake of marrying Tommy, she was not going to lose that chance. Curly was her sort of man. She knew it at once. Curly knew it, too. He pressed her arm.

"How about being my cheese for a change?" he asked, half seriously as they walked to the door, and they laughed together.

Jordan True, whose pale blue eye missed neither incomings nor outgoings, remarked later to Doris: "It appears that Curly has got back into the juvenile delinquent class when he's old enough to be declared an habitual. The vagaries of human affection are inestimable," he said oracularly. "But what's it all amount to in the end?" From the wisdom of experience he shook his head. "Bull, just bull."

"That's his look-out," Doris said acidly.

# III

Racing a rival taxi back to the rank late one night Tommy failed to notice that the municipal watering cart had just covered the stretch of street down which he was driving at fifty miles an hour. The cab skidded, whirled round and turned over, all in the space of a few seconds, and Tommy was taken to hospital with a fractured shoulder and concussion.

The thought of Tommy lying unconscious in the hospital should have melted Neicie; but it didn't. She merely regarded Tommy's mishap as a providential opportunity to slip out of her life with him; and having packed Robert John off to his grandmother, she gathered her favourite possessions together and left for good.

Tommy's feelings when he heard the news were more than half relief. He was profoundly grateful she had not taken Robert John.

"I don't know 'ow it is," Old Bob said huskily, "that the rest of the bunch turned out all right and Neicie, that we thought was the top of 'em," he fumbled with his hat, "ain't. She shouldn't uv gone off while you was laid up. She might of waited till you got better."

Tommy closed his eyes.

"Me an' Mamie," Bob continued, " 'll be pleased as punch to look after Bunny. If you like to settle in wiv us, Tommy, we'd be 'appy to 'ave you."

"I don't know yet," Tommy said slowly. "I don't know what I'll do."

His head ached at the idea of getting a divorce. Neicie had sent a message asking for a separation; she didn't want a divorce. After all, Tommy meant money in time of need, and it was a pity to waste him.

"She can do what she likes," Tommy had replied drearily. He did not want to marry anyone else. He was cured of that. He did not realize that, by allowing Neicie a separation and losing his chance of a divorce, he was putting himself into her sharp, little claws.

The first experience of those claws was some nine months later, when Neicie quite callously and rather foolishly threatened to send him to jail for non-payment of arrears of maintenance. And then Tommy really did get mad.

"If she thinks," he said, "that I'm going to work myself blue, blind and purple to pay her money, she's mistaken." He was living with the old people and Mamie and Bob had been good to him. They, he felt, were his family and they had first call on any money. Bob was having a hard time of it. It looked as though the old horse and cart he had kept by him all these years would have to go. Yet here was Neicie insisting on her pound of flesh.

"She doesn't care," Tommy said bitterly, "as long as she's all right." He couldn't and wouldn't pay Neicie's allowance any longer. If she tried to send him to jail, she was just killing the goose that, if it didn't lay golden eggs, had paid down so much a month. Thereafter, he realized, his life must be complicated by this struggle to pay Neicie's and lawyer's fees when she sued him for custody of Robert John, lawyer's fees if she sued him for arrears, and more lawyer's fees if he tried to get a divorce. He meditated throwing the taxi over.

"While I'm working," he explained to Bramley, "she thinks she can get something out of me. If I get on the dole, there's nothing doing, and she knows it."

Anyway, he would get his divorce and, as he could prove Neicie was living with a criminal, there was no fear of her getting Robert John. But as far as women were concerned he was through. He had never realized how sound Bramley was in keeping clear of them. He said as much to his brother.

Bramley did not reply for a minute. He was leaning on the window of the taxi which Tommy had drawn into the kerb. "Look here," he said, "you're out and about some queer places. See if you can pick up any trace of Linda Montague."

"Why, I thought she was living with Bud Pellager."

"She was — in a way. But she cleared out after her mother died. Bud was arrested the same time." Bramley's manner was confused in his effort to appear casual. "Jimmy's been searching for her high and low."

Tommy scratched his head. "Rather a tall order these days. Like looking for a lost ha'penny at the mint. What's the idea?"

"Rolfe's keen on her," Bramley said deliberately.

Tommy gave him a shrewd look with some of his old mischief in it: all his trouble with Neicie had failed to break that boyishness in him. "Strikes me he isn't the only one." He grinned. "I always thought you'd a soft spot for that sour-looking piece." He snapped his fingers. "They're all the same. I suppose she got all she could out of Bud."

Bramley said nothing. It was not his habit to discuss women, more especially Linnie, with a hard case like Tommy.

"Love 'em and leave 'em," the hard case grinned. "You're a mug if you don't."

Bramley shook his head. "It's not good enough," he said slowly. There was something in his blue eyes that stirred all the sore hurt of Neicie that Tommy thought had healed.

"I did but see her passing by," he murmured derisively, "and yet I love her till I die. That's your line, eh? Let me tell you, son, that's all you ever will do if you don't hop in and start before it's too late. Staying pure gets to be a habit."

"How's Robert John?" Bramley asked. He hated Tommy's views on virginity.

"The Rabbit's fine." The old boyish look flashed back to Tommy's brown face. "And talk! You ought to hear him."

"And how's the Taxi-drivers' Union?"

"That's fine, too," Tommy responded.

It was strange, Bramley thought, that Tommy, cured of matrimony, should take to organizing a union. He, Bramley, had been cured of organizing. As for matrimony, he shrugged. The only thing these days that mattered was trying to hold your job.

# CHAPTER 8

## I

The extraordinary confusion that the depression brought upon
the landlords and agents in Foveaux was due to the fact that,
whereas there were many fine new flat buildings, such as those
twin white elephants erected so lovingly by Bross, Massingham
and Twyford, the general run of the population could not
afford to live in them. People were giving up even the
moderately priced flats and looking for something cheaper.
Tenants of houses were going into rooms. Others were sharing
houses or looking for smaller ones. The first idea that occurred
to the desperate clerk, with a salary cut so that it resembled
a lettuce, was that he could find a "cheaper place". And following the exodus of tenants, the rents began to come down
with a run. Impoverished landlords, left with empty houses on
their hands, were offering them at half rent, sometimes charging only a nominal sum to keep tenants in the houses to
protect them from stray "squatters" who, evicted from some
other landlord's roof and desperate for a dwelling, were likely
to walk in and defy removal.

Other landlords were struggling with erstwhile good-paying
tenants who had nowhere to go and no money to pay rent.
Even Mr Bross found himself in a difficult position. He was
able to get any number of tenants because his houses were the
cheapest apologies for a dwelling that it was possibe to find.
His chief trouble was to get people out when they could not
pay. There was always a large floating population in the Bross
houses ready to steal away, leaving considerable arrears of
unpaid rent. But now some of the oldest residents were catching the complaint. Not that they could find anything cheaper
and nastier. The only choice below one of Mr Bross's houses
was a tent.

How many non-paying tenants Mr Bross did manage to

drive into rooms or unemployed camps he himself could not
tell. One woman was luckily removed just in time. Otherwise
she might have caused him trouble by a long and sympathy-
rousing convalescence in his house. The rent-collector got her
out protesting and destitute and she was delivered of a child
in a tent in the rain with her other children crying around her.
As Mr Bross said, he wasn't a hard man; but he couldn't have
the woman pleading impoverished circumstances to the
magistrate and playing on the new baby and living rent-free
in his house when he could be letting it.

"I remember poor old Joe Burke saying to me once," Mr
Bross remarked to his son, "that if it wasn't one thing a
tenant'd put over you, it was another. There was a man for you
— he's gone now, God-rest-'is-soul and a great fun'ral they
gave 'im, the Grand Master of the Lodge there and Sir
Whatsisname Eccleston and all the nobs. Though I don't s'pose
you'd really count it as a fun'ral, seein' they only recovered
part of the body. 'E told me 'imself that 'e was goin' over the
cliff but 'e 'oped the insurance wouldn't find it out an'
naturally, God-rest-'is-soul I wouldn't tell the company. I'd
a felt I was lettin' down an old friend if I prevented 'is widow
collectin' on 'im—"

"Dad," his son broke in on Mr Bross's wanderings, "I want
a loan."

Mr Bross's look of soulful sentiment vanished. "What's up
now?" he said tartly.

"I'll give you my personal security. Those flats. . . ."

"Not good enough," Mr Bross, Senior, responded shortly.
"I'm sick of the sound of them flats of yours. I wouldn't 'ave
'em on me mind."

"Look, dad, we're in a hell of a mess. You know what
prices are. There's no sale for land. We might as well close
down, all the business we're doing. Massingham's just about
mad. We weren't working on a big margin and now the insurance company's likely to close down on their mortgages. We
staked a lot on those flats."

"More fools you."

"I know, I know. Don't dig it in. They're just a loss. We
equipped them with cocktail sets and silver and linen galore

and this fashionable mob got in and gave parties. They'd break one of the cocktail glasses and when they moved out the week after, the new tenant'd want a new cocktail set. And someone leaves a cigarette butt on the centre table. Nice little scar on the edge. Next tenant won't take it without a new table. Or one of the serviettes is missing. New lot of serviettes or you'll have them squealing. It's costing a fortune to keep the fittings in decent nick."

His father had been listening with a glazed and contemptuous eye. "I always told you you took after y'r mother," he put in. "What's the use of all y'r swank? If I 'ad them flats, I'd make 'em pay. I'd make 'em pay right in the middle of this 'ere depression."

"You would? How'd you do it?"

Mr Bross was conveniently silent. "I'm willing to do you a good turn, Billy. After all, you're me son, even if you ain't got any 'ead for business. Too 'igh falutin'. Lookin' down on terraces. You seem to fergit you was born down at the foot of Lennox Street over the grocer's shop an' your mother, God-rest-'er-soul, accusin' me of flirtin' with the midwife, an' you lyin' squallin' there all red an' raw-looking'. 'Gawd-struth, woman,' I says to y'r mother—"

"Yes, I know." Bill Bross had heard the story before. It had the genuine Foveauvian touch. Not that he was squeamish; but the old man's stories were a bit rough and ready. "What about these flats?"

"I been thinkin'. What'd it cost to get Massingham and Twyford out?"

"They'd sell out for next to nothing to be free of them."

Old Mr Bross almost chuckled. "Good. I'm buying their shares. But you're goin' to buy 'em for me, Billy. After all, you're my son, an' I feel like doin' you a good turn. You get me those shares."

Bill Bross went red. "Where do I come in?"

"When I got those shares," his father answered affably, "I'll show yer."

"And you won't give a loan?"

"No," Mr Bross responded blandly. "I won't. I'll do yer a good turn instead."

Bill Bross cursed silently. "It means that I'm back in the old cow's hands," he said bitterly to Bramley Cornish. "Once he gets control, he'll turn those flats — good, exclusive flats, even if they aren't paying their way at present — into a horse stables or a dancing academy or something. I know him."

"I've been meaning to ask you, Mr Bross," Bramley said, "if you could give me an idea of how long the firm will be needing my services. These rumours of dissolution. . . ."

Bross stared. "So it's got about, eh?"

"Not through me. I just asked if you thought I'd be doing wrong to look for another job."

"By all means look," Bross said gloomily. "If there's one to be had. I bet my socks there's not a job in Sydney for a pig-washer without about three hundred apply."

Bramley swallowed. "If you hear of anything," his pride hurt his throat as it went down, "I'd be grateful if you'd let me know."

"Yes, yes," Bross said, hurriedly rising. Other people's misfortunes are an annoyance. "See what I can do. If I hear of anything." He wandered out, a middle-aged, bald man, rapidly going to flesh.

Bramley looked after him bitterly. "If I had had half your chance," he thought, "this business wouldn't be on the rocks." They had practically thrown it away, like a good ship with a drunken captain. But he, Bramley Cornish, was only a fore-mast hand looking for a spar to cling to. Bill Bross would float. His father would see to that. Those flats were probably, if Bross only knew it, a comfortable lifebelt.

Bramley's pencil flashed across his blotting pad. If he had a thousand pounds, even five hundred, he could transform those flats, he could make them into a semblance of what he and Jimmy had hoped the Porpoise might be. He could make neat, efficient homes out of them, let them to people at a reasonable rental and make the place pay for itself. There wouldn't be much profit, but there would be enough coming in for repairs, lighting, rates and so forth. But what was the use? He tapped the pencil despondently. No money.

Again his brain lit with an idea. Old Bross was interested in Bill's white elephants. Perhaps, if the idea were put to him —

there was just a chance. Bramley seized his hat. "I'll be back in an hour, Miss Bevis," he called.

He did not even ring Old Bross for an appointment, knowing the old man's habits. At the moment he would be eating his after-dinner digestive tablet, a vile pink pill that he bought by the half-pound box from a dirty herbalist's shop at the bottom of Murchison Street.

Bramley walked straight in. "Could I see you for a minute, Mr Bross?" he asked, standing over the old man, a tall figure in navy blue, very correct with his pince-nez and his aloof look.

"Well, it depends what you've come about," Mr Bross said deliberately. "If yer want to see me about a job, you can git out."

"It's about the flats, Your son was telling me you're interested in them."

"Take a seat." Bross shoved a chair out with his foot.

"There's a big chance going to waste there," Bramley said almost eagerly. "They may not look it, but they're a sound investment, Mr Bross."

"I don't need you to tell me that."

"But not as flats for rich people." Bramley was talking quickly in a low voice. "For people who can pay a moderate rent, they could be the beginning of a big thing—"

"Who brought you into this?" Bross asked abruptly.

"I brought myself. Your son said you had some idea of turning the place — into something or other — and I thought I could offer you a scheme."

"Why?"

"Well. . . ." Bramley began to go red. "It was something I wanted to do myself and I hadn't the money to do it. You have. I've passed the idea on. I don't want anything out of it." He had meant to ask the old man for a job, but his gorge rose against the thought.

"Heh!" Mr Bross grunted disbelievingly. "As old Andy Kennedy used to say (he's gone, poor feller, went off in nineteen hundred with a camel team west of Bourke. They found his gold teeth in a creek bed. Sold 'em too) . . . as old Andy used to say, when a feller tells you 'e don't want anything, clutch yer wad hard." He eyed the stiff figure in front of him almost jeeringly.

"Since you stuck yer nose into this, I'll tell yer what's goin'
to 'appen to them flats, seein' you don't want anythin' out of
it. I'm going to take 'em over an' make 'em pay. Not," again
the jeering note caught Bramley, "not that I aim at any slum
clearings an' model dwellings an' such. No. I'm goin' to stick
in some partitions an' gas grillers an' so on. Jus' like your idea
only better. Let 'em as rooms, bachelor flats. Ha, ha. That's
the idea. Modern residential."

Bramley was aghast. "But you're going to make them a
slum!"

"A slum?" Old Bross chuckled. "That's only your way of
puttin' it."

Bramley stood up. "I'm only wasting your time and mine,"
he said. "Good afternoon."

"Marble-tiled bathrooms for the workers," old Bross
crooned. "Suites of plush free for 'em to put their boots on.
That's your idea." He, too, was on his feet. "I seen it in you
when yer first came into this office. When you was a kid.
Lookin' at me like a blue-eyed baa lamb, frosty and dis-
approvin'. I'd 'alf a mind to give yer the sack many a time, but
I says: 'Bill thinks a lot of 'im and 'e's only a kid.' " He was
close to Bramley looking up at him maliciously. "You and
your Slum Clearance gang. Where did that get yer? Nowhere.
Not that I lost anything through you. What're you goin' to do
now? Let yer old woman keep you? That's all Bill's been doin'.
Livin' on 'is old woman's money that I put in 'er name an' she
left to Bill."

He seemed to sink back behind those wrinkled, reptilian
eyelids. They blinked and moved like a lizard's. "Try it out an'
see how you like it. When you get yer bellyful, you can come
an' ask me an' maybe I'll give you a job. Maybe I won't." He
mimicked his ex-office boy's clear-cut speech. "I don't want
anything out of it. That's you all over. Too damn stuck-up to
eat." He tapped himself on the chest. "Look at me. I was born
an' reared in one of them little houses at the Foot you swanky
bastards called slums. Bill was born in one of them. An' what
was good enough for me is good enough for a lot of other
people who 'ave to put up with what they're damn lucky to

get." He was wheezing with suppressed emotion. "There ain't nothin' wrong with them houses. I lived in 'em an' I know. Wantin' marble bathrooms! Jus' swank, that's all it is. Swank."

"Good afternoon," Bramley said politely. He was almost sorry for the old man. "I might," he thought as he walked through the outer office, "be crawling in to beg for his damn job any day now." And he mentally added: "I'd probably get turned down," and more bitterly: "I'd have to risk it."

## II

Mrs Cornish in the depression acted much as she had always done in a high gale at sea. Then she had insisted on going up on deck with a neat little gossamer veil tied firmly to keep her hat on. Now she bustled round preparing to take lodgers, to be helpful, to do her small part to keep the ship afloat.

Almost proudly she eyed the notice "Vacancies" in the corner of the front window. She had kept it by her, a faded legacy from Mrs Webb, and it had come in handy, just as she had prophesied. With the trepidation of a hungry little spider on a leaf she settled down to wait for her bread and butter to ring and ask to see the rooms.

Bramley was out day after day doing the rounds of the offices, answering advertisements, being polite to head clerks, applying for everything from bar tender to salesman wherever he thought there might be a chance. He had in a fit of devilish pride kept from his mother that Old Bross had taunted him with being unemployed and had half jeeringly dangled the promise of a job. Bross would like nothing better than the chance to knock him back, to humiliate him.

Bramley preferred even going round from door to door advertising breakfast goods and distributing sample packets of "Cruncho, It Tastes Like Foam", having doors slammed in his face and dogs sniffing at his ankles.

From a temporary job of this nature he returned one night to find that the beaming Mrs Cornish had let the front upstairs room to two "young ladies". It was not for him to be censorious, he thought, when he met the two young ladies on the stairs. They had paid in advance. When one of the young ladies returned home the next night in a taxi, Mrs Cornish, peeping from behind the window curtain, was much impressed. Then she realized that the taxi-driver had alighted to assist the young lady out, for she was too hopelessly drunk to do anything but cling to the two bottles in her arms. One of them fell and rolled unbroken in the roadway; but she merely jerked her head for the taxi-driver to pick it up and lurched across the road to the front gate, while he followed meekly in the rear. Mrs Cornish thanked heaven it was not Tommy driving the taxi. She had not realized before what terrifying things taxi-drivers must encounter in the course of their daily round. The driver deposited his fare on the veranda, touched his cap and drove away. Mrs Cornish opened the door terrified.

"I 'ad a few drinks, ma," the young lady said with maudlin affection. " 'Ere, one of them's for you." She dumped the bottles into Mrs Cornish's arms. "I've 'ad trouble, dear," she continued thickly, patting Mrs Cornish on the shoulder and breathing wine down at her. "A boy friend of mine, you might of heard of him, dear, Joe Collins, 'is name is, has just been framed." She shook her head sadly, dribbling over the last word. "Framed," she repeated, swaying slightly. "It wasn't what you would call entering. They give 'im a month. It's 'ard, dear." She patted Mrs Cornish again. "It's 'ard just to come out yourself and then 'ave them pinch your boy."

Mrs Cornish's hair almost rose on her head. For years now she had been carefully searching her room each night for burglars, and here was her new lodger, not only alcoholic but an admitted fraternizer with the kind of person who, Mrs Cornish felt sure, would think nothing of lurking under her bed. Nevertheless, she helped the girl upstairs.

"What else could I do?" she asked Bram almost tearfully. "We can't afford to have the rooms empty. Oh, dear, oh dear. They've been singing and shouting and calling to young men in the street. I'm sure the police will come and take them away, and it won't be a bit like Mr Duncan who was a respectable man, even if he did write for the papers."

Bramley went upstairs and was received with a storm of abuse.

"We paid our rent, ain't we? You try and shift us. l ike hell you will."

"Your room is required from next week," Bramley said sternly. "If you make any more noise, I'll call the police."

This effectually quieted the young ladies for the time being. Next morning they were full of apologies; but little Mrs Cornish, divided between dislike of scenes, fear of a police visit, and the terror of finding a possible burglar under her bed, was adamant.

Bramley, the same morning, was waiting in the Bross outer office before the old man got in. "I'm busy," Bross croaked as he passed through. "I ain't got no time to see you."

"Mr Bross. . . ." Bramley followed him insistently. "I wish you'd allow me a few minutes. I won't keep you." He dogged Bross into his office. "I want to ask you to consider me if you have vacancies on the staff." He was eating dirt and knew it. "Your son knows that I am competent and he'll tell you that his firm had no fault to find—"

"Nothin' doin'," Bross snapped.

"I've been eighteen years working, Mr Bross, five for you and thirteen for your son. I think that entitles me to ask you to consider my application."

"You think it entitles you to a lot." Mr Bross sank back in his leather chair. "There's men with longer service out of work today and as likely to get work." Bramley picked up his hat and turned towards the door. "Swank," Mr Bross said unpleasantly. "If I let yer take over some of me rent-collectin's, you'd be that far above it, you'd look like one of the 'Imalayas."

"I'd be glad of any sort of a job, Mr Bross."

"All right." Bross was business-like. "You can start on Monday. Be here Friday to get the run of things. You still don't drink?"

"No."

"Nor gamble, nor go with bad women? I know. Pure an' 'oly." His tone was satirical. "You'll be getting the basic wage jus' like any ordinary chap." Bramley almost bit his lip. "If you got anything to say, now's yer time."

"You said Friday, Mr Bross?"

"Yeah."

Bramley gave almost a queer little bow. "Thank you; I'll do my best."

"See Simons when you come. He'll tell you what to do. I'm busy."

As he went out Bramley wondered why he did not feel anything but kindly towards Old Bross. Somehow the old chap regarded him as a symbol of an alien civilization to that of Foveaux. He was taking revenge on Bramley as he might have hacked at Jimmy's unbuilt Porpoise with a knife. He and Bross recognized, disliked and yet admired something in the other, a certain warped pride; Old Bross in being of the Foot earthy, and Bramley in accepting a situation and quietly putting up with it.

" 'E's honest," Old Bross said to his son. "Too bloody stupid to be anythin' else."

Bill Bross moved uneasily. He felt he might have done better for Bramley.

"Glad you made room for him," he muttered. "Deserves something."

### III

The young lady who came home in taxis was very condescending to Bramley when she and her friend packed and left.

"Don't you get the idea you got us out. We were only here for the time being. We got a place in Foveaux Flats." She winked at Bramley. "Any time you feel like dropping in to see us."

Bramley smiled. The idea struck him as humorous. He had a mental picture of himself very solemn in his navy suit and pince-nez glasses ringing their bell.

"You'll like it, honest you will," the lady said brightly.

"You may be seeing me," Bramley said, still smiling. "I will probably collect your rent."

The lady's expression changed. "Oh," she said icily, "well, g'bye. Come on Jean. Let's get out of here."

"Oh dear," Mrs Cornish mourned after her ex-lodgers, "it does seem a terrible thing to think that those young girls are

. . . not nice." She hesitated on the word. Far be it from her
to condemn. But when she went upstairs to put their room
to rights, her opinion was strengthened and confirmed.
"Look," she called, horror-stricken, to Bramley. "Look."
She was holding out a small brown object. "A b———! They
must have brought it with them." She would not say the word.
She would not mention the enemy against whose insidious
hosts she and all other landladies of Foveaux waged war un-
ceasing. "They'll get in the walls," she wailed, "and we'll have
all the trouble over again that we had at Mrs Webb's place."

"Cheer up," Bramley said with a grin. "They'll probably
take a few to their new quarters."

The idea of Bill Bross's once beautiful flats, now cut up into
rooms and half-flats and bedsitting-rooms, becoming infested
with tiny inhabitants did not cause him any regret. "Serve them
right," he muttered. Old Bross had refused to put in any more
bathrooms. He had termed his drastic carving up of floor space
"alterations and repairs". A flat that had been intended to
house a family was now housing three. People were sub-
letting rooms and even beds on the good old Foveaux tradition. The place still looked all right from the outside, but inside
there was a difference. Loud voices echoed down the stairs.
There were cigarette butts in the palm-stand in the hall. Neighbours complained of the noise and the quarrelling that went on.
The police swooped round silently and collected a group of
sly-grog sellers from the second floor. The tenants strung
clothes-lines across the windows and aired their linen in
full view of the street. As long as you paid your rent you
could live in Foveaux Flats and no one was particular how
you got it. No longer were they advertised as exclusive or quiet
or select; they were just residentials with a blaring chorus of
gramophones.

Another of old Bross's innovations had been to run up a big
parking garage on what he called the "wasted ground" at the
back where the tenants had formerly hung their washing and
the children and lap-dogs had taken an airing. The roar
of the cars from the lane came in at the flat windows. All day
and night the noise seemed to continue. It was as though the
flats themselves were shouting like barrowmen, proclaiming

their hard, loud creed of indifference to the universe in general.

There was no privacy in the flats. The thin partitions might have been of matchwood, so little did they muffle sound. There was no friendship, each flat-dweller claiming a self-sufficient suspicion like a hermit in a desert and furious at the people above and below. However sunny it might be in Lennox Street, with the leaves of Honest John's debatable plane-trees casting a flickering embroidery on the paths, many of the tenants always had on the electric light because their rooms looked out on a dark lift-well or a blank wall. You could get a bachelor flat, admittedly lacking light and air, but with hot water laid on, for a little above what you would pay for a room around the Foot.

When three shrill, bepainted women climbed into Tommy's cab one night he took one genial glance at them and said, "How's trade?"

"Bloody awful," one of them responded, pushing her hat back. "D'you ever get any mugs in your cab?"

"Sometimes."

"Lumber them down to my place." The woman gave him a meaning nod. "I'll make it worth your while."

"Where are you?"

"Foveaux Flats." She slipped him a card. "You know the big place at the top of the hill. Don't forget."

Tommy mentioned the encounter casually to Bramley. "The flats are getting a stinking bad name," he remarked. "You might tell the old fool so from me."

Bramley shook his head. "What does he care? They're making money."

It was not only the atmosphere of the flats that had altered during the depression. Foveaux was a wreckage of empty shops, dwellings, with "To Let" and "For Sale" notices, deserted factories with their windows smashed by stones. A place could not stay empty long without being wrecked and some landlords were even glad to bargain with the unemployed trespassers they might find camping in their empty houses to stay there until the house was let on the condition that they guarded it from thieves and kept it clean. This was less expensive in the long run than prosecuting them for breaking in.

A general air of desolation and neglect was more and more noticeable around Foveaux although the noise seemed to have increased. All day long the great lorries thundered through Lennox and Mark streets; they backed cautiously, or not so cautiously, out of little lanes and obscure entrances; they charged hot and shining down the black roads. Women still strolled bare-legged and in slippers up to Dennison Square to buy from the vegetable barrows on Friday afternoons and look at the shops. Or on Saturday mornings they attended the meat auctions to bid for a coveted piece of pork and some sausages. The fish and chip vendors still sieved their sizzling fat, and down-and-out, thin-faced men still hung about the doors of the cafés that took dole tickets, waiting hungrily for five o'clock when they would open.

Barrowmen up and down every little lane and street collected their usual buyers on credit-till-dole-day. Children still screamed together as they played along the footpaths. Nothing had altered, except that there was a general impoverishment, a gradual, easy assumption of the standards of the Foot as the population of the Foot crowded into the houses farther up the hill, driving out more and more of the more respectable residents. They had energy and vigour on their side. Foveaux was their native heath and they looked almost with contempt on those persons of our alien civilization who did not attend the greyhound races or spend their Wednesday and Saturday afternoons in the wine bar listening to the races.

The gradual tide of the Foot was rising up, was drowning out the old gentility in a hard-mouthed, loud, cheerful, brutal flood. People who might still work occasionally, or who had not worked for years, people who never intended to work and still made enough money out of other people's trustfulness to eat three times a day, ladies of easy virtue and easier conversation, all types on the border-line of respectability or just over that border-line, made for Foveaux, living all up and down Lennox Street, without realizing that their place was round the Foot, as it had been in the old days when the old demarcations held.

They lived as they had always lived, from hand to mouth, and spent what they had on picture shows and beer. Mrs

Cornish, regretting the departure of Mr Budin and his wife, was shocked by the morals of the people next door. There were so many people living there and they dumped their tin cans and old rubbish all round the yard where Mr Budin had grown flowers. They had three cats who came over in a body and fell upon Darkie. They had two dogs always lying in front of the house and attacking passers-by. There was an aggregate of nine children for the three families always playing noisily on the footpath.

"You never saw such people," Mrs Cornish would say to Bramley. "Screaming and swearing and carrying on. I'm sure I don't know what your father would have said. He was always very particular about bad language."

Bramley had to walk most of the day collecting rents. He usually came home too tired, after listening to excuses, complaints or just boring gossip from Mr Bross's tenants, to pay much attention to Mrs Cornish's murmurs of horror. Only one thing, he vowed, he would get out of Foveaux. He would shake the dust of the accursed place off his feet for ever.

If only they could have enough money to get a home of their own somewhere along the harbour or the sea front, he would die happy. Only to get out of Foveaux, the smell of it, the feel of Foxeaux closing round him like an invisible, mysterious jail, of which the chimney-tops and towers were spikes to wall him in. To be away from the humiliation of working for Bross and hating him with a corrosive dislike that was beginning to mark deep lines beside his mouth. Sometimes he thought that if he did not get away from Foveaux he would murder some of these gabbling dirty women who kept him talking on their doorsteps in the hot sun, these slouching men sitting along the gutters, these snotty brats playing around the dustbins.

"Things are so dear," Mrs Cornish would go prattling on with her little pieces of news, as they ate their tea. "I had to go to three butchers before I could get a set of brains, and if it hadn't been for that young boy in the shop at the corner knew me, I wouldn't have been able to get them then. Pussy caught a bird this morning and the feathers were all over the lawn. It must have been a pigeon by the size of the feathers. Will you have some more gravy?"

"No, thank you, mumsy," Bramley would respond mechanically. Even sitting at the kitchen table in the old suit he wore for tramping around Foveaux, he looked infinitely correct and cool and at ease. Mrs Cornish watched him happily, her son who had so justified her affection, who had never spoken a hard word to her, who was always efficient and quiet and calm. There were not many mothers, she thought, with such a quiet, good-tempered son. He was becoming quieter and quieter these days, but perhaps that was because he worked so hard. Later, she was sure, he would get a better position and be more carefree.

Bramley, however, realized that he would never be free. He was thirty-two; he was shy; he was set in a complicated network of little habits. He liked his food cooked in certain ways; he always made his own bed and swept his room, and he would resent it otherwise. His queer loneliness, certain little austerities he had, were set hard, a part of him now. He was not adaptable any longer. He had grown stiff.

Even so his queer dreams of getting out of Foveaux persisted. Once he had hoped to change Foveaux, to mould it to his own pattern of a certain clean austerity. But he was not even like that himself now. He felt that his mind was only a whited sepulchre, clean and efficient on the surface, but seething below with hate and passion and unpleasant longing he knew not for what. He had to keep a determined grip on himself to prevent those back alleys in his mind from sending out tenants into the more conscious reasoning parts.

He had formed a queer, unconscious habit of clenching and unclenching his hands. More and more of his initiative and nerve was being worn away as his boot-leather was worn tramping the hot pavements from one terrace of hovels to the next.

"I don't think the bird is really well," Mrs Cornish was saying. "He screeches such a lot, but perhaps it's those children teasing him through the fence."

"I'll clean his cage on Saturday," Bramley said mechanically. If only he could get away from Foveaux. A vision rose to his mind of blue water and unclouded miles of beach and scrub. "How would you like to go away for the week-end, mumsy?" he asked. "Stay at a boarding-house near the beach."

Mrs Cornish looked doubtful. "Where would we leave the bird?" she asked. "There'd be no one to feed Darkie. And I don't think it's altogether safe to go away with those people next door."

"Perhaps you're right," Bramley said slowly. "Perhaps you're right." But he said it so strangely that Mrs Cornish looked at him puzzled. She wondered if she ought not to get some kind of tonic from the chemist.

# BOOK IV

---

# THE ROCKS

# CHAPTER 1

I

With the depression the Reverend Adam Atwater's talents, so long limited by the round of church functions, had found their proper outlet in organized benevolence. He had started with a soup kitchen in the church hall and, finding that many of those who came to it had nowhere to go at night, he allowed a limited number to sleep in the church hall thereby much disturbing the insurance company. The numbers, however, who were turned away, decided Mr Atwater that something must be done on a bigger scale.

The black four-square bulk of an empty factory in Joyous Street caught his eye, and it was not long before he was pouring out his idea to the factory owner. While the place was not being used the owner was agreeable to accept a nominal rent on the understanding that improvements were made and that all rates and taxes fell on the shoulders of the Church Relief Committee which Mr Atwater with his customary vision decided to form.

"We can be certain of the liberal support of our church people," the Reverend Adam burbled enthusiastically. "We have had no trouble so far in collecting all the food we need from the big shops and factories. The men, I know, will be only too willing to help by contributing their dole and their labour they will also give, willingly — willingly. And think what an opportunity, my dear sir, what a marvellous opportunity for improving the morale of these men — their spiritual view — their, as it were, religious sense."

He was equally enthusiastic towards government officials whose aid he enlisted.

"Take all these poor fellows camping in the Domain. Wet nights, little tents and caves, that sort of thing. Much better if they had some real home where their self-respect could be

developed." Little did Mr Atwater know that the Domain
dossers with a view of the harbour would not speak to the
inferior campers with only a view of the docks.

"Doesn't sound such a bad idea," the official said thoughtfully. "They're a confounded nuisance, what with people going
down to give them things, and other people whining about the
pitiful plight of the unemployed. Besides, they make the place
look untidy."

"Exactly. Exactly." Mr Atwater was ready to agree with
any view in support of his scheme. "Poor chaps. They can't
help it, of course."

"Well, if you get your property rent free and light free and
food free, and pay only a nominal rent," the official said
presently, "I suppose you'll be feeding them for nothing, eh?"

"Not at all," Mr Atwater said firmly. "The men must be
given some feeling of independence and responsibility. They
must not be allowed to subsist on charity. It saps the morale."

Later, for the same reason, though partly because the cook
complained, Mr Atwater decided that the hostel should serve
only two meals a day, breakfast and tea. "If they don't go out
and forage for themselves," he argued, "they'll get slack. It
gives them an incentive."

To his delight, Mr Atwater found that not only did the
Church Relief Committee receive hearty support from all
quarters, but it made a handsome profit. Sixty men to a dormitory and five dormitories to the hostel with an average of
six and sixpence a week allowed him to clear, over and above
the scanty wages of the cook and the officials, some forty
pounds a week. This, he considered, was full and ample proof
of the efficiency of his methods of benevolence. He was able
to administer the money well enough to furnish, with donations
another men's home and a third hostel for married people who
had been evicted.

In this hostel there were some objections from people
ignorant of the true facts. They seemed to think it was unhealthy for a mother and father and six children to share a
room. Mr Atwater explained that it was possible to allow only
one room to each family. They furnished it themselves and
provided their own food, the Church Relief Committee charg-

ing a small rental for the room. Mr Atwater pointed out that most of the people in the hostels were quite used to such arrangements.

"Necessity, my dear chap. I admit I don't like it myelf, but it's better than leaving the poor creatures on the streets."

For all the effort and thought and enthusiasm he put into planning the homes, Mr Atwater, as their administrator, was not as happy as when he was running paltry church bazaars that gave no real scope for his powers. The extraordinary hostility and ingratitude of those he sought to benefit and bring back from what he termed "the lowest depths" troubled him.

He had been by chance one of the crowd at a meeting of unemployed and the howl of hate and rage that went up when his name was mentioned cut him to the heart. They regarded him as the symbol of all their miseries because it was to his hostels that the police sent them. He strove to make their lot more tolerable. He preached that only Christian love and trust could bring them to a better state of things.

"We can only do our best," he would say. "Everyone is doing his best. The Government is doing all it can for you men and you must have patience."

He trusted the officials in charge of his hostels. They seemed sincere Christian men. He would not give heed to scandals against them. Whenever he visited the hostels they seemed in excellent order. The wooden tables were scrubbed, the tin dishes washed, the men respectful. And yet he was not happy.

"If there's ever a revolution in this country," one man had shouted at him, shaking his fist (admittedly the man was drunk and undesirable and he was being ejected), "you'll be the first to get stood against a wall and shot. I 'ope I'm there to put a bullet through you."

Mr Atwater did not prosecute the man for his abuse. He took up a Christian attitude that the fellow was one of those types it was impossible to lift from their degradation. Yet the thought of such hatred troubled him. He had only done his best and he felt, he truly felt, that there was something wrong with human nature when it would not recognize his best as good.

# I I

Unemployed single men usually found their way sooner or later to the Joyous Street hostel. It was therefore natural that one wet dripping night Jimmy Rolfe should tramp into the entrance and broach the matter of a bed to the official at the hall desk.

"Eightpence the night, fourpence breakfast and fourpence tea," the official said with polite decision. "If you're on the dole, you can just put in your ticket."

"I had an idea that I could get a night's shelter for nothing."

"You'd have to see Mr Atwater and you can only see him between ten and twelve and two and four."

Rolfe felt ruefully in his pocket. He had no desire to see the Reverend Atwater or be subjected to his warm bubbling sympathy. He paid for bed and breakfast.

"Come far?" the official asked familiarly as he made out the ticket.

"Perth."

"Thasso? If you have any valuables you'd better leave them here. C42's your bed."

"I think I'd better keep the crown jewels," Rolfe said thoughtfully. "I always sleep with them under my pillow."

"This way, old man, straight up the stairs." The man's cordiality was almost worse than hostility.

Dormitory C, to which Rolfe was directed, had oddly enough quite a domestic atmosphere. It would have been a repellent place unoccupied. It was a long, cold whitewashed factory floor with a roof too low and windows tight shut. The washroom was at the end opposite the entrance door and between the washroom and himself were sixty beds so close together that there was only just space between them for a man to stand. The occupants of the beds were some of them already under the clothes, some had gathered in groups arguing in a friendly way. Others bent over a pack of cards or a racing paper. The domestic atmosphere was enhanced by little lines of washing strung between the posts supporting the roof. From home-made clothes pegs depended the spare shirt and socks of the bed owners. One glance convinced Rolfe his sheets were much in need of the same treatment. He decided to sleep in his clothes.

There was only one old gentleman on that floor who sported pyjamas. He wore them ostentatiously and they looked conventional enough from a front view. Seen from behind, they were tattered ribbons and less actual covering than the all-predominant shirt.

Having discovered bed forty-two, Rolfe took off his boots and sat down gingerly on the side of it to take stock of his neighbours. Very few of them were worse dressed than he was. One man was carefully placing his trousers under the thin straw mattress of his bed; another was cleaning his boots with a little home-made boot-brush. There were all the evidences of independence and cleanliness about these men, a friendliness mixed with reserve that surprised him. Here were none of the "lowest depths" but a set of men making the best of what little remained, whether it be the shreds of an old pair of clean pyjamas or a worn-out pride.

An old gentleman with white hair was solemnly doing his physical culture exercises in the little space just inside the washroom door. "Fifty-six?" he was saying, chuckling to a younger man. "Why, I'm seventy-two, and look at me. Never had a day's illness."

The man in the bed next but one to Rolfe was exhibiting to his friends a home-made electric torch. He had connected an old cast-off torch to a set of discarded dry cells assembled in a butter-box. He had also a home-made wireless set, the earphones of which were adjusted over the head of the man in the next bed who had gone to sleep with them on. These home-made wireless sets, Rolfe later discovered, were fairly common in "Eden", as the hostel inmates bitterly named their refuge. It was not uncommon to find the owners or their mates listening, not only to the racing news, but also to symphony concerts with every sign of enjoyment. None of the wireless sets was licensed. When a visit from the postal inspector was due, a notice would be posted warning all wireless owners to stow their property out of sight.

"How about my things?" Rolfe demanded of a wizened bottle-nosed citizen in the next bed. "Will they be all right?"

"A chap 'ud have to be pretty tough," his companion
remarked, "before he'd start pinching things from us here."
He eyed Rolfe curiously. "I s'pose they been telling you it's a
case of first up, best dressed, and that you got to put the bed-
posts inside your boots to keep 'em from walking?"

Rolfe shook his head. "I don't know anything about the
joint," he said.

"Everybody bludges and robs," the leathery-looking citizen
drawled. "They have to make a crust. In business it's supposed
to be reasonable profit. But it's just robbery." He smiled.
"They don't rob you here because you ain't worth it. Except
for grabbin' your dole." He heaved the blanket up round his
shoulder and turned over. "It's nice," he added, "to be in out
of the rain, ain't it?"

"Yes," Rolfe said shortly.

"When I think of some poor chaps," the leathery citizen
continued, "who ain't got homes to go to. Ever been on the
track?"

"No."

"You ain't missed nothing."

The lights gave a warning blink and Rolfe discarded his
coat, vest and socks, and turned into bed just as they went out.

When a late-comer stumbled in, the electrical expert with
the torch proudly switched it on and directed the beam on the
stranger while he undressed and climbed into bed. The newcomer recognized that the gesture was well meant. "Thanks,
mate," he called into the darkness. The torch blinked out and
only the light from the washroom, which stayed on all night,
faintly illuminated the floor.

As the dormitory settled down into comparative silence,
Rolfe began to notice the chorus of coughing which was to
keep him awake most of the night. He could grow used to the
lack of air, to the ever-restless procession pacing by all night
to the washroom, but not to that interminable coughing. The
men in the hostel were never really well. Bad food and too little
of it kept them constantly undernourished and wakeful. Some
sat up most of the night coughing and silently smoking an
occasional cigarette. The many-toned snores were nothing to
the coughing. It was as though the unspoken protest these men

had not made broke from their throats in the darkness, a muffled reproach to the civilization which bred them to be herded here like cattle waiting to die. They did not complain. They were dignified with their small pieces of soap and their carefully preserved razors. They only lay awake and coughed at night, thinking.

Rolfe found himself thinking also. His mind flickered back over the resolve he had taken to leave Foveaux eighteen months before. With Linnie gone, God alone knew where, he had decided to break with the place, and after memorizing empty cabins in the shipping company's office, had gone aboard a boat for Fremantle.

Rolfe's stowing away had been a work of art. At the last possible moment he rushed up the second-class gangway, asked to be directed to the first-class, went quietly to the cabin he had selected and stayed there until dinner-time. That meal was the crucial test. Having waited until everyone was at dinner he marked down an empty seat and waved aside the steward who came forward for his table reservations.

"It's quite all right," he said confidently. "That's my seat. Over there." His manner carried him through.

Rolfe didn't really care what became of him. He was over forty and he had begun to look it. He did not care. Almost before he was off the boat he was trying for a job having made friends with two of the stewards. They introduced him to another steward who knew the head-waiter of one of Perth's biggest hotels. A fortnight after he landed, Rolfe, in a stiff white mess jacket, was carrying round trays of coffee and liqueurs in the hotel lounge. It was a stroke of luck he had not bargained for, and had it not been for the pain in his inside, he might have been almost happy. He even attempted to save money, a thing he had never done before. Inevitably he made friends. Wherever Jimmy Rolfe went, he made friends, and his life was by no means lonely. But the pains in his stomach nine months after his introduction to the art of waiting bade fair to put an end to that career.

The doctor's emphasis regarding the necessity of removing part of his intestine he repudiated. He was not, he said, "going to have any tucks put in him". Finally he collapsed and was removed to hospital, where his condition after the operation was described as critical.

It seemed to Rolfe, tossing in the stuffy dormitory, that it might have been better if he had died in Perth. He was getting old, he was sick and weak. He had no one in the world who cared twopence for him.

"A long sea voyage, a milk diet and complete rest," the doctor had said unctuously.

"And no worry," Jimmy said sardonically. "I know."

Why he had decided to come back to Sydney he could not say. Although he laughed at himself for the idea, he had a conviction that Linnie was still there somewhere, carrying on in her lonely, independent way. Foveaux, besides, had always had an attraction for him; a baffling mixture of dislike and homesickness for that dirty locality filled him. He cursed himself for his decision to return. Almost against his will he was being drawn back to Foveaux. "So be it," he vowed. "I will take my place with the other wrecks." He would not struggle any longer or make fighting efforts to wrench comfort from fortune before it was too late. He would enjoy being a failure in peace, high and dry on the lee shore, gradually disintegrating.

With this resolve he gathered the shreds of his old impudence and repeated the manoeuvre which had brought him round the continent. The only trouble was that no single cabin was vacant on the homeward-bound boat he had chosen, so he fixed on an empty berth in a two-berth cabin and flung himself on the mercy of the Englishman who had paid good money for the other berth.

"So if you want to have me hauled off to the dungeons," he had concluded his story, "now's your chance." But the Englishman had been delighted.

"I say, have you got a dress suit?" he asked.

Rolfe shook his head. He had had one until recently.

"You must let me lend you one of mine," the Englishman said eagerly. "And you'd better come down to dinner with me. Make it look much more authentic, don't you think?"

The effort of boarding the boat had taken the last ounce of energy out of Rolfe. When he landed in Sydney he did not want to see anyone he knew. He only wished to crawl into a hole and die. The next best thing to a hole seemed to be "Eden". As he lay weak and exhausted in the dirty bed, he wondered just how long it would be before his wish came true.

The night dragged on. A grim grey light outlined the window-panes. When finally he trooped down with the others to breakfast he found that he could not eat. There was a tin mug full of something that might have been either tea or dirty dish-water, a slab of bread that had been stale three days ago, a dish of porridge without milk or sugar but with plentiful remains of yesterday's porridge still sticking to the bottom of it and a plate on which reposed a leathery fragment that, by the taste, must once have been horse. To attack these delicious viands he was provided with a spoon and fork. His neighbour was endeavouring to chop off a corner of the horseflesh with an old razor blade; but the main method of attack was to hold the fragment up on the end of the fork and eat round the edges.

Rolfe pushed his away and immediately one of the others pounced on it hungrily. The sight of the food made him ill, and after trying out the alleged tea, he rose and went out, grinning as he noticed that the attendant forestalled the wolves by snatching up the bit of bread he had not eaten, dusted it carefully and carried it off in triumph to be used on some other occasion.

In a week Rolfe would be looking forward to the porridge at least, later perhaps, even to the gate-hinge masquerading as meat. Meanwhile he made his way to a small café close by where, for sevenpence, the waitress brought him bacon and eggs, toast and coffee. She was not in any way like Linnie. Still she was a woman, she spoke to him, she laid out knives and forks and brought him food. It was the first domestic touch, the first kindly word a woman had spoken to him, it seemed, for years.

Thereafter Rolfe came to that café, not for food, but because the waitress knew him and smiled to him as "a regular". He had joined the thousands of men who wait in loneliness for the meal times when a woman will speak to them, the only woman's voice of all their day, who go to the same mean eating-house because the waitress knows them and may address them by a Christian name, may even fling a remark about the weather. They crave with a terrible loneliness, as they crave food, the domestic presence of a woman. They wait until their own waitress is free to serve them, and they resent the ministerings of any other than their own.

That day and many succeeding days Rolfe spent sitting in the sun. Always there was "Eden" at night and a meal or so by day. When he gained strength, he would try to get work. Meanwhile he was beginning to be recognized as "a regular", not only at his café, but in "Eden" where the more exclusive circles now deigned to enter into conversation with him.

The mysterious leathery neighbour who rose and left at dawn became almost friendly. Old Snow showed him some of the physical culture exercises, and Josh Capple, the mechanic with the wireless set, let him listen in to the opera broadcasts. He was even admitted to the exclusive poker school in the corner where, as in jail, they played for stakes of tobacco. Little by little he came to know them all.

He and Grandpa Brophy and the leathery Herb Jones in the next bed formed almost a little club of their own with Herb's mate, a big hulking country lad, who was always threatening to go back "up to Bellinger", because the water in Sydney tasted funny. It wasn't like river water at all. He complained that Sydney didn't smell like the Bellinger either but nobody seemed in the mood to rectify the mistake. He and Herb were barrowmen, hence the early rising. Old Grandpa Brophy made a pittance hawking bootlaces, soap and darning wool in a battered old suit-case. Almost from the first he took Rolfe under his protection.

"I can see," he wheezed, "that you're like meself. I've had the money, you know, but I've spent it. Ah, that's the trouble, I've spent it. I can remember Sir Frederick Wickers saying to me when I was a lad—a great favourite of his, I was — 'Brophy, my boy,' he would say, 'ah, the fairest and best of women come between friends and remember, my boy, your best friend is in your pocket.' A grand man, Sir Frederick. Did I ever tell you about the time he and I took the late King out fishing?"

It was impossible to prevent Grandpa Brophy from producing an anecdote to fit any prominent person mentioned. Always Grandpa had met them or outshone them under peculiar circumstances which he would proudly relate.

"Sir Joseph Banks," he would say with a gleam in his eye, "now a curious thing about Sir Joseph Banks, it's a fact that, I suppose, only I know, and never having told anyone, the secret, when I die, will go to the grave with me. I remember when we were boys, we used to go down to a boatshed kept by a chap called Joe Banks, and a funny thing about him was that he was never known to wear boots. Later, my dear wife (God bless 'er) came to me one day and said: 'The woman who comes in to clean floors, Minnie Banks, her name is, says that she's Sir Joseph Banks' daughter and Joe Banks is her brother.' 'Why, if this is true,' I said, 'what an astonishing thing!' "

Grandpa Brophy, all the time holding his audience with a rheumy blue eye, would emphasize the suspense with his pipe stem. " 'I must see her,' I said. And I did see her. 'Is it a fact, my good woman,' I says, 'that you are related to Sir Joseph Banks who came out with Captain Cook?' 'It's as true as I'm standing here, sir,' she said, 'and the mystery of it is that neither my brother nor I have ever been able to get our rights. After father died mother was turned out of Government House, we don't know why, and we was brought up in poverty. That's why Joe always goes about without boots.' Remarkable mystery, eh? The daughter of Sir Joseph Banks scrubbing floors!"

"Too right," put in Herb Jones, who had been listening with keen interest to this recital.

"Ah, but the mystery didn't rest there. Not at all. I mentioned the matter to a solicitor friend of mine and he said: 'Harry, me boy, if what you say is a fact, I feel I'm on a big thing.' Apparently he sees Joe Banks and establishes that his grandfather is the Earl of Absolt, and he determines he'll take Joe home to England to claim his rights."

"Without no boots?" Herb's pal put in.

"Ah, that was the crux of it. My friend had bought Joseph a pair of boots out of his own pocket, but Joe had to walk half across Sydney to catch the boat, and he couldn't walk properly in boots. Here's the solicitor leaning over the rail anxiously and scanning the wharf because he thinks Joe'll miss the boat, and at the last minute Joe comes strolling down, his boots round his neck tied together by the laces.

" 'Why haven't you got 'em on, you ruffian?' the lawyer shouts. 'Disgracin' me and your noble name.'

" 'Couldn't walk in the damn things,' says Joe."

Grandpa would pause halfway in a yarn on some pretext or other to draw more listeners to the group or work up interest.

"And how did the belted Earl take it?" Rolfe felt he should show some appreciation.

"The Earl, his grandfather? Ah, well, I'm going to tell you. And this is where the mystery is cleared up."

"Get on with it before I faint," Herb said with a grin.

"My friend the solicitor told me when he returned how he interviewed the Earl and the Earl was certainly very gracious. 'If,' he said, 'if he had been my grandson, perhaps, I might see some point in keeping a damn dirty fellow that can't even wear boots after the many years he has spent among the natives of Australia. But, my dear sir,' the Earl says, 'I am about to reveal the reason why I have no intention of recognizing him as my heir. His mother was not my daughter, she was my wife. And that damned low scoundrel of a Sir Joseph persuaded her to elope with him to Australia when his friend Cook discovered the place. And do you think I'm going to have that rascal's rascally offspring claiming me as a relative? Why, if it wasn't for one thing and another, I would have been off to Australia years ago looking for Sir Joseph Banks. And, sir, I was taking a horsewhip with me.' " Grandpa Brophy paused sadly. His audience relaxed.

"So 'e didn't clean up on the Earl?" Herb inquired.

"No, sir. To this very day the son of Sir Joseph Banks may be seen fishing barefooted off the end of the wharf and the secret of his lineage," Grandpa continued solemnly, "resides with me alone and will probably die with me. And the tragedy of it all is that Lady Banks who lies in a grave at Waverley Cemetery isn't Lady Banks at all."

"Well, if that isn't too bad." Herb winked at the grinning Rolfe.

"Up on the Bellinger wharves," his mate said wistfully, "you can get fish just by leaning over and scooping them out."

"Ar, hell!" Herb said disgustedly. "You and the Bellinger."

It was a few nights later that Herb came gloomily into the dormitory, sat down and pulled off his boots without saying a word to anyone.

"What's up?" asked Rolfe. "Somebody sandbagged your mate?"

"That's just it," the leathery Mr Jones said nastily. "He's gone back to 'is bloody Bellinger, and I hope," he concluded viciously, "that he drowns in it." He accepted Rolfe's tobacco. "We came out of jail cleanskins this morning," he began again. "And he says, 'Herb, before we get any more blues for obstructin' the traffic, there's something I want to tell you. I am going,' he says, 'back—' "

"I know. Back to Bellinger next week. Tough luck."

"With a barrer," Herb said gloomily, "you need a side-kick you can trust." He glanced at Rolfe sidelong. "I don't suppose you've ever been on a barrer?"

"No. Can't say I have."

"How about giving it a burl?"

"Do I get anything out of it or is it honorary?"

"Fifty-fifty," Herb said cautiously. "Strikes me you'd be pretty good on calling them up. You know —'Step this way, ladies, look at these brussels sprouts, you won't see brussels sprouts like those anywhere in Sydney today. Sixpence, lady. Thank you, lady.' "

"It sounds all right," Rolfe reflected.

"Of course out of every month you spend a week in slow. We halve the warrants between us." Rolfe did not look so happy. "That ain't really anything to worry about. Take a look at these blues." With a flourish he produced a wad of grey summonses which he shuffled like a pack of cards. "Thirty of 'em there. They come in handy in the washroom sometimes."

Rolfe looked over Herb's shoulder. "Hereinafter called the defendant," he murmured. "Between the hours of 8.30 a.m. and 6.30 p.m. did conduct a vehicle, to wit, a hand cart. . . . Why, to wit?"

"Search me." Herb shook his head.

"Which, owing to its loading, was unable to perform its

journey at a pace faster than a walk along Pitt Street. . . ."

"Sounds as though I was being cruel to that there little barrer, don't it?" Herb grinned. He flicked the summonses with a dirty thumb. " 'Ere's another. Did use a standing vehicle for the purpose of offering for sale certain goods, to wit, strawberries." He shuffled rapidly. "To wit, pineapples, to wit, celery, to wit, sprouts — and so on."

"What do they do? Lug you up to the station?"

"Some silly copper might be mug enough to take a chap up to Central and get ticked off by the seargeant for leaving 'is beat. Usually, you push the barrer down to the city and pick a good spot. The John comes up and says: 'Take that bloody barrow out of here.' And you say: 'You bloody well try and shift us.' Well, after you've called each other everything for a while, he books you for obstructin' the traffic."

"Then I suppose you appear and so forth?"

"You don't have to appear on a traffic summons." Herb looked pained at his new mate's ignorance. "Of course, you could get one of these lawyers who hang round pubs to appear for you for the price of a beer, but it ain't worth it. Say, you're fined two and six with eight shillings costs, or a pound, option, three days. Well, you ask for time, and get a week."

"What good is that?"

"You can go to work in the meantime and get some more bookings," Herb explained. "It takes three or four days to issue a warrant, and when you've got about ten bookings and ten warrants, you can't work any more, so you go into smoke for a week." Rolfe looked dubious.

"After about a week you ring up all the stations, Darlinghurst and Clarence Street, and say: 'Any warrants out for me? All right. Send them all in to Central, will you? I want to give meself up.' "

Rolfe felt it would be better not to interrupt. The picture of giving himself up rose in his mind.

"Well, they send your warrants in, and you go to the pictures on Saturday night all comfortable. . . ."

"Sort of glow of conscious virtue?"

"Yeah. Well, after the pictures, you word the paper-boy to send your paper up to Central in the morning and you walk in and give yourself up."

"With a dramatic flourish?" Rolfe suggested.

Herb was forming a habit of ignoring his interjections. "They can't send you out to the Bay on a Sunday, so you spend Sunday yarning with the chaps at Central and then Monday morning at six you get out to the Bay and put in your week."

"Only a week! I thought it would have taken a couple of years to work out the summonses."

"They're concurrent," Herb said simply. "That's the idea of getting as many as you can before you go in. I've known fellers cut out thirty in one week. Go in Saturday and come out cleanskins on the Friday." He looked at Rolfe questioningly. "It ain't a bad life."

"After living in this damned hole," Rolfe declared, "jail seems good for a change."

The signal for lights out came in its usual unexpected manner.

"Are you on?" Herb asked impatiently as he began to remove his coat.

"I'll give it a go."

"Right-o. G'night, Jimmy." Mr Jones obviously considered the matter settled.

"It certainly restores the self-respect," Rolfe murmured to himself as the light blinked out, "to have the prospect of a job again."

### III

Being Herb Jones's "side-kick", Rolfe discovered, was hard work. Really too hard for him. He was almost glad when the price of fruit rose to ten shillings a case and the barrowmen could not work. At other times he and Herb were able to go to their "bank", a big, fat, shrewd Jew, who hired the barrows and scales, and demand an extra fiver when they saw a "nick" in the market.

There was the triumphant day when they sold forty cases of passionfruit and cleared a profit of seven pounds ten between them. On another occasion when walnuts were dear, they bought half a load, filling up the rest of the barrow with cheap new potatoes. Shovelling the potatoes and walnuts into the bags together and selling them as walnuts, they did a roaring trade.

Herb was an expert at sleight of hand. Many a time Jimmy saw him flick ten bananas into a bag and take the money for a dozen. When one lady came back and complained, Herb was courteous and apologetic.

"Verry sorry, lady. I dunno how it could uv happened. Now look, you watch me. Two — four . . . six — eight . . . ten — twelve, and extra one for coming back."

When the woman got home there were only nine in the bag.

"You got to jink the public to live," Herb maintained. "Why, we'd make about fourpence profit on a case, if we didn't dud 'em up."

Rolfe was becoming an expert at arranging apples where they made a tempting show in front. Behind these toppers were the inferior fruit that had to be mixed in with the good. He learnt all the tricks from putting saw-dust with the peas to sticking a half-pound weight under the scales. He could just touch a paper bag with his finger so that it turned the scales when he was giving light weight, and his manners were charming.

"When a barrowman, do as barrowmen do," was his motto. He and Herb would make what they thought was a good day's profit and then go to the races. They always had a standing debt with their "bank". But, as Herb explained, "Look at the money he makes out of the fruit cases the barrowmen dump in 'is yard. Why I've known Sam the Jew clear six pounds case money in a week."

The only trouble about jail was, as Rolfe expected, that it interfered with his milk diet. He became hardened to it after a while. When he and Herb were making money, they lived well. When they hit a lean patch, they could always go back to "Eden".

"It's the apples sends us there," was one of Herb's favourite jokes. "Not gets us put out."

Herb was contented with his queer new mate who had "trouble with his stummick" and used long words. Rolfe had acquired a good grip, however, of the language of Foveaux and could talk, as Herb graciously admitted, "like a real knock-about". He would describe the police "sweating on them like a mob of vultures" and he gave money its rightful designation of "chaff", "sugar" or "hay".

"An' when I come acrost you," Herb would remind him, "you was about as much use as a dead cat."

"True, true," Rolfe would respond.

He had a habit Herb could not understand of probing into all kinds of odd nooks and corners. He would search the faces of the crowd passing their barrow always as though he expected to see someone. Apart from Herb, old Duncan and Bram Cornish, he had no friends.

"It's such a silly sort of game to waste your life on," Bramley argued. "In and out of jail all the time. You know, Jimmy, you could do pretty well now if you made the effort."

"I know. I know. But I might just as well be a barrowman as anything else."

"It's a waste."

"So are you," Jimmy retorted. "You ask your mother. She's still certain you're going to be Prime Minister."

Bramley grinned and dropped the subject.

When times were bad, Jimmy had discovered ways and means of coming by free food. He got to know every "hand out" in Sydney. Only to one of these did Herb refuse to accompany him, and that was when Rolfe paid an occasional visit to Ogham Street Mission.

IV

One of Rolfe's first discoveries had been the Mission. He had gone there with Grandpa Brophy one Wednesday night and found that most of the congregation were men from "Eden". This had puzzled him until it was announced that tea was handed out after the service. Bench by bench they sat there, all the broken, ageing, shabby men with stolid, wrinkled faces, leaning forward looking at their clumsy worn boots, while half the amateur preachers in Sydney talked about "love" and exhorted them to receive it.

They were waiting, not for love, but for the tea and bread and butter, the due reward for hearing all the platitudes they had heard before. The iron-jawed, scrubby old missioner rubbed redemption into them like salt; the fat young student smeared it over them like melted butter, the visiting preachers hurled it at them; but it always bounced back off that patient mob waiting for the tea and bread, from the tolerance and hard wisdom of these men whose eyes said so plainly: "He's young. Let him talk. There's always the supper."

And the preachers knew it. They knew that their flock was waiting to be fed, that without the bribe of a cup of tea and a thick sandwich, their hall would be empty, and their pleadings fall on empty air. As far as the Foot was concerned, it had been proven all too often that, without inducements of a material nature, the inhabitants preferred to remain heathen, playing two-up at the back of the hotels. As for horse-racing, it would take all the religious-minded in Sydney preaching twenty-four hours a day in shifts to keep one housewife from putting her sixpence on the chosen horse, and then they would only prevent her so doing, if they could prove they knew a better chance than the one she had picked.

There was a certain good-humour mixed with the tolerance extended by the congregation to the gospel bringers. The men loved to sing hymns. Rival singers would pick sides and shout at the top of their voices against each other. As Grandpa Brophy said, he liked "hymns with plenty of guts in them", and the swing of some of the hymn tunes was certainly admirable. Rolfe found himself bellowing with the rest:

> *"Where will you spend Eternity?*
> *That question comes to you and me!*
> *Tell me, what shall your answer be —*
> *Where will you spend Eternity?*
> *Eternity! Eternity!*
> *Where will you spend Eternity?"*

"Have you ever thought on that question, friends," the missioner grated at them as they sat down. "Ah, where will we spend eternity? Where indeed? Some of you men know, or

think you know, where you are going. But do any of us know?
Only trusting, trusting, accepting His mercy and love, can we
be sure we will save ourselves from the result of our sins.
Where will your present life lead you? Ask yourself that?"

To another week in jail, Rolfe thought. Probably the week
after next. He was beginning to be bored by this aimless
existence, in and out of jail.

"Some of you men," the missioner said stridently, "will sing
yourselves into hell. You refuse the Love of God when it is
offered. Ah, time and again you have sung of it. But have you
really accepted it?"

"George's in form tonight," someone behind Rolfe whispered huskily.

"We will ask Brother Loftus to take us to the Lord in
prayer," the rock-jawed bringer of love said harshly.

The comfortably covered man, sitting on a chair a little in
front of the crowd, rose and shut his eyes. Most of the congregation sat with theirs open watching him interestedly as he
worked up a sufficiency of fervour. It was Mr Loftus's habit
to pray with his elbows, his eyebrows, his waistcoat. His glasses
moved up and down on his little snub nose and the perspiration
broke out on his brow as he remembered any number of little
faults in the universe which it might be worth recommending
to the notice of their Creator. But particularly was he annoyed
at the prevalence of sin. He spoke about it at some length,
one eye on the door at the back of the hall through which he
expected the visiting preacher to appear at any moment.

It was a sustained effort worthy of more attention than it
received, the congregation, when the first interest in him wore
off, having settled down to its prayer-time occupation of
reviewing the occupants of "Magdalene Row" where, under
charge of a small stiff matron in squeaky shoes, the inmates
of the Little Clee Street Home for Destitute Women always
sat. The two front rows were their by right. There they were
carefully segregated from any tendency to immoral glances
on the part of the "Eden" residents. All that could be observed
of the Little Clee Street inmates were the backs of their necks
or an occasional side view, but from long gazing at these
salient points, the men from "Eden" had come to distinguish

the characters and personalities of Magdalene Row from the Matron to little Timmy. It was as much a diversion as hymn-singing to speculate about the mysterious group as they walked in two by two and out again at the end of the service, un-approachable and guarded by the stiff, small matron. The congregation always sat silent until the women had gone out, eyeing them speculatively.

"I'm sorry for them girls," Grandpa Brophy would whisper. "The little one with the kid isn't looking so spry tonight."

"Did you notice the one on the end looking round," a white-haired old veteran would ask. "A very flighty lookin' girl I'd say."

Mr Loftus with a final wave of his elbows, a final rush of protestations concerning their attitude to the primordial force of creation, "humbly returned", as he said, "from the throne of Grace to resume this earthly life". He mopped his brow and sat down. A hymn was announced to fill the gap; but the tardy speaker, a small apologetic man with thinning hair, galloped up the aisle and took the rostrum, shuffling his notes.

"Well now, boys," he began affably, "let's begin with a hymn. Come on, which hymn do you want?" He did not know which hymns had already been sung.

There was a difference of opinion, one group wanting one hymn, and one another. Finally, on the request of an old fellow in the front, "Throw Out the Life Line" won the day.

"But first," the preacher was playing desperately for time. "Before we sing our hymn, boys, I will ask Mr Loftus to lead us to the throne."

Mr Loftus, relaxed in his chair, started up and convulsively swallowed the peppermint with which he was solacing himself.

"Wot, again?" moaned the back bench.

Mr Loftus shut his eyes and said with unaccustomed severity:

"We come before thee, O Lord for the *second* time this night. Thou knowest O Lord, our needs. It is not for us to remind thee. We would, however, ask. . . ." And he covered the grounds of his former petitions with considerable dispatch, the speaker meanwhile studying his notes and the audience studying the speaker.

The method of the visiting preacher was, as he said, "the scientific approach". He investigated the Love of God with a little geological hammer and tapped at it in sharp-nosed investigation. Then he went on to lay bare the probable mental, physical and spiritual strata of those present, pointing out pressure faults and erosion. He then turned his little hammer on their attitude to the scientifically established Love of God and intimated that it was as hard as sandstone but friable.

"Stony-hearted," he rapped. "Once I was stony-hearted myself. But the love got me, boys, the love got me."

"It can have him," a heathen behind Rolfe announced hoarsely. The meeting was always restless towards the end of the sermon. There was a general impatient shuffling of boots that brought a sour frown to the face of the director.

"There is a tide," the preacher began to work up to his peroration, "that, taken at the flood, will float you. You know the wonderful old saying, men. Don't miss the tide. I plead with you not to miss that tide. It is the cleansing tide of The Blood. Don't let that tide go out without you. Don't be left stranded in sin. Think of it floating you to your Heavenly Home, to the golden sea, and the eternal rest of the saved. Our last hymn," there was a general sigh of relief, "Hymn Three Hundred and Ninety-Seven, 'Are you coming Home tonight?' A wonderful hymn, boys, a beautiful hymn. 'Will you trust His precious promise? Are you coming Home tonight?' "

Due to the fact that very few of the congregation had homes, the hymn was a favourite. They enjoyed the irony of it and gave it full voice.

> "Are you coming Home tonight?
> Are you coming Home tonight?" they bellowed.
> "Are you coming Home to Jesus,
> Out of darkness into light?
>
> Will you trust His precious promise?
> Are you coming Home tonight?"

One of the women in the front row had a very deep voice. It rang out through the roars of the male unemployed. Rolfe located the voice's owner as a shabby, lean woman, fourth from the end of the front row.

In the silence that followed the final prayer all the men sat expectantly waiting for the women to go before the stampede for supper took place. Every face in the hall was turned to them curiously as, with eyes cast down, they filed out. The matron tramped behind to the door and the spell was broken. "Ready, boys," the stout Mr Loftus beamed and there was a rush and thundering of heavy boots down the stairs. Rolfe was not among the throng. He was struggling towards the entrance of the hall and the retreating file of destitute females, his eyes fixed on one in particular, the woman in a shabby black beret who was Linnie Montague.

# CHAPTER 2

## I

When Linda Montague left the court after Bud's trial she realized she was lucky not to be leaving it in a prison van. Her release was due mainly to the Reverend Adam Atwater, who had testified to her character with warmth and vigour.

"You'll keep in touch with me, won't you?" he asked as he shook hands. "All friends you know, Linnie . . . all ready to help . . . only too glad. And here's Bram Cornish's splendid little mother offering you a home!

"And I'm sure with your capabilities. . . . Have you any plans, at all, Linnie?"

"Get a room," Linda said briefly. "Get a job."

There had been no word from her father or Oscar. Bud, in jail, did not seem very pleased to see her, had told her to keep away. She felt she could not accept shelter from the Cornishes knowing how nervous her mere presence made Mrs Cornish. Bramley's mother was afraid that Linda might want to take Bramley. She would heave a sigh of relief at Linda's refusal however much Bram might protest.

Linnie had a little money from the sale of the furniture. Neatly she packed her clothes, listed what possessions remained to be sold. Then very carefully she made herself out some references, not in the name of Linda Montague, but of Linda Allen. Her plans for shedding her old skin were complete.

She was done with Foveaux, with her old life. Not even Jimmy or Bram should know where she was going. It must be a clean break from Foveaux. She shrank from anyone who knew Linda Montague. She did not want to be Linda Montague any longer. To disappear in the city of Sydney you need move only a few streets. Linda went to the other side of the city. She moved from room to room as she found out the drawbacks of each. One was so infested with bugs that she slept there only one night and that in the bath. At another the landlord beat his children so that their screams echoed all over the house. In a third the landlord tried to make love to her, or, as she termed it, "put the hard word on her". Linnie was no stranger to the hard word; but in her case it had never softened her to any endearment more promising than a black look. She finally settled down in a dim dark back room in a cheap residential run by a Mrs Spurge.

There were hundreds of typists walking around Sydney with the soles worn from their shoes and, finding her typing references of little value, Linda made out some more for herself as a waitress.

Her first position was scrubbing floors in a café. It was only a part-time job, bringing in fifteen shillings a week. For all the economists say, it is impossible to live on fifteen shillings, even when paying only five shillings rent to share a room with another girl who is likely enough to walk in in the middle of the night with a gentleman friend ready and willing to contribute substantially in return for his night's entertainment. Linnie preferred a room to herself and that cost her seven and sixpence, leaving a shilling a day for food, which sounds ample until you try to exist on it.

"I tell you what I'll do," a generous, stout butcher had said when she applied for work. "I can't give you a job, but any time you want meat, you can come here and get all you like for nothing."

"Thanks," Linnie said briefly. The offer was a good one. The problem was to cook a steak without her landlady's knowledge. If her landlady caught Linnie cooking steak, she would immediately demand arrears of rent on the assumption that people who ate steak must be affluent.

For some time it was Linnie's habit to knock on the window of the ground-floor back room to gain admittance. The inmate, an ex-commercial artist, called Harris, was also dodging the landlady, and Linnie found it convenient to pass through his room as a means of ingress. They used to drink cocoa together. They had little food, no money, no milk or sugar, but Harris, from some mysterious source, had supplies of cocoa. They almost lived on it. "Here's luck," they would say, smiling at each other over the rim of their cups. And, "Better luck next time," each would echo when the other returned jobless.

Then Linda secured another job as a "part-time waitress" from five o'clock until nine at night. This brought in a pound a week and she would rise with the early daylight, go out to her scrubbing, come back and rest for a few hours and start out again to work until the last diner had left.

She did not mind work, but she was so lonely that even an infrequent kind word from a customer made her grateful. All her life she had cared for and tended and managed someone and she missed her mother, her mother's dependence and small demands.

It was after months of hard work and abiding loneliness that she met Mabel. She had gone to bed as soon as she came in one night, but was awakened a little before eleven by a noise in the room above.

One of the girls, she thought with a half smile, bringing home a friend. The residential seemed to be mostly inhabited by young ladies who brought home friends. Then she realized that someone was moaning in the room overhead. She was certain of that. Half hesitating, she dressed, crept up the dark stairs and knocked.

"Hullo," she asked softly. "Anything I can do?" The moaning stopped. "What is it?" she asked through the door panel. "Can I come in?"

Another groan answered her. Linnie opened the door cautiously.

"Put the light on," the girl in the bed whispered. "The matches are on the wash-stand."

The house of the amiable Spurge had only gas light. Under its weak flare, Linnie anxiously approached the bedside. She had passed the girl on the stairs, often enough. Mrs Spurge called her Mabel. A bepainted, plump little minx, with frizzy hair, she had not appealed to Linnie particularly. But now she was paintless and bedraggled.

"I gotta get to the hospital," she said, raising herself on her elbows.

"I'll call the ambulance," Linnie said firmly.

"Not on yuh life. They'll want ten shillings. If you give me a hand to get some clothes on. . . ." She was seized with a spasm of pain. "I'm going to have a baby."

The girl could not have alarmed Linnie more if she had said she had the Black Death. Anxiously the visitor searched her mind for any scraps of obstetric information. Hot water and towels, she knew she should procure, but apart from that, what did you do? The girl saw her perplexity and smiled weakly.

"It's all right," she said. "You needn't look like that. S'long as I get to hospital."

"I can't get a taxi," Linnie explained. "No money."

"Same here. Just give us a hand with this skirt." Mabel had taken command of the situation. "I haven't slept for nights," she said. "The fleas is terrible here. Many in your room?"

"A few."

"I do like a clean room. Spurgie's a dirty old thing, though she's let me have this room for next to nothing all of six months. She could uv put me out." Mabel wiped her eyes with the corner of a dirty towel and proceeded to cover her ravaged face with rouge and face powder. "Gee, I feel crook."

Linnie was anxious. She had a feeling that the girl might have a child any minute, and that would be terrible. Mabel seemed maddeningly slow.

"How are you going to get to the hospital?" she asked.

"Walk," Mabel said grimly.

"You can't."

Mabel grinned. "Watch me, gee! Don't worry like that. Why, when I get to the hospital, they'll bath me and clean me and take hours just messing about. They don't give a damn."

"Here lean on me." Linnie was helping her in her slow progress to the door.

They were halfway down the street before Mabel had another spasm of pain and sat down in the gutter to rest. A beautiful green limousine cruising past slowed down and the driver tried to attract their attention. This struck Mabel as richly humorous.

"He's trying to pirate us," she giggled. "If he only knew where we're going, he'd sheer off."

The persistent citizen in the limousine hung about hopefully until it became apparent that neither of the ladies was interested in him. By that time Mabel was hysterical from laughing.

"There he is again," she would say joyfully. "Shows I'm pretty good, don't it, when I've got guys trying to pick me up right on the steps of the hospital."

"Get the man to drive us up," Linnie suggested.

"No chance. He'd go for his life, if we asked him," Mabel said hardly.

Linnie began to be angry. The whole thing was a nightmare. There was the car and this girl needed help. She dashed across the road.

"Look here," she said. "My friend's sick. Will you drive us to the hospital?"

The man put his car into gear, without a word, and roared away, leaving Linda standing in the road.

"What did I tell you?" Mabel said with a grin. She was entirely without rancour. "You must be from the country." Painfully and with many stops they made their way to the hospital.

The Gresham Hospital for women was like most other public hospitals. It was conveniently situated so that all the noises of trams and traffic that could possibly disturb a patient would be quite close. One of those tall dirty grey buildings that spread like a fungus, it budded new wards with the rapidity of yeast, at unsuitable and inconvenient angles. The long roll of honour in the vestibule attested to the number of worthy citizens who had sold tickets for most enjoyable balls raising funds so that mothers might bear children within the gloomy precincts of the Gresham. It had all the welcoming benevolence of a hygienic jail.

"Well, so long," Mabel said. "Thanks."

"What's your other name?" Linnie asked.

"Why?"

"Thought I might come and see you."

"Mabel Marsh. G'night and thanks again."

Mabel turned unconcernedly towards the lift the night watchman indicated.

## II

"I want to get off at seven," Linda said obstinately. "I'll work back any other night, George."

"You no care as long as you all rrright," her employer growled. "O.K." He shook his finger. "Onlee tonight." Anyone would think he was granting her leave for a month on full pay.

Linda hurried to the hospital. Almost shyly she bought a bunch of violets from a flower seller by the door. Up in the lift and down a long corridor she went, down another corridor and then to the left through the wards. It seemed to her that every bed with its white cocoon of a swaddled woman and the smaller white cradle beside it had been repeated a hundred times in an ever receding mirage of mirrors within mirrors. There were so many beds, so many wards, infinitely repeating the same monotonous white bed. There was nothing lovely or gracious about motherhood here. This was a mass process, turning out mass babies in the thousand, like a factory, a clean, hygienic, impersonal factory, keeping down costs and keeping up production. So many babies per year, so many deaths, so many mothers discharged. What became of the mothers and babies was no concern of the factory. The mothers would go back into circulation and the children would go to the kindergarten with its steel wire and steel swings and then to a public school, four storeys high, with a rim of asphalt playground in which the new product would shriek with all the other hundreds of similar grimy little products of the Gresham.

The old crones, loafing by the doorways round the Foot of Foveax, with their antiquated, dirty methods of bringing babies into the world, were better than this. You might die under their care, but at least you would die in human surroundings, not as part of the factory machinery for increasing the population.

"How's things?" Linda said gruffly, stalking to the bedside of Mabel Marsh, now lying, a white cocoon with a small white cradle beside her.

Linnie inspected the occupant of the cradle distantly. Rich people, she thought bitterly, as she handed Mabel the tiny bunch of violets, could have children in beautiful places with green trees outside their windows and the view of blue water.

"What is it?" she asked with a lump in her throat, she was so sorry for Mabel in her cheap embroidered nightgown. "Boy or a girl?"

"A girl," Mabel smiled. "She's lovely." Better if they drowned the baby like a kitten, Linnie thought. "You're mummy's little lamb, aren't you," Mabel cooed. "Patty's her name."

"Hullo, Patty," Linnie said softly. They bent over the cradle.

"Like to nurse it?" Mabel asked; but a nurse swooped down on them.

"You must let the baby sleep, Mrs Marsh," she snapped.

Mabel scowled. "Gee, they're tough in this place, and the food's terrible," she complained. "Wake you before daylight to wash you. Can't get the bedcover untidy or they bounce you. They'll come up ten times to smooth your sheets, but if you want anything — urgent like — they don't take a bit of notice. Anyway, thank God, I'll be out in eight days."

"Eight days?" Linnie said, aghast. "But isn't that too soon?"

"Oh, they want the bed. And I'm strong." Anything that happened to Mabel she accepted. She had had a long practice in accepting unpleasant facts.

"Then what are you going to do?"

Mabel gave her a sidelong look. "Oh, just what I was doing before."

"With the baby?"

"The baby's got to eat. So've I."

Again that impotent rage surged up in Linnie.

"Spurge'll let me have my room back," Mabel said reflectively. "She may try to chuck me out, of course." She contemplated the prospect without concern.

"She'd better not," Mabel's new friend said warmly. When Mabel returned there was an epic row with Mrs Spurge. Linda stood by trying to stem the landlady's flow of filthy language. "Look here," she persuaded. "How about you coming in with me, Mabel, just for the time being. The room's big enough. If Mabel shares my room and I pay an extra shilling a week rent will that suit you, Mrs Spurge?"

Mabel gave her a suspicious stare. "What's the catch?" she asked.

"Until you're stronger," Linda urged. "Until you can get a job. . . ."

Mrs Spurge had quietened somewhat.

"Well, I must say you're a very kind girl, Miss Allen. Not that I've got anything against Mabel, but I can't have my house getting a *name*."

Linda's look disconcerted her.

"I'll tell you what I'll do," she said effusively. "I'll let you have the double bed I've got stored under the stairs. 'Tisn't doin' any good where it is." She left a little afraid of Miss Allen. When she encountered her on the stairs a few days later she was still effusive. "Them poor young girls, love," Mrs Spurge confided. "Them poor young girls. I dunno 'ow they manage. Of course, it's different with you, Miss, and I know I always get me money when you have it, but I wonder you don't ever bring home your gentleman friends, love. I'm sure I wouldn't mind. I'm not the kind of woman to think evil."

Linda bit her lip. "I have no friends," she said abruptly.

The woman's expression altered from affability to menace.

"I don't like to 'ave nothing underhand," she said meaningly. If the girl had another place she might as well go and live there.

Linda climbed the stairs with a bitter smile. A landlady who wanted part of the proceeds of her non-existent immoralities touched her hard sense of humour.

It was through Mabel that Linnie first came into contact with Kingston, the Child Welfare Inspector, who arrived to investigate Mabel's claim for the allowance for Patty. He and Mabel had a long and dogmatic argument over the affiliation.

Kingston looked more like a cowboy than an affiliation officer. He called Mrs Spurge "ma" with contemptuous familiarity, and he was "taking no nonsense" from Mabel as he told her.

"Come on," Kingston said sternly. "I haven't all day. What's the man's name?"

Mabel gave it, sullenly.

"Address?" She gave that too, reluctantly.

"When did you last see him?"

"That's my business."

Kingston threw down his note-book. "Now stop shilly-shallying," he said fiercely. "I suppose you think I like this sort of thing, huh?"

The inquisition continued.

" 'Tisn't as though my bloke wouldn't marry me," Mabel told Linnie. "But he's only on relief. Anyway, the first kid don't count for anything on the relief, and it's eight and six from the Child Welfare."

"That means you're better off for staying single with a child?"

Mabel nodded. "I'm that scared of them taking the kid away," she worried.

"They can't."

"Oh, can't they just. You don't know." Mabel began to pour out highly coloured stories of what had happened to various friends of hers. Then there was Neicie Thompson. She was married to a taxi-driver before she took up with Curly, and she tried to get her kid back from its father. Terrible time she had, and couldn't get the kid after all. Then she had another kid, Curly's, and the Child Welfare mob came down like a ton of hot bricks, and threatened to take it away because the neighbours heard her screaming when Curly got drunk and threatened to cut her throat. They said they could take the kid because she was living with a criminal, and she had to go to a lot of trouble and divorce her husband and marry Curly because she was so scared of them. Terrible people they were.

The worst fear that haunts poor people is that of having their children removed. This dread, Linda was to discover, motivated many inexplicable actions, such as their sudden removals to distant suburbs for no apparent reason. It was a sword over their heads. Mothers would threaten small boys who stayed away from school. "The Child Welfare Man'll take you and put you in a home and you'll never be seen again." This fear beset them unreasonably in their ignorance of legal procedure and the rights of citizens. They regarded the Child Welfare "Man" and the Children's Court, and the Child Welfare Department with animal fear and horror. A vicious neighbour had only to ring up the Department and complain that someone's children were allowed to play in the street or were ill-treated and the Child Welfare Officer would be there on the doorstep, more fearful than the dole inspector because all-powerful in their eyes.

III

Mabel, having assured herself that she was not expected to give anything in return for Linnie's hospitality, adjusted herself to the situation with her usual placidity. She did not attempt to look for work. She sat all day long looking at herself in the mirror or reading cheap novelettes. Sometimes she did not get up at all, and let Linda bring her meals. The room, unless Linda cleaned it, was always untidy and almost any hollow article would be sure to have a deposit of cigarette ash in the bottom of it.

"I don't see what you make such a fuss about," Mabel grumbled, while Linda washed the baby's clothes. "They only get dirty again."

Shrill bepainted young women would come in to "keep Mabel company", and it was usual for Linnie to get home from her scrubbing and find the room thick with cigarette smoke, the window shut, the bed unmade and Mabel sitting quite happy in the midst of her friends as she had sat all the morning.

"She don't deserve to have a job," Mabel was proud to exhibit the queer manners of her room-mate. "Why, she knocks back the boss where she works, if he gets gay."

The assembled "poor young girls" expressed their surprise and disgust at such behaviour.

"You must be soft," Wilma said scornfully. "Remember May, Joan? She had a job as a waitress, and the boss wanted to sleep with her. She says to him: 'Look here, if you think I'm going to work all day and all night too for these wages, you got a big shock coming.' She thinks it out, see, and does the sensible thing. Tells him it's either work or sleep with him, but not both. If she did both, it would be bringing down the wage rates for other girls. A unionist, she was. She's a good-looking girl, so he gives her a flat and anything she wants. She made herself expensive all right. Then when she's saved enough of his dough, she dumped him and walked out."

The anecdote was received with every mark of respect as illustrating the correct procedure in such cases.

"Well, look at Bee," Joan struck in. "She'd been in the game five years, and she quit and started a shop. Supported her kid all the time, too."

"There isn't no man any good," Anne put in cheerfully. "The only thing to do is to get as much out of them as you can, then chuck them."

This statement was apparently agreeable to everyone except Linnie. "Don't see that," she protested. "Decent chaps about. Few and far between."

"You wait," Anne said wisely, "till you've had them coax your last half crown out of you and spend it on booze."

To look at Anne, you would have though she was no more than sixteen. She was not attractive, but everything had been done to make her defects less noticeable. Her eyebrows were plucked, her hair curled, her shabby stilt-heeled shoes were cheap but stylish. She had been twice jailed for vagrancy.

She smiled at Linnie maliciously. "Gee, Linnie sticking up for men! Who is he? What's he like? We'll have her bringing him home one night."

"Silly goats," Linnie said shortly.

"She's never had a man," Joan said shrewdly. "That's why she thinks they're such wonders."

"Never said I did. Fact remains there are some decent blokes going about. I knew two or three once." She pictured the austere blue eyes of Bramley sweeping the group of girls. What would he say if he saw her now? On the other hand, Rolfe would probably make friends with Mabel and Joan and Anne. Rolfe always did make friends.

"Come on. Tell us," they coaxed.

"Nothing to tell. Decent blokes, that's all."

The gang was obviously disappointed. I wonder, Linda thought, whether I wouldn't go out and get men as these girls do, if it were not that I've known a different sort of man? She

352

deserted the problem as she had done before. Perhaps, if she
were hungry enough, one of these nights, she might. Something
within her said, No. No matter how hungry she might be. It
was something deeper than morals. Not if she were hungrier
than she had ever been. Never. Never! It was her sense of
justice. A woman should not be forced into pretending love,
lying and cheating at love for a trade.

The gathering of poor young girls was debating the possibility of the existence of Plato's ideal "good man".

"I tell you there ain't no such thing," Anne said warmly.
"There's some chaps better than others, but they're all crooks.
Marie was saying to me just before she married that Chinese
out at Waterloo that, whatever he was like, she couldn't get
a worse spin than she'd had from the white men."

"And look at her now," Joan agreed. "Rings on her fingers
and bells on her toes. She breeds greyhounds and races them.
Simply rolling in it. He gives her money to do the housekeeping and she puts it into her bank account."

"They have rows," Wilma disagreed. "Why, when I went
out there to see if I could touch her for a loan, the wall was
all covered with raspberry jam where he'd thrown it at her."

"Terrible mean, she is now," Joan agreed. "She used to be
pretty free with her money when she hadn't any, but since she's
married him, she's as mean as dirt."

Meanness was not a quality the poor young girls cultivated.
Wilma in particular was accustomed to bring home suit-cases
full of clothes for Patty, toys and sweets, and little rugs and
woollies. The baby had quite a trousseau.

"How do you do it?" Linnie asked one night.

"Nick them off the counter," Wilma said briefly. Shoplifting
was only a sideline of hers.

It was not only clothes for the baby Wilma brought home.
Sometimes they would all have had nothing to eat had it not
been for her mysterious power of wafting goods out of shops.

And then two months later to the disgust of Mabel, Linda
lost her job scrubbing. She fell behind with the rent, and Mrs
Spurge became less and less effusive.

"If you can wait just a few weeks," Linda begged. "I've
got the promise of a job." There had been only a vague word

from the manager of a department store that he would remember her next time they were putting on girls.

"I've heard that tale before," the woman said contemptuously. "I don't mind Mabel. When she lumbers a gay she splits fair. But you don't even pay your rent."

Linda was heart-sick.

"Mabel," she said sharply, when she reached their room. "Have you been bringing men here?"

Mabel's eyes narrowed. "What d'you mean?"

"I'm telling you," Linda said quietly. "Cut it out."

Mabel was glad to drop the subject. Linda represented a small but certain income. Mabel knew that even if Linda went hungry Patty would be fed. They could not all live on Linda's pound a week, but Mabel made no effort to get work. Her greatest inspiration in a time of dearth was the suggestion that Linda could pawn the typewriter. Much to Mrs Spurge's disgust Mabel did "cut it out". Linda was too valuable . . . why, she was practically a gift.

A month later Linda lost her job as a waitress.

"Practically threw it away," as Mabel remarked scornfully.

She had been alone in the café kitchen with George, the proprietor, and any girl who worked for George he considered fair game. He was therefore all the more astonished by the vicious manners of this employee who, when he followed his usual procedure neither giggled nor screamed but struck out with an exceedingly firm fist. George thought he must have been mistaken and he came up again, and was smitten heavily in the diaphragm. It takes muscle to polish floors and Linda was not surprised to find herself suddenly jobless. She took down her shabby coat.

"All right," she said briefly. "I heard you."

George relapsed into Greek.

Mrs Spurge was not long in finding out and she acted with creditable promptitude. There was nothing worth taking, she decided, having inspected the room when Linda and Mabel were both out. Everything was in pawn with Linda's typewriter. So Mrs Spurge went downstairs again and rang the police.

Linda and Mabel walked into the ambush and found them-

354

selves in the grip of two heavy policemen, and under suspicion of having no visible means of support. There was nothing new to Mabel in "being vagged". She accepted it as she accepted most other things, but her parting remarks to Mrs Spurge showed that Mabel had unsuspected talents.

"And not paying any rent for months," Mrs Spurge was saying volubly, "and that poor little baby there starving and crying and them bringing men in at all hours of the day and night—"

"You filthy old gutter cat. . . ." Mabel began again, but was hustled off in the middle of her farewell.

At Central they were charged and there separated. Mabel, who was apparently well known, went out to Glebe being under eighteen, while Linda waited at Central until next morning when she should be removed to "the Bay". Bramley, she knew, might have bailed her out. But what was the use?

"Haven't I seen you somewhere before?" The policewoman had one of those departmental memories.

"No," Linda managed to gulp. "No."

"Yes I have," the policewoman maintained. "It was the Salamoa case. Sure I remember. You were living with the man. I say, Harry, remember the Salamoa case? That's her."

"So you changed your name, eh, Montague?" the sergeant said. "I don't wonder."

Linda went out to Long Bay Gaol as Linda Montague.


IV

The Little Clee Street Home for Destitute Women had only one room into which the sunlight shone and that was the matron's sitting-room. Across the lane Methered's Knitted Silk Factory loomed up and blotted out the light from all the other windows. When the whistle blew at seven in the morning for the hands to start work, the Home vibrated with the blast. All day long that piercing whistle shivered its dirty old walls making nervous inmates jump. Besides the whistle there was the humming and clicking of the machines, a never-to-be-forgotten accompaniment for the morning and evening prayers.

From the narrow lane, mostly inhabited by Chinese, the Home's entrance opened into a dark little hall which led off to a big stone kitchen and the matron's room. From this dark hallway also the staircase rose threateningly like a wounded snake, beneath which was a hollow cupboard in which the matron locked with a great clicking of keys the pitiful, battered suit-cases of the women who slept at the Home.

The basement door from Little Clee Street was used only by the women who lived in the Home. There was another entrance from Ogham Street which gave on to the set of offices on the floor above. This floor was forbidden ground to the Home inmates. Here were the typewriters and printing presses of those good people who had set out to redeem Foveaux, and especially the Foot, by investigation, prayer, admonition, distribution of tracts and, occasionally, old clothes. It was the happy hunting ground of the faddist, the fanatic and the social science student.

"I dunno why it is that most of them that go about redeemin' people," Brownie remarked to Linnie as they were scrubbing the dormitory one chilly morning, "are the kind that you wouldn't pick up with a clothes prop." It was Miss Brown who had suggested to Linda that they try the Home. They had come out of Long Bay the same day, Brownie having been doing a stretch as drunk and disorderly. "Look at 'em," she continued, wiping back a wisp of greying hair. "Lumpy fat fools, with no chins and big feet—"

"S . . .ssh." Thelma, in the bed at the end of the dormitory, was dressing her little boy, Teddy. "One of them'll hear you."

"I don't care," Brownie said defiantly. She was not much to look at herself, were it not for the humorous twinkle in her rather bleary eye. "They can't do anything to me. I don't know whether the goodness brings them out in pimples or the pimples keep 'em good."

Thelma looked disapproving. She had been living at the Home a long time, ever since Teddy was a baby. The atmosphere had her beaten.

"Matron's not so bad," she said weakly.

"That don't alter the fact," Brownie was scrubbing under

the bed, "that it brings them out in pimples."

Of the women in the Home Linda liked Miss Brown by far the best. There were not many women there. As Brownie said, "They don't come here if they can find anywhere else to go." There was only one dormitory with a dozen beds in it. Of these, Mrs Hurst, a woman fashioned of grey blubber, greasy and stupid, occupied the end bed beside which her small son Timmy slept in a cot he was fast outgrowing. Opposite, Thelma and her baby had the bed by the window. Next to her was Brownie, and then Mrs McLean, tired, dusty-looking, bitter about her broken shoes and sore feet, a woman praying for a job so that she could be with her husband again. He was living at "Eden" and the two of them met sometimes when they were supposed to be looking for work, pathetically like young lovers under the green trees in the park. They would sit hand in hand, saying nothing, happy in each other's presence. "It's the hope of being together again keeps us going," Mrs McLean would say. "If it wasn't for that. . . ."

Brownie had no hope of anything better, and she knew it. "I always come back, even if I'm drunk, because the matron isn't as down on drink as she is about you staying out all night. Thinks you're with some man. Why one night I stayed out, I told her I was at the Y.W.C.A., and she rang up to find out if I was. Trying to trap me, see? I'm scared of losing me bed here. After all, it is a place to sleep, and there's even sheets. You get so it's home after a while." She was quite contented in a tolerant, humorous style. Every now and then Brownie mysteriously scraped together enough to buy wine and she would come back beautifully drunk. The week after that she would go about assuring the others that she "was off it for life". "Never again, dear, not if I know it. I'd hate to tell you what that paint did to my stomach."

The thing Brownie most hated about the Home was her turn to go out on Sunday morning with one of the others and bring the milk can from the depot of the milk company. Brownie was not alone. All the other women hated lugging the heavy milk can through the streets. "You got no idea what all this exercise is doing to my inside," Brownie panted to Linnie, who was upholding the other side of the milk can. "If I don't get home soon. . . ."

No one could help laughing at Brownie staggering along
with the milk can and admonishing a stray black and white cat
running along beside them.

"Now, go on. Leave us alone. Matron'll murder us if we go
givin' you milk. Look out! Gee, it nearly tripped me!" She
sat the can down while the cat rubbed against her legs. "S'pose
we better give it some," she grumbled. "See if you can find
an empty tin, kid." There were no empty tins about. Whereupon Brownie took off her old battered hat. "Can't make it
worse than it is. Here, you give it a drink, kid. I can't bend,
not with my inside."

They made a queer group, Linnie thought, as she knelt there
offering the milk in Brownie's old felt hat. No one would set
them up as a statue group of Charity, two weary, shabby
women feeding a shabby pussy.

"I'm glad I didn't get picked with May," Brownie remarked
as they started off again. "Wouldn't she moan!"

May was a born moaner. She lost jobs because she was
always whining. She was continually complaining about everything, from the holes in her stockings to the fact that she
thought she was carrying more than her share of the milk can.

"Now, I ain't heard you say hardly a word," Brownie said
reflectively, glancing at Linnie. "All the time you've been
here."

Linda made no reply. What was the use? She would laugh
at Brownie's bawdy jokes, play with Timmy who was a darling,
nurse Teddy, who was not, or help Mrs Hurst and listen to her
horrible stories about her husband and why she had to leave
him. But the Home was acting on her like a tonic. Little by
little, the listless apathy that had beset her since Angelique's
death was being burnt out in a clear flame of hate, a smoulder-
ing corroding core of white hot fury. It had blazed up first
when the matron smacked the kitten so hard that it screamed
because the kitten had climbed into the ashes by the fire and
had a glorious little game there.

"You dirty beast," the matron said determinedly. "I've told
you not to do that. There!"

What a perfect statement, Linnie thought, of her system of

# 358

charity. She would keep the kitten and feed it scraps; but the kitten must conform. Linda's mind flashed to the cats who lived in Foveaux Park, who reared little litters of kittens as wild as themselves under the bandstand. Their food was either stolen from the dustbins or else they hunted birds. But they lived, and lived well, compared to the Home kitten who was always being made to feel a deep sense of sin.

Linda decided that she was not made for the life of a tame cat. She had stood it long enough. This clear flame of hate was what made criminals, the wild cats and outlaws, the vagrants, the outcasts, the free. Better prison than this half confinement, this being let out on a string.

Every morning the inmates were roused at half-past five. The sleepy women would dress, make their beds and straggle yawning down to the kitchen where, to the accompaniment of May's grumbling that someone had stolen the bit of sacking she knelt on to scrub, they would read the list laid out on the table.

"Bessie Brown:—Scrub stairs and half kitchen.
Linda Montague:—Half dormitory and half Meeting Hall.
Mrs McLean:—Clean upper hall.
May Teakle:—Clean offices. . . ."

Wisely had the managers of the Home decided to keep it open. It held only sufficient women to supply a competent labour force for the cleaning of the Board's premises. Had the Benevolent Board decided to pay for the cleaning, it would have cost at least thirty shillings a week. By allowing these women to sleep in its attic and eat in its basement the expense of cleaning could be saved and at the same time their reputation for benevolence increased. The women did not cost anything because what food they had was donations. The matron was honorary. It was a beautiful example of what can be done to economize and be charitable at the same time.

After an hour's scrubbing, to the tune of clanking buckets and more of May's grumbling, they would struggle back to the kitchen to wait until Matron should get up and hold morning prayer. It was impossible, however faint and hungry they might be, to begin breakfast before Matron squeaked in with the heavy Bible under her arm, her keys chinking. Then there was a long and usually uninteresting passage to be read from the Bible. Matron had a habit of sucking her false teeth between words, as though she were swallowing them and finding them unsatisfactory nourishment. Her hungry audience was always particularly sullen about the Bible reading. No one is the more endeared to religion when it is made a substitute for breakfast. After the reading they must again go down on their sore knees, reddened and stiff from scrubbing, to wait while Matron communicated her wishes in a fervent monologue to her Maker. Then there was the Lord's Prayer. Then Matron squeaked out, leaving them to breakfast, her own being carried in to her on a tray.

Breakfast, except when the milk was sour, was bearable. It consisted of porridge with brown sugar, tea and stale bread and dripping. The inmates of the Home were then at liberty to go seeking a job where and when they might find it. Most of them would wander about aimlessly all day asking for work, limping in their worn shoes, unable to afford a twopenny tram fare. They knew they could not get a position if they had not the five shillings to register at an agency, and they had not the five shillings. Even if they had registered, their chances were slight, they were such a shabby set of women, starved-looking and weak. Long undernourishment did not contribute to their efficiency as prospective domestic servants.

"I'm not going out today," May said sullenly. "What's the use? I sat in the park most of yesterday. If it hadn't been that some people got up and left some sandwiches on the seat, I would've been too faint to walk back."

"You didn't eat them?" Mrs McLean said in a shocked tone.

"Too right I did," May responded defiantly. "Egg sandwiches they were."

"I've seen people do that," Mrs McLean said wonderingly. "I saw a man in a rest'rong once get up and take a scone another man had left. But I couldn't do that. I couldn't take other people's leavings."

"Take a look at this," Brownie held up a sausage roll and extracted from it a piece of sausage that had gone green.

"What do you call that, if it isn't a leaving? All the stuff we get here's left over."

She carefully unwrapped the pastry from the remainder of the sausage and plastered some marmalade on it.

"Remember them meat pies we had for tea one night, May? You ought to of seen them, Linnie. I says to May, 'Leave 'em alone and they'll walk by themselves.' "

On Sundays there was meat, "donated meat", and some stringy beans. All the time Linnie was at the Home she never saw butter or white sugar or really appetizing food. The skim milk the dairies failed to sell came to the Home. The food was mostly old meat pies or sausage rolls sent by the pastry shops when they had lost all usefulness as merchandise. Occasionally there were sandwiches from the same source resembling wet tissue paper and as tasteless. There was no midday meal. If you could not provide your own, you did without. If any of the inmates came back at midday, they might grudgingly be provided with a cup of tea and a slice of bread and dripping; but the custom of needing food in the middle of the day was discouraged.

"I see," Brownie said, looking up from the old newspaper that served as tablecloth for breakfast, "that the Riordan wedding breakfast was served to sixty guests. The bride wore magnolia satin and carried a sheaf of lilies-of-the-valley and orchids. I'd have liked," she said appreciatively, "to a seen her. Must've looked real pretty."

"Some lovely weddings there's been lately," Mrs McLean joined in, brightening over the thought. "One young girl was married in pink tulle. Now that'd be unusual."

"I wouldn't like it," May said decisively. "Pink 'ud look funny on a bride. Talk about weddings. I only wish I had the money they spend on the bookay."

"What'd you do with it?" Brownie jeered.

"I wouldn't get boozed," May retorted sharply. She sighed. "What I'd like right now is a pork chop and a new pair of stockings."

"A big feed of steak and chips and a coat for the winter," Mrs McLean chimed in wistfully. "Not a second-hand coat either. A new one."

"I'd get a push cart for Teddy," Thelma contributed. "He's getting that heavy to carry about."

"I'd stand meself some plonk," Brownie said with a wink at Linnie. "Not the cheap stuff that'd take the lining off me stummick. What's your choice, kid?" she made a sweeping gesture. "You on'y got to ask for it — I don't think."

Linnie mused a minute. "Don't want anything," she said shortly. "What's the use," she said, pushing back her chair, "of ice-cream in hell?"

"Well, I don't know what you want to go talking about hell in that way," Mrs Hurst said stiffly. "You ought to of been here when the last matron used to get drunk and the beds were full of bugs. Then you might uv talked."

"There's worse places," Thelma put in. "Take the South Street Home. All the good sorts go there."

The others nodded agreement. "Good sorts", as they knew them, were women who made their living when and how they could. At least, the Little Clee Street Home was respectable. They looked sideways at Linda and Brownie. It was whispered that they were not.

"If there's anything more likely to turn a girl bad," Linnie said fiercely to Brownie as the two left the home together on their daily mockery of looking for work, "it's religion before breakfast, prayers at every meal, the services you have to go to on Sundays and Wednesdays." She glowered at Brownie. "One more service and I'll go and sleep in the gutter for preference."

"Well, tonight's Wednesday again," Brownie said, cocking a humorous eye at her. "And there's plenty of empty gutters." Her face lengthened. "Gee, I hope that rat don't come out again."

Ever since Brownie had awakened one night to find the animal sitting on her pillow she had filled the dormitory with gloomy speculations as to whether it would bite them when they were asleep.

"I won't stay in that home until it beats me into a crawling slave too scared to open my mouth," Linnie said tensely. "I want to go out and smash windows and smash people. I could smash the Matron with ease."

"Gee, you're some basher," Brownie said humorously. Her voice went hard. "It's all right when you're young. If you don't get a job, you can find some mug to keep you. But when you get as old as me and there ain't no jobs and you're not interested in men any longer, you're glad enough of a bed out of the rain and the bread and drippin'."

Linda's first visit had been to Mrs Spurge. The landlady refused to give up her clothes and demanded back rent. Day by day the girl walked the city inquiring desperately for work. It was not until she had been in the Home nine days that she went once more to the Department Store whose manager had promised to remember her.

"What happened to you?" he said sharply. "We wrote a fortnight ago to tell you to start. It's no good now. I've filled the vacancy."

Linda clutched the table hard. She was feeling faint and sick. It was disappointment as much as lack of food.

"Didn't get the letter," she said weakly. "Landlady must have kept it. I . . . moved."

The manager was not a hard man. He had liked the look of Miss Allen; her clothes, even her shoes were worn out, but there was a kind of pride about her.

"I can't do anything in the sales department," he said abruptly. "But the caretaker mentioned he wanted more help with the cleaning. If you would care to see him. . . ."

"I would."

"I'll ring through to him."

Linda left the store walking on air.


V


Somehow the Little Clee Street Home did not seem so dreadful when she knew she was leaving it. Linda was thinking, as she stood in the front row of the Mission singing hymns, that there was any number of trades you could try before actually descending to the level of the Home and its forcible spirituality, you could sing in the streets, for instance, or peddle matches.

*"Are you coming Home tonight?"* she sang strongly.
*"Are you coming Home tonight?*
*Are you coming Home to Jesus,*
*Out of darkness into light?"*

Linda had wondered in the old days why Captain Cornish had been so fierce when his family were all so hungry and someone had "investigated" him. Now she understood. It was the tradition of freedom that she, too, had inherited from her middle-class parents. Working-class people were accustomed all their lives to the police or charity workers or church authorities "investigating" them. They had come to expect it. When they were out of work, they were fair game, and they knew it.

Rich people did not have authorities constantly prying, asking how often they washed their children's ears, and why wasn't the baby brought more regularly to the clinic. They did not know what it felt like to be spied on and bullied by regulations. Over the dinner table they could discuss the incidence of malnutrition in comfort, if they were not absorbed in the more pressing topics of bridge scores or golf.

Against all the people who did not know or care Linda's hatred rose. Doling out charity through these religious organizations! Keeping poor creatures like Brownie and Mrs McLean from actually starving!

The front row was filing out past the matron like caterpillars crossing a road one behind the other. Linda strolled down the alley-way between the seats, her eyes fixed on Brownie in front. Never a glance did she cast at the flotsam and jetsam crowding the hall.

As she went down the steps that she had washed herself that morning from the meeting hall into the street, she noticed absently how muddy boots had left grit on them. They would have to be washed again tomorrow morning, patiently washed for years and years by other women, dispirited women, broken, dull slaves.

"Linnie," a voice called behind her. She half turned her head.

"Jimmy!"

They were on the footpath together, oblivious of the gaping inmates of Little Clee Street Home, of the loafers around the door. She clutched him with the strength of the drowning as they stood there, a shabby thin woman and a man going grey, shabby also and unshaven.

"Linnie, I've been looking for you everywhere." He was holding both her hands. "My God, I can't believe it's you."

There was a clinking and squeaking beside them and the stiff little matron at Linda's elbow was requesting her to "catch up with the others, please Linda".

Rolfe smiled down at the matron. "Madam," he said splendidly, "if you will allow me one minute."

The matron strangely melted. Secretly the remnants of romance in her stirred. "Well, just a minute," she said folding her hands and waiting stiffly to intercept any wrongful word.

They were both talking at once, explaining, arguing, trying to bridge the years they had been apart.

"I'll be waiting outside for you tomorrow morning," Rolfe said, reluctantly releasing her. "Then we can talk. Oh, Lightning, I'll never let you go again. Never, never, never."

"I trust," the small matron said, her round toes squeaking along beside Linnie. "I trust, Linda, that you will not be foolish enough to do anything rash." He plain face looked almost pleadingly at the tall girl. "You don't want to let yourself be led away into anything you may regret."

Looking down at her Linda smiled suddenly. This woman she had loathed was after all only kindly, elderly, somewhat wistful and drab, cheated of the fair and splendid things of life. The hate that had been gnawing at her like a pain was now strangely love and tolerance of all the world, of all its mistakes and dirt and stupidity. Before the astonished Home, waiting on the doorstep for the matron to come and unlock the doors, she bent and exultantly kissed the plain, surprised face turned up to her, no longer hating, but as she might have kissed Angelique.

"Matron," she said gently, "I'm going to marry that man."

"In that case, Linda," the matron said primly, "I shall trust you."

# CHAPTER 3

## I

It was a consignment of cauliflowers that married Rolfe. He and Herb had what Herb called a "big clean-up".

"I'm taking the day off tomorrow," Jimmy informed Herb, surveying his share of the takings.

"Where you going — races?" Herb asked.

"I'm going to get married," Rolfe said, loosening the collar of his shirt uneasily.

Herb expressed his opinion. "An' don't ask me to be no witness," he finished. "I'm not going to pool any cobber of mine into a jam like that."

"Maybe you're right," Rolfe agreed with a grin. "Thanks for the congratulations."

Herb grunted disgustedly. "You'll maybe recover before it's too late."

"I think it's too late now," Rolfe responded.

"She's got you hooked," Herb shook his head. "One of them nearly got me once." He rubbed the unshaven stubble on his countenance. "But I got away."

"Hard luck on her," Rolfe agreed.

"Aren't you being tremendously quixotic?" Jimmy had sighed to Linda. "After all, I have some scruples and bigamy is not among those crimes that have hitherto landed me in jail. I much prefer taking a 'to wit, loaded vehicle at a pace which owing to its loading,' etc."

They had formed a habit of meeting in the Gardens, not as friends who had been parted and met by chance, but almost shyly, as lovers, distressed that so many long hours lay between them and the next day.

"I'm going to marry you," Linnie said decidedly. "You haven't seen your fool wife for years and she may have been lost at sea. I want to marry you."

She pressed his hand as it lay along the rough wooden bench where they sat under the trees by the water. With Little Clee Street a nightmare behind her — with a job and a room of her own — the world was a paradise to Linnie.

"I repeat that you are being tremendously quixotic." He regarded her gravely. "It's madness, sheer madness."

"It isn't. I've got a job, I tell you. With the permissible income regulation you'll probably have to live on what I earn," she informed him. "And you're going to. I won't have you going to jail."

"Sheer madness," he repeated, smiling rather sadly. "Listen, Linnie, to reason. I'm not young any longer. I'm a sick man, old, broke, tired, too far gone to make an effort and climb back."

"Tomorrow," Linnie said definitely, "I'll be waiting for you outside the Registrar's at eleven-thirty."

Rolfe fell back on his last line of defences. "I won't," he said, "not tomorrow. If you like to make it the next day, Herb and I are dwelling on a consignment of cauliflowers. I may have the money to pay for the licence. I'm damned if I'll get married otherwise."

"That's better," Linnie encouraged. "That's more the spirit I like to see." Suddenly the raillery dropped away from her. "You remember that night when Angelique died?" She paused. "And I asked you what I should do?" Her face was fierce. "I wanted you to say you loved me. I wanted to marry you then."

"But, Lightning, how could I? I was broke."

"I didn't care," she said sternly. "You had no right to tell me to stay with Bud. You could have hit me in the face and I wouldn't have minded. But that was the last straw."

He shook his head. "I was a fool," he said in a low voice.

"And now," she pleaded, "don't you see I must change my luck? Jimmy, we're nothing by ourselves. We drift. Remember how you said Foveaux was the place of wrecks — the lee shore for jettisoned hope. Well, you can strand one person, but two means they're not stranded, they're — they're — content." She gripped those mobile, long fingers on the rough bench back. "Change my luck for me, Jimmy."

"If you must be bigamous," he sighed, "at least you can

wait until those confounded cauliflowers come to light. And even then I only promise to think it over."

He kissed her, a stooped, ashen, tired working-man kissing a woman slightly shabby, in the weak sunshine and bleak publicity of the Gardens with its shouting children and disinterested swans.

"You're lovely, Lightning," he said with a lump in his throat. "You're brave."

But for all Linda's bravery Rolfe hesitated as he waited for her under the disapproving shadow of the cathedral with the gay taxi-rank opposite and the lounging drivers all seeming to grin at him, the man selling oranges and peanuts with a little peanut roaster that whistled derisively at him. If it had not been for her determination, he would have taken the easier course and walked away. But she came across the green park with the fountain behind her like a spray of white flowers and Rolfe's heart leapt. "There's a tide in the affairs of men," his brain said strangely. Why shouldn't he take a chance? She was willing and foolish. Once before he had tried to be wise for her and it was a tragic wisdom. There was something well-omened in this mad marriage.

The old white-headed registrar regarded them almost pleadingly through his glasses. "But why not get married in a church?" he said persuasively. "You know it really is so much finer and more — more to be remembered." He looked at them wistfully. "You have only one wedding day, you know, and it is a pity, my dear young lady, to waste it on a place like this. If you would only wait and be married in a church."

"Your appeal," Linnie said solemnly, "is in vain. I've had enough trouble getting him here as it is."

The old gentleman gave her a nervous glance. "Oh, in that case," he said hurriedly, "I suppose. . . ." He broke off. "Where are your witnesses?"

They had not remembered a little detail like witnesses. Rolfe's heart sank.

"The taxi drivers—" the kindly official pointed out, "very often the taxi drivers will act as witnesses. For ten shillings. . . ."

Linnie and Rolfe looked aghast. Ten shillings! Two weeks' room rent!

"I'll see," Rolfe muttered and dashed outside. He looked with dismay at the group of uniformed men lounging on the corner. Then again his heart leapt like a song. A car had swished into the rank and from it, hard, lean and smiling, a very god from the machine, stepped Tommy. He strolled casually across to the group on the corner and slapped a fellow driver on the shoulder with his glove. Almost before the man could turn Rolfe had reached the spot.

"Tommy," he whispered, "come over here for the love of Mike."

Tommy allowed himself to be led away. "For crying out aloud," he said, "where the hell have you sprung from, Jimmy?"

"Look, I need two witnesses for my marriage," Rolfe said desperately.

Tommy roared with laughter. He laughed so that his fellow-drivers on the corner eyed him curiously.

"You're not trying to put one over me?" he asked incredulously.

"No. Quick." Rolfe was making for the steps of the Registrar's building. "I can't keep the old bird waiting any longer. And remember, Tommy, you're not getting anything for this vulture's job. You're donating your services."

He hurried up the steps of the building. Tommy still chuckling beckoned another driver and the two followed Rolfe.

Rolfe gave a sigh of relief when the service was over. After paying for the licence he would have enough for a week's rent and food and that would be about all.

"Thanks, Tommy," Linnie said, as they stood together somewhat embarrassed on the steps.

"And I suppose you think you are going to vanish again," Tommy said sardonically.

"No," Linda said, her head high. "Why?"

"I'll call for you Sunday," Tommy declared. "Mamie and Bob and I invite you to Sunday dinner."

Linda's eyes were afraid. She still disliked the memory of Foveaux; and then she stiffened. She must face and beat it, not skulk in other places.

"Mr and Mrs Rolfe," she said, smiling, "have much pleasure in accepting your kind invitation."

## II

They drew up with a swish before the narrow doorway of a prim dark house in a dirty little terrace. A swarm of small children came forth and clambered unhesitatingly on to Tommy's car.

"You're not to touch anything in front," he warned. "Hector, you're in charge. Hullo there, Bunny."

"Visitors, ma," Tommy announced. "You know Jimmy Rolfe and this is Mrs Rolfe who was Miss Montague."

"Ah, many a pound of spuds I sold 'er mother when she was alive," old Bob put in huskily over his wife's shoulder. "Ah, an' a nicer spoken woman you wouldn't wish to meet. It was always: 'A nice day, Mr Noblett, an' a little 'otter than it should be this time of the year.' Always a pleasant word she 'ad."

Tears sprang to Linnie's eyes. "Made us come," she said gruffly, nodding at Tommy.

"He was quite right," Mamie said warmly. "Come in an' please don't mind my sewing bein' littered about. It's not often we 'ave a weddin' breakfast, not with our lunch."

Old Bob had vanished to reappear proudly a few seconds later with two bottles of beer.

"My shout," he announced, "An' 'ere's to the bride." He met Mamie's look half defiantly. "I ain't touched it, Mamie, since I was converted. But you can trust me, Mamie."

"Too right you can," Tommy concurred. "The old devil knows I'll knock his block off if he takes one gulp too many." He smiled at the little group paternally. "Here's luck."

"I'm sorry I can't drink it," Rolfe apologized, but he looked at Linnie. "Here's a change of luck."

"An' now," old Mamie said kindly after lunch when Rolfe and Bob went off to inspect the horse, "if it wouldn't be stickybeaking, dear, I was wonderin' what sort of a 'ouse you was gettin'."

"House?" Linnie stared at her. "Why, we haven't any furniture or crockery or anything." She shrugged. "I hate living in a room, but what else is there?"

"Bob and me," Mamie said, "started much the same. On'y me mother give me a bed. 'You've made it, me girl,' she said, 'an' you must lie on it.' A good bed it was, too. I let the boys 'ave it when they got too big for the cot." She looked at Linnie with a gentle compassion. "I'd give you a bed if you liked. It's an old one we keep in case one of the boys drops in."

"You're sweet, Mrs Noblett," Linnie protested. "But it isn't only a bed."

"For ten shillings," Mamie said temptingly, "there's a place down in Paradise Street that Tommy's brother 'as the lettin' of. 'E give it you like a shot. An' you've got a job. You could pay the rent."

Linnie paled. Ten shillings a week, and then they had to pay for food on top of that.

"Think," Mamie pleaded, much in the tone of the old registrar appealing to them to get married in a church, "you'd 'ave three rooms, two an' the kitchen, an' you could let the upstairs room unfurnished. That 'ud be an extra four shillings." She touched the girl's arm. "I've got ever so many things, dearie, that I don't want. Don't go in a room, dear. It's that miserable not 'avin a place of your own."

Linnie hesitated. "I haven't any things," she said again weakly.

"It wouldn't do any 'arm to look at it," Mamie said eagerly. "Just while they're out in the yard. It's on'y round the corner an' I could drop in any time."

She was smiling as she got down her old black straw hat.

"Where are you going?" Rolfe said, catching sight of them.

"Going to look at a house," Linnie called.

She allowed herself to be propelled into the narrow alley, and viewed the dirty hovel, in which Mamie proposed she should live, with dismay. It was the usual one-room pattern, a kitchen stuck at the back and an attic on top reached by a narrow stair. The key was with the next-door neighbour, Mrs Flaherty, who gave them a calculating stare and gathered a little group of women on the footpath to watch them go in.

"There was a murder committed," she said cheerfully, "in the backyard. That's why they're reducing it to seven-an'-six."

Linnie shivered. She had lived in miserable enough rooms, but to live in an alley with a house such as this was as new a life as living at the North Pole. The floor and walls were filthy, the little backyard, six feet by twelve, was cluttered with rubbish and smelt of cats, burnt rubber and old rotten rags. A dismal heritage to which to bring a new husband.

"Tomorrow I could go down and see Tommy's brother," Mamie was planning. "Or maybe, 'e could fetch 'im down tonight an' I'll 'ave it ready an' cleaned by tomorrow night for you."

"I'll ask Jimmy," Linnie said weakly. She did not like to offend this kindly old woman. But she had sworn that never, never again would she live in Foveaux. Then suddenly she was tempted. Why should she not have a house, a real house of her own? Mamie was dying to give her the bed and really you didn't need more than a bed to start housekeeping. She had a crazy desire to acquire Number Ten Paradise Street and live in it.

Jimmy would have to be down at the markets with daylight to meet Herb; she herself would be polishing floors about the same time; but they stayed to tea at Mamie's, they sat up late talking. They were arguing about the house when Bramley arrived, shy, somewhat hesitant, but eager with congratulations.

"Good luck, you two," he greeted the guests, his eyes shining. "You deserve it."

There were a hundred questions to answer at once, but by common consent they were of the future. Tommy repeated at least three times how Rolfe had pounced on him as a witness. Mamie insisted loudly that she had set her heart on seeing Linnie installed just around the corner in Paradise Street.

"It's not much of a place," Bramley said gravely. "The drains are in a dreadful condition. No, the murder wasn't in the backyard. It was outside the back-gate."

Linnie drew a breath of relief. "Doesn't matter about the drains so much," she said. "It was the murder I didn't like."

"Well, if you like to come to the office tomorrow morning,

I'll fix it up for you," Bramley said. "Sorry I can't get the Old Man to reduce it below seven-and-six. He claims the place is worth fifteen shillings. He was going to repair it a bit and raise the rent." Linnie looked dismayed. "It's all right. I'll fix that."

Tommy drew his brother to one side when he was leaving. "I'll go you halves in getting the gas and light installed," he offered.

His elder brother, tall in the dark shadow of the doorway, looked down at him. "Thought you were against marriages from the word go?"

"I am," Tommy said unblushingly. "But seeing they're married, there's no reason to penalize them for it."

In the darkness he pressed his elder brother's arm hard. It was half comforting, half a caress, restoring between them the understanding they had had when Tommy was a small boy and Bramley his big brother, his loving protector. Only now the positions were reversed. It was Tommy who was the comforter. Tommy who knew the hidden ache under Bramley's generous front. But no word of these things was spoken.

Instead Bramley said: "Right-o, I'll fix up about the gas and light."

"I'm going to Brisbane next month, old son," Tommy said abruptly. "I'm pretty sweet with the manager and he's offered me a good opening on the garage side of the Brisbane depot. I'd be a mug to let it go." He stopped, then said diffidently: "Keep an eye on the kid, will you? I'm leaving him with Bob and Mamie for the time being."

"Of course I will. That's great news, Tommy."

"I don't know," Tommy mused, "how it'll turn out. Anyway, I'll be glad to get out of this damn hole."

As Bramley walked up Lennox Street he began to plan to send the repairs boss down to put in the copper and a new lavatory door. Some enterprising neighbour had removed the lavatory door, probably for firewood. With any luck he might be able to get through an order for a coat of kalsomine over the miserable mildewed, sky-blue kitchen.

So it was that Linnie took what she called a bus-driver's holiday, scrubbing out the accumulation of dirt in Number

Ten. One of Bramley's stout-hearted repair contractors arrived to fix a hole in the floor and made the pleasing discovery that a rat had gnawed through the lead joint of the water pipe and that all drainage for a long, long time had accumulated under the house.

"You can complain when the rent-collector comes round and maybe they'll fix it," he said discouragingly.

Linnie rang Bramley and a plumber was whistling over the job next morning.

Once having decided on the house there seemed to be no limit to the number of things old Mamie Noblett discovered were of no use to her. She was panting round every day with some odd bits of crockery or an old saucepan that might come in handy. Bob created a sensation when he arrived leading the horse and cart piled with the bed and bedding, two wooden chairs, a table, which he explained had stood in the backyard "that long it was a shame", and a present from Freddy who was earning good money now as a joiner, the present taking the shape of two sets of shelves.

The neighbours collected on the footpath to watch the furniture move in. "They certainly ain't got much," one housewife leaning on her broom remarked to the woman opposite. But to Linnie it was a palace. She told Rolfe so when he returned tired and sick from standing all day shouting his wares on the hot street.

"I was imprisoned in a palace in Bessarabia once," he said, glancing round with haggard appreciation, "that had a lot less in it than this."

They were eating their dinner of bread and frankfurters off the table covered with newspapers.

"A bed," Linnie glowed, "and a table and two chairs. Curtains, mind you, and shelves."

"I've got some stuff stored with Bramley's mother," Rolfe said absently. "Never thought to collect it again. I'll get him to send it down."

At the week-end there descended upon them Mrs Cornish, somewhat shy and ready to run, but holding a bowl of custard which she had brought because of "Mr Rolfe's stomach trouble", and Bramley grimly lugging two heavy suit-cases

full of Rolfe's papers and books. It was quite a family party,
with Mamie running in with some more curtains she had discovered, and Bunny tugging at Mrs Cornish's skirts for attention, and Bramley and Rolfe arguing over where the bookshelves ought to go. Linnie pounced with a cry of delight on a
bit of Mexican embroidery wrapped round some old plans, a
glowing thing of brown and gold and white and scarlet.

"Like it?" he asked.

"It's going on the wall," she declared. "There. Right across
the front room."

"But you can't hang it up yet," Bramley protested. The
walls had at one time been covered with brown wallpaper
decorated by blue tulips. This had only been half covered by a
later attempt, obviously amateur work, to paste up another
wallpaper in designs of pink roses on a yellow and blue trel-
lis. "The only thing to do," he declared, eyeing the wall
speculatively, "is to rip it all down and whitewash the whole
blinking room. I'm not going to wait for the repair boss
either."

Bramley was as absorbed in Number Ten Paradise Street as
if he had just moved in himself. He was out seeing about
brushes and kalsomine when whitewash proved impossible.
He borrowed a pair of old trousers from Bob Noblett and set
to work himself.

"Hate to think I'm improving the Old Man's property for
nothing," he muttered with a grin. "But there's no sense
waiting until I've persuaded the firm to get it done. Might have
to wait years."

Little Mrs Cornish watched, a trifle sadly. Bram was so
generously happy setting Mr Rolfe's home to rights, so
enthusiastic. He had, she realized, somewhere choked up in
him an urge to make a home that expressed itself in this paint-
ing of floors and furniture, just as it had once expressed itself
in that committee for abolishing slums. Yet Bramley was
contented enough. He had settled down. He would not be
willing to change, to marry as poor Mr Rolfe had done, reck-
lessly and without due provision for the future. She was very
glad for Bramley's sake that he was not marrying a girl who
refused the offer of little mantel ornaments and a curtain of

strands of coloured raffia to hang across her doorway. He could surely never have been happy in this bare place. Mrs Cornish liked little things and snug like the cabin of a ship with everying within reach. Linnie's idea of a room seemed to be to have as little in it as possible.

By the end of the next week the front room was the pride of Linnie's heart. The floor had been stained brown and there were two brown and white mats across it. The window curtains were brown and white. Across one wall flamed the Mexican embroidery and pen and ink drawings, relics of Rolfe's more affluent days, decorated the other walls. On either side of the fireplace the two tall bookshelves just filled one wall. The table was under the window flanked by the two chairs. On the mantelpiece a cheap brown earthenware vase filled with marigolds from Mrs Cornish's garden somehow managed to harmonize with the whole.

"Why, it might have been planned," Linnie breathed. She had a home. It did not matter that the kitchen was also the bedroom, if she had one part of the house that really did her credit. Here she would not be ashamed to bring anyone. For the time being, she decided, they must sleep in the kitchen. The gaping hole in the ceiling of the upstairs room did not conduce to restful slumber. Besides it was easier to wake in the kitchen in the morning.

Linda sighed thankfully. So far, apart from the fact that Jimmy was looking ill and would probably be "cutting out his warrants" at the end of the week, they could say that everything was going more than well. Pausing there in the comfort of her clean brown and white room, Linnie shuddered and then wondered why. When you are drowning, she thought, battered by waves, your bleeding fingers slipping from their hold on the weed and wet rocks, you do not realize how terribly the cold bites your bones. It is afterwards, when you crawl out on the rocks, that you can feel sick and faint in the memory of terror. She shrugged her shoulders, dismissing the nightmare.

"Very nearly starved once," she told Rolfe, as they sat happily by the ricketty plank on boxes that served as the kitchen table. "Had one meal in three days. Too faint to walk about. Then a girl I knew came in and took me out to dinner.

Some men friends of hers paid for it. Don't know who they were, but that dinner carried me over a couple more days." She smiled. "Seems queer now."

He pressed her hand. "Not sorry you married me?"

"Never. Never. Never. Haven't had time to see you. People coming all day laden up with gifts like camels. Haven't a minute to ourselves."

"Love me?"

"Ever so."

The little catechism went on.

"Oh, well," Rolfe said contentedly, "so far I'm slightly dazed. Maybe when the tumult and the shouting dies, and the gift-bringers depart, we can really take stock of how we stand."

### III

Paradise Street had so far held aloof. It could not quite settle its mind about the newcomers. The woman was a skinny-looking thing who went out scrubbing, and the man, it was rumoured, had been in jail. This latter piece of news rather warmed the community's attitude, because any number of the breadwinners of the street had been there, too. However, they would certainly wait and see if the new arrivals were orthodox in the matter of backing the right horses on Wednesday afternoon, or if he beat her when he got drunk.

The neighbours received their first shock over the glimpse they had of Linnie's front room. It was so entirely different from all the other front rooms of the neighbourhood. There were no big plush chairs bought on time-payment, no wireless set, no carpet or linoleum on the floor.

"They must be hard up, all right," was the general verdict.

"A terribly funny-looking room it is," reported Mrs Flaherty, who lived next door, and had better opportunities than anyone else for observation. She had struck up a conversation with Mrs Rolfe the very first day and lent her a box of matches. On the strength of this she posed as an authority.

One point in Linnie's favour was that she did not mind the

children sitting on her doorstep and littering her bit of foot-path with scraps of paper. Realizing this, they all came to play outside Number Ten. The local cats sat unreprimanded on her window sill or boldly walked in to miaow for food. Stray, friendly hounds would come inside the front door wagging their tails, and these when driven forth, would return and curl up on the doorstep among the children.

Linnie's was the sunny side of the street, and all Mrs Dempsey's six infants preferred it to their own place opposite. They played their favourite games of gun-men and police up and down the gutter, imitating the sirens of the police cars in detective films until the noise was almost unbearable. The street was so narrow that only one cart could come down it at a time, and if another vehicle decided to approach from the opposite end, there was all the stir and confusion of making the horse shift up on to the fifteen-inch footpath and guiding the wheels so that they would not interlock; and the children and dogs and housewives would gather round to watch and encourage. It never occurred to the wood-and-coal man, the bottle-o or the rabbit-o, or whoever it was in difficulties, to back his cart out of the street. No, the carts must pass, if it took the united efforts of all present. One of the tremendous spectacles of Paradise Street was to see the garbage wagon come down, its mudguards almost brushing the walls on either side, while the garbage men ran along, tossing up the dirt bins to their fellows, who cheerfully trampled down, the piled-up filth on the truck and shouted pleasantries to all the wives of Paradise Street. It was the habit of the garbage men to cheer each other on with "Heave-o's. Here she comes Bill. Look out," and sundry unintelligible but amiable roars. All the time a fine full-flavoured smell and drifting clouds of dust rolled forth, setting the onlookers coughing, even as they admired the superb balance of the jugglers. To throw a weighty dustbin up in the air and catch it as it descends empty is no mean feat. The skill and grace of the men on top of the load also, their neatness in trampling the garbage into its place, deserved the acclaim they received.

Nor was Paradise Street neglected by the street singers who with guitar and unmelodious voice did full justice to the latest love song even if they knew only half the chorus. Paradise Street, there was no disguising it, was noisy, from the time before dawn when the trucks of Carrier Johnstone on the corner began roaring out of their garage until the shouts of the various vendors died down with daylight to be replaced by glaring outbursts of wireless dance music; and on Saturdays and Wednesdays the shrieks of some hapless wife "getting it", as the street expressed it, "in the neck".

Then old Mrs Fuller's drunken son would come home to torment his mother for money. When she shut the door on him, he would sing and dance and shout in the street and call her names until she burst into tears. Then again there was Mrs Metting. Millie Metting, having been dispossessed by the demolition of Plug Alley, had been leading a migratory existence until she settled on Paradise Street like some fell blight. She regarded the letting of Number Ten with interest. It would possibly mean someone new to fight with. Mrs Metting's powers of invective had not diminished with age. She still cherished the delusion that her large family of brothers and sisters were after her "mother's money". The poor old lady found that none of her children would visit her for fear of meeting Millie who insisted on coming round every morning to see if she was comfortable and scold her if she wasn't. Millie quarrelled with all her mother's landladies also, so that the poor, fat old woman was forced to shift to a new room almost weekly.

Not that Millie's mother was rich. She existed on a microscopic pension which her daughter was determined to inherit. Millie would call upon her brothers and sisters to reproach them with their neglect of their mother and if they bolted the door in time, she would stand on the front doorstep to revile them, tracing back their criminal careers to the time when they abetted in theft of jam from the pantry. Millie even penetrated into the St Matthew's choir practice in search of a sister whom she described to the rector as "a spotted viper".

"Oh, I know her!" she shrieked. "Comes singing here so sweet, would think butter wouldn't melt in her mouth. Oh, yes. And there's her poor old mother could die as far as she's concerned without ever seein' her. But you can bet as soon as mother's in her grave, they'll all be crawlin' round tryin' to lick up what she's left."

"Hadn't you better go?" the rector said sternly. "This is not the place for such remarks."

It said a good deal for the young rector that Mrs Metting, after accusing him of neglecting his flock because he had not called on her mother for three days, actually departed.

The first Linda heard of Mrs Metting was from the scared Mrs Dempsey opposite. "You want to watch out for her," Mrs Dempsey advised. "She come down the other day and said my Ted was taking her Gwenda out to pitchers, and then she said his father was a Chinaman. My boy wouldn't be seen dead with that Gwenda. I says so. I says 'is father wasn't a Chinaman and she says some terrible things back at me. She tries to make me fight her and near knocked the baby out of me arms."

"Then I come over," Mrs Flaherty chimed in from the opposite doorway, "and said to 'er: 'You leave Mrs Dempsey alone.' I was scared she'd take to me. An old bloke came down 'ere one night to collect a debt off 'er, all in 'is best soot and watch chain and bowler 'at, she 'it at 'im over the 'ead with a pot stick. An' one of 'er relatives come 'ere once and she chased the woman all up the street pullin' 'er 'air and screamin' and swearin'. Something awful, she is."

Linnie's first encounter with Mrs Metting occurred one morning as the new resident was returning tired from her cleaning. Noticing Mrs Metting watching her, she nodded politely. "Nice day," she said.

"A very nice day, beautiful, lovely day," Mrs Metting answered sourly, "for any landlord's pimps that can go sneakin' about."

Linnie passed on, leaving Mrs Metting triumphant. She cackled like a hen to the street about having "told off the dirty spy in Number Ten".

The very next day she accosted Linnie again and in front of the enthralled audience of neighbours called her a few of the choicer epithets she usually reserved for relations. Linnie did not even trouble to reply but a less belligerent woman than Mrs Metting would have taken warning from her eyes.

"If you don't get out of my way," Mrs Rolfe said calmly,

"I will call the police."

"Ah, I knew yer was a police pimp," Mrs Metting sneered. "You 'aven't fooled me. Oh, no." She pushed Linnie violently. "Don't you come tryin' to put yer bounce over me," she shouted.

It was all Linnie had been waiting for. She seized the astounded Mrs Metting securely by the shoulders and shook her, shook her hard. It was the suddenness of the attack that disconcerted Mrs Metting. She tried to strike at Linnie, but there seemed to be nothing but two iron hands that gripped her shoulders in a vice and shook her as she had never been shaken before. Her grey, wispy hair fell over her eyes and she nearly swallowed her false teeth when the breathless Mrs Rolfe flung her against the wall and said grimly as she passed on: "Don't say that again."

It was a glorious moment for the neighbours. Mrs Flaherty was observed to embrace Mrs Dempsey joyously as she gurgled: "I wouldn't 'ave missed it for quids."

"I'll have you prosecuted!" Mrs Metting screamed after Mrs Rolfe's departing back; but her husband when he came home took a different view.

"Serves you damn well right," he growled. "You been lookin' for it. Shut yer mouth and give me a bit of peace."

It was a bitter, a crushing defeat for Mrs Metting. She could not stay in Paradise Street with all the women giggling. The following week she moved bag and baggage with a last vindictive shriek about police pimps, spitting on the Rolfe doorstep as she passed.

Mrs Dempsey came over with congratulations and a plate of fish her husband had caught that morning. "Gets up at four every day and goes off fishing. We make a bit sometimes by little Bert's sellin' them round Dennison Square. Just thought you and Mr Rolfe might like some. We got more than we want."

It was the accolade. The street approved the new arrivals. It was their coming that had rolled away the terrible cloud of Mrs Metting. Again the sun shone, again old ladies and cats came running on the footpath and women chatted in their doorways unmolested. The children played over Mrs Metting's hitherto inviolate doorstep and Mrs Dempsey's Bert heaved a heartfelt stone through the window of the empty house, expressing the feelings of the whole street.

With one pest gone, there were others demanding attention. All the neighbours had assured the newcomers that the bugs would not bite until November when the warm weather really began to work in their blood; but Linnie did not like the look of the vermin.

"They ain't 'ad a good feed for so long, dear," Mrs Flaherty remarked encouragingly. "You got to remember they've got their feelin's same as you."

Everybody in the street had a patent bug-killer, but there was one old lady with a simple remedy. She lived alone with two cats, one to sleep at her back and one on her feet. Having no occasion to keep the remedy secret, she willingly passed it on to the new member of the Doorstep Club.

"If you've got beer in your blood," she declared, "they won't bite yuh."

Mrs Noblett's method was more elaborate. After anxious consultation over the expense Rolfe and Linnie spent days brewing noxious potions in an old tin can. They bought a big howitzer spray and placing one bug on the window sill, they puffed at it with Mrs Noblett's remedy. The bug merely twitched its whiskers. Then, as Linnie was giving way to despair, it rolled over and expired. There was great rejoicing.

"Talk about large-scale murder," Jimmy told old Bob. "It would give you some idea of the next war to see us."

"Jimmy," Linnie said firmly, "let the matter drop."

"This fight with the hidden foe," Rolfe went on perversely, "continues as a kind of theme through all our daily dealings. The motif in B flat running through the symphonic prelude to living. I remember going out to the Bay once, there was a chap in the van, and he was bottle green and lousy from sleeping in the park."

"Rolfe!" Linnie said reproachfully.

"He scratched himself for a bit, and then said: 'Hey, mate, I'll swap you two commonos for a stripey one.' We look down our noses now," he finished contentedly, "when we see those chaps who came round selling phenol on Saturdays."

382

"Jimmy," Linda said, when Bob had departed, "you should not make light of serious matters."

Rolfe grinned. "You're very middle-class in your attitude to things. No one would believe you were brought up in Foveaux."

"I wonder," Linnie said slowly, "was I right to come back here?" She looked anxiously at Rolfe. "Don't seem to be able to keep away from the place."

"Places are like that," Rolfe said. "Why worry?"

"I don't — with you." She was absently eyeing the Mexican embroidery. "That's valuable, isn't it?"

"You're not going to sell it?"

"Didn't mean that. I could make things like it, though. Ought to sell."

Rolfe stared at her. "How d'you mean?"

"Exclusive shops. Build up a trade. Get a factory of my own some day."

Jimmy grinned. "Capitalist, eh?"

Linnie nodded quite soberly. "They try to buy things like that cheap and sell them for about four guineas. Might be a start if I let them sweat me." She looked at her long hands and sighed. They were soiled and broken with work. "Don't believe any of those advertisements about things that take the dirt out," she said ruefully. "I've tried 'em all."

"You shall sit on a cushion," Rolfe vowed, "one of these days, and sew a fine seam. And dine upon. . . ."

She smiled. She had no illusions as to who was the practical one of the partnership. She did not ever want Rolfe to be practical. With him to back her, she would tear Foveaux apart. She was shrewd and strong and she could work. Oh, how she would work!

"Still love me?" he asked.

"Seen any signs of failing affection?"

"Mrs Roolllffe," Mrs Flaherty was howling over the back fence. "Mrs Roolllffe."

"One of these days," Linnie said, "we really will have a minute to ourselves."

# CHAPTER 4

## I

For years Bramley Cornish and that genial bandit, Kingston of the Child Welfare Department, had been accustomed to start their Tuesday morning rounds in the Foot together. Sometimes they would meet in the tram if Bramley had gone into the office; sometimes they would encounter each other on the corner of Slazenger Street. Bramley could cover a street in the time it took Kingston to investigate a couple of families, but they kept fairly level. It did not do for Mr Bross's rent-collector to seem hand-in-glove with the Child Welfare officer; still they always managed to meet for lunch together. Kingston, in his methodical way, had made inquiries about Bramley before ever he sought his acquaintance and had decided that, among rent-collectors, he was a rarity. A man who battled with his boss in the tenants' interests was either, he decided, a fool or a friend. They had been friends now for years; and there was nothing about which they agreed except on liking each other.

"There's a rent collector in Glebe," Kingston remarked laconically as he overtook Bramley in Slazenger Street, "who gets up at half-past six and does his rounds before breakfast. Why not try it?"

"No chance," Bramley grinned. "It would make me too unpopular."

Kingston grunted. "Every time I come to this dump," he said disparagingly, "it looks worse. I don't know how the devil you keep cheerful. At least I do get away to the country part of the year."

"I ought to look cheerful," Bramley responded. "Yesterday the old man offered to get me a car."

Kingston twisted his face into an expression of disbelief. "Get out!" he said.

"And he also raised my emolument somewhat," Bramley continued. "In fact he just about doubled it."

"How come?"

"The result of beautiful bluff. I will stand lunch today on the strength of it." Bramley could have gone home to lunch but it was their custom to spend the midday break together. "It was like those things you read about: The Power of the Eye and Take Our Three Courses of Memory Training and Bully Your Chief for the Rest of Your Life. Never thought it would work."

"What sort of a car do you get," Kingston was no longer disbelieving.

"Don't know that I want one."

"You're a mug," Kingston said caustically. "Never fit a gift horse out with a set of false teeth."

He was ready to advise Cornish about cars. Advice was Kingston's strong point. It came almost mechanically to him after years of the Child Welfare Department to advance an authoritative opinion on any subject the minute it was mentioned.

"If I get a car, the Old Man will expect me to do the rent collecting in about three suburbs, and what's more, he'll put a couple of chaps off so I can."

"Use your bluff. By the way, what was the bluff?"

"I told him I had been offered another job at a better screw."

"Good enough. And he swallowed it."

"I had been offered another job as a matter of fact," Bramley said reflectively. "In an accountancy department. And the pay looked good."

"Well, why didn't you take it?"

"I'm too old," Bramley said sedately. "I've been with the firm since I was a pup."

Why should he tell Edward Kingston of all the struggles of the past years? The early, gloomy hatred of the daily round of the office, his personal dislike of old Bross and his hero-worship of Bross's son. The time he had spent in the land and estate firm of Bross, Twyford and Massingham loaded with office drudgery, fretting because he would have been able to do so much better on his own, if only he had the money to start.

Then there had been the breaking up of the partnership during the depression and his own return to the dark offices of Bross, so dark that he was glad to be out rent-collecting to escape them.

There was his antagonism to the Old Man. They had never seemed able to meet without abuse on Bross's side and stiff resentment from Bramley. Finally, when the chance came of a job in the accounts department of a big wholesale firm, he had been almost too discouraged to care. It was chiefly the thought of the extra small comforts he might buy his mother that led him to consider the offer. Then there had come the vision of giving notice to Bross, the thought of having the opportunity to fling at Bross all the hatred that had been choking him for years, to feel the satisfaction of unleashing the madness and passion he had restrained so long.

It was the moment he had waited for when he tramped into Bross's office and the old chap had looked up and growled: "What the hell's up now?"

"I'm getting out," Bramley had responded. "I've got the offer of a better job and a better screw, and you, you damn old rack-renter, can go to hell and take your slums with you."

Old Bross had been no whit perturbed.

"How much are they going to give yer?" he croaked.

"None of your business now, but it's five-ten a week and the chance of promotion."

Bross had snapped his fingers suddenly, disconcertingly. "I'll give you the same to stay," he said.

"Not on your life," his rent-collector said determinedly.

"If you're too bloody 'aughty to go rent-collectin' on foot, you can get yourself one of them cars to do it in," Bross sneered. "That's your whole trouble. Lowerin' yer dignity rent-snatchin'. You'd sooner sit on yer backside for the rest of yer life addin' up figgers. All right, you can sit in this office and add to your 'eart's content."

"No good. I'm fed up to the back teeth."

"Siddown." The Power of the Eye had not been all on Bramley's side. He hesitated, looked at the door, then sat sullenly. "Ever since you was a kid," Bross said ruminatingly, "you been the same. Too big for your boots." He eyed Bramley sourly. "I know what you're goin' to say. If you 'adn't 'ad a mother to keep, you wouldn't 'ave stopped 'ere two days. All right, you 'ave stopped 'ere. You been 'ere longer than anyone an' now you learnt everything I've taught you, you're going' to clear off and leave me."

The sheer effrontery of this attack took his rent-collector's breath away. "Why you. . . ." he began.

"There's Bill," old Bross continued. "Comes into the office about an hour a day, then goes out to golf. 'Don't think I'll be in tomorrow,'" he mimicked, "'Got to motor up to see old Jack Hutchison.' If it isn't that, it's something else. Can't depend on 'im." There was an open note of pleading in his voice. "They're all livin' off me. Every damn one of them. Me wife's family, me brother Ernest and 'is kids, and now Bill. I 'ad 'opes Bill'd come to 'is senses." Bramley Cornish was impatient. The old cow was spoiling his exit with this last minute bathos. "I been watchin' you, Cornish. I been sayin' to meself: 'There's a feller you can depend on.' I know you 'ate me very guts and you 'ave for years, but that ain't nothing. I've said: 'There's a chap that don't lie. 'E earns what 'e gets.'"

"Three-ten a week," Bramley said bitterly. "You can't blame me for wanting to go. I've made up my mind."

"To hell with your mind! You ain't got one. It's all run to nobility the way a cabbage runs to seed." Mr Bross was wheezing in his customary bad temper. "Maybe you ain't been over-paid. I don't say you 'ave. But if you stay, I'll see you don't suffer."

"I asked for a rise a month ago and you turned me down," Bramley said stubbornly.

"Ah, but you wasn't goin' to get out then," old Bross responded craftily. "If you 'ang on, you can 'ave six quid a week to go on with and the car."

"What's the catch?" Bramley said nastily.

"There ain't none, I'm tellin' you. But you got to understand that I may want yer to do more'n the rent-collectin'," old Bross continued hastily. "If I raise your screw, I expect you to do more work. Bit by bit you can drop the rent-snatchin' and get in the office 'ere with me."

"That," Bramley said, almost with a smile, "would be wonderful. We could fight all day." He had dropped his anger. It was not natural for him to be angry long.

"Well, what about it?"

"I'll think it over," Bramley said, rising.

"You won't do nothin' of the sort. Make up your mind now or never."

"They'll keep the job open for a bit," Bramley said coolly. "I'll see how I feel in a couple of weeks."

Secretly he was relieved. The thing that had galled him most about old Bross had been the contemptuous hints that he could dispense with his rent-collector's services any time. Bross knew that Bramley Cornish was valuable, tactful, and, until this crisis, cheap. In Bramley's mind flamed like a beacon the idea that the old man really depended on him. The sour old fossil actually was willing to allow him some measure of control, to let him gather the threads of those hundreds of houses and hovels into his hands. He would be Prime Minister, he thought, but it would be for old Bross. If the old man really meant it, and it was fairly evident that he did, there was no limit to which Bramley could not go. He had learnt how to treat Bross, to answer him, argument for argument and word for word, instead of hating him coldly and in silence. The old chap wasn't such a bad old devil even if he was a mean, dirty, foul-mouthed reprobate.

## I I

"By the way," Kingston growled as he consulted his lists. "Traves over in Newtown has a perfect fiend of a woman in his territory and I know for a fact he's trying to shift her into mine. So far she won't go, but if she comes in and wants one of your houses, look out for her. Her husband's a jail-bird and she's just as rough as a couple of chaff-bags. Name of Neicie Thompson. I'm not going to have her in my territory if I can help it."

"I don't think she'd want to live in Foveaux again," Bramley said quietly. "She lived here once before."

"Good job. I've met her. God, what a tongue! She'll be

another Mother Metting when she gets older. By the way," he widened in a grin as they stopped at the first house in Ogham Street, "Elaine has twins!"

"No!" Bramley was astounded. "Twins!"

"It's a fact," Kingston said happily. "I said to her: 'Elaine, you don't know what's in store for you, my girl, carrying on the way you do.' And by gosh," he said happily, "I was right." His face darkened. "Is this one of the places your boss won't fix?"

"It is," Bramley said in a hard tone. "He told me that he could get twelve and six for it as it stood, so why should he renovate it."

It was easier to step through the sagging wooden palings of the fence beside the lane than to open the broken gate. Kingston always followed this procedure, because the inmates would bar the door if they saw him coming and pretend to be out. Coming through the side fence he had a chance of catching them.

"Hey, anyone at home?" he shouted. A tousled fair girl in a dressing gown lounged out the door. "Hullo, Jessie. Where's Elaine? Where's Joyce?"

"They're somewhere about," the girl said sullenly.

"Tell them I want to see them."

Kingston walked into the kitchen and pulled out the only chair. Bramley stood by the door.

"Elaine's got your money, Mr Cornish," Jessie informed him. "I'll let her know you're here." She gave him a smile.

"Thank you," said Bramley politely. "Can I see the twins?"

"Sure," the girl nodded, glancing sidelong at Kingston, the look of a tiger towards the man with the whip. "Hey, Elai-aine."

A small dark girl appeared with two bundles, one in a mauve and one in a blue shawl. She smiled at Bramley, showing a set of bad teeth.

"I've got it, Mr Cornish," she said, holding out a ten shilling note and waiting for the receipt. "Here, Jess, hold the kids." Proudly she displayed the two red infants. "They're girls," she beamed. "I always wanted a girl."

Elaine, Bramley reflected, at the age of nineteen had now

four children. Joyce had one and Jessie two. None of them had a husband. It was out of the child endowment money that Bross's rent would come. Bross would be buying that car out of Elaine's earnings.

Kingston was sorting his papers. "Elaine," he said with half a smile, "you can't say I didn't warn you."

The girl smiled back, a hard twisted smile. Either you got hard about these things or else you broke your heart and were no more use. It was easier to get hard.

Bramley lifted his hat to the small mother. "They're beautiful babies," he said, knowing as much about babies as he did of rare vintages. "Good morning." He stepped through the fence.

Kingston, his sombrero hat pushed back on his forehead, reflected that Bram Cornish was really on a better wicket than he was. Cornish was the rent man, inevitable, to be greeted without animosity, to be propitiated. He had seen Cornish handle recalcitrant tenants and admired his never-failing self control.

"You must remember that poor Mr Bross has suffered very much since the depression, Mrs Quine," Bram would say sadly, "but I'll see if I can get the window fixed."

And Mrs Quine would tell her neighbours that "Mr Cornish was a nice man" and that if anything could be got out of Mr Bross, he would get it. Bramley was an intermediary. They knew he was not responsible for the horrible state of their dwellings, for the dark, smelly rooms without windows, the galvanized iron roofs full of rust holes, the damp walls, the paper peeling off, the dilapidated tubs emptying into the cesspool in the backyard. "If Mr Cornish had the handling of it, things would be different," the tenants told each other. They did not blame him. Was he not as much at the mercy of Bross as they were?

But Kingston was a foeman to be treated with treachery if possible, or truth, if it paid better. The neighbourhood watched Kingston as a native tribe might watch the white man with a gun in his pocket and gifts in his hands. He was authority, a demon in human form who led a lovely life harrying poor people and taking their children away. Kingston had never yet

390

removed one child; but the fear and hate were there all the same, mixed with a kind of grudging admiration. Kingston knew everything. With the job of Child Welfare officer he combined that of chief quarrel adjudicator, lord high admonisher, inquiry agent, policeman and censor.

"Here comes Kingie!" small boys would shout and the street in a minute would be as empty as last year's bird's-nest. The people of Foveaux were Kingston's "Warrigals", as he said with a contemptuous affection, and he carried the White Man's Law among them. They might not love him but they respected his word.

It was to the rent-man that the warrigals gossiped. If Kingston stopped to talk, they knew he wanted information about the woman next door and the way she treated her children. He would work the conversation round that way and the neighbours would give him details readily and with spite. But they knew all the time he sat yarning that it was information he was after.

On the other hand they talked to Bram Cornish as they did to the rector, for the love of talking. Bramley had to listen to long family histories with one foot off the doorstep and his mind agile to make a break from the monologue.

"It was the same with my cousin's boy, Harry, the one who was on the milkcart. First 'e thinks 'is teeth is causing it, and 'e pays a lot of money to 'ave them out — that was when 'e 'ad a job of course. But it didn't do a bit of good. Then 'e got little startin' pains down 'is legs. Then they come up in the groin and back. Something terrible the back pains was, 'e told me."

"Well, I hope he's feeling better next week," Bramley would say cheerfully but firmly. "Remember me to Miss Greta." And he would be off before any further symptoms could be added.

"What do you favour for Saturday?" old Mr Stevens would invariably ask, mending watches as he sat on the gas box on his front veranda.

And Bramley, scribbling out the rent receipt, would respond: "Jack Hooper tells me Viper is a good thing." Bramley had never backed a horse in his life.

He would be met with complaints about the kitchen sink or

the leak in the roof or the banister giving way under Gramma's weight. He would be taken in to inspect the rusted kitchen stove or the hole in the copper. To Bramley the running sores of Foveaux were always unwrapped. All day long he moved in the sour stench of misery, the dirt, the sweaty, clammy nastiness of diseased people and decayed houses. Sometimes he felt as though he was putting his hand on slime. His gorge rose with it. He was degraded with the degradation of these lounging, sunken-eyed men, these tired, stooping women, the children perpetually running at the nose and with black, bare feet and legs covered with sores.

Kingston at lunch was never very cheering. He would discuss congenital syphilis over the soup and tuberculosis with dessert. His account of his morning round was always lurid.

"So I said: 'You go and get that leg seen to, Mrs Williams.' The old devil will have to have it off if she doesn't go soon. 'I can't make up me mind,' she whined. 'I've always been a healthy woman bar the knee. Long life runs in the family, Mr Kingston.' She had the hide to tell me: 'Aunt Susan pinched a man off a much younger girl when she was sixty and me father was murdered in his bed at ninety-three.' " Kingston mimicked the Foveaux diphthongs to perfection.

Bramley continued his dinner while Kingston began to puzzle out aloud why Keith's stepfather had informed the police that the lad was implicated in the robbery of Snowy Breen. A lie, Kingston decided, inspired by the stepfather's desire to stand in well with the police. There was also the fact that Keith had stopped his stepfather beating the little girl. In the middle of his monologue Kingston stopped.

"You don't seem as cheerful as you were this morning?"

"I was thinking of the Fergusons," Bramley answered. "They're paying fifteen shillings for that filthy hole."

Ferguson was a thin, scrawny idler who was dying of tuberculosis. He sat on the front doorstep all day, with the youngest of his eleven children playing about his feet.

"Castration," Kingston said with a didactic cheerfulness, as though he was commenting on the salad. "That's the only cure. Compulsory castration. All subnormals."

Bramley stiffened. "And for all unemployed," he asked

coldly, "who can't provide for their families?"

They were on Kingston's pet theory, their favourite quarrel. "Not necessarily *all*. Have a board of appeal." Kingston realized that Bramley would never regard his theory as scientifically correct. But then Cornish would argue that the people in these slums were not subnormal. He did not recognize an I.Q. when he saw it, and maintained that to test a child on how many trees stand in a field when the child was terrified and had never heard of a field in its life, was not a test of intelligence. "I still maintain," Kingston said deliberately, "the poor should have no children. Children are not born to this place — they're damned to it."

"That's what you say because you have to tramp round doling out the cash for them," Bramley retorted.

"I could poison off the whole human race," Kingston agreed, "sometimes."

Bramley nodded. One's view did become warped under the eternal attack of other people's pain. You breathed it in, you got it in your lungs, and your mind and your bloodstream, a composite horror. Sleeping with a corpse would be pleasant to living day by day with the slow death of these streets. Kingston, doing ten men's work with five men's kindness and justice, was just not normal on the matter of slum children.

"Take this morning," Kingston said bitterly. "Only spark of humour is Elaine having twins when I'd told her to be a good girl and she had promised me she would. I offered Jess a job out at Maroubra, told her she could take the kids with her. She wouldn't go. I asked Joyce. Same answer. Why? They're fighting over a man and each is scared if they go off and take a job, the other'll get him." His eyes hardened. "They're perfectly contented to live quarrelling and fighting and starving like a set of wild she-cats when they could be working. They're all quite content. Quite." He looked straight at Bramley. "It's a fact, isn't it?"

Bramley shook his head. "Not content. Resigned. They know there's no rescue ship." The terrible resignation of the poor like the resignation of the dying hurt more than anything else.

"Resigned then," Kingston nodded, his grey eyes hard.

"They're no good to themselves or other people. They need to be wiped out like diseased animals. They're not educated or clean or human. There's a subnormal woman in the next street. She's got eight children and she doesn't know who their eight fathers are. I asked her straight out: 'Would you have had that last child if it wasn't for the eight-and-six from the Department?' and she said: 'No bloody fear, I wouldn't.' " He took a hearty bite of bread and butter. "It sickens you. Only thing is to take it as a matter of course. They want the money so they breed children. Be businesslike."

Bramley nodded. "Business," he said sardonically, "is business."

Kingston lit his after-lunch cigarette. "Can't make you out," he grunted at Bramley. "I'm tough enough, God knows, but when I see all their faces twisted with disease and cunning and drink, it makes me sick."

He sighed, thinking of the Chief sitting in his office. Bramley reminded him of the Chief sometimes when he put on that kindly, half humorous smile. The Chief could tell just by the voice of someone ringing him on the telephone whether a complaint was genuine or not. They all had to be investigated, but the old man knew. He had tramped his boot soles off, had the Chief, round all the dirty dens in Sydney. He knew them inside out, but it had not made him hard or bitter or mean. He sat there, an old kindly man, and the misery and filth and poverty flowed into him in a never ending loathly stream. He had stayed clean in his mind and kind.

Kingston straightened. "It doesn't do any harm having lunch with you, young Cornish," he said. Bramley was older than he was. "Particularly when you pay for it." His mind reverted to his earlier thought. "Still I can't understand your sticking to this job."

"A man can serve two masters," Bramley said. "If I can make the old man put in a new floor-board occasionally, I have not lived in vain." He twisted his tea-cup. "They hate charity," he said reflectively. "I was born here. I know. My family hated charity, too. You're not charity, of course, you're the government," he hastened to add. "You're a legitimate source of income."

Kingston rose. "The minute I get out of this swarming, pullulating, festering mess of lanes and dirt," he said, reaching for his hat, "I try to forget it."

"The only people who do," said Bramley, "are the people who have never seen it."

Kingston nodded. "You're right," he said. "But there's nothing can be done."

Bramley did not answer.

"Got to call in at the clinic," Kingston remarked. "Going that way?"

# III

It cheered them up to call on the baby clinic. There were probably not two lovelier looking women in the world than the matron and sister. A shame to waste them on the Foot, Kingston thought. The sister, at least ought to marry. She was so delicate, so pale and flower-like under her white veil. The matron, grey-haired and blue-eyed, had the same clear dignity. They greeted the two men smilingly.

"What do you know about Elaine having twins!" Kingston said with a guffaw.

"Wasn't it wonderful, Mr Kingston?" the sister cried. "We were so pleased."

"They're marvellous children," the matron chorused. "She ought to be very proud of them."

"But look here," Kingston protested with the pained reproach of one who had been outed on a foul, "you've got to realize the girl's got no means of support."

"I don't care." The pale, delicate face of the sister was defiant. "They're glorious children, and they weigh," she added triumphantly, "eleven pounds."

The incomprehensible attitude of females towards their erring sisters baffled Kingston. He growled, and dropped the subject. "Has Mrs Whistler brought the baby in?" he asked.

"I'll see," the matron said hurriedly. "No, she hasn't been in for a month."

"I've got to see her this afternoon and I'll remind her."

The wind was still blowing down the streets with a vindictive sting in it, throwing dust in Kingston's eyes as deliberately as any of his pensioners. The two-up school on the corner took no notice of Bramley and Kingston. The only thing that really disturbed the streets was "the blue-bird", the police car on its rounds. Then, indeed, there would be a stir among the warrigals.

Bramley touched his hat to Mrs Tracey as she hurried past. He wondered if her husband was in jail again. Mr and Mrs Tracey were among the most loving and peaceable couples round the Foot, but when things "got tough", as they expressed it, it was their habit to stage a glorious row, and Mrs Tracey would be able to send Mr Tracey to jail for charges ranging from language to hitting her with a sauce bottle. During Mr Tracey's term his wife would be supported by the Child Welfare Department. It was much better than the dole. Kingston knew, but he felt that such heroic measures merited their reward.

Anyway the Traceys weren't as bad as the Hendersons. Kingston had a suspicion that Mrs Henderson's husband was living just around the corner on the money his wife was paid for being deserted.

Kingston started frowning at his little pocket book. "I'll leave you here, Bram," he said abruptly. "So long."

"So long."

Bramley turned to the heart-rending job of convincing a terrace of haggard women that there was nothing he could do about the rent being raised from seventeen-and-six to a pound.

"We just won't pay it, that's all," one bony woman said desperately. "Mrs Rolfe says if we all refuse to pay it, he can't force us."

Bramley set himself to the task of wringing the half-crown out of them. It was his job, and business, he told himself bitterly, was business.

"Mr Bross owns these houses," he said, "and he has a right to say what they are worth. I'm employed to collect his rents and I'm supposed to collect a pound. If you don't pay it, you'll have to move."

This comes of Linnie living down here, he thought.

"We'll have to move anyway," the woman said fiercely.

"The place is falling to bits round our ears. Tell him he can have his old ruins. I'll pay you seventeen-and-six and not a penny more."

"Very good," said Bramley, and wrote out the receipt for the amount.

He passed on and rang the bell of the next house. There was no answer. Those who did not fling open defiance, shut their doors and were not at home. Finally he gave it up and rang Bross.

The old man over the telephone was bitter. "You want a damn wet' nurse," he cursed. "Lettin' them put it over you like that."

"All right. Come and get it out of them yourself," Bramley retorted. "The places aren't worth five bob."

There was an indignant croak from the other end of the telephone.

"It isn't how much a place is worth. It's how much you can get for it."

"Well, what am I to tell them?" Bramley asked coolly.

"Tell them to go to hell."

"I'll tell you something, too," Bramley said furiously, all the pent-up wretchedness of the day bursting forth. "If you don't let these miserable women off the rise, you can come down and do your own rent-collecting. I'm not asking them any more for it."

"That's it. That's it. Let me down and side with them. I s'pose you want to see me starvin' in the gutter?"

"Are you going to hold out for the quid?"

There was a silence. "What chance is there of getting it? Honest now, Brammy?"

Bramley considered. "If you insist, they'll give in," he said coldly. "You've got the whip hand. Half of them will leave, the rest won't be able to. But it will cost you the houses empty and you'll have to reduce the rent in the long run."

There was a short silence.

"All right," Bross croaked. "Never say I ain't treated them well. You can tell 'em I'll let 'em off the extra two-and-six for the time being."

# CHAPTER 5

## I

It was a point of honour in Foveaux to attend meetings of some kind. The tradition was so strong that if two Foveauvians were wrecked on some desolate coast, as soon as they staggered ashore they would hold a formal meeting to arrange for the distribution of the salvaged tin of biscuits.

Those Foveauvians who did not attend the meetings of the A.L.P. Branch, the British Israelites, the vestry, the two-up school, the gymnasium in the cellar of Jordan True's wine bar, the Christian Youth Council or the Gaelic song rallies, could always find a meeting going on in Dennison Square, Friday, Saturday or Sunday night, often several meetings at once. But most of the meetings had their hallowed and traditional gathering places.

There was any number of halls in Foveaux; the letting of them was a staple industry, and they ranged from exclusive big ballrooms like the Foveaux Assembly Hall, decorated with white and gold woodwork, to the disused corn and fodder store where the Foveaux Unit held its meetings.

The Foveaux Unit of the Communist Party was spending its Friday night revelling in an orgy of self-criticism. Every once in a while the Foveaux Unit had one of these bacchanalian revels wherein the members vied with each other in confessing political sins. Usually the accusation was the mysterious formula that they had been "too leftist"; but tonight Jamieson had a new explanation why the Unit in Foveaux had slipped.

"We're tailing behind the masses," he said accusingly. "We have completely lost touch with them. It's getting to the stage where the same members turn up to each meeting and there's no real attempt made to rally new members."

"We haven't had that kind of campaign for a long time," Mrs Stanchen said stiffly. "Last time the committee decided it should be a Better Morals Campaign. We were to have the slogan 'A Hundred Per Cent Morality by June' and 'Bring Your Domestic Troubles to the Party instead of the Divorce Court'." She looked accusingly at Emily Anseer. "We only fulfilled ninety per cent of our quota."

"I'm not talking about morals or distributing circulars or anything like that," Jamieson said impatiently. "Our organizing is all wrong. We have lost touch."

"I don't agree with you, Comrade Chair," a lean youth with protruding teeth put in. "There was a Party member admitted only last July."

"And what happened?" Jamieson demanded fiercely. "Comrade McCullemy follows him about to discover if he's a spy or not and the new comrade becomes incensed and retires from Party work altogether."

"When I was in jail in nineteen-twenty-nine," McCullemy reminisced, "Jack and I heard a joker with a stutter just like his talking to the police sergeant. Didn't we, Jack? We didn't see the chap, but I could swear to the stutter."

"Ay, ay," Jamieson said impatiently. "I dare say. But the point tonight is we're getting nowhere in Foveaux." He smote the rickety table with his fist. "Nowhere. We're tailing behind the masses."

"What makes you say that, comrade?"

"This Progress Association," Jamieson declared fiercely. "The thing started only last month and they've a membership of several hundred, a hall given them rent-free and they've started a paper. There's organizing for you."

Emily Anseer laughed shrilly. "But look at the people running it! Old Duncan who, as everyone knows, has never been more than a Left Laborite—"

"Half the disgruntled A.L.P. are in it," Jamieson interrupted. "All the real old diehards, the radicals—"

"The petty-bourgeoisie," Emily Anseer said disdainfully.

"You're wrong. There's a large element of factory workers. Men who've refused to become Unit members are working in the Progress Association."

"But it's bourgeois," Emily shrilled. "And that Mrs Rolfe — the woman has a hopelessly bourgeois outlook. Besides she used to be connected with a group of intellectuals who have gone Trotskyite. And wasn't there something funny about her marriage?"

"Mrs Rolfe," Jamieson said sternly, "is a solid member of her union and a good influence where she lives."

"Oh, of course—" Emily was beginning angrily, but Jamieson took no notice.

"We've got to get over this idea," he said emphatically, "that because we're members of the Communist Party, people necessarily recognize us as the spearhead and vanguard of the workers. They don't unless we actually are doing the job. At present, the spearhead and vanguard in Foveaux is the Progress Association which has led the fight against increased rentals and won."

There was a silence.

"May I remind you, comrades, that the policy we are endeavouring to follow is not an isolationist policy, it is a policy of co-operation with any body which is willing to follow our line."

"But the Progress Association don't want to follow our line. They want to have *their* way—"

Jamieson swept on over the interruption. "Our line at the moment is the improvement of the living conditions of the masses, the actual improvement of their status."

"But I thought," someone suggested, "that the closer the masses were to starvation the more likely a revolutionary situation was."

"Wrong," Jamieson snapped. "And you know your dialectics are wrong. I wish you'd attend a class again, comrade. It's not because the people's living conditions are worsened that a revolution occurs, but because there is an educated class-conscious vanguard ready to lead the people."

The congregation nodded solemnly at this orthodox statement of the position. Jamieson's theory was always impeccable.

"That is probably why in such places as Foveaux," Jamieson pursued, "you find the depressed middle classes, when they are ground into the position of unemployed workers, either becoming Fascist or left revolutionaries. They are more ready to fight than that section of the proletariat which has been forced into a resignation, almost contentment, by a long period of oppression and malnutrition."

"But, comrade, the leadership of the revolution must always be with the proletariat—"

"Who's talking about the revolution?" Jamieson demanded impatiently. "I'm talking about the day-to-day struggle here in Foveaux and the best way of using that section of the middle class which is ready to struggle because it is struggling for what it once enjoyed." He shook his shoulders impatiently. "Here we are arguing theoretical points while the Progress Association celebrates its victory in the Rent Campaign."

"They never asked us to co-operate. They asked the Unemployed Committee."

"Must we wait for an invitation?" Jamieson asked impatiently. "We should have had our members in the Progress Association when it started and had them elected to executive positions."

"I don't agree that this Progress Association is such a good idea." Comrade Anseer said pettishly. "I remember they had something like a slum abolition campaign or something — but it failed. They're only lumpen proletariat round this area. They get interested like children, then forget." She remembered another point. "Most of the people who were purged out of the Unit for years back have gone into the Progress Association."

Jamieson sighed. "We must form a broad united front," he said patiently, "with the Progress Association, with the mothers' guild, with the Sunday School picnic if necessary, as long as we popularize our movement among the masses. It's the Party line, comrades."

To these last awful words the meeting acquiesced in respectful silence. Then—

"I don't see," Emily Anseer said acidly, "how we're going to be the spearhead of the working class if we let the Progress Association steal our thunder."

"We will work in and through it. It is the duty of every member of the Unit to join. It's our job to lead the masses. If the Progress Association is leading them in Foveaux, we should be in it."

"S'pose Rolfe and his gang get offended?"

"There's no need. As long as we can use them, let us be tactful."

"Butter their feet," McCullemy suggested lazily.

"If you like. Be courteous. Be tactful. Don't offend their susceptibilities. After all," he moodily twisted the agenda paper, "they're good types."

"Not Duncan," Miss Anseer said bitterly. "I remember once when a comrade just returned from Russia came to address a meeting in Foveaux, someone stole his overcoat, and old Duncan said that he had no right to be so upset about it, because after all Foveaux wasn't enlightened like Russia."

"Order!" Jamieson snapped. "I'll call for a motion." Foveaux, he thought, a bitter place, a disappointing place, but after all — his place. "Will someone move the motion?"

The Foveaux Unit had not paid the rent for the corn and fodder store for several years. Its typewriters were secured on a deposit and used until the typewriter firms, despairing of another payment, took them back. Nevertheless, confident of its ability to lead the masses, the Foveaux Unit voted unanimously to join the Progress Association and become elected to positions of trust.

## II

There was another gathering in progress that night in the shabby brick building beside St Matthew's Church. This hall was referred to as the "New Sunday School Hall", although it had been put up long ago when Lennox Street was cut across the corner of the church grounds into Errol Street.

There the hoary Fathers of the United Ancient Order of Druids met in all the glory of their regalia under the piercing gaze of an old portrait of Queen Victoria, one of those portraits that are seen nowhere outside reformatories or Foveaux. The austerity of the wooden benches and the royal countenance was mitigated by the brilliant backdrop of the platform at one end of the hall. The artist who painted the backdrop had obviously glanced at Queen Victoria and determined that something must be done to offset that portrait. The wings of the stage depicted a stone wall of ruby-coloured brick over which a hollyhock was clambering in a manner more resembling virginia creeper. Behind the stone wall a sheaf of wheat the size of an oak-tree provided a riotous yellow contrast. The backdrop displayed a ten-sixty-six castle on a mountain top with a vivid blue lake in the foreground. The surface of the lake would quiver and the castle shake to its topmost turret when Miss Josie Selkirk's tap-dancing troupe gave an item.

On the fiftieth anniversary of the foundation of the Foveaux Lodge you could hardly get in the Sunday School door for the crowds of druids, druidesses and their friends, many of whom had come from lodges far off in the outer suburbs to celebrate the occasion. Invitations had been issued to famous druids who graced the Foveaux Lodge in the long ago; and the lodge officers, clustered around the door, were kept busy shaking hands with visiting brothers, falling upon them in a torrent of welcome and friendliness as they entered, shouting to make themselves heard above the efforts of the dance band, whose syncopation kept the stage backdrop in a constant state of agitation and swung the younger druids and druidesses around the hall in a whirlpool of cheerful noise.

Seated around the walls on wooden forms, the elder druidesses conversed together placidly and criticized the fox-trotting, gum-chewing, cigarette-smoking element in the middle of the dance floor. The elderly women did not wear evening dress, but the young girls did, cheap, pretty taffeta frocks that they bought for a pound or so on the lay-by. Their partners in their best suits had discarded their dungarees and working clothes, though some of them still retained the traditional Foveaux woollen sweater instead of a waistcoat.

"Looks like being a good turn-out," Brother Isenberg, the lodge secretary, greeted the ex-worthy-arch-brother Sutton who came mildly into the middle of the noise, a somewhat stooped old man, well into his seventies.

"It does. Yes, it does," Brother Sutton responded. "Ah, it takes the Foveaux Lodge to show them how to run a dance."

He chuckled good-naturedly at the proud and happy secretary and turned off towards an obscure corner where sat his friend, Mr Budin, sedately eating peppermints. Now that Hildebrand Sutton was really getting his garden into decent condition after the upsetting move of twenty years ago, he was specializing on roses. His Lady Slazenger, a splendid cream standard with orange veining, was in all the catalogues. His Foveaux Folly was coming into popularity, a rich deep crimson, very hardy and vigorous. Mr Sutton was seventy-eight; but that did not prevent his travelling in every second Tuesday to attend his lodge meeting in Foveaux. He was too proud to order out the big car, which his chauffeur used mainly for the benefit of his lady friends, though tonight his rheumatism was annoying him again. Mr Sutton would drift round quietly until supper time and then just as quietly return to his big, empty house and his acres of roses. He left the welcoming and hand-shaking to Isenberg and the other officers who were being more than necessarily loud and jolly as they greeted the notable Brother Foxteth, K.C., and Brother Agnew.

Close behind them came Honest John Hutchison. He came in with such a roar of goodwill that everyone turned to watch him as the committee fell upon the long-lost brother and smote him on the back and pumped his hand and poured upon him the sanctifying oil of good fellowship.

"Well, you old devil," the district president said as he bore down upon him, "you're looking no worse for the change."

"Never felt better, Joey. You fellers got no idea what it's like just to sit back and let things slide. Any time you want to see something of the simple life you make for the mountains and I'll show you. Ha, ha. You couldn't get me back in Sydney if you dragged me on a rope. And talk about living high! I've got a baths there and, believe me, those old Roman emperors would take one look and go green with envy. You let me know and I'll meet you at the station."

The gala night was an event for Honest John. His daughters had disapproved of his coming, his doctor had disapproved, everybody seemed determined to keep him immured in the mountain fastnesses about which he lied so bravely. To be back in Foveaux, to breathe the atmosphere of crowds and friendliness, and hear the dance band, and feel other men deferring to him, made life worth living once more.

Honest John's bungalow on the mountains was a resort of hard drinking old battlers who lived at his expense and kept him company. He sometimes invited up the once notorious Bud Pellager who had taken to a mild and lucrative form of bushranging as owner of a garage on the Main Western Highway. But Bud and Honest John could seldom meet without a brawl and every fresh invitation had to be preceded by an apology for what happened last time. One such invitation was delayed for months until Honest John in high dudgeon secured from England a copy of his birth certificate and enclosed it with the invitation as a gentle reminder that the last time Bud had called him a "quarrelsome old bastard".

When Honest John was first forced to retire, it was feared that he would pine away. He did nothing but walk round the boundaries of his property with a forbidden cigar between his teeth and a dejected air about him very much like a solemn old goldfish finning round his bowl. Nothing would comfort him. Then one day, looking over his fence with the glazed eye of sorrow, it suddenly struck him that, if the fence were moved slightly, it would enclose a little creek which ran through the adjacent block of crown land.

The idea was like an electric battery to a racehorse. In an hour Honest John was digging post-holes, swearing and raving at a group of his friends who had come, as they pointed out, to comfort him, not to act as navvies. They just leant on their shovels and drank beer, while Honest John, who was not allowed beer, swore and sweated and dug.

He next busied himself on the excavation of what his pals described as "a young quarry", which he lined carefully with cement. Into this he diverted the Government's little creek and, behold, a baths, a veritable baths!

"Dug it meself! With me own hands!" he crowed proudly. "Took me six weeks to do it."

Half the business world of Sydney had been up to swim in Honest John's baths, and the only people who did not know about it were the Crown Land authorities.

Everyone crowded round to welcome Honest John. In their attitude there was no hint of censure. He was a "smart man". He had made money and had never actually been caught.

Besides, he belonged to Foveaux, and in some obscure way they were proud of him.

"So you're married now," he was saying to one pretty little druidess. "How's Walter? Still riding that infernal motor-bike? And Cissie's married, too. Well, well. Marvellous how time flies! How about having a dance with an old man who remembers when you had hair-ribbons?"

He puffed gallantly round the floor, treading on the feet of the fairest.

"How about a drink?" Isenberg whispered hoarsely in the ear of Brother Foxteth.

"Well, Ise, I'd probably get you off it if you were caught giving me one," Brother Foxteth responded imperturbably.

"Me wife's over there," Isenberg said, looking round cautiously. "Don't know why they had to have a dance. I voted for a smoke-o, plenty of comic turns and more refreshments. As it is, we only got two kegs of beer. Letting these women in mucks things up."

"All these old daddies," the secretary of the ladies' lodge was saying scornfully, discussing lodge politics with a group of fellow druidesses. "If they think the women's lodges are going to take a back seat, they're mistaken." She broke off to wave a friendly hand. "I saw you, Angus. I'll tell John I saw you flirting."

Angus McErchin was dancing with painful precision with old Mrs Isenberg.

The band paused thankfully and the worthy arch announced that the pupils of Miss Josie Selkirk would entertain with a song. Three shrill-voiced, leggy children broke into an example of the "Lonely for Yew" type of ballad so favoured in Foveaux, throwing the backdrop into a state of tremor as they danced.

"That's Mrs Ashley's Jessie, the little one with the curls," one stout matron confided to another. "I don't think she's doing the best for Jessie curling her hair like that. It's as straight as a stick naturally. It gives the child too much of an opinion of herself."

"I do think Josie Selkirk brings them on well," her neighbour remarked. "My sister's little girl is going after Christmas for the tap-dancing. My sister says she wants her child to have some accomplishments."

"I think it's nice for the children, mind you," the stout lady agreed. "These lodge turn-outs give them a chance to show their little dances."

The applause was deafening. A long succession of items would follow in the course of the evening, from Miss Melston singing "Parted" to a highly paid patter-and-comic-song professional who would come after his turn at the theatre as a favour to his friend, the lodge secretary.

The band struck up a waltz and the eye of many a hoary druid brightened as he glanced round for some dainty girl willing to be trampled on.

"The trouble with the soil around Foveaux," Mr Sutton was saying through the music to his friend, Mr Budin, "is that it's never forgotten Foveaux was once sandhills. I can remember when they had the quarry down where the Claribel Lane Steps are today. The owner sold the quarry for a barrel of rum. Just below Ogham Street it was a marsh. Salt, it was, all salt. The paperbark-trees standing in water and the weedy lagoon and sandhills all round it. Nothing growing but a bit of tea-tree blown flat by the wind. You couldn't expect to get the best out of roses here."

"But for carnations," Mr Budin argued, "it's good soil."

"Oh, I'll give you the carnations in, but roses need something with more body, not that loose grit."

"I get all the little boys to go out and shovel manure for me off the roads," Mr Budin said wistfully. "But there's very few horses about nowadays. I'm not able to afford superphosphate."

"You couldn't do better than horse manure," Mr Sutton said warmly, "provided it's liquid. I get mine and pour water on it and leave it standing."

"Hullo, hullo, hullo," Mr Hutchison beamed down on them. "How's the new house, Brother Budin?"

Brother Budin acknowledged that the new house was watertight and that he was lucky to get it so cheaply. "The missus snapped it up, Jack, just at the last minute. It was a bit of a mess when we went in but I'm straightening it up by degrees."

"Fine, fine," Honest John said heartily. "I hear you're a rose expert these days, Brother Sutton. You ought to see the rose I've got up at my shack. I've got a beauty growing by the gate. Sort of whitey thing."

"Silver Coronel," Mr Sutton hazarded. His heart bled for that rose. It probably had aphis all over it.

"Dunno what you call it, A goat came in chewed the tag off. Nearly finished the tree, too, all but the one bud. And you ought to see it. 'S round as this."

Honest John hoped he was rousing anguish in the heart of the rose expert. "Still thinks he owns the blasted place," he told himself. "Needs taking down a peg." He was diverted from this worthy intention by the band striking up another waltz.

"Well, there's that pretty little Alice Fox sitting by herself. Fine girl, fine girl."

He waddled off in her direction.

Old Mr Bross by the doorway was trying to make himself heard above the music. The secretary was being asked so many questions by so many people that Mr Bross had to repeat himself three times before the secretary got the strength of his remarks.

"A chap from my office," Mr Bross shouted. "I told 'im to come. 'E lives in Foveaux. I thought 'e ought to join and I says to 'im, if I'm late, I says, see the secretary and say I sent you. 'As 'e been?"

"Not yet," replied the secretary. "What name?"

"Cornish," Mr Bross said sadly. "I thought livin' 'ere, 'e ought to be a druid. A nasty cold sort of fish 'e is. Not what you'd call a mixer."

"Hullo," one of the young ladies called. "I thought you were going to bring your son, Mr Bross. You said you'd bring him to the anniversary."

"Bill? Bless you, you couldn't get Bill to anythin' as low as the things 'is ole dad goes to. I did try," Mr Bross grumbled, "to get a stuck-up fossil that works in the office to come. But I guess 'e was scared when I told 'im there was girls galore."

The secretary moved away and Mr Bross, still grumbling under his breath, cast round for somebody who would give him a hearing. In the midst of these laughing, dancing chattering young persons, he felt left out in the cold. There were, however, lodge members from other branches who had not had the pleasure of his conversation or been warned against him. He selected a mild-looking gentleman who admitted that he came from the Rose of Australia Lodge in an outer suburb and Mr Bross proceeded to give the history of the Foveaux Lodge from its inception.

"You ought to a seen us in the ole days when we 'ad a procession every year — done up like a sore toe with banners and floats. Some wonderful men in it there were," he was saying after ten minutes' monologue. "There was old Bert Robinson — God-rest-his-soul — 'e's gorn now, poor fellow. Ever 'eard of Bert Robinson? No, I don't suppose you would. 'E kept a livery stable down at the Foot. I s'pose you've 'eard of the Four-bob Robbos, then? The chaps used to go an' hire a cart for four bob and take it round loaded with vegetables. The kids used to call after 'em, 'Four Bob Robbo, Four Bob Robbo.' Old Bob Noblett, 'e's an old man now, but I can remember when Bob Noblett was a four-bob Robbo. 'E was a great boxer, Bob Noblett. Did you ever 'ear the time 'e knocked out Big Paddy behind the Rose of Denmark? No, I don't s'pose you'd 'ave 'eard of that. I was there the day it 'appened."

He paused complacently for the murmur of congratulation. A hunted look was beginning to appear in the eye of the visitor. He fully expected that he would have to follow the champion through every round.

"Ah, Foveaux was *some* place in those days! Even now you got no idea the real bang-up people who come from Foveaux, doctors and sirs and silvertails of all sorts. I remember old Johnny Hennessy sayin' to me that Foveaux had bred more men that never come back from the war than any other place in Australia.

"I didn't tell you about the Gold Brick Society we 'ad, did I? I was one of the original gold bricks. You may or may not know it but when the King came out 'ere, 'e was made a gold brick. They give 'im a little gold brick with a diamond to 'ang on 'is watch chain. Yes, my boy, the King was a gold brick."

He broke off and his fellow druid seized the respite.

"Wait a minute," Mr Bross said, brightening, "I thought I saw a young feller come in the door I invited 'ere tonight. A very cold sort of young feller 'e is. 'E reminds me of Tommy Brady, the man that made all the money out of funerals."

Deserting his prey, he was off questing towards the door. "So you did come," he croaked. "I says to meself, 'The feller's too busy courtin' or 'e's dead drunk or somethin'.' Lemme introduce you to the secretary." There was almost a fondness in old Bross's tone. "Hey, Charlie, ere's the feller I said I was goin't bring along tonight. 'Ow would 'e do for a druid, eh?" He gripped Bramley's arm.

The secretary greeted the visitor hurriedly but warmly. "An' look at the medical benefits," Bross was breathing in Bramley's ear. "If you fall sick, you get a doctor free. You get buried free. 'Ow about joinin' up next lodge night?"

"I'm not joining," Bramley said firmly.

Old Bross's face fell. "Why not?" he demanded.

"I'm insured. I don't drink, I don't dance and I've never joined anything. I'm too old to begin."

As usual Mr Bross began to be incensed. He waved his hand at the dancers. "You can't even dance after I take the trouble to bring yer. You mean y' don't wanter. Why, if I was twenty years younger, I'd a been the life and soul of a turn-out like this. I was always a great one for the girls. That's where Bill gets it."

"I said I'd come," Bramley said patiently, "because you made me promise."

Old Bross was suddenly piteous. "You'll stay for the supper?" he queried. "They 'ave a good feed."

Bramley smiled. "I'll stay for the supper."

"Right-o." Mr Bross cheered up again. He clutched Bramley like a leech. "Lemme introduce you to Brother Agnew A big man Agnew is. Made 'is money out of plumbers' fittin's."

Mr Bross was enjoying himself. He no longer felt lonely. If Bill had been half a decent son, he would have accompanied his old father, but Bram Cornish was an excellent substitute. Of course he had far too much bounce for a mere employee; but the old antagonism between them seemed to be much more a friendly hostility than it used to be.

"I'm not joining your damn secret society, chief," Bramley said amiably. "You can drown it with your slums."

"Slums!" the old man shrilled. "Fat lot you know. You go drivin' round in the new car. Ain't I give yer a car?"

"And I can hardly get it down some of the streets—"

"You go drivin' round in that car — nothin' to do all day while I'm there in the office, worryin' me guts out to make ends meet and pay your wages, and then you call my 'ouses slums. Lemme introduce you to Brother Hutchison; 'e's a real 'ard case, Honest John."

Mr Bross doddered through the dancers in the manner of a hen walking over an ants' nest. Bramley followed grimly. The reason he had come was to try to get Bross to see reason about Number Ten Paradise Street.

"I know," Bross piped. "Got the idea I'm made of money. Marble armchairs free in the front sittin'-room."

"Get out. You know the old ruin's on its last legs. Put in a bath anyway."

"Put in a bath!" Bross screamed. "Listen, they're only payin' seven-and-six a week and you want me to put in a bath. You're mad, you're tryin' to ruin me. Hey, Brother Hutchison, meet Bram Cornish, young feller from my office, clever, but one of them cheeky young devils. Oh, you've met 'im. Where you been?"

"Hullo, Sid. They tell me you've been had up as co-respondent in the divorce court again," Hutchison winked at Bramley. "You're a gay old hound, Sid, if ever there was one."

"Ha, ha!" Mr Bross was highly pleased.

"Did I tell you about the baths I put in at my place? . . ."

Hutchison and Bross stood halfway out on the floor with a little eddy of dancers swirling round them. Bramley, tall and formal, had been separated from his patron by a group of Foveaux matrons.

"Don't talk to me about baths, Jack, there's young frost-face over there layin' down the law about puttin' in baths in places where they are not payin' ten bob a week. It's enough to break yer 'eart. We never 'ad no bath at our place. A tin tub in the kitchen was good enough when we were kids."

"I dunno, Sid. You've got to move with the times. You can get some pretty cheap second-hand baths and move 'em out when the people go. How's Bill?"

"All right," Bross said sourly. Everyone seemed to be against him. He had a good mind to sack that long streak of a Cornish.

"How about those baths?" his guest demanded when next they came together. "I was talking to the health inspector and he says—"

"Hey, can't you enjoy yourself for once? You and your damn slum clearance."

"How about it?" Bramley said grimly.

"I'll think it over. You can give me an estimate of 'ow much it'd be."

"Miss Kitty Whitehead will favour us with a song," the M.C. announced. " 'My Baby Just Cares for Me'."

Bramley backed against the wall satisfied. He had achieved something by attending this gathering of the Foveaux clan. Behind him two old gentlemen were discussing the theory that, if you planted seeds with the moon waxing, they grew better than they did when the moon was on the wane.

"You can say what you like," the voice of Mr Budin insisted through the saxophone and drums, "but there's something in it. Now take my brother up on the Clarence River. Durin' the depression we were up there for a while. He had a crop of lucerne and. . . . Hullo, Mr Cornish, I ain't seen you in a dog's age." Mr Budin was shaking hands vigorously. "How's your little mother? And my respects to her. As fine a little lady as you'd wish to meet, Brother Sutton. Meet Brother Sutton, Mr Cornish."

"The idea's all bunkum," Mr Sutton said, shaking hands absent-mindedly. "When you investigate these things, you find they're all bunkum."

"Come and sit down." Brother Budin in his turn gripped Bramley's arm.

Mr Bross turning round to look for his charge felt a spasm of jealousy. He had brought the young fellow there, hadn't he? He employed him, didn't he? And there he was talking to old Sutton, a fellow that had more money than was good for him, and loafed about nursing a lot of plants. There was almost a wistfuless in Bross's rheumy eye as he stood undecidedly amid the fringe of wallflowers.

" 'Aving a nice time I see," he said sarcastically when Bramley rejoined him. "You get in among the money right from the start. Next thing I know you'll be buyin' yerself a dress soot and diamond studs."

"Chief," Bramley said firmly, "you're a cranky old cow." He heaved Bross out of the path of two young persons practising a rhumba. "I want to talk to you about that terrace in Slazenger Street. You're going to lose money on it if you don't give it a coat of paint."

Mr Bross was secretly pleased to be noticed. Nobody had been paying any attention to him; no one had shown any anxiety to listen to his stories or even do more than nod and sheer off before he could clutch them. He was as anxious for attention as a debutante. Women looked at Bramley Cornish. Men like Sutton were friendly to him.

"All right," he grumbled with a show of reluctance. "I s'pose since you come 'ere, I've got to let you get it off your chest. Why the 'ell you couldn't keep it for the office I don't know. Old Eddy Summers used to say—"

"Can't get you to listen in the office," Bramley said shortly. "You scream like a wounded bandicoot if I mention repairs."

"Now listen to me — I ain't goin' to 'ave you talk like that."

"Come on over here. You're in the way of the dancers."

"You're a frost-bitten, purple-toed snake, suckin' me life blood."

"The same to you," Bramley continued imperturbably. "Now about that terrace in Slazenger Street. . . ."

"Speaking of slugs," Mr Budin was saying. "Have you ever wondered why it is that slugs and snails, as it were, alternate. Now you'll get a run of slugs and then a run of snails. . . ."

The dancers in the middle of the floor continued to mill round unregarding.

"Dunno what these old birds come here for," one high-heeled, arch-browed damsel remarked to her swain who worked in the same radio factory. "All they do is stand round the wall and yarn to each other."

"I suppose," her gentleman friend answered sagely, "that the old buffers get a kick out of just bein' here watchin' us. After all, Millie, you can't expect them just to die off."

"It wouldn't," Millie chewed her gum reflectively as she swept a scornful eye over those druids, the bald druids, the fat and lame and elderly and wrinkled fathers who stood or sat round the wall, "it wouldn't be much loss." She revolved the idea in her mind. "They ain't as young as they used to be," she added in justification. "Sort of burnt out."

# CHAPTER 6

Bramley Cornish had made for his Saturday mornings a definite set pattern to which, however bright and shining, they must conform. They might come in with a frolicking wind blowing tatters of cloud, like the torn grey towels hanging over the rail of Barret's the barber; with a sky the colour of an asphalt pavement; or blue, divinely smiling. Bramley began all Saturdays the same by rising at five and doing the washing. He prepared his mother's breakfast tray, a few fingers of toast, crisp as she liked it, a cup of hot water and an orange. For himself, he reserved the news section of the paper, placing on the tray only those portions relating to household management and fashions which, he was convinced, his mother enjoyed; and, indeed, after so many years of waking to them, she had become accustomed to reading hints on cleaning furs and preserving old felt hats from the moths.

After a breakfast of bread and milk he would proceed methodically to wash up, clean the house and polish the linoleum. On this particular Saturday the parrot was still showing signs of bad temper which, Bramley had been told, indicated that the bird was suffering from red mites. He therefore sprayed Cocky deliberately with red-mite killer without apparent improvement in the creature's temper.

Then there were the messages to do, the buying of the supplies for the week-end, though this was not the epic task the rest of Foveaux made it. Saturday morning, Dennison Square and Murchison Street were at their busiest. Ample matrons waddled carefully from shop to shop selecting the family food supplies on the principle that the cheaper it was the better it must be. Butchers in white coats and striped aprons stood at the doors of their shops, auctioning choice cuts with enough chops and sausages thrown in to supply the family requirements over the week-end. The crowds pushed and jostled round the butchers' windows picking out the special tray of sausages and shoulder of mutton, or pork chops and round of beef, for which they intended to bid. Even those people who preferred to buy their fruit and vegetables "at the door" from visiting barrowmen, went into the greengrocers' shops to turn over the bruised and damaged apples, the "specks", as they were called. You could get four specks for the price of one sound apple and stewed specks were a staple dessert in Foveaux. In the alcoves of buildings and empty shops flower-sellers and vegetable men had set their baskets and boxes. Even if you had bought all you could afford, there was the entertainment of looking in the windows. Thin, hard-faced girls with their hair in curl-pins and their bare feet in slippers with a couple of children each would stroll slowly past the dress shops commenting on the display.

There were the pastrycook shops with windows full of yellow sponge cakes, cream cakes, chocolate cakes with coloured jellies decorating them, rainbow cakes, plum cakes, jam rolls, ginger cakes, nut loaves, bun loaves, and a wafted smell from the doorway of hot meat pies and fresh bread. There were florists with a wet confusion of buckets of green bush and broken dahlia stems and radio shops a-blare with music. Of all the shops the Blue Bird, where you could get a three-course meal for ninepence or any kind of small goods, had a window that positively ravished the appetite with a magnificent nude turkey in the middle decorated with strings of sausages and surrounded by a tight-packed mound of cauliflowers. Around this centrepiece were arranged noble sirloins of raw beef on a background of parsley and pats of butter, fowls, rabbits, plates of giblets, cooked mutton-bird, Tasmanian scallops, slabs of brawn, coils of black-pudding and patent breeds of sausage. Little red strings of frankfurts dipped in festoons round the glass and a profusion of eggs, marked "First Quality, 1s. 4d." made a pearly pavement for the heaped splendour of tomatoes. There were bottles of pickles and bottles of onions and bottles of gherkins and capers and jam. There were hams and little mounds of chicken in jelly. There were smoked salmon and yellow mountains of cheese.

Bramley passed all this without a glance. His mother's diet was mainly vegetarian so when he ate meat it was a lone chop.

Masses of food did not interest him even theoretically. To-wards the salt bacon and sawdust smell of the grocer's he directed his way, to wait patiently among the thin young women with little carboard suitcases and food orders to whom the shop assistants did not defer. These customers could wait. Bramley always seemed to be among those whom any shop assistant decided on sight would never push forward and thunder on the counter for attention. He would be elbowed out of the way by hot fat females and thin sharp females demand-ing their rights; he would stand for about ten minutes at least before he was noticed; and then it might be another ten minutes before he was served, despite the lightning speed of wrapping and running, the high jumps and miraculous slides of the sawdust which seemed to be part of the grocery routine. By the time he staggered out of the grocer's he was in no mood to bid for meat at the auction and preferred to purchase his chops at a quieter butchery in a back street where he was known. The hurly-burly of Dennison Square on a Saturday, the noise of the traffic, and people, he shook off as soon as pos-sible. Saturday was too precious to waste round shops.

Hurrying home with a sigh of relief and all the preliminaries completed, he prepared to enjoy his free morning. His mother watched him anxiously, as he rolled up his towel and trunks.

"You won't be too late?"

"No, I'll be back at one."

"What pudding would you like for lunch, boy? I thought of making a little custard."

"Good."

"What kind of custard would you like? Would you like a plain custard or a bread-and-butter custard or a sago custard?"

"Oh, any sort."

"But which would you rather have?"

"Oh, you make whichever's the easiest."

"Would you like a plain custard, then?"

Bramley saw he would have to give the orders as usual.

"Yes, a plain custard."

"You're sure you wouldn't prefer sago?"

"Sure."

"Or a bread-and-butter custard? You can have whichever

you like, boy."

He took her gently by the shoulders. "Don't fuss," he said, kissing her. "Bread-and-butter."

Mrs Cornish was relieved. The momentous question was settled. She pattered to the door to see him off and wave him good-bye.

Bramley strode happily to the baths. It was fine and hot and he would enjoy his one luxury of lying in the sun like a cat. A wet Saturday meant a whole week without a swim.

The nudist club that met in the sheltered corner of the baths was one of the most long-standing institutions of its kind. The baths were a strictly masculine baths. They were a sanctuary, never violated by makers of custards. Here old gentlemen long retired read the papers and played rummy. Wars might come and go and civilization pass; but the old gentlemen would still be basking securely on the warm boards, winning a glorious stake of half a dozen matches.

One old gentleman had never failed for twenty years to climb every Saturday morning to the very top platform of the diving tower. He would pose there for a while conscious of the sensation he was creating and the shouts of encouragement and then come hurtling down, to land with a terrific wallop flat on his stomach. He dived only once a week but it was his hope that some day he would make a really perfect dive.

Other members such as Grandpa Brophy did their physical culture exercises, although there was a good deal of grunting over the toe-touching, and chaff when a fat old chap, clad only in white moustache, failed to do it without bending his knees.

The nudist club had one hated foe, an elderly maiden lady who, from the topmost flat of a tall grey building overlooking the baths, was in the habit of training a pair of binoculars on them in the cause of morality. When she had the joy of discovering that some withered ancient had discarded the customary shred of clothing, she would rush to the telephone and inform the police. Of late, however, the nudist club had nearly driven her wild by holding their newspapers in such a way she could not tell whether the members were naked or not.

"She must admire me figger," old Mr Keyne always guffawed. The tradition that their foe was hopelessly in love with old Billy Keyne was elaborated with fictitious and somewhat rude descriptions of his courtship and the jilting of the revengeful maiden lady.

There was always the excitement of discussing what they would do if the police ever really did arrest anyone; and here the old gentleman referred to as Pop would pipe up:

"If ever they got me into court on a charge of indecent exposure and the magistrate says: 'Any previous convictions?' I'm going to draw meself up and say: 'Yes, your worship, I was fined for indecent exposure on Newcastle Beach in 1878 and I'm proud of it.' "

The others who had not been fined regarded the pioneer enviously.

Besides this ever-present topic, the nudist club was not unmindful that their views on the political, economic and international events of the day were of value and should be freely disseminated. First in importance as news came bathing costume regulations, then broken swimming records with illustrations from the feats of past champions, then wars and rumours of wars, with illustrations of what happened at Spiney Kop in the Boer War. Some wars the nudist club approved, occasionally censure motions were passed on the Government for allowing a perfectly good war to go to waste without getting into it. As the nudist club pointed out, Australia was only next door to China and there were some remarkably fine massacres going on in China with no Australians to participate. "Death or Glory" might well have been the club's motto, with a pair of bathing trunks rampant.

It was that morning at the baths that Bramley decided that his hair was getting thin on top. This is always a turning point in a man's life. Will he fight the long, slow, losing fight with hair oils or will he resign himself to the inevitable? Bramley yawned and rolled over on his back, reflecting that it didn't matter much, except that it would be a bit cold when he got really bald. In that brief reflection did he bid farewell to youth, although he did not realize it? He was pleasurably occupied with the sunny happiness of basking, with his arm behind his head and the rough wooden beams making a not unpleasant print on his hide. He licked his wrist reflectively and decided that he liked the taste of salt. There was so little needed, he thought, to make a man happy. Sunshine and clear water to swim in were luxuries enough. Perhaps one of the reasons why Jamieson found trouble organizing the unemployed was that, although they might not have adequate food or shelter, many of them could go swimming. There is not much comfort in swimming when you are sick and hungry but it was strange, he thought, how the water washed the bitterness out of you.

He had been grimed with bitterness all the week. Bitterness against things he was powerless to alter. All that had dissolved in salt water. The ache, the futility of his life washed off him, the wasted years doing work that did not count when he knew he had the ability for better things. That was what hurt. He had not wanted happiness, but he had wanted to work hard at a worthwhile job. He had not had that chance. It was no use being bitter. It was his own fault for not being hard enough to push people out of his way. That would have brought one sort of happiness, but this was another perhaps more to be desired.

Bramley opened his eyes, rolled over, and surveyed the pale green water through a chink in the runway. Presently he would dive in again and feel the sudden cool shock of it and climb out and lie once more pleasantly lazy with the water drying off him in the sun. Thank God he wasn't ever likely to get fat or pot-bellied. As he grew older he would be scrawny with a long wrinkled neck like the old chap in the corner. However, the day when he could not do his five hundred yards was still a long way off.

A stout dark man near by, having noticed Bramley open his eyes, immediately rustled his paper as a prelude to conversation.

"I see the Government's going to abolish slums," he remarked tentatively.

Bramley almost sighed. Now why of all things must the ass make a remark like that? He grunted: "Zat so?"

"It's got the report here." Again the bather rustled his paper. "Wonder what the idea is?"

Bramley made no answer.

"Can't tell me they haven't got something up their sleeve."

It was obvious that he would go on talking. Bramley decided

he would force himself into politeness.

"They were talking about it some time ago," he said blandly. "As a matter of fact in nineteen-twelve. Maybe in another twenty to fifty years they might. . . ."

The other shook his head. "Now, I'm in a position to know," he said authoritatively, depressing his plump chin. He was the kind of man whose pelt would make an excellent doormat. "It seems to me that a lot of these chaps are beginning to realize that there's money to be made out of big flats close to the city."

Bramley grunted again.

"Let the people who live in hovels live in them further away. Move the factories out. They're nearly as unsightly as the slums. Move them all out. Keep our city clean. Ha, ha."

Bramley shut his eyes again; but his new acquaintance did not seem to realize that his conversation was not required.

"I'd be willing to bet that inside ten years all these slum places down near the water and round the inner suburbs are torn down and there'll be ten- and twelve-storey flats going up in their places. It stands to reason. Creates a boom in building, keeps people busy. And businessmen are realizing what mugs they are to be wasting petrol driving in to town every day when they could have a flat five minutes from their business. Have a week-end place in the country, of course."

Bramley opened one eye. What were these things to him? The wheels of the Juggernaut would roll on grinding any human plans to powder.

"Is there anything about war in Europe?" he asked to divert the talker.

The stout man was happy. "Yeh. Here, wait a minute. I've lost the page. Hitler says . . ." he mumbled, turning the sheets. "Here it is. 'War in Spain. Air Raid on Madrid.' "

"Huh, huh," Bramley said peacefully. Dimly he could hear his new acquaintance reading him extracts of news and then the voice faded away. In a minute, he thought, he would have another swim and then go home. Mummy would be fussing about that custard.

After lunch it was Bramley's habit to sleep all the afternoon, but this particular Saturday happened to be the anniversary of his father's death. Therefore he slipped a pair of grass clippers, carefully wrapped in brown paper, into his hip pocket with the worthy intention of cleaning up the grave. It had looked scraggy and neglected on the last visit he had paid some weeks before with his mother. As Mrs Cornish felt it was too hot to go out Bramley hesitated and then decided to establish a precedent. He would call for young Robert John and take him out to the cemetery. Mamie would probably welcome the offer.

A hot westerly had sprung up and was rustling the leaves of the plane-trees as he passed along the footpath down the hill under their shade. In all the seasons the plane-trees were a delight to him; in summer when they were green and friendly overhead, and in winter when their crisp leaves rasped noisily underfoot. The street sweepers cursed the plane-trees as they tried with unwieldy brooms to assemble the fallen leaves in heaps. They gave themselves a liberal allowance of strayed leaves to every tree and scowled at the old gentleman who, in carpet slippers, with his own small domestic broom, herded from the footpath by his gate a flock of leaves. He would shepherd his collection to the foot of the plane-tree in triumph and lean upon his broom while the council men contemptuously dumped the little brown and yellow heap of contributions into a bin.

Bramley Cornish liked to watch the leaves as he walked to work in the morning. As they moved they made a small dry whispering. They did not flutter or go swirling round, dancing on the corners. It was as though they marched the pavement, an army without plans. Sometimes one leaf would trundle forward and overtake another or stop as if for rest and then go on again. In a tireless, surging, dry horde, the leaves, rustling over the footpaths, went on their own ghostly and lifeless way, powerless but still talking with grey tongues, a myriad syllables scraping the asphalt, lisping over the gutter, sibilant across the street.

The leaves this hot Saturday afternoon were green, the sky bright over the stretch of city below, the same city whence the tall factories had advanced and climbed the slopes, until now there were factories all over the hill of Foveaux. It struck Bramley suddenly how muddled the view was, a bit of this and a bit of that, like washing drying on a line; here a great ten-storey building, and there a dirty little dumpy factory, then a large residential or a terrace of mean houses. The bald patch where Plug Alley had been still showed with Honest John's streets running wide and straight through a fantastic desert of weeds and broken stones. Outside the hotels of Ogham Street the Saturday afternoon crowds sat in the gutters waiting for the race results and playing two-up with a look-out posted for the police.

Looking over the roofs and streets in the hard, hot sunlight, Bramley Cornish's thoughts turned in the direction of Paradise Street. Suddenly he felt bitter and hard and old. He had failed in life. His failure was heavy and conclusive. Love, he thought, looking down at those roofs wavering in the heat, even that had passed him by. Tommy's words came back to him so that his throat hurt with the memory. "I did but see her passing by, and yet I love her till I die."

He had loved Linnie once but what was the use of remembering it? He clenched his teeth. Was he too arrogant, too aloof, too proud to snatch and weep like other people? He leant on the railing at the top of the steps and looked down at that bit of waste land his efforts had helped to lay bare. Even when the mud closed over you, he thought, you never quite lost the resentment of mud and apathy, of the steady sucking down into an inglorious old age.

He straightened his shoulders, realizing that these incidentals did not matter. He had loved Foveaux. He had been Foveaux's solitary lover when she was beautiful. He still loved Foveaux. He liked the dirty, tragic, cheery people, their bravery and their horrible patience, contented in hell. He liked the streets and the very muddle of factories and houses and lanes where everything was unexpected. He liked the funny little squares where cats sat amid staghorns on the curious pillars outside houses nearly a hundred years old. He loved these old stairs and the curious blends of half tones, dull grey and white, and red and brown and yellow that all looked grey.

There were other patriots, other people who loved Foveaux and would rather a day in her pits than a year in palaces; but they were inarticulate about it as he was. He knew that he had loved Foveaux, that he had possessed the place. "He does not

die that can bequeath some influence to the land he knows."
Bramley smiled. Perhaps he had left himself a memorial in that
dirty bit of resumed land that the city did not yet know how
to use. A few seconds it had taken for his thoughts to flash
through all these things, but his mind had cleared like a pool
in which sediment stirred, then settled.

"Could I take young Robert John out to Waverley?" he
asked, standing shy and tall, on Mamie's doorstep. "Thought
it would do the little beggar good."

"Of course, Mr Cornish. I got 'im all cleaned up. 'E
was. . . ." Mamie hesitated. " 'E was goin' to the pictures with
the little boy next door."

Young Bunny showed a tendency to sulk which Mamie
promptly frowned upon. He could go to the silly old pictures
any time. He was going out with his Uncle Bramley if he
was a good boy and kept himself clean and didn't tread on the
toe of one shoe with the toe of the other. Bunny had to have
his hair wet and brushed and his face cleaned again and his
nose wiped; but finally he was ready and set out hand in hand
with his uncle for the tram stop.

"What's a cemetery?" Bunny asked loudly going out in
the tram.

"It's a place where people are buried."

Bunny jigged on the seat in a manner which brought a disapproving frown to the face of the lady next to him.

"Can I cut the grass?" he asked. Chiefly on the promise of
being allowed to cut the grass had he been won over to the idea
of coming. Bramley was somewhat at a loss with his small
nephew who had such shrewd black eyes and the impudence of
his father.

"Daddy's going to go off in a boat," Bunny told him. "Did
you know?"

"Yes, I knew."

The tram rounded a bend and Bunny had to climb up on
the seat to see the sea. "Like scales on a fish," he said after
lengthy thought. "When you flick them off with a knife."

Bramley glanced out the window. The kid was right. The
sea did look like a flickering of scales.

Walking to Waverley he had to shorten his stride to allow

424

Bunny to keep up. Bramley began to wonder whether Robert
John was an asset on such a trip. He would probably howl to
go home shortly.

The cemetery, however, completely enchanted Robert John.
He wandered about, collecting pebbles off the different graves
and asking questions. After a few clips of the grass clippers he
confined himself to weeding, pattering with his small patent
leather sandals over his grandfather's last resting place.

"That's the sea daddy's going on?" he asked, pointing over
the white headstones to the dark blue that, from their perch on
the cliff top, was no longer silver scaled.

Bramley put down his grass clippers. "That's the very same
sea," he answered.

"Where does it go to?"

"Everywhere."

"I went for a swim," Robert John piped. "I swum in it."

"Why don't you go away on a boat?" he asked next.

Bramley shook his head. "I have to stay ashore," he said,
"to look after grannie."

"I'm going away on a boat," Robert John announced.
"Some day."

He was off again to peer through the iron railings of a large
vault. Over the dark spikes of the headstones, the dark spikes
of the pines, a crew of seagulls drifted sideways towards the
edge of the cliff. It was all very peaceful with the water like
a wall of blue roughcast above the green and white of the
graveyard.

The Saturday afternoon procession of ships passed at slow
intervals from the Heads. The great overseas liners, coming
early and going proudly by as though the water were a blue
velvet carpet under them, then the interstate liners, and a
miscellaneous following of cargo boats, little coastal steamers,
the small tubs running lonely sea-errands.

From the close-clipped green of the grave the scent of cut
grass was warm and pleasant. Bramley carefully dug out a last
dandelion with the sharp point of the shears. It was getting late.
He put his clippers back in their brown paper, rolled them
carefully, and slipped them into his pocket again. The shadow
of the gravestones was growing longer. He sat there for a time

looking towards the cliff edge.

This place, he thought, was perhaps apart from Foveaux Stairs, the one he liked best in the world. The orderly arrangement of white gravestones appealed to his methodical mind. There was no passion in it, no loud overtones. Even the sea was only a blue background on which painted ships went by. A man's mind could rest here quietly and never ache again. He thought of his father, long dead and blind for ever. There had been no rescue ship for his father as there was none for him.

Small Robert John was beginning to grow impatient. He had explored all the nearby paths. The people were going away, the sea had darkened, but the sky cleared and brightened as the sun went down.

"I suppose," Robert John said casually, treading one toe of his sandals on the other, "we'd better be going home."

His Uncle Bramley was still sitting on the edge of the grave, leaning forward. His eyes had a far-away look.

"Gran has tea at six o'clock," Robert John mentioned.

At the sound of his nephew's voice Bramley turned and his eyes lit kindly.

"Come on," he said. "I'll carry you. Jump up."

As he had once carried Bunny's father, so he now hoisted the small boy on his shoulders. There flashed to his mind that day long ago when Tommy had wanted to see the procession. Now he and Bunny were the procession and it was the gravestones, the white clouds, that watched them go. The gravel crunched beneath his feet cheerily.

"We'll be home in no time, son," he said, setting Bunny on his feet again. "If we have to wait for a tram, I'll shout you an ice-cream."

They passed out of the great iron gates together.

# OTHER SIRIUS PAPERBACKS

## BY

# KYLIE TENNANT

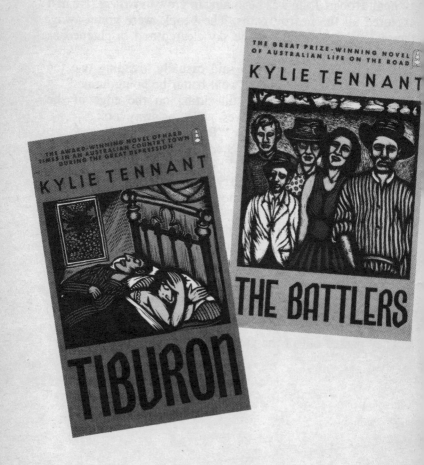

THE AWARD-WINNING NOVEL OF HARD
TIMES IN AN AUSTRALIAN COUNTRY TOWN
DURING THE GREAT DEPRESSION

KYLIE TENNANT

TIBURON

THE GREAT PRIZE-WINNING NOVEL
OF AUSTRALIAN LIFE ON THE ROAD

KYLIE TENNANT

THE BATTLERS